Writing
for My Life

Writing *for* My Life

THE VERY BEST *of*
RUSKIN BOND

Ruskin Bond

PENGUIN BOOKS

An imprint of Penguin Random House

PENGUIN BOOKS

USA | Canada | UK | Ireland | Australia
New Zealand | India | South Africa | China

Penguin Books is part of the Penguin Random House group of companies
whose addresses can be found at global.penguinrandomhouse.com

Published by Penguin Random House India Pvt. Ltd
4th Floor, Capital Tower 1, MG Road,
Gurugram 122 002, Haryana, India

Penguin
Random House
India

This edition published in Penguin Books by Penguin Random House India 2021

ISBN 9780143454458

Typeset in Minion Pro by Manipal Technologies Limited, Manipal
Printed at Thomson Press India Ltd, New Delhi

www.penguin.co.in

MIX
Paper
FSC FSC® C010615

CONTENTS

·Contents

Contents

RETURN TO INDIA

TO THE HILLS

THE RIPLEY-BEAN MYSTERIES

ENVOI

Contents

INTRODUCTION

It has been over twenty-five years since Penguin Random House India brought out *The Best of Ruskin Bond*, and I am grateful to see (from my royalty statements) that it is still one of the most popular titles. But there were many good things that couldn't get into it; and there have been many stories, essays, poems and memories written in recent years, from which a selection of the 'best' can easily be made. And with the help of Premanka Goswami, my editor, I have made a selection of some of my own favourites and some that have elicited a favourable response from my readers.

My grandson Gautam wants to know if I'm going to give a title to this collection, apart from the rather staid 'Volume 2' . . .

'What would you suggest?' I ask.

'Rocky Two,' he replies.

Obviously, he's a fan of Sylvester Stallone.

The memories of the school boxing-ring are not as inspiring. A black eye and a broken tooth were my rewards for putting on the gloves. I was better at football and had a good left-footed kick. Had kick-boxing been an approved sport, I might have fared better.

Games and other physical and Spartan activities were compulsory in my dear old school, and when I wanted to escape P.T. or the marathon run, I'd slip away and take refuge in the school library. I would enter by the French windows, which I could open without a key. Reading was almost a secret activity.

That's how I became a writer. Hundreds of books at my disposal! Classics, modern novels, plays, biographies, story collections, crime fiction, I had my pick—and I picked freely. Hardly anyone used the library.

There were even those early Penguins, and it was through them that I discovered many contemporary authors. There was Somerset Maugham's *The Moon and Sixpence*; Graham Greene's *Brighton Rock*; Compton Mackenzie's *Carnival*; Arthur Machen's *Holy Terrors*; Maurice Collis's *Trials in Burma*; and a host of others.

I resolved that I, too, would be a Penguin author one day, and this dream was realized when, in the early 1970s, my children's story *Angry River* appeared in the Puffin list. Then, in 1986, Penguin came to India, and I adopted that floppy literary bird and persuaded it to publish no less than seventy of my titles, in the Penguin, Puffin and Penguin Random House format.

~

The first story was published in the *Illustrated Weekly of India* in 1951, the year after I finished school. My first novel was published in 1956 by Andre Deutsch, in London, and later reprinted by Penguin India. I have been writing for seventy years, and for most of that time I've made a living from it. Is that a boast? Well then, as Walt Whitman wrote: 'Do I celebrate myself? Very well then, I celebrate myself!'

After a lifetime of sitting at a sunny desk, putting words to paper, I think I'm allowed a small boast. And if no one else will pat me on the back, I shall stand against the wall with my back to it, and rub myself like a cat.

~

Speaking of cats, a lot of my stories have been about big cats—leopards and tigers—and other wild creatures, and the hills and forests in which they survive. I have also written a lot about childhood—my own and others'—and stories about lonely people and their dreams. And I like going back in time and recreating scenes from the past.

Some of these stories are here. And many in which I celebrate the world of Nature, which has meant so much to me. We are fortunate to be living on a green planet, probably the only one in our galaxy. But over the centuries humans have done their best to desecrate it, to strip it of its forests and grasslands and its clean sparkling streams. We must try to reverse this process, so difficult in the face of a proliferation of the human race. Nature has always rewarded us when we have respected its presence. Destroy it, and we destroy ourselves.

DREAMS *of* CHILDHOOD

FARAWAY
PLACES

A nil and his parents lived in a small coastal town on
the Kathiawar peninsula, where Anil's father was
an engineer in the Public Works Department. The boy
attended the local school but as his home was some way
out of town, he hadn't the opportunity of making many
friends.

Sometimes he went for a walk with his father or
mother, but most of the time they were busy, his mother
in the house, his father in the office, and as a result he was
usually left to his own resources. However, one day Anil's
father took him down to the docks, about two miles from
the house. They drove down in a car, and took the car right
up to the pier.

It was a small port, with a cargo steamer in dock, and a
few fishing vessels in the harbour. But the sight of the sea
and the ships put a strange longing in Anil's heart.

The fishing vessels plied only up and down the Gulf. But the little steamer, with its black hull and red and white funnel held romance, the romance of great distances and faraway ports of call, with magical names like Yokohama, Valparaiso, San Diego, London . . .

Anil's father knew the captain of the steamer, and took his son aboard. The captain was a Scotsman named Mr MacWhirr, a very jolly person with a thunderous laugh that showed up a set of dirty yellow teeth. Mr MacWhirr liked to chew tobacco and spit it all over the deck, but he offered Anil's father the best of cigarettes and produced a bar of chocolate for Anil.

'Well, young man,' he said to the boy with a wink, 'how would you like to join the crew of my ship, and see the world?'

'I'd like to, very much, captain sir,' said Anil, looking up uncertainly at his father.

The captain roared with laughter, patted Anil on the shoulder, and spat tobacco on the floor.

'You'd like to, eh? I wonder what your father has to say to that!'

But Anil's father had nothing to say.

Anil visited the ship once again with his father, and got to know the captain a little better; and the captain said, 'Well, boy, whenever you've nothing to do, you're welcome aboard my ship. You can have a look at the engines, if you like, or at anything else that takes your fancy.'

The next day Anil walked down to the docks alone, and the captain lowered the gangplank especially for him. Anil spent the entire day on board, asking questions of the captain and the crew. He made friends quickly, and the following day, when he came aboard, they greeted him as though he was already one of them.

'Can I come with you on your next voyage?' he asked the captain. 'I can scrub the deck and clean the cabins, and you don't have to pay me anything.'

Captain MacWhirr was taken aback, but a twinkle came into his eye, and he put his head back and laughed indulgently. 'You're just the person we want! We sail any day now, my boy, so you'd better get yourself ready. A little more cargo, and we'll be steaming into the Arabian Sea. First call Aden, then Suez, and up the Canal!'

'Will you tell me one or two days before we sail, so that I can get my things ready?' asked Anil.

'I'll do that,' said the captain. 'But don't you think you should discuss this with your father? Your parents might not like being left alone so suddenly.'

'Oh, no, sir, I can't tell them; they wouldn't like it at all. You won't tell them, will you, captain sir?'

'No, of course not, my boy,' said Captain MacWhirr, with a huge wink.

During the next two days Anil remained at home, feverishly excited, busily making preparations for the voyage. He filled a pillowcase with some clothes, a penknife and a bar of chocolate, and hid the bundle in an old cupboard.

At dinner, one evening, the conversation came around to the subject of ships, and Anil's mother spoke to her husband, 'I understand your friend, the captain of the cargo ship, sails tonight.'

'That's right,' said the boy's father. 'We won't see him again for sometime.'

Anil wanted to interrupt and inform them that Captain MacWhirr wouldn't be sailing yet, but he did not want to arouse his parents' suspicions. And yet, the more he pondered over his mother's remark, the less certain he felt. Perhaps the ship was sailing that night; perhaps the captain had mentioned the fact to Anil's parents so that the information could be passed on. After all, Anil hadn't been down to the docks for two days, and the captain couldn't have had the opportunity of notifying Anil of the ship's imminent departure.

Anyway, Anil decided there was no time to lose. He went to his room and, collecting the bundle of clothes, slipped out of the house. His parents were sitting out on the verandah and for a while Anil stood outside in the gathering dusk, watching them. He felt a pang of regret at having to leave them alone for so long, perhaps several months; he would have liked to take them along, too, but he knew that wouldn't be practical. Perhaps, when he had a ship of his own . . .

He hurried down the garden path, and as soon as he was on the road to the docks, he broke into a run. He felt sure he had heard the hoot of a steamer.

Anil ran down the pier, breathing heavily, his bundle of clothes beginning to come undone. He saw the steamer, but it was moving. It was moving slowly out of the harbour, sending the waves rippling back to the pier.

'Captain!' shouted Anil. 'Wait for me!'

A sailor, standing in the bow, waved to Anil; but that was all. Anil stood at the end of the pier, waving his hands and shouting desperately.

'Captain, oh, captain sir, wait for me!'

Nobody answered him. The sea gulls, wheeling in the wake of the ship, seemed to take up his cry. 'Captain, captain . . .'

The ship drew further away, gathering speed. Still Anil shouted, in a hoarse, pleading voice. Yokohama, Valparaiso, San Diego, London, all were slipping away forever . . .

He stood alone on the pier, his bundle at his feet, the harbour lights beginning to twinkle, the gulls wheeling around him. 'First call Aden, then Suez, and up the Canal.' But for Anil there was only the empty house and the boredom of the schoolroom.

Next year, sometime, he told himself, Captain MacWhirr would return. He would be back, and then Anil wouldn't make a mistake. He'd be on the ship long before it sailed. Captain MacWhirr had promised to take him along, and wasn't an adult's word to be trusted? And so he remained for a long time on the pier, staring out to sea until the steamer went over the horizon. Then he picked up his bundle and made for home. This year, next year, sometime . . . Yokohama, Valparaiso, San Diego, London!

THE WOMAN *on*
PLATFORM NO. 8

It was my second year at boarding school, and I was sitting on Platform no. 8 at Ambala station, waiting for the northern bound train. I think I was about twelve at the time. My parents considered me old enough to travel alone, and I had arrived by bus at Ambala early in the evening; now there was a wait till midnight before my train arrived. Most of the time I had been pacing up and down the platform, browsing through the bookstall, or feeding broken biscuits to stray dogs; trains came and went, the platform would be quiet for a while and then, when a train arrived, it would be an inferno of heaving, shouting, agitated human bodies. As the carriage doors opened, a tide of people would sweep down upon the nervous little ticket collector at the gate; and every time this happened I would be caught in the rush and swept outside the station. Now tired of this game, and of ambling about the platform,

I sat down on my suitcase and gazed dismally across the railway tracks.

Trolleys rolled past me, and I was conscious of the cries of the various vendors—the men who sold curds and lemon, the sweetmeat seller, the newspaper boy—but I had lost interest in all that was going on along the busy platform, and continued to stare across the railway tracks, feeling bored and a little lonely.

'Are you all alone, my son?' asked a soft voice close behind me.

I looked up and saw a woman standing near me. She was leaning over, and I saw a pale face and kind dark eyes. She wore no jewels, and was dressed very simply in a white sari.

'Yes, I am going to school,' I said, and stood up respectfully. She seemed poor, but there was a dignity about her that commanded respect.

'I have been watching you for some time,' she said. 'Didn't your parents come to see you off?'

'I don't live here,' I said. 'I had to change trains. Anyway, I can travel alone.'

'I am sure you can,' she said, and I liked her for saying that, and I also liked her for the simplicity of her dress, and for her deep, soft voice and the serenity of her face.

'Tell me, what is your name?' she asked.

'Arun,' I said.

'And how long do you have to wait for your train?'

'About an hour, I think. It comes at twelve o'clock.'

'Then come with me and have something to eat.'

I was going to refuse, out of shyness and suspicion, but she took me by the hand, and then I felt it would be silly to pull my hand away. She told a coolie to look after my suitcase, and then she led me away down the platform. Her hand was gentle, and she held mine neither too firmly nor too lightly. I looked up at her again. She was not young. And she was not old. She must have been over thirty, but had she been fifty, I think she would have looked much the same.

She took me into the station dining room, ordered tea and samosas and jalebis, and at once I began to thaw and take a new interest in this kind woman. The strange encounter had little effect on my appetite. I was a hungry school boy, and I ate as much as I could in as polite a manner as possible. She took obvious pleasure in watching me eat, and I think it was the food that strengthened the bond between us and cemented our friendship, for under the influence of the tea and sweets I began to talk quite freely, and told her about my school, my friends, my likes and dislikes. She questioned me quietly from time to time, but preferred listening; she drew me out very well, and I had soon forgotten that we were strangers. But she did not ask me about my family or where I lived, and I did not ask her where she lived. I accepted her for what she had been to me—a quiet, kind and gentle woman who gave sweets to a lonely boy on a railway platform . . .

After about half an hour we left the dining room and began walking back along the platform. An engine was shunting up and down beside Platform no. 8, and as it approached, a boy leapt off the platform and ran across the rails, taking a short cut to the next platform. He was at a safe distance from the engine, but as he leapt across the rails, the woman clutched my arm. Her fingers dug into my flesh, and I winced with pain. I caught her fingers and looked up at her, and I saw a spasm of pain and fear and sadness pass across her face. She watched the boy as he climbed the platform, and it was not until he had disappeared in the crowd that she relaxed her hold on my arm. She smiled at me reassuringly and took my hand again, but her fingers trembled against mine.

'He was all right,' I said, feeling that it was she who needed reassurance.

She smiled gratefully at me and pressed my hand. We walked together in silence until we reached the place where I had left my suitcase. One of my schoolfellows, Satish, a boy of about my age, had turned up with his mother.

'Hello, Arun!' he called. 'The train's coming in late, as usual. Did you know we have a new headmaster this year?'

We shook hands, and then he turned to his mother and said: 'This is Arun, Mother. He is one of my friends, and the best bowler in the class.'

'I am glad to know that,' said his mother, a large imposing woman who wore spectacles. She looked at the woman who held my hand and said: 'And I suppose you're Arun's mother?'

I opened my mouth to make some explanation, but before I could say anything the woman replied: 'Yes, I am Arun's mother.'

I was unable to speak a word. I looked quickly up at the woman, but she did not appear to be at all embarrassed, and was smiling at Satish's mother.

Satish's mother said: 'It's such a nuisance having to wait for the train right in the middle of the night. But one can't let the child wait here alone. Anything can happen to a boy at a big station like this—there are so many suspicious characters hanging about. These days one has to be very careful of strangers.'

'Arun can travel alone though,' said the woman beside me, and somehow I felt grateful to her for saying that. I had already forgiven her for lying; and besides, I had taken an instinctive dislike to Satish's mother.

'Well, be very careful, Arun,' said Satish's mother looking sternly at me through her spectacles. 'Be very careful when your mother is not with you. And never talk to strangers!'

I looked from Satish's mother to the woman who had given me tea and sweets, and back at Satish's mother.

'I like strangers,' I said.

Satish's mother definitely staggered a little, as obviously she was not used to being contradicted by small boys.

'There you are, you see! If you don't watch over them all the time, they'll walk straight into trouble. Always listen to what your mother tells you,' she said, wagging a fat little finger at me. 'And never, never talk to strangers.'

I glared resentfully at her, and moved closer to the woman who had befriended me. Satish was standing behind his mother, grinning at me, and delighting in my clash with his mother. Apparently he was on my side.

The station bell clanged, and the people who had till now been squatting resignedly on the platform began bustling about.

'Here it comes,' shouted Satish, as the engine whistle shrieked and the front lights played over the rails.

The train moved slowly into the station, the engine hissing and sending out waves of steam. As it came to a stop, Satish jumped on the footboard of a lighted compartment and shouted, 'Come on, Arun, this one's empty!' and I picked up my suitcase and made a dash for the open door.

We placed ourselves at the open windows, and the two women stood outside on the platform, talking up to us. Satish's mother did most of the talking.

'Now don't jump on and off moving trains, as you did just now,' she said. 'And don't stick your heads out of the windows, and don't eat any rubbish on the way.' She allowed me to share the benefit of her advice, as she probably didn't think my 'mother' a very capable person. She handed Satish a bag of fruit, a cricket bat and a big box of chocolates, and told him to share the food with me. Then she stood back from the window to watch how my 'mother' behaved.

I was smarting under the patronizing tone of Satish's mother, who obviously thought mine a very poor family; and I did not intend giving the other woman away. I let her take my hand in hers, but I could think of nothing to say. I was conscious of Satish's mother staring at us with hard, beady eyes, and I found myself hating her with a firm, unreasoning hate. The guard walked up the platform, blowing his whistle for the train to leave. I looked straight into the eyes of the woman who held my hand, and she smiled in a gentle, understanding way. I leaned out of the window then, and put my lips to her cheek and kissed her.

The carriage jolted forward, and she drew her hand away.

'Goodbye, Mother!' said Satish, as the train began to move slowly out of the station. Satish and his mother waved to each other.

'Goodbye,' I said to the other woman, 'goodbye— Mother . . .'

I didn't wave or shout, but sat still in front of the window, gazing at the woman on the platform. Satish's mother was talking to her, but she didn't appear to be listening; she was looking at me, as the train took me away. She stood there on the busy platform, a pale sweet woman in white, and I watched her until she was lost in the milling crowd.

SO WELL-
REMEMBERED: MISS
KELLNER *and the*
MAGIC BISCUIT TIN

There are some people who, because of their personality or circumstances, stand out in this writer's memory more vividly than those who seemed more important in many ways. Childhood influences are often the most lasting, and people who once seemed peripheral to my life now take on a deeper meaning. They did not know it, but they made a lasting impression on a growing boy.

Miss Kellner must have been in her sixties when I first saw her. She was my grandmother's tenant, and a valued tenant at that. I must have been seven or eight at the time, spending that winter in my grandmother's house. She too was in her late sixties, a heavily built woman with Nordic features. She seldom smiled, and I never heard her laugh, and I don't think she was particularly fond of small boys, but she put up with me more as a matter of family duty than anything else. I stayed out of her way as much as I could. But at lunchtime (or 'tiffin', as we called it), she would be present at the dining table, making sure that I did not overeat or use the wrong knife or drop gravy on the tablecloth. My table manners had to be perfect. This rather took my appetite away.

'Don't play with your food,' Granny would say. 'And if you don't finish your vegetables, you won't get any custard afterwards.' As a result, I took a permanent dislike to vegetables, especially those that were supposed to be 'good for a growing boy'—turnips, cabbage, spinach and lettuce. A famous children's author called Beatrix Potter wrote little books about cute rabbits being kept out of the farmer's lettuce patch. As far as I was concerned, the rabbits were welcome to all the lettuce in the world.

All the same, I did not really miss out on all those vital green vitamins as there were several guava trees in the garden. These were easy to climb and I spent a fair amount of time in them, guzzling guavas until my stomach ached.

It was while I was in one of these guava trees that I noticed the old lady in the armchair, sunning herself at the far end of the garden. She was there every morning, a small table beside her, and an ayah in attendance. I asked Dhuki, the gardener, about her.

'She can't walk,' said Dhuki. 'Can't stand up. And her hands and arms are all crooked too. Poor lady, she had an accident when she was a child. But she can read and write, and maybe she'll talk to you if you go and see her.'

I approached the old lady with some caution. As I came closer, I noticed she had a beaky nose and bright-blue eyes. Her head was covered by a small straw hat. I was quite close before she noticed me. Without looking up she said, 'You must be Edith's son,' (Edith being my mother's name); so she was aware of my presence.

'Yes, Miss—' I began.

'Kellner,' she said. 'I am Miss Kellner. You must be having your holidays.'

'Yes, Miss Kellner.'

'And getting bored?'

'A bit. There's not much to do.'

'No books in the house?'

'Only religious books.'

'But you like guavas, I notice.' (She noticed everything.)

'Only when I'm hungry.'

'And are you hungry now?'

'Just a little.'

'I see you're a truthful boy. Ayah, fetch the biscuit tin!'

Ayah, a stalwart lady with a paan-stained mouth, went indoors and came back with a very large tin, the size of a bucket, and placed it on the side table.

'Have a biscuit', said Miss Kellner. 'Have two. They are all different.'

It was a collection of all sorts of biscuits—ginger biscuits, cream crackers, biscuits with sugary tops, cream-filled biscuits, chocolate biscuits, cheese biscuits . . .

I helped myself to a ginger biscuit, and followed this up with something soft and buttery. The magic biscuit tin was then taken indoors.

'Sit down and talk to me,' said Miss Kellner.

I sat down on a cushioned mora and tried to think of something intelligent to say. But the old lady was full of questions, so I didn't have to think much. She told me a little about herself, but not much—and I refrained from asking her how she became a cripple. Her hands and fingers were all twisted, but she could hold a pen and a pack of cards. When she wasn't writing letters, she told me, she was playing cards with herself.

'Do you know any card games?' she asked, and when I shook my head, she said, 'I'll teach you some easy ones.' And producing a pack of well-worn cards she taught me a simple but lively game called 'Snap'.

And another called 'Beggar My Neighbour'. I was never going to become a card player—too much of sitting in one place—but I enjoyed playing with Miss Kellner, and the time passed quickly.

'Tiffin time!' called Granny's khansama from the kitchen, and I had to say goodbye to Miss Kellner and hurry back to our side of the house. Granny did not like my being late for meals—or for anything.

~

I had the temerity to ask my grandmother how Miss Kellner got her injuries, but I was told not to pry into the affairs of older people. The cook told me she'd been in a carriage accident in Kolkata when she was a girl, but Dhuki the gardener gave me a different story. According to him, when Miss Kellner was a baby, a fond uncle had been playing with her by tossing her up in the air and catching her as she came down. Distracted by a loud noise behind her, he failed to catch the baby on her descent, and she fell on the floor, breaking her limbs and injuring her spine.

I did not talk to Miss Kellner about it. She would not have remembered such incidents from her early childhood. Her condition was something that she accepted, having known nothing better. And she was fortunate in that she had money of her own, her father having left her with ample means and investments. She could afford servants and a comfortable home. Once a week she was put into her rickshaw and taken off to play bridge with her friends.

There were four rickshaw boys—poor boys from a village near Tehri in the hills—and although they ran barefoot, they were smartly turned out in sky-blue uniforms. The boys were always laughing and chatting among themselves, even as they sped along Dehra's narrow lanes.

Most people went about in tongas (horse-drawn buggies) and there were hundreds of tongas plying in the town in the 1940s. They were uncomfortable contraptions, and Miss Kellner would not have been able to ride in one of them. Cars were then as rare as rickshaws; so she had her own little hand-pulled carriage, and a pretty sight it was, the boys in blue, pattering along the metalled Rajpur Road, and going quite fast as Miss Kellner was no weight at all.

I went over to talk to her about twice a week, and she seemed glad to see me; young people seldom came her way. The magic biscuit tin was always sent for, and it was always full. It was like a lucky dip. I would take a chance and take out the first biscuit that came to hand. I wasn't fussy!

There were other surprises too. The occasional meringue or lemon tart. And there were marzipans kept in a glass jar. My culinary education was in full flow.

Sometimes Miss Kellner asked me to read to her. All that letter writing tired her eyes, she said.

Although I was only eight, I could read quite well. Miss Kellner produced a book that she had loved as a girl—*Black Beauty*, the story of a horse (as told by the horse)—and I read to her in my shrill, unformed voice. Presently she fell asleep, but I kept on reading—first out loud, then to myself—the story enthralled me, and when she woke up she rewarded me with a chocolate soldier. Yes, they made chocolate soldiers in those far-off days!

My visits to Miss Kellner become more frequent. She seemed to have an unlimited store of confectionery. I suspect she had a sweet tooth herself. Occasionally I found her sucking a lemon drop or a bull's eye. As she never went out shopping, I presume she received parcels from distant friends and relatives. But the baker came regularly.

Mohammed Sharif had a small bakery in the Dilaram Bazaar, and he made all kinds of biscuits and cakes, including the most delicious soft nankatties. He supplied Granny with bread and, sometimes, vegetable patties, but Miss Kellner went in for more exotic items—pastries and curry puffs and meringues—and I suspect she was his favourite customer.

Those were the days of the 'box man'. Sundry vendors would roam the residential areas with tin trunks balanced on their heads (or on the heads of their assistants), selling everything from household articles to fruits and vegetables.

The baker or his boy came every day. So did the sabzi-wallah with his basket of fresh fruit or vegetables. So did the box man with combs and ribbons, soaps and scents, cups and saucers, almost anything that the householder might find useful or decorative. Sometimes they kept stationery too, and I remember buying a little notebook and using it to make lists of various things—the names of flowers and trees, the titles of famous books, the names of cities and countries. I think my writing career started with those lists I used to make.

In this way the winter holidays passed quickly. But I was soon back in boarding school, and when my next holidays came around I went to my father in New Delhi.

It was two or three years before I came to Dehradun again, and then it was to stay with my mother and stepfather in another part of town.

A lot had happened in the interval. My parents had separated; my father, who had been taking care of me, had died suddenly; and I had to adjust to a new home and a different, and sometimes difficult, life.[*]

But I hadn't forgotten Miss Kellner.

Hiring a bicycle, I rode over to Granny's house. She was out of town, visiting one of her daughters in Ranchi; but Dhuki the gardener was still there, and so was Miss Kellner.

But she was not the same. Her eyesight had deteriorated and her hands trembled. She did not know who I was until I spoke to her. And then, of course, she did remember me, and she said, 'You're Ruskin, the boy who used to play Snap with me. Come and sit down.'

---

[*] I have written about this period in *Looking for the Rainbow* (Puffin, 2017) and *Till the Clouds Roll By* (Puffin, 2017).

I sat beside her, and she chatted away, her mind as alert as ever. But I got the feeling that she was not as well off as before. Her clothes were old, and there was no sign of the rickshaw boys. She had stopped going out to bridge parties, and the boys had gone home to their village. The rickshaw stood in the back verandah gathering dirt and cobwebs.

Still, she hadn't forgotten my healthy appetite.

'Fetch the biscuit tin, ayah.'

The magic biscuit tin arrived, and I dipped my hand into it.

It was less than half full, but I came up with a ginger biscuit. And after a little while I left and cycled home.

I did not see Miss Kellner again. I made friends with some boys in my locality, and there were cricket matches and cycle rides and visits to the cinema to keep me busy. A few months after returning to school, my mother wrote and informed me (casually, and among other bits of news) that Miss Kellner had passed on.

Ships that pass in the night.

I did dream of her once. I saw her riding through the sky in her colourful rickshaw, leaving behind a trail of marzipans.

A boy's dream.

And now, seventy-five years later, I pay this little tribute to one who befriended a lonely boy.

Farewell, Miss Kellner!

THE
CANAL

We loved to bathe there, on hot summer afternoons—Sushil and Raju and Pitamber and I—and there were others as well, but we were the regulars, the ones who met at other times too, eating at chaat-shops or riding on bicycles into the tea-gardens.

The canal has disappeared—or rather, it has gone underground, having been covered over with concrete to widen the road to which it ran parallel for most of its way. Here and there it went through a couple of large properties, and it was at the extremity of one of these—just inside the boundaries of Miss Gamla's house—that the canal went into a loop, where it was joined by another small canal, and this was the best place for bathing or just romping around. The smaller boys wore nothing, but we had just reached the years of puberty and kept our kachhas on. So Miss Gamla really had nothing to complain about.

I'm not sure if this was her real name. I think we called her Miss Gamla because of the large number of gamlas or flowerpots that surrounded her house. They filled the verandah, decorated the windows, and lined the approach road. She had a mali who was always watering the pots. And there was no shortage of water, the canal being nearby.

But Miss Gamla did not like small boys. Or big boys, for that matter. She placed us high on her list of Pests, along with monkeys (who raided her kitchen), sparrows (who shattered her sweet-peas), and goats (who ate her geraniums). We did none of these things, being strictly fun-loving creatures; but we did make a lot of noise, spoiling her afternoon siesta. And I think she was offended by the sight of our near-naked bodies cavorting about on the boundaries of her estate. A spinster in her sixties, the proximity of naked flesh, no matter how immature, disturbed and upset her.

She had a companion—a noisy peke, who followed her around everywhere and set up an ear-splitting barking at anyone who came near. It was the barking, rather than our play, that woke her in the afternoons. And then she would emerge from her back verandah, waving a stick at us, and shouting at us to be off.

We would collect our clothes, and lurk behind a screen of lantana bushes, returning to the canal as soon as lady and dog were back in the house.

The canal came down from the foothills, from a hill called Nalapani where a famous battle had taken place a hundred and fifty years back, between the British and the Gurkhas. But for some quirky reason, possibly because we were not very good at history, we called it the Panipat canal, after a more famous battle north of Delhi.

We had our own mock battles, wrestling on the grassy banks of the canal before plunging into the water—it was no more than waist-high—flailing around with shouts of joy, with no one to hinder our animal spirits . . .

Except Miss Gamla.

Down the path she hobbled—she had a pronounced limp—waving her walnut-wood walking-stick at us, while her bulging-eyed peke came yapping at her heels.

'Be off, you chhokra-boys!' she'd shout. 'Off to your filthy homes, or I'll put the police on to you!'

And on one occasion she did report us to the local thana, and a couple of policemen came along, told us to get dressed and warned us off the property. But the Head Constable was Pitamber's brother-in-law's brother-in-law, so the ban did not last for more than a couple of days. We were soon back at our favourite stretch of canal.

When Miss Gamla saw that we were back, as merry and disrespectful as ever, she was furious. She nearly had a fit when Raju—probably the most wicked of the four of us—did a jig in front of her, completely in the nude.

When Miss Gamla advanced upon him, stick raised, he jumped into the canal.

'Why don't you join us?' shouted Sushil, taunting the enraged woman.

'Jump in and cool off,' I called, not to be outdone in villainy.

The little peke ran up and down the banks of the canal, yapping furiously, dying to sink its teeth into our bottoms. Miss Gamla came right down to the edge of the canal, waving her stick, trying to connect with any part of Raju's anatomy that could be reached. The ferrule of the stick caught him on the shoulder and he gave a yelp of pain. Miss Gamla gave a shrill cry of delight. She had scored a hit!

She made another lunge at Raju, and this time I caught the end of the stick and pulled. Instead of letting go of the stick, Miss Gamla hung on to it. I should have let go then, but on an impulse I gave it a short, sharp pull, and to my horror, both walking-stick and Miss Gamla tumbled into the canal.

Miss Gamla went under for a few seconds. Then she came to the surface, spluttering, and screamed. There was a frenzy of barking from the peke. Why had he been left out of the game? Wisely, he forbore from joining us.

We went to the aid of Miss Gamla, with every intention of pulling her out of the canal, but she backed away, screaming, 'Get away from me, get away!' Fortunately, the walking-stick had been carried away by the current.

Miss Gamla was now in danger of being carried away too. Floundering about, she had backed away to a point where a secondary canal joined the first, and here the current was swift. Even the boys, big and small, avoided that spot. It formed a little whirlpool before rushing on.

'Memsahib, be careful!' shouted Pitamber.

'Watch out!' I shouted. 'You won't be able to stand against the current.'

Raju and Sushil lunged forward to help, but with a look of hatred Miss Gamla turned away and tried to walk downstream. A surge in the current swept her off her legs. Her gown billowed up, turning her into a sail-boat, and she moved slowly downstream, arms flailing as she tried to regain her balance.

We scrambled out of the canal and ran along the bank, hoping to overtake her, but we were hindered by the peke who kept snapping at our heels, and by the fact that we were without our clothes and approaching the busy Dilaram Bazaar.

Just before the Bazaar, the canal went underground, emerging about two hundred metres further on, at the junction of the Old Survey Road and the East Canal Road. To our horror, we saw Miss Gamla float into the narrow tunnel that carried the canal along its underground journey. If she didn't get stuck somewhere in the channel, she would emerge—hopefully, still alive—at the other end of the passage.

We ran back for our clothes, dressed, then ran through the Bazaar, and did not stop running until we reached the exit point on the Canal Road. This must have taken us ten to fifteen minutes.

We took up our positions on the culvert where the canal emerged, and waited.

We waited and waited.

No sign of Miss Gamla.

'She must be stuck somewhere,' said Pitamber.

'She'll drown,' said Sushil.

'Not our fault,' said Raju. 'If we tell anyone, we'll get into trouble. They'll think we pushed her in.'

'We'll wait a little longer,' I said.

So we hung about the canal banks, pretending to catch tadpoles, and hoping that Miss Gamla would emerge—preferably alive.

Her walking-stick floated past. We did not touch it. It would be evidence against us, said Pitamber.The dog had gone home after seeing his mistress disappear down the tunnel.

'Like Alice,' I thought. 'Only that was a dream.'

When it grew dark, we went our different ways, resolving not to mention the episode to anyone. We might be accused of murder! By now, we *felt* like murderers.

A week passed, and nothing happened. No bloated body was found floating in the lower reaches of the canal. No Memsahib was reported missing.

They say the guilty always return to the scene of the crime. More out of curiosity than guilt, we came together one afternoon, just before the rains broke, and crept through the shrubbery behind Miss Gamla's house.

All was silent, all was still. No one was playing in the canal. The mango trees were unattended. No one touched Miss Gamla's mangoes. Trespassers were more afraid of her than of her lathi-wielding mali.

We crept out of the bushes and advanced towards the cool, welcoming water flowing past us.

And then came a shout from the house.

'Scoundrels! Goondas! Chhokra-boys! I'll catch you this time!'

And there stood Miss Gamla, tall and menacing, alive and well, flourishing a brand new walking-stick and advancing down her steps.

'It's her ghost!' gasped Raju.

'No, she's real,' said Sushil. 'Must have got out of the canal somehow.'

'Well, at least we aren't murderers,' said Pitamber.

'No,' I said. 'But she'll murder us if we stand here any longer.'

Miss Gamla had been joined by her mali, the yelping peke, and a couple of other retainers.

'Let's go,' said Raju.

We fled the scene. And we never went there again. Miss Gamla had won the Battle of Panipat.

CHACHI'S
FUNERAL

Chachi died at 6 p.m. on Wednesday, 5 April, and came to life again exactly twenty minutes later. This is how it happened.

Chachi was, as a rule, a fairly tolerant, easy going person, who waddled about the house without paying much attention to the swarms of small sons, daughters, nephews and nieces who poured in and out of the rooms. But she had taken a particular aversion to her ten-year-old nephew, Sunil. She was a simple woman and could not understand Sunil. He was a little brighter than her own sons, more sensitive, and inclined to resent a scolding or a cuff across the head. He was better looking than her own children. All this, in addition to the fact that she resented having to cook for the boy while both his parents went out to office jobs, led her to grumble at him a little more than was really necessary.

Sunil sensed his aunt's jealousy and fanned its flames. He was a mischievous boy, and did little things to annoy her, like bursting paperbags behind her while she dozed, or commenting on the width of her pyjamas when they were hung out to dry. On the evening of 5 April, he had been in particularly high spirits and, feeling hungry, entered the kitchen with the intention of helping himself to some honey. But the honey was on the top shelf, and Sunil wasn't quite tall enough to grasp the bottle. He got his fingers to it but as he tilted it towards him, it fell to the ground with a crash.

Chachi reached the scene of the accident before Sunil could slip away. Removing her slipper, she dealt him three or four furious blows across the head and shoulders. This done, she sat down on the floor and burst into tears.

Had the beating come from someone else, Sunil might have cried; but his pride was hurt and, instead of weeping, he muttered something under his breath and stormed out of the room.

Climbing the steps to the roof, he went to his secret hiding place, a small hole in the wall of the unused barsati, where he kept his marbles, kite string, tops and a clasp knife. Opening the knife, he plunged it thrice into the soft wood of the window frame.

'I'll kill her!' he whispered fiercely. 'I'll kill her, I'll kill her!'

'Who are you going to kill, Sunil?'

It was his cousin Madhu, a dark, slim girl of twelve, who aided and abetted him in most of his exploits. Sunil's chachi was her mami. It was a very big family.

'Chachi,' said Sunil. 'She hates me, I know. Well, I hate her too. This time I'll kill her.'

'How are you going to do it?'

'I'll stab her with this.' He showed her the knife. 'Three times, in the heart.'

'But you'll be caught. The CID is very clever. Do you want to go to jail?'

'Won't they hang me?'

'They don't hang small boys. They send them to boarding schools.'

'I don't want to go to a boarding school.'

'Then better not kill your chachi. At least not this way. I'll show you how.'

Madhu produced pencil and paper, went down on her hands and knees, and screwing up her face in sharp concentration, made a rough drawing of Chachi. Then, with a red crayon, she sketched in a big heart in the region of Chachi's stomach.

'Now,' she said, 'stab her to death!'

Sunil's eyes shone with excitement. Here was a great new game. You could always depend on Madhu for something original. He held the drawing against the woodwork, and plunged his knife three times into Chachi's pastel breast.

'You have killed her,' said Madhu.

'Is that all?'

'Well, if you like, we can cremate her.'

'All right.'

She took the torn paper, crumpled it up, produced a box of matches from Sunil's hiding place, lit a match and set fire to the paper. In a few minutes all that remained of Chachi was a few ashes.

'Poor Chachi,' said Madhu.

'Perhaps we shouldn't have done it,' said Sunil, beginning to feel sorry.

'I know, we'll put her ashes in the river!'

'What river?'

'Oh, the drain will do.'

Madhu gathered the ashes together and leant over the balcony of the roof. She threw out her arms, and the ashes drifted downwards. Some of them settled on the pomegranate tree, a few reached the drain and were carried away by a sudden rush of kitchen water. She turned to face Sunil.

Big tears were rolling down Sunil's cheeks.

'What are you crying for?' asked Madhu.

'Chachi, I didn't hate her so much.'

'Then why did you want to kill her?'

'Oh, that was different.'

'Come on, then, let's go down. I have to do my homework.'

As they came down the steps from the roof, Chachi emerged from the kitchen.

'Oh, Chachi!' shouted Sunil. He rushed to her and tried to get his arms around her ample waist.

'Now what's up?' grumbled Chachi. 'What is it this time?'

'Nothing, Chachi. I love you so much. Please don't leave us.'

A look of suspicion crossed Chachi's face. She frowned down at the boy. But she was reassured by the look of genuine affection that she saw in his eyes.

'Perhaps he does care for me, after all,' she thought and patted him gently on the head. She took him by the hand and led him back to the kitchen.

THE BOY WHO
BROKE *the* BANK

Nathu grumbled to himself as he swept the steps of the Pipalnagar Bank, owned by Seth Govind Ram. He used the small broom hurriedly and carelessly, and the dust, after rising in a cloud above his head, settled down again on the steps. As Nathu was banging his pan against a dustbin, Sitaram, the washerman's son, passed by.

Sitaram was on his delivery round. He had a bundle of freshly pressed clothes balanced on his head.

'Don't raise such dust!' he called out to Nathu. 'Are you annoyed because they are still refusing to pay you an extra two rupees a month?'

'I don't wish to talk about it,' complained the sweeper boy. 'I haven't even received my regular pay. And this is the twentieth of the month. Who would think a bank would hold up a poor man's salary? As soon as I get my money, I'm off! Not another week do I work in this place.' And

Nathu banged the pan against the dustbin several times, just to emphasize his point and give himself confidence.

'Well, I wish you luck,' said Sitaram. 'I'll keep a lookout for any jobs that might suit you.' And he plodded barefoot along the road, the big bundle of clothes hiding most of his head and shoulders.

At the fourth home he visited, Sitaram heard the lady of the house mention that she was in need of a sweeper. Tying his bundle together, he said, 'I know of a sweeper boy who's looking for work. He can start from next month. He's with the bank just now but they aren't giving him his pay, and he wants to leave.'

'Is that so?' said Mrs Srivastava. 'Well, tell him to come and see me tomorrow.'

And Sitaram, glad that he had been of service to both a customer and his friend, hoisted his bag on his shoulders and went his way.

Mrs Srivastava had to do some shopping. She gave instructions to the ayah about looking after the baby, and told the cook not to be late with the midday meal. Then she set out for the Pipalnagar marketplace, to make her customary tour of the cloth shops.

A large, shady tamarind tree grew at one end of the bazaar, and it was here that Mrs Srivastava found her friend Mrs Bhushan sheltering from the heat. Mrs Bhushan was fanning herself with a large handkerchief. She complained of the summer which, she affirmed, was definitely the hottest in the history of Pipalnagar. She then showed Mrs Srivastava a sample of the cloth she was going to buy, and for five minutes they discussed its shade, texture and design. Having exhausted this topic, Mrs Srivastava said, 'Do you know, my dear, that Seth Govind Ram's bank can't even pay its employees? Only this morning I heard a complaint from their sweeper, who hasn't received his wages for over a month!'

'Shocking!' remarked Mrs Bhushan. 'If they can't pay the sweeper they must be in a bad way. None of the others could be getting paid either.'

She left Mrs Srivastava at the tamarind tree and went in search of her husband, who was sitting in front of Kamal Kishore's photographic shop, talking to the owner.

'So there you are!' cried Mrs Bhushan. 'I've been looking for you for almost an hour. Where did you disappear?'

'Nowhere,' replied Mr Bhushan. 'Had you remained stationary in one shop, I might have found you. But you go from one shop to another, like a bee in a flower garden.'

'Don't start grumbling. The heat is trying enough. I don't know what's happening to Pipalnagar. Even the bank's about to go bankrupt.'

'What's that?' said Kamal Kishore, sitting up suddenly. 'Which bank?'

'Why the Pipalnagar Bank, of course. I hear they have stopped paying employees. Don't tell me you have an account there, Mr Kishore?'

'No, but my neighbour has!' he exclaimed; and he called out over the low partition to the keeper of the barber shop next door. 'Deep Chand, have you heard the latest? The Pipalnagar Bank is about to collapse. You better get your money out as soon as you can!'

Deep Chand, who was cutting the hair of an elderly gentleman, was so startled that his hand shook and he nicked his customer's right ear. The customer yelped in pain and distress: pain, because of the cut, and distress, because of the awful news he had just heard. With one side of his neck still unshaven, he sped across the road to the general merchant's store where there was a telephone. He dialled Seth Govind Ram's number. The Seth was not at home. Where was he, then? The Seth was holidaying in Kashmir. Oh, was that so? The elderly gentleman did not believe it. He hurried back to the barber's shop and told Deep Chand: 'The bird has flown! Seth Govind Ram has left town. Definitely, it means a collapse.' And then he dashed out of the shop, making a beeline for his office and chequebook.

The news spread through the bazaar with the rapidity of forest fire. At the general merchant's it circulated amongst the customers, and then spread with them in various directions, to the betel seller, the tailor, the free vendor, the jeweller, the beggar sitting on the pavement.

Old Ganpat, the beggar, had a crooked leg. He had been squatting on the pavement for years, calling for alms.

In the evening someone would come with a barrow and take him away. He had never been known to walk. But now, on learning that the bank was about to collapse, Ganpat astonished everyone by leaping to his feet and actually running at top speed in the direction of the bank. It soon became known that he had a thousand rupees in savings!

Men stood in groups at street corners discussing the situation. Pipalnagar seldom had a crisis, seldom or never had floods, earthquakes or drought; and the imminent crash of the Pipalnagar Bank set everyone talking and speculating and rushing about in a frenzy. Some boasted of their farsightedness, congratulating themselves on having already taken out their money, or on never having put any in; others speculated on the reasons for the crash, putting it all down to excesses indulged in by Seth Govind Ram. The Seth had fled the state, said one. He had fled the country, said another. He was hiding in Pipalnagar, said a third. He had hanged himself from the tamarind tree, said a fourth, and had been found that morning by the sweeper boy.

By noon the small bank had gone through all its ready cash, and the harassed manager was in a dilemma. Emergency funds could only be obtained from another bank some thirty miles distant, and he wasn't sure he could persuade the crowd to wait until then. And there was no way of contacting Seth Govind Ram on his houseboat in Kashmir.

People were turned back from the counters and told to return the following day. They did not like the sound of that. And so they gathered outside, on the steps of the bank, shouting, 'Give us our money or we'll break in!' and 'Fetch the Seth, we know he's hiding in a safe deposit locker!' Mischief makers who didn't have a paisa in the bank joined the crowd and aggravated the mood. The manager stood at the door and tried to placate them. He declared that the bank had plenty of money but no immediate means of collecting it; he urged them to go home and come back the next day.

'We want it now!' chanted some of the crowd. 'Now, now, now!'

And a brick hurtled through the air and crashed through the plate glass window of the Pipalnagar Bank.

Nathu arrived next morning to sweep the steps of the bank. He saw the refuse and the broken glass and the stones cluttering the steps. Raising his hands in a gesture of horror and disgust he cried: 'Hooligans! Sons of donkeys! As though it isn't bad enough to be paid late, it seems my work has also to be increased!' He smote the steps with his broom scattering the refuse.

'Good morning, Nathu,' said the washerman's boy, getting down from his bicycle. 'Are you ready to take up a new job from the first of next month? You'll have to I suppose, now that the bank is going out of business.'

'How's that?' said Nathu.

'Haven't you heard? Well, you'd better wait here until half the population of Pipalnagar arrives to claim their money.' And he waved cheerfully—he did not have a bank account—and sped away on his cycle.

Nathu went back to sweeping the steps, muttering to himself. When he had finished his work, he sat down on the highest step, to await the arrival of the manager. He was determined to get his pay.

'Who would have thought the bank would collapse!' he said to himself, and looked thoughtfully into the distance. 'I wonder how it could have happened . . .'

RUSTY
and
FRIENDS

RUSTY
PLAYS HOLI

In the early morning, when it was still dark, Ranbir stopped in the jungle behind Mr Harrison's house, and slapped his drum. His thick mass of hair was covered with red dust and his body, naked but for a cloth round his waist, was smeared green; he looked like a painted god, a green god. After a minute he slapped the drum again, then sat down on his heels and waited.

Rusty woke to the sound of the second drum-beat, and lay in bed and listened; it was repeated, travelling over the still air and in through the bedroom window. Dhum! . . . a double-beat now, one deep, one high, insistent, questioning . . . Rusty remembered his promise, that he would play Holi with Ranbir, meet him in the jungle when he beat the drum. But he had made the promise on the condition that his guardian did not return; he could not possibly keep it now, not after the thrashing he had received.

Dhum-dhum, spoke the drum in the forest; dhum-dhum, impatient and getting annoyed . . .

'Why can't he shut up,' muttered Rusty, 'does he want to wake Mr Harrison . . .'

Holi, the festival of colours, the arrival of spring, the rebirth of the new year, the awakening of love, what were these things to him, they did not concern his life, he could not start a new life, not for one day . . . and besides, it all sounded very primitive, this throwing of colour and beating of drums . . .

Dhum-dhum!

The boy sat up in bed.

The sky had grown lighter.

From the distant bazaar came a new music, many drums and voices, faint but steady, growing in rhythm and excitement. The sound conveyed something to Rusty, something wild and emotional, something that belonged to his dream world, and on a sudden impulse he sprang out of bed.

He went to the door and listened; the house was quiet, he bolted the door. The colours of Holi, he knew, would stain his clothes, so he did not remove his pyjamas. In an old pair of flattened rubber-soled tennis shoes, he climbed out of the window and ran over the dew-wet grass, down the path behind the house, over the hill and into the jungle.

When Ranbir saw the boy approach, he rose from the ground. The long hand-drum, the dholak, hung at his waist. As he rose, the sun rose. But the sun did not look as fiery as Ranbir who, in Rusty's eyes, appeared as a painted demon, rather than as a god.

'You are late, mister,' said Ranbir, 'I thought you were not coming.'

He had both his fists closed, but when he walked towards Rusty he opened them, smiling widely, a white smile in a green face. In his right hand was the red dust and in his left hand the green dust. And with his right hand he rubbed the red dust on Rusty's left cheek, and then with the other hand he put the green dust on the boy's right cheek; then he stood back and looked at Rusty and laughed. Then, according to the custom, he embraced the bewildered boy. It was a wrestler's hug, and Rusty winced breathlessly.

'Come,' said Ranbir, 'let us go and make the town a rainbow.'

~

And truly, that day there was an outbreak of spring.

The sun came up, and the bazaar woke up. The walls of the houses were suddenly patched with splashes of colour, and just as suddenly the trees seemed to have burst into flower; for in the forest there were armies of rhododendrons, and by the river the poinsettias danced; the cherry and the plum were in blossom; the snow in the mountains had melted, and the streams were rushing torrents; the new leaves on the trees were full of sweetness, and the young grass held both dew and sun, and made an emerald of every dewdrop.

The infection of spring spread simultaneously through the world of man and the world of nature, and made them one.

Ranbir and Rusty moved round the hill, keeping in the fringe of the jungle until they had skirted not only the European community but also the smart shopping centre. They came down dirty little side-streets where the walls of houses, stained with the wear and tear of many years of meagre habitation, were now stained again with the vivid colours of Holi. They came to the Clock Tower.

At the Clock Tower, spring had really been declared open. Clouds of coloured dust rose in the air and spread, and jets of water—green and orange and purple, all rich emotional colours—burst out everywhere.

Children formed groups. They were armed mainly with bicycle pumps, or pumps fashioned from bamboo stems, from which was squirted liquid colour. And the children paraded the main road, chanting shrilly and clapping their hands. The men and women preferred the dust to the water. They, too, sang, but their chanting held a significance, their hands and fingers drummed the rhythms of spring, the same rhythms, the same songs that belonged to this day every year of their lives.

Ranbir was met by some friends and greeted with great hilarity. A bicycle pump was directed at Rusty and a jet of sooty black water squirted into his face.

Blinded for a moment, Rusty blundered about in great confusion. A horde of children bore down on him, and he was subjected to a pumping from all sides. His shirt and pyjamas, drenched through, stuck to his skin; then someone gripped the end of his shirt and tugged at it until it tore and came away. Dust was thrown on the boy, on his face and body, roughly and with full force, and his tender, under-exposed skin smarted beneath the onslaught.

Then his eyes cleared. He blinked and looked wildly round at the group of boys and girls who cheered and danced in front of him. His body was running mostly with sooty black, streaked with red, and his mouth seemed full of it too, and he began to spit.

Then, one by one, Ranbir's friends approached Rusty.

Gently, they rubbed dust on the boy's cheeks, and embraced him; they were so like many flaming demons that Rusty could not distinguish one from the other. But this gentle greeting, coming so soon after the stormy bicycle pump attack, bewildered Rusty even more.

Ranbir said: 'Now you are one of us, come,' and Rusty went with him and the others.

'Suri is hiding,' cried someone. 'He has locked himself in his house and won't play Holi!'

'Well, he will have to play,' said Ranbir, 'even if we break the house down.'

Suri, who dreaded Holi, had decided to spend the day in a state of siege; and had set up camp in his mother's kitchen, where there were provisions enough for the whole day. He listened to his playmates calling to him from the courtyard, and ignored their invitations, jeers, and threats; the door was strong and well barricaded. He settled himself beneath a table, and turned the pages of the English nudists' journal, which he bought every month chiefly for its photographic value.

But the youths outside, intoxicated by the drumming and shouting and high spirits, were not going to be done out of the pleasure of discomfiting Suri. So they acquired a ladder and made their entry into the kitchen by the skylight.

Suri squealed with fright. The door was opened and he was bundled out, and his spectacles were trampled.

'My glasses!' he screamed. 'You've broken them!'

'You can afford a dozen pairs!' jeered one of his antagonists.

'But I can't see, you fools, I can't see!'

'He can't see!' cried someone in scorn. 'For once in his life, Suri can't see what's going on! Now, whenever he spies, we'll smash his glasses!'

Not knowing Suri very well, Rusty could not help pitying the frantic boy.

'Why don't you let him go,' he asked Ranbir. 'Don't force him if he doesn't want to play.'

'But this is the only chance we have of repaying him for all his dirty tricks. It is the only day on which no one is afraid of him!'

Rusty could not imagine how anyone could possibly be afraid of the pale, struggling, spindly-legged boy who was almost being torn apart, and was glad when the others had finished their sport with him.

All day Rusty roamed the town and countryside with Ranbir and his friends, and Suri was soon forgotten. For one day, Ranbir and his friends forgot their homes and their work and the problem of the next meal, and danced down the roads, out of the town and into the forest. And, for one day, Rusty forgot his guardian and the missionary's wife and the supple malacca cane, and ran with the others through the town and into the forest.

The crisp, sunny morning ripened into afternoon.

In the forest, in the cool dark silence of the jungle, they stopped singing and shouting, suddenly exhausted. They lay down in the shade of many trees, and the grass was soft and comfortable, and very soon everyone except Rusty was fast asleep.

Rusty was tired. He was hungry. He had lost his shirt and shoes, his feet were bruised, his body sore. It was only now, resting, that he noticed these things, for he had been caught up in the excitement of the colour game, overcome by an exhilaration he had never known. His fair hair was tousled and streaked with colour, and his eyes were wide with wonder.

He was exhausted now, but he was happy.

He wanted this to go on for ever, this day of feverish emotion, this life in another world. He did not want to leave the forest; it was safe, its earth soothed him, gathered him in, so that the pain of his body became a pleasure . . .

He did not want to go home.

THE CROOKED
TREE

'You must pass your exams and go to college, but do not feel that if you fail, you will be able to do nothing.'

My room in Shahganj was very small. I had paced about in it so often that I knew its exact measurements: twelve feet by ten. The string of my cot needed tightening. The dip in the middle was so pronounced that I invariably woke up in the morning with a backache; but I was hopeless at tightening charpoy strings.

Under the cot was my tin trunk. Its contents ranged from old, rejected manuscripts to clothes and letters and photographs. I had resolved that one day, when I had made some money with a book, I would throw the trunk and everything else out of the window, and leave Shahganj forever. But until then I was a prisoner. The rent was nominal, the window had a view of the bus stop and rickshaw stand, and I had nowhere else to go.

I did not live entirely alone. Sometimes a beggar spent the night on the balcony; and, during cold or wet weather, the boys from the tea shop, who normally slept on the pavement, crowded into the room.

Usually I woke early in the mornings, as sleep was fitful, uneasy, crowded with dreams. I knew it was five o'clock when I heard the first upcountry bus leaving its shed. I would then get up and take a walk in the fields beyond the railroad tracks.

One morning, while I was walking in the fields, I noticed someone lying across the pathway, his head and shoulders hidden by the stalks of young sugar cane. When I came near, I saw he was a boy of about sixteen. His body was twitching convulsively, his face was very white, except where a little blood had trickled down his chin. His legs kept moving and his hands fluttered restlessly, helplessly.

'What's the matter with you?' I asked, kneeling down beside him.

But he was still unconscious and could not answer me.

I ran down the footpath to a well and, dipping the end of my shirt in a shallow trough of water, ran back and sponged the boy's face. The twitching ceased and, though he still breathed heavily, his hands became still and his face calm. He opened his eyes and stared at me without any immediate comprehension.

'You have bitten your tongue,' I said, wiping the blood from his mouth. 'Don't worry. I'll stay with you until you feel better.'

He sat up now and said, 'I'm all right, thank you.'

'What happened?' I asked, sitting down beside him.

'Oh, nothing much. It often happens, I don't know why. But I cannot control it.'

'Have you seen a doctor?'

'I went to the hospital in the beginning. They gave me some pills, which I had to take every day. But the pills made me so tired and sleepy that I couldn't work properly. So I stopped taking them. Now this happens once or twice a month. But what does it matter? I'm all right when it's over, and I don't feel anything while it is happening.'

He got to his feet, dusting his clothes and smiling at me. He was slim, long-limbed and bony. There was a little fluff on his cheeks and the promise of a moustache.

'Where do you live?' I asked. 'I'll walk back with you.'

'I don't live anywhere,' he said. 'Sometimes I sleep in the temple, sometimes in the gurdwara. In summer months I sleep in the municipal gardens.'

'Well, then let me come with you as far as the gardens.'

He told me that his name was Kamal, that he studied at the Shahganj High School, and that he hoped to pass his examinations in a few months' time. He was studying hard and, if he passed with a good division, he hoped to attend a college. If he failed, there was only the prospect of continuing to live in the municipal gardens . . .

He carried with him a small tray of merchandise, supported by straps that went round his shoulders. In it were combs and buttons and cheap toys and little vials of perfume. All day he walked about Shahganj, selling odds and ends to people in the bazaar or at their houses. He made, on an average, two rupees a day, which was enough for his food and his school fees.

He told me all this while we walked back to the bus stand. I returned to my room, to try and write something, while Kamal went on to the bazaar to try and sell his wares.

There was nothing very unusual about Kamal's being an orphan and a refugee. During the communal holocaust of 1947, thousands of homes had been broken up, and women and children had been killed. What was unusual in Kamal was his sensitivity, a quality I thought rare in a Punjabi youth who had grown up in the Frontier provinces during a period of hate and violence. And it was not so much his positive attitude to life that appealed to me (most people in Shahganj were completely resigned to their lot) as his gentleness, his quiet voice and the smile that flickered across his face regardless of whether he was sad or happy. In the morning, when I opened my door, I found Kamal asleep at the top of the steps. His tray lay a few feet away. I shook him gently, and he woke at once.

'Have you been sleeping here all night?' I asked. 'Why didn't you come inside?'

'It was very late,' he said. 'I didn't want to disturb you.'

'Someone could have stolen your things while you slept.'

'Oh, I sleep quite lightly. Besides, I have nothing of special value. But I came to ask you something.'

'Do you need any money?'

'No. I want you to take your meal with me tonight.'

'But where? You don't have a place of your own. It will be too expensive in a restaurant.'

'In your room,' said Kamal. 'I will bring the food and cook it here. You have a stove?'

'I think so,' I said. 'I will have to look for it.'

'I will come at seven,' said Kamal, strapping on his tray. 'Don't worry. I know how to cook!'

He ran down the steps and made for the bazaar. I began to look for the oil stove, found it at the bottom of my tin trunk, and then discovered I hadn't any pots or pans or dishes. Finally, I borrowed these from Deep Chand, the barber.

Kamal brought a chicken for our dinner. This was a costly luxury in Shahganj, to be taken only two or three times a year. He had bought the bird for three rupees, which was cheap, considering it was not too skinny. While Kamal set about roasting it, I went down to the bazaar and procured a bottle of beer on credit, and this served as an appetizer.

'We are having an expensive meal,' I observed. 'Three rupees for the chicken and three rupees for the beer. But I wish we could do it more often.'

'We should do it at least once a month,' said Kamal. 'It should be possible if we work hard.'

'You know how to work. You work from morning to night.'

'But you are a writer, Rusty. That is different. You have to wait for a mood.'

'Oh, I'm not a genius that I can afford the luxury of moods. No, I'm just lazy, that's all.'

'Perhaps you are writing the wrong things.'

'I know I am. But I don't know how I can write anything else.'

'Have you tried?'

'Yes, but there is no money in it. I wish I could make a living in some other way. Even if I repaired cycles, I would make more money.'

'Then why not repair cycles?'

'No, I will not repair cycles. I would rather be a bad writer than a good repairer of cycles. But let us not think of work. There is time enough for work. I want to know more about you.'

Kamal did not know if his parents were alive or dead. He had lost them, literally, when he was six. It happened at the Amritsar railroad station, where trains coming across the border disgorged thousands of refugees, or pulled into the station half-empty, drenched with blood and littered with corpses.

Kamal and his parents were lucky to escape the massacre. Had they travelled on an earlier train (they had tried desperately to get into one), they might well have been killed; but circumstances favoured them then, only to trick them later.

Kamal was clinging to his mother's sari, while she remained close to her husband, who was elbowing his way through the frightened, bewildered throng of refugees. Glancing over his shoulder at a woman who lay on the ground, wailing and beating her breasts, Kamal collided with a burly Sikh and lost his grip on his mother's sari.

The Sikh had a long curved sword at his waist; and Kamal stared up at him in awe and fascination—at his long hair, which had fallen loose, and his wild black beard, and the bloodstains on his white shirt. The Sikh pushed him out of the way and when Kamal looked around for his mother, she was not to be seen. She was hidden from him by a mass of restless bodies, pushed in different directions. He could hear her calling, 'Kamal, where are you, Kamal?' He tried to force his way through the crowd, in the direction of the voice, but he was carried the other way . . .

At night, when the platform was empty, he was still searching for his mother. Eventually, some soldiers took him away. They looked for his parents, but without success, and finally, they sent Kamal to a refugee camp. From there he went to an orphanage. But when he was eight, and felt himself a man, he ran away.

He worked for some time as a helper in a tea shop; but, when he started getting epileptic fits, the shopkeeper asked him to leave, and he found himself on the streets, begging for a living. He begged for a year, moving from one town to another, and ended up finally at Shahganj. By then he was twelve and too old to beg; but he had saved some money, and with it he bought a small stock of combs, buttons, cheap perfumes and bangles; and, converting himself into a mobile shop, went from door to door, selling his wares.

Shahganj was a small town, and there was no house which Kamal hadn't visited. Everyone recognized him, and there were some who offered him food and drink; the children knew him well, because he played on a small flute whenever he made his rounds, and they followed him to listen to the flute.

I began to look forward to Kamal's presence. He dispelled some of my own loneliness. I found I could work better, knowing that I did not have to work alone. And Kamal came to me, perhaps because I was the first person to have taken a personal interest in his life, and because I saw nothing frightening in his sickness. Most people in Shahganj thought epilepsy was infectious; some considered it a form of divine punishment for sins committed in a former life. Except for children, those who knew of his condition generally gave him a wide berth.

At sixteen, a boy grows like young wheat, springing up so fast that he is unaware of what is taking place within him. His mind quickens, his gestures become more confident. Hair sprouts like young grass on his face and chest, and his muscles begin to mature. Never again will he experience so much change and growth in so short a time. He is full of currents and countercurrents.

Kamal combined the bloom of youth with the beauty of the short-lived. It made me sad even to look at his pale, slim body. It hurt me to look into his eyes. Life and death were always struggling in their depths.

'Should I go to Delhi and take up a job?' I asked.

'Why not? You are always talking about it.'

'Why don't you come, too? Perhaps they can stop your fits.'

'We will need money for that. When I have passed my examinations, I will come.'

'Then I will wait,' I said. I was twenty-two, and there was world enough and time for everything.

We decided to save a little money from his small earnings and my occasional payments. We would need money to go to Delhi, money to live there until we could earn a living. We put away twenty rupees one week, but lost it the next when we lent it to a friend who owned a cyclerickshaw. But this gave us the occasional use of his cycle, and early one morning, with Kamal sitting on the crossbar, I rode out of Shahganj.

After cycling for about two miles, we got down and pushed the cycle off the road, taking a path through a paddy field and then through a field of young maize, until in the distance we saw a tree, a crooked tree, growing beside an old well.

I do not know the name of that tree. I had never seen one like it before. It had a crooked trunk and crooked branches, and was clothed in thick, broad, crooked leaves, like the leaves on which food is served in the bazaar.

In the trunk of the tree there was a hole, and when we set the bicycle down with a crash, a pair of green parrots flew out, and went dipping and swerving across the fields. There was grass around the well, cropped short by grazing cattle.

We sat in the shade of the crooked tree, and Kamal untied the red cloth in which he had brought our food. When we had eaten, we stretched ourselves out on the grass. I closed my eyes and became aware of a score of different sensations. I heard a cricket singing in the tree, the cooing of pigeons from the walls of the old well, the quiet breathing of Kamal, the parrots returning to the tree, the distant hum of an airplane. I smelled the grass and the old bricks round the well and the promise of rain. I felt Kamal's fingers against my arm, and the sun creeping over my cheek. And when I opened my eyes, there were clouds on the horizon, and Kamal was asleep, his arm thrown across his face to keep out the glare.

I went to the well, and putting my shoulders to the ancient handle, turned the wheel, moving around while cool, clean water gushed out over the stones and along the channel to the fields. The discovery that I could water a field, that I had the power to make things grow, gave me a thrill of satisfaction; it was like writing a story that had the ring of truth. I drank from one of the trays; the water was sweet with age.

Kamal was sitting up, looking at the sky.

'It's going to rain,' he said.

We began cycling homeward; but we were still some way out of Shahganj when it began to rain. A lashing wind swept the rain across our faces, but we exulted in it, and sang at the top of our voices until we reached the Shahganj bus stop.

Across the railroad tracks and the dry riverbed, fields of maize stretched away, until there came a dry region of thorn bushes and lantana scrub, where the earth was cut into jagged cracks, like a jigsaw puzzle. Dotting the landscape were old, abandoned brick kilns. When it rained heavily, the hollows filled up with water.

Kamal and I came to one of these hollows to bathe and swim. There was an island in the middle of it, and on this small mound lay the ruins of a hut where a nightwatchman had once lived, looking after the brick kilns. We would swim out to the island, which was only a few yards from the banks of the hollow. There was a grassy patch in front of the hut, and early in the mornings, before it got too hot, we would wrestle on the grass.

Though I was heavier than Kamal, my chest as sound as a new drum, he had strong, wiry arms and legs, and would often pinion me around the waist with his bony knees.

65

Now, while we wrestled on the new monsoon grass, I felt his body go tense. He stiffened, his legs jerked against my body, and a shudder passed through him. I knew that he had a fit coming on, but I was unable to extricate myself from his arms.

He gripped me more tightly as the fit took possession of him. Instead of struggling, I lay still, tried to absorb some of his anguish, tried to draw some of his agitation to myself. I had a strange fancy that by identifying myself with his convulsions, I might alleviate them.

I pressed against Kamal, and whispered soothingly into his ear; and then, when I noticed his mouth working, I thrust my fingers between his teeth to prevent him from biting his tongue. But so violent was the convulsion that his teeth bit into the flesh of my palm and ground against my knuckles. I shouted with the pain and tried to jerk my hand away, but it was impossible to loosen the grip of his jaws. So I closed my eyes and counted—counted till seven—until consciousness returned to him and his muscles relaxed.

My hand was shaking and covered with blood. I bound it in my handkerchief and kept it hidden from Kamal.

We walked back to the room without talking much. Kamal looked depressed and weak. I kept my hand beneath my shirt, and Kamal was too dejected to notice anything. It was only at night, when he returned from his classes, that he noticed the cuts, and I told him I had slipped in the road, cutting my hand on some broken glass.

66

Rain upon Shahganj. And, until the rain stops, Shahganj is fresh and clean and alive. The children run out of their houses, glorying in their nakedness. The gutters choke, and the narrow street becomes a torrent of water, coursing merrily down to the bus stop. It swirls over the trees and the roofs of the town, and the parched earth soaks it up, exuding a fragrance that comes only once in a year, the fragrance of quenched earth, that most exhilarating of smells.

The rain swept in through the door and soaked the cot. When I had succeeded in closing the door, I found the roof leaking, the water trickling down the walls and forming new pictures on the cracking plaster. The door flew open again, and there was Kamal standing on the threshold, shaking himself like a wet dog. Coming in, he stripped and dried himself, and then sat shivering on the bed while I made frantic efforts to close the door again.

'You need some tea,' I said.

He nodded, forgetting to smile for once, and I knew his mind was elsewhere, in one of a hundred possible places from his dreams.

'One day I will write a book,' I said, as we drank strong tea in the fast-fading twilight. 'A real book, about real people. Perhaps it will be about you and me and Shahganj. And then we will run away from Shahganj, fly on the wings of Garuda, and all our troubles will be over and fresh troubles will begin. Why should we mind difficulties, as long as they are new difficulties?'

'First I must pass my exams,' said Kamal. 'Otherwise, I can do nothing, go nowhere.'

'Don't take exams too seriously. I know that in India they are the passport to any kind of job, and that you cannot become a clerk unless you have a degree. But do not forget that you are studying for the sake of acquiring knowledge, and not for the sake of becoming a clerk. You don't want to become a clerk or a bus conductor, do you? You must pass your exams and go to college, but do not feel that if you fail, you will be able to do nothing. Why, you can start making your own buttons instead of selling other people's!'

'You are right,' said Kamal. 'But why not be an educated button manufacturer?'

'Why not, indeed? That's just what I mean. And, while you are studying for your exams, I will be writing my book. I will start tonight! It is an auspicious night, the beginning of the monsoon.'

The light did not come on. A tree must have fallen across the wires. I lit a candle and placed it on the windowsill and, while the candle spluttered in the steamy air, Kamal opened his books and, with one hand on a book and the other hand playing with his toes—this attitude helped him to concentrate—he devoted his attention to algebra.

I took an ink bottle down from a shelf and, finding it empty, added a little rainwater to the crusted contents. Then I sat down beside Kamal and began to write; but the pen was useless and made blotches all over the paper, and

I had no idea what I should write about, though I was full of writing just then. So I began to look at Kamal instead; at his eyes, hidden in shadow, and his hands, quiet in the candlelight; and I followed his breathing and the slight movement of his lips as he read softly to himself.

And, instead of starting my book, I sat and watched Kamal.

Sometimes Kamal played the flute at night, while I was lying awake; and, even when I was asleep, the flute would play in my dreams. Sometimes he brought it to the crooked tree, and played it for the benefit of the birds; but the parrots only made harsh noises and flew away.

Once, when Kamal was playing his flute to a group of children, he had a fit. The flute fell from his hands, and he began to roll about in the dust on the roadside. The children were frightened and ran away. But the next time they heard Kamal play his flute, they came to listen as usual.

That Kamal was gaining in strength I knew from the way he was able to pin me down whenever we wrestled on the grass near the old brick kilns. It was no longer necessary for me to yield deliberately to him. And, though his fits still recurred from time to time—as we knew they would continue to do—he was not so depressed afterwards. The anxiety and the death had gone from his eyes.

His examinations were nearing, and he was working hard. (I had yet to begin the first chapter of my book.) Because of the necessity of selling two or three rupees' worth of articles every day, he did not get much time for studying; but he stuck to his books until past midnight, and it was seldom that I heard his flute.

He put aside his tray of odds and ends during the examinations, and walked to the examination centre instead. And after two weeks, when it was all over, he took up his tray and began his rounds again. In a burst of creativity, I wrote three pages of my novel.

On the morning the results of the examination were due, I rose early, before Kamal, and went down to the news agency. It was five o'clock and the newspapers had just arrived. I went through the columns relating to Shahganj, but I couldn't find Kamal's roll number on the list of successful candidates. I had the number written down on a slip of paper, and I looked at it again to make sure that I had compared it correctly with the others; then I went through the newspaper once more.

When I returned to the room, Kamal was sitting on the doorstep. I didn't have to tell him he had failed. He knew by the look on my face. I sat down beside him, and we said nothing for some time.

'Never mind,' said Kamal, eventually. 'I will pass next year.'

I realized that I was more depressed than he was, and that he was trying to console me.

'If only you'd had more time,' I said.

'I have plenty of time now. Another year. And you will have time in which to finish your book; then we can both go away. Another year of Shahganj won't be so bad. As long as I have your friendship, almost everything else can be tolerated, even my sickness.'

And then, turning to me with an expression of intense happiness, he said, 'Yesterday I was sad, and tomorrow I may be sad again, but today I know that I am happy. I want to live on and on. I feel that life isn't long enough to satisfy me.'

He stood up, the tray hanging from his shoulders.

'What would you like to buy?' he said. 'I have everything you need.'

At the bottom of the steps he turned and smiled at me, and I knew then that I had written my story.

AS TIME
GOES BY

Prem's boys are growing tall and healthy, on the verge of manhood. How can I think of death, when faced with the full vigour and confidence of youth? They remind me of Somi and Daljit, who were the same age when I knew them in Dehra during our schooldays. But remembering Somi and Dal reminds me of death again—for Dal had died a young man—and I look at Prem's boys again, haunted by the thought of suddenly leaving this world, and pray that I can be with them a little longer.

Somi and Dal . . . I remember: it was going to rain. I could see the rain moving across the hills, and I could smell it on the breeze. But instead of turning back, I walked on through the leaves and brambles that grew over the disused path, and wandered into the forest. I had heard the sound of rushing water at the bottom of the hill, and there was no question of returning until I had found the water.

I had to slide down some smooth rocks into a small ravine, and there I found the stream running across a bed of shingle. I removed my shoes and socks and started walking up the stream. Water trickled down from the hillside, from amongst ferns and grass and wild flowers, and the hills, rising steeply on either side, kept the ravine in shadow. The rocks were smooth, almost soft, and some of them were grey and some yellow. The pool was fed by a small waterfall, and it was deep beneath the waterfall. I did not stay long, because now the rain was swishing over the sal trees, and I was impatient to tell the others about the pool. Somi usually chose the adventures we were to have, and I would just grumble and get involved in them; but the pool was my own discovery, and both Somi and Daljit gave me credit for it.

I think it was the pool that brought us together more than anything else. We made it a secret, private pool, and invited no others. Somi was the best swimmer. He dived off rocks and went gliding about under the water, like a long, golden fish. Dal threshed about with much vigour but little skill. I could dive off a rock too, but I usually landed on my belly.

There were slim silver fish in the waters of the stream. At first we tried catching them with a line, but they usually took the bait and left the hook. Then we brought a bedsheet and stretched it across one end of the stream, but the fish wouldn't come near it. Eventually Somi, without telling us, brought along a stick of dynamite, and Dal and I were startled out of a siesta by a flash across the water and a deafening explosion. Half the hillside tumbled into the pool, and Somi along with it; but we got him out, as well as a good supply of stunned fish which were too small for eating.

The effects of the explosion gave Somi another idea, and that was to enlarge our pool by building a dam across one end. This he accomplished with Dal's and my labour. But one afternoon, when it rained heavily, a torrent of water came rushing down the stream, bursting the dam and flooding the ravine; our clothes were all carried away by the current, and we had to wait for night to fall before creeping home through the darkest alleyways, for we used to bathe quite naked; it would have been unmanly to do otherwise.

Our activities at the pool included wrestling and buffalo riding. We wrestled on a strip of sand that ran beside the stream, and rode on a couple of buffaloes that sometimes came to drink and wallow in the more muddy parts of the stream. We would sit astride the buffaloes, and kick and yell and urge them forward, but on no occasion did we ever get them to move. At the most, they would roll over on their backs, taking us with them into a pool of slush.

But the buffaloes were always comfortable to watch. Solid, earthbound creatures, they liked warm days and cool, soft mud. There is nothing so satisfying to watch than buffaloes wallowing in mud, or ruminating over a mouthful of grass, absolutely oblivious to everything else. They watched us with sleepy, indifferent eyes, and tolerated the pecking of crows. Did they think all that time, or did they just enjoy the sensuousness of soft, wet mud, while we perspired under a summer sun . . .? No, thinking would have been too strenuous for those supine creatures; to get neck-deep in water was their only aim in life.

It didn't matter how muddy we got ourselves, because we had only to dive into the pool to get rid of the muck. In fact, mud fighting was one of our favourite pastimes. It was like playing snowballs, only we used mud balls.

If it was possible for Somi and Dal to get out of their houses undetected at night, we would come to the pool and bathe by moonlight, and at these times we would bathe silently and seriously, because there was something subduing about the stillness of the jungle at night.

I don't exactly remember how we broke up, but we hardly noticed it at the time. That was because we never really believed we were finally parting, or that we would not be seeing the pool again. After about a year, Somi passed his matriculation and entered the military academy. The last time I saw him, about twenty-five years ago, he was about to be commissioned, and sported a fierce and very military moustache. He remembered the pool in a sentimental, military way, but not as I remembered it.

Shortly after Somi had matriculated, Dal and his family left town, and I did not see him again, until after I returned from England. Then he was in Air Force uniform, tall, slim, very handsome, completely unrecognizable as the chubby little boy who had played with me in the pool. Three weeks after this meeting I heard that he had been killed in an air crash. Sweet Dal . . . I feel you are close to me now . . . I want to remember you exactly as you were when we first met. Here is my diary for 1951 (this diary formed the nucleus of my first novel, *The Room on the Roof*), when I was sixteen and you thirteen or fourteen:

September 7: 'Do you like elephants?' Somi asked me.

'Yes, when they are tame.'

'That's all right, then. Daljit!' he called. 'You can come up. Ruskin likes elephants.'

Dal is not exactly an elephant. He is one of us.

He is fat, oh, yes he is fat, but it is his good nature that is so like an elephant's. His fatness is not grotesque or awkward; it is a very pleasant plumpness, and nothing could suit him better. If Dal were thin he would be a failure.

His eyes are bright and round, full of mischievousness and a sort of grumpy gaiety.

And what of the pool?

I looked for it, after an interval of more than thirty years, but couldn't find it. I found the ravine, and the bed of shingle, but there was no water. The stream had changed its course, just as we had changed ours.

I turned away in disappointment, and with a dull ache in my heart. It was cruel of the pool to disappear; it was the cruelty of time. But I hadn't gone far when I heard the sound of rushing water, and the shouting of children; and pushing my way through the jungle, I found another stream and another pool and about half-a-dozen children splashing about in the water.

They did not see me, and I kept in the shadow of the trees and watched them play. But I didn't really see them. I was seeing Somi and Daljit and the lazy old buffaloes, and I stood there for almost an hour, a disembodied spirit, romping again in the shallows of our secret pool. Nothing had really changed. Time is like that.

THE PLAYING
FIELDS *of* SIMLA

It had been a lonely winter for a twelve-year-old boy.
I hadn't really got over my father's untimely death two
years previously; nor had I as yet reconciled myself to my
mother's marriage to the Punjabi gentleman who dealt in
second-hand cars. The three-month winter break over,
I was almost happy to return to my boarding school in
Simla—that elegant hill station once celebrated by Kipling
and soon to lose its status as the summer capital of the Raj
in India.

It wasn't as though I had many friends at school.
I had always been a bit of a loner, shy and reserved,
looking out only for my father's rare visits—on his brief
leaves from RAF duties—and to my sharing his tent or air
force hutment outside Delhi or Karachi. Those unsettled
but happy days would not come again. I needed a friend
but it was not easy to find one among a horde of rowdy,

pea-shooting fourth formers, who carved their names on desks and stuck chewing gum on the class teacher's chair. Had I grown up with other children, I might have developed a taste for schoolboy anarchy; but, in sharing my father's loneliness after his separation from my mother, I had turned into a premature adult. The mixed nature of my reading—Dickens, Richmal Crompton, Tagore and *Champion* and *Film Fun* comics—probably reflected the confused state of my life. A book reader was rare even in those pre-electronic times. On rainy days most boys played cards or Monopoly, or listened to Artie Shaw on the wind-up gramophone in the common room.

After a month in the fourth form I began to notice a new boy, Omar, and then only because he was a quiet, almost taciturn person who took no part in the form's feverish attempts to imitate the Marx Brothers at the circus. He showed no resentment at the prevailing anarchy, nor did he make a move to participate in it. Once he caught me looking at him, and he smiled ruefully, tolerantly. Did I sense another adult in the class? Someone who was a little older than his years?

Even before we began talking to each other, Omar and I developed an understanding of sorts, and we'd nod almost respectfully to each other when we met in the classroom corridors or the environs of dining hall or dormitory. We were not in the same house. The house system practised its own form of apartheid, whereby a member of, say, Curzon

House was not expected to fraternize with someone belonging to Rivaz or Lefroy! Those public schools certainly knew how to clamp you into compartments. However, these barriers vanished when Omar and I found ourselves selected for the School Colts' hockey team—Omar as a fullback, I as goalkeeper. I think a defensive position suited me by nature. In all modesty I have to say that I made a good goalkeeper, both at hockey and football. And fifty years on, I am still keeping goal. Then I did it between goalposts, now I do it off the field—protecting a family, protecting my independence as a writer . . .

The taciturn Omar now spoke to me occasionally, and we combined well on the field of play. A good understanding is needed between goalkeeper and fullback. We were on the same wavelength. I anticipated his moves, he was familiar with mine. Years later, when I read Conrad's *The Secret Sharer*, I thought of Omar.

It wasn't until we were away from the confines of school, classroom and dining hall that our friendship flourished. The hockey team travelled to Sanawar on the next mountain range, where we were to play a couple of matches against our old rivals, the Lawrence Royal Military School. This had been my father's old school, but I did not know that in his time it had also been a military orphanage. Grandfather, who had been a private foot soldier—of the likes of Kipling's Mulvaney, Otheris and Learoyd—had joined the Scottish Rifles after leaving home at the age of seventeen. He had died while his children were still very young, but my father's more rounded education had enabled him to become an officer.

Omar and I were thrown together a good deal during the visit to Sanawar, and in our more leisurely moments, strolling undisturbed around a school where we were guests and not pupils, we exchanged life histories and other confidences. Omar, too, had lost his father—had I sensed that before?—shot in some tribal encounter on the Frontier, for he hailed from the lawless lands beyond Peshawar. A wealthy uncle was seeing to Omar's education. The RAF was now seeing to mine.

We wandered into the school chapel, and there I found my father's name—A.A. Bond—on the school's roll of honour board: old boys who had lost their lives while serving during the two World Wars.

'What did his initials stand for?' asked Omar.

'Aubrey Alexander.'

'Unusual names, like yours. Why did your parents call you Ruskin?'

'I am not sure. I think my father liked the works of John Ruskin, who wrote on serious subjects like art and architecture. I don't think anyone reads him now. They'll read me, though!' I had already started writing my first book. It was called *Nine Months* (the length of the school term, not a pregnancy), and it described some of the happenings at school and lampooned a few of our teachers.

I had filled three slim exercise books with this premature literary project, and I allowed Omar to go through them. He must have been my first reader and critic. 'They're very interesting,' he said, 'but you'll get into trouble if someone finds them. Especially Mr Oliver.' And he read out an offending verse:

Olly, Olly, Olly, with his balls on a trolley,
And his arse all painted green!

I have to admit it wasn't great literature. I was better at hockey and football. I made some spectacular saves, and we won our matches against Sanawar. When we returned to Simla, we were school heroes for a couple of days and lost some of our reticence; we were even a little more forthcoming with other boys. And then Mr Fisher, my housemaster, discovered my literary opus, *Nine Months*, under my mattress, and took it away and read it (as he told me later) from cover to cover. Corporal punishment then being in vogue, I was given six of the best with a springy malacca cane, and my manuscript was torn up and deposited in Fisher's waste-paper basket. All I had to show for my efforts were some purple welts on my bottom. These were proudly displayed to all who were interested, and I was a hero for another two days.

'Will you go away too when the British leave India?' Omar asked me one day.

'I don't think so,' I said. 'My stepfather is Indian.'

'Everyone is saying that our leaders and the British are going to divide the country. Simla will be in India, Peshawar in Pakistan!'

'Oh, it won't happen,' I said glibly. 'How can they cut up such a big country?' But even as we chatted about the possibility, Nehru and Jinnah and Mountbatten and all those who mattered were preparing their instruments for major surgery.

Before their decision impinged on our lives and everyone else's, we found a little freedom of our own—in an underground tunnel that we discovered below the third flat.

It was really part of an old, disused drainage system, and when Omar and I began exploring it, we had no idea just how far it extended. After crawling along on our bellies for some twenty feet, we found ourselves in complete darkness. Omar had brought along a small pencil torch, and with its help we continued writhing forward (moving backwards would have been quite impossible) until we saw a glimmer of light at the end of the tunnel. Dusty, musty, very scruffy, we emerged at last on to a grassy knoll, a little way outside the school boundary.

It's always a great thrill to escape beyond the boundaries that adults have devised. Here we were in unknown territory. To travel without passports—that would be the ultimate in freedom!

But more passports were on their way and more boundaries.

Lord Mountbatten, Viceroy and Governor-General-to-be, came for our Founder's Day and gave away the prizes. I had won a prize for something or the other, and mounted the rostrum to receive my book from this towering, handsome man in his pinstripe suit. Bishop Cotton's was then the premier school of India, often referred to as the 'Eton of the East'. Viceroys and Governors had graced its functions. Many of its boys had gone on to eminence in the civil services and armed forces. There was one 'old boy' about whom they maintained a stolid silence—General Dyer, who had ordered the massacre at Amritsar and destroyed the trust that had been building up between Britain and India.

Now Mountbatten spoke of the momentous events that were happening all around us—the War had just come to an end, the United Nations held out the promise of a world living in peace and harmony, and India, an equal partner with Britain, would be among the great nations . . .

A few weeks later, Bengal and Punjab provinces were bisected. Riots flared up across northern India, and there was a great exodus of people crossing the newly drawn frontiers of Pakistan and India. Homes were destroyed, thousands lost their lives.

The common-room radio and the occasional newspaper kept us abreast of events, but in our tunnel,

Omar and I felt immune from all that was happening, worlds away from all the pillage, murder and revenge. And outside the tunnel, on the pine knoll below the school, there was fresh untrodden grass, sprinkled with clover and daisies, the only sounds the hammering of a woodpecker, the distant insistent call of the Himalayan barbet. Who could touch us there?

'And when all the wars are done,' I said, 'a butterfly will still be beautiful.'

'Did you read that somewhere?'

'No, it just came into my head.'

'Already you're a writer.'

'No, I want to play hockey for India or football for Arsenal. Only winning teams!'

'You can't win forever. Better to be a writer.'

When the monsoon rains arrived, the tunnel was flooded, the drain choked with rubble. We were allowed out to the cinema to see Lawrence Olivier's *Hamlet*, a film that did nothing to raise our spirits on a wet and gloomy afternoon—but it was our last picture that year, because communal riots suddenly broke out in Simla's Lower Bazaar, an area that was still much as Kipling had described it—'a man who knows his way there can defy all the police of India's summer capital'—and we were confined to school indefinitely.

One morning after chapel, the headmaster announced that the Muslim boys—those who had their homes in what was now Pakistan—would have to be evacuated, sent to their homes across the border with an armed convoy.

The tunnel no longer provided an escape for us. The bazaar was out of bounds. The flooded playing field was deserted. Omar and I sat on a damp wooden bench and talked about the future in vaguely hopeful terms; but we didn't solve any problems. Mountbatten and Nehru and Jinnah were doing all the solving.

It was soon time for Omar to leave—he along with some fifty other boys from Lahore, Pindi and Peshawar. The rest of us—Hindus, Christians, Parsis—helped them load their luggage into the waiting trucks. A couple of boys broke down and wept. So did our departing school captain, a Pathan who had been known for his stoic and unemotional demeanour. Omar waved cheerfully to me and I waved back. We had vowed to meet again some day.

The convoy got through safely enough. There was only one casualty—the school cook, who had strayed into an off-limits area in the foothill town of Kalka and been set upon by a mob. He wasn't seen again.

Towards the end of the school year, just as we were all getting ready to leave for the school holidays, I received a letter from Omar. He told me something about his new school and how he missed my company and our games and our tunnel to freedom. I replied and gave him my home address, but I did not hear from him again. The land, though divided, was still a big one, and we were very small.

Some seventeen or eighteen years later I did get news of Omar, but in an entirely different context. India and Pakistan were at war and in a bombing raid over Ambala, not far from Simla, a Pakistani plane was shot down. Its crew died in the crash. One of them, I learnt later, was Omar.

Did he, I wonder, get a glimpse of the playing fields we knew so well as boys?

Perhaps memories of his schooldays flooded back as he flew over the foothills. Perhaps he remembered the tunnel through which we were able to make our little escape to freedom.

But there are no tunnels in the sky.

RUSTY *and* KISHEN
RETURN *to* DEHRA

Before the steps and the river tank came to life, Kishen and Rusty climbed into the ferry boat. It would be crossing the river all day, carrying pilgrims from temple to temple, charging nothing. And though it was very early, and this the first crossing, a free passage across the river made for a crowded boat.

The people who climbed in were even more diverse than those Rusty had met on the train: women and children, bearded old men and wrinkled women, strong young peasants—not the prosperous or mercantile class, but the poor—who had come miles, mostly on foot, to bathe in the sacred waters of the Ganges.

On shore, the steps began to come to life. The previous day's cries and prayers and rites were resumed with the same monotonous devotion, at the same pitch, in the same spirit of timelessness; and the steps sounded to the tread of many feet, sandalled, slippered and bare. The boat floated low in the water, it was so heavy, and the oarsmen had to strain upstream in order to avoid being swept down by the current. Their muscles shone and rippled under the grey-iron of their weather-beaten skins. The blades of the oars cut through the water, in and out; and between grunts, the oarsmen shouted the time of the stroke.

Kishen and Rusty sat crushed together in the middle of the boat. There was no likelihood of their being separated now, but they held hands.

The people in the boat began to sing.

It was a low hum at first, but someone broke in with a song, and the voice—a young voice, clear and pure—reminded Rusty of Somi; and he comforted himself with the thought that Somi would be back in Dehra in the spring.

They sang in time to the stroke of the oars, in and out, and the grunts and shouts of the oarsmen throbbed their way into the song, becoming part of it.

An old woman, who had white hair and a face lined with deep ruts, said: 'It is beautiful to hear the children sing.'

'Then you too should sing,' said Rusty.

She smiled at him, a sweet, toothless smile.

'What are you, my son, are you one of us? I have never, on this river, seen blue eyes and golden hair.'

'I am nothing,' said Rusty. 'I am everything.' He stated it bluntly, proudly.

'Where is your home, then?'

'I have no home,' he said, and felt proud of that too.

'And who is the boy with you?' asked the old woman, a genuine busybody. 'What is he to you?'

Rusty did not answer; he was asking himself the same question: what was Kishen to him? He was sure of one thing, they were both refugees—refugees from the world . . . They were each other's shelter, each other's refuge, each other's help. Kishen was a jungli, divorced from the rest of mankind, and Rusty was the only one who understood him—because Rusty too was divorced from mankind. And theirs was a tie that would hold, because they were the only people who knew each other and loved each other.

Because of this tie, Rusty had to go back. And it was with relief that he went back. His return was justified.

He let his hand trail over the side of the boat: he wanted to remember the touch of the water as it moved past them, down and away: it would come to the ocean, the ocean that was life.

He could not run away. He could not escape the life he had made, the ocean into which he had floundered the night he left his guardian's house. He had to return to the room, *his* room; he had to go back.

The song died away as the boat came ashore. They disembarked, walking over the smooth pebbles; and the forest rose from the edge of the river, and beckoned them.

Rusty remembered the forest on the day of the picnic, when he had kissed Meena and held her hands, and he remembered the magic of the forest and the magic of Meena.

'One day,' he said, 'we must live in the jungle.'

'One day,' said Kishen, and he laughed. 'But now we walk back. We walk back to the room on the roof! It is our room, we have to go back!'

They had to go back: to bathe at the water tank and listen to the morning gossip, to sit in the fruit trees and eat in the chaat shop and perhaps make a garden on the roof; to eat and sleep; to work; to live; to die.

Kishen laughed.

'One day you'll be great, Rusty. A writer or an actor or a prime minister or something. Maybe a poet! Why not a poet, Rusty?'

Rusty smiled. He knew he was smiling, because he was smiling at himself.

'Yes,' he said, 'why not a poet?' So they began to walk

Ahead of them lay forest and silence—and what was left of time . . .

REUNION
at the REGAL

If you want to see a ghost, just stand outside New Delhi's Regal Cinema for twenty minutes or so. The approach to the grand old cinema hall is a great place for them. Sooner or later you'll see a familiar face in the crowd. Before you have time to recall who it was or who it may be, it will have disappeared and you will be left wondering if it really was so-and-so . . . because surely so-and-so died several years ago . . .

The Regal was very posh in the early 1940s when, in the company of my father, I saw my first film there. The Connaught Place cinemas still had a new look about them, and they showed the latest offerings from Hollywood and Britain. To see a Hindi film, you had to travel all the way to Kashmere Gate or Chandni Chowk.

Over the years, I was in and out of the Regal quite a few times, and so I became used to meeting old acquaintances or glimpsing familiar faces in the foyer or on the steps outside.

On one occasion I was mistaken for a ghost.

I was about thirty at the time. I was standing on the steps of the arcade, waiting for someone, when a young Indian man came up to me and said something in German or what sounded like German.

'I'm sorry,' I said. 'I don't understand. You may speak to me in English or Hindi.'

'Aren't you Hans? We met in Frankfurt last year.'

'I'm sorry, I've never been to Frankfurt.'

'You look exactly like Hans.'

'Maybe I'm his double. Or maybe I'm his ghost!'

My facetious remark did not amuse the young man. He looked confused and stepped back, a look of horror spreading over his face. 'No, no,' he stammered. 'Hans is alive, you can't be his ghost!'

'I was only joking.'

But he had turned away, hurrying off through the crowd. He seemed agitated. I shrugged philosophically. So I had a double called Hans, I reflected; perhaps I'd run into him some day.

I mention this incident only to show that most of us have lookalikes, and that sometimes we see what we want to see, or are looking for, even if on looking closer, the resemblance isn't all that striking.

But there was no mistaking Kishen when he approached me. I hadn't seen him for five or six years, but he looked much the same. Bushy eyebrows, offset by gentle eyes; a determined chin, offset by a charming smile. The girls had always liked him, and he knew it; and he was content to let them do the pursuing.

We saw a film—I think it was *The Wind Cannot Read*—and then we strolled across to the old Standard Restaurant, ordered dinner and talked about old times, while the small band played sentimental tunes from the 1950s.

Yes, we talked about old times—growing up in Dehra, where we lived next door to each other, exploring our neighbours' litchi orchards, cycling about the town in the days before the scooter had been invented, kicking a football around on the maidan, or just sitting on the compound wall doing nothing. I had just finished school, and an entire year stretched before me until it was time to go abroad. Kishen's father, a civil engineer, was under transfer orders, so Kishen, too, temporarily did not have to go to school.

He was an easy-going boy, quite content to be at a loose end in my company—I was to describe a couple of our escapades in my first novel, *The Room on the Roof*. I had literary pretensions; he was apparently without ambition although, as he grew older, he was to surprise me by his wide reading and erudition.

One day, while we were cycling along the bank of the Rajpur canal, he skidded off the path and fell into the canal with his cycle. The water was only waist-deep; but it was quite swift, and I had to jump in to help him. There was no real danger, but we had some difficulty getting the cycle out of the canal.

Later, he learnt to swim.

But that was after I'd gone away . . .

Convinced that my prospects would be better in England, my mother packed me off to her relatives in Jersey, and it was to be four long years before I could return to the land I truly cared for. In that time, many of my Dehra friends had left the town; it wasn't a place where you could do much after finishing school. Kishen wrote to me from Calcutta, where he was at an engineering college. Then he was off to 'study abroad'. I heard from him from time to time. He seemed happy. He had an equable temperament and got on quite well with most people. He had a girlfriend too, he told me.

'But,' he wrote, 'you're my oldest and best friend. Wherever I go, I'll always come back to see you.'

And, of course, he did. We met several times while I was living in Delhi, and once we revisited Dehra together and walked down Rajpur Road and ate tikkis and golguppas behind the clock tower. But the old familiar faces were missing. The streets were overbuilt and overcrowded, and the litchi gardens were fast disappearing. After we got back to Delhi, Kishen accepted the offer of a job in Mumbai. We kept in touch in desultory fashion, but our paths and our lives had taken different directions. He was busy nurturing his career with an engineering firm; I had retreated to the hills with radically different goals—to write and be free of the burden of a ten-to-five desk job.

Time went by, and I lost track of Kishen.

About a year ago, I was standing in the lobby of the India International Centre, when an attractive young woman in her mid-thirties came up to me and said, 'Hello, Rusty, don't you remember me? I'm Manju. I lived next to you and Kishen and Ranbir when we were children.'

I recognized her then, for she had always been a pretty girl, the 'belle' of Dehra's Astley Hall.

We sat down and talked about old times and new times, and I told her that I hadn't heard from Kishen for a few years.

'Didn't you know?' she asked. 'He died about two years ago.'

'What happened?' I was dismayed, even angry, that I hadn't heard about it. 'He couldn't have been more than thirty-eight.'

'It was an accident on a beach in Goa. A child had got into difficulties and Kishen swam out to save her. He did rescue the little girl, but when he swam ashore he had a heart attack. He died right there on the beach. It seems he had always had a weak heart. The exertion must have been too much for him.'

I was silent. I knew he'd become a fairly good swimmer, but I did not know about the heart.

'Was he married?' I asked.

'No, he was always the eligible bachelor boy.'

It had been good to see Manju again, even though she had given me bad news. She told me she was happily married, with a small son. We promised to keep in touch.

And that's the end of this tale, apart from my brief visit to Delhi last November.

I had taken a taxi to Connaught Place and decided to get down at the Regal. I stood there a while, undecided about what to do or where to go. It was almost time for a show to start, and there were a lot of people milling around.

I thought someone called my name. I looked around, and there was Kishen in the crowd.

'Kishen!' I called, and started after him.

But a stout lady climbing out of a scooter-rickshaw got in my way, and by the time I had a clear view again, my old friend had disappeared.

Had I seen his lookalike, a double? Or had he kept his promise to come back to see me once more?

LIFE *with* MY FATHER

LIFE *with* MY
FATHER

During my childhood and early boyhood with my
father, we were never in one house or dwelling for
very long. I think the 'Tennis Bungalow' in Jamnagar (in
the grounds of the Ram Vilas Palace) housed us for a couple
of years, and that was probably the longest period.

In Jamnagar itself we had at least three abodes—a
rambling, leaking old colonial mansion called 'Cambridge
House'; a wing of an old palace, the Lal Bagh I think it was
called, which was also inhabited by bats and cobras; and
the aforementioned 'Tennis Bungalow,' a converted sports
pavilion which was really quite bright and airy.

I think my father rather enjoyed changing houses,
setting up home in completely different surroundings. He
loved rearranging rooms too, so that this month's sitting
room became next month's bedroom, and so on; furniture

would also be moved around quite frequently, somewhat to my mother's irritation, for she liked having things in their familiar places. She had grown up in one abode (her father's Dehra house) whereas my father hadn't remained anywhere for very long. Sometimes he spoke of making a home in Scotland, beside Loch Lomond, but it was only a distant dream.

The only real stability was represented by his stamp collection, and this he carried around in a large tin trunk, for it was an extensive and valuable collection—there was an album for each country he specialized in: Greece, Newfoundland, British possessions in the Pacific, Borneo, Zanzibar, Sierra Leone; these were some of the lands whose stamps he favoured most . . .

I did share some of his enthusiasm for stamps, and they gave me a strong foundation in geography and political history, for he went to the trouble of telling me something about the places and people depicted on them—that Pitcairn Island was inhabited largely by mutineers from *H.M.S.Bounty;* that the Solomon Islands were famous for their butterflies; that Britannia still ruled the waves (but only just); that Iraq had a handsome young boy king; that in Zanzibar the Sultan wore a fez; that zebras were exclusive to Kenya, Uganda and Tanganyika; that in America presidents were always changing; and that the handsome young hero on Greek stamps was a Greek god with a sore heel. All this and more, I remember from my stamp-sorting sessions with my father. However, it did not form a bond between him and my mother. She was bored with the whole thing.

~

My earliest memories don't come in any particular order, but most of them pertain to Jamnagar, where we lived until I was five or six years old.

There was the beach at Balachadi, and I remember picking up seashells and wanting to collect them much as my father collected stamps. When the tide was out I went paddling with some of the children from the palace.

My father set up a schoolroom for the palace children. It was on the ground floor of a rambling old palace, which had a tower and a room on the top. Sometimes I attended my father's classes more as an observer than a scholar. One day I set off on my own to explore the deserted palace, and ascended some wandering steps to the top, where I found myself in a little room full of tiny stained-glass windows. I took turns at each window pane, looking out at a green or red or yellow world. It was a magical room.

Many years later—almost forty years later, in fact—I wrote a story with this room as its setting. It was called

*The Room of Many Colours** and it had in it a mad princess, a gardener and a snake.

~

Not all memories are dream-like and idyllic. I witnessed my parents' quarrels from an early age, and later when they resulted in my mother taking off for unknown destinations (unknown to me). I would feel helpless and insecure. My father's hand was always there, and I held it firmly until it was wrenched away by the angel of death.

That early feeling of insecurity was never to leave me, and in adult life, when I witnessed quarrels between people who were close to me, I was always deeply disturbed—more for the children, whose lives were bound to be affected by such emotional discord. But can it be helped? People who marry young, even those who are in love, do not really know each other. The body chemistry may be right but the harmony of two minds is what makes relationships endure.

Words of wisdom from a disappointed bachelor!

I don't suppose I would have written so much about childhood or even about other children if my own childhood had been all happiness and light. I find that those who have had contented, normal childhoods, seldom remember

---

* In *Time Stops at Shamli and Other Stories* (first published by Penguin Books India, 1989).

much about them; nor do they have much insight into the world of children. Some of us are born sensitive. And, if, on top of that, we are pulled about in different directions (both emotionally and physically), we might just end up becoming writers.

No, we don't become writers in schools of creative writing. We become writers before we learn to write. The rest is simply learning how to put it all together.

~

I learnt to read from my father but not in his classroom.

The children were older than me. Four of them were princesses, very attractive, but always clad in buttoned-up jackets and trousers. This was a bit confusing for me, because I had at first taken them for boys. One of them used to pinch my cheeks and hug me. While I thought she was a boy, I rather resented the familiarity. When I discovered she was a girl (I had to be told), I wanted more of it.

I was shy of these boyish princesses, and was to remain shy of girls until I was in my teens.

~

Between Tennis Bungalow and the palace were lawns and flower beds. One of my earliest memories is of picking my way through a forest of flowering cosmos; to a five-year-old they were almost trees, the flowers nodding down at me in friendly invitation.

Since then, the cosmos has been my favourite flower—fresh, open, uncomplicated—living up to its name, *cosmos*, the universe as an ordered whole. White, purple and rose, they are at their best in each other's company, growing almost anywhere, in the hills or on the plains, in Europe or tropical America. Waving gently in the softest of breezes, they are both sensuous and beyond sensuality. An early influence!

There were of course rose bushes in the palace grounds, kept tidy and trim and looking very like those in the illustrations in my first copy of *Alice in Wonderland*, a well-thumbed edition from which my father often read to me. (Not the Tenniel illustrations, something a little softer.) I think I have read *Alice* more often than any other book, with the possible exception of *The Diary of a Nobody*, which I turn to whenever I am feeling a little low. Both books help me to a better appreciation of the absurdities of life.

There were extensive lawns in front of the bungalow, where I could romp around or push my small sister around on a tricycle. She was a backward child, who had been affected by polio and some damage to the brain (having been born prematurely and delivered with the help of forceps), and she was the cross that had to be borne by my parents, together and separately. In spite of her infirmities, Ellen was going to outlive most of us.

~

Although we lived briefly in other houses, and even for a time in the neighbouring state of Pithadia, Tennis Bungalow was our home for most of the time we were in Jamnagar.

There were several Englishmen working for the Jam Saheb. The port authority was under Commander Bourne, a retired British naval officer. And a large farm (including a turkey farm) was run for the state by a Welsh couple, the Jenkins. I remember the verandah of the Jenkins home, because the side table was always stacked with copies of the humorous weekly, *Punch*, mailed regularly to them from England. I was too small to read *Punch*, but I liked looking at the drawings.

The Bournes had a son who was at school in England, but he had left his collection of comics behind, and these were passed on to me. Thus I made the acquaintance of Korky the Kat, Tiger Tim, Desperate Dan, Oor Wullie and other comic-paper heroes of the late thirties.

There was one cinema somewhere in the city, and English-language films were occasionally shown. My first film was very disturbing for me, because the hero was run through with a sword. This was Noel Coward's operetta, *Bitter Sweet*, in which Nelson Eddy and Jennette MacDonald made love in duets. My next film was *Tarzan of the Apes*, in which Johny Weissmuller, the Olympic swimmer, gave Maureen O'Sullivan, pretty and petite, a considerable mauling in their treetop home. But it was to be a few years before I became a movie buff.

Looking up one of my tomes of Hollywood history, I note that *Bitter Sweet* was released in 1940, so that was probably our last year in Jamnagar. My father must have been over forty when he joined the Royal Air Force (RAF), to do his bit for King and country. He may have bluffed his age (he was born in 1896), but perhaps you could enlist in your mid-forties during the War. He was given the rank of pilot officer and assigned to the cipher section of Air Headquarters in New Delhi. So there was a Bond working in Intelligence long before the fictional James arrived on the scene.

The War wasn't going too well for England in 1941, and it wasn't going too well for me either, for I found myself interned in a convent school in the hill station of Mussoorie. I hated it from the beginning. The nuns were strict and unsympathetic; the food was awful (stringy meat boiled with pumpkins); the boys were for the most part dull and unfriendly, the girls too subdued; and the latrines were practically inaccessible. We had to bathe in our underwear, presumably so that the nuns would not be distracted by the sight of our undeveloped sex! I had to endure this place for over a year because my father was being moved around from Calcutta to Delhi to Karachi, and my mother was already engaged in her affair with my future stepfather. At times I thought of running away, but where was I to run?

Picture postcards from my father brought me some cheer. These postcards formed part of Lawson Wood's 'Granpop' series—'Granpop' being an ape of sorts, who indulged in various human activities, such as attending cocktail parties and dancing to Scottish bagpipes. 'Is this how you feel now that the rains are here?' my father had written under one illustration of 'Granpop' doing the rumba in a tropical downpour.

I enjoyed getting these postcards, with the messages from my father saying that books and toys and stamps were waiting for me when I came home. I preserved them for fifty years, and now they are being looked after by Dr Howard Gotlieb in my archives at Boston University's Mugar Memorial Library. My own letters can perish, but not those postcards!

I have no cherished memories of life at the convent school. It wasn't a cruel place but it lacked character of any kind; it was really a conduit for boys and girls going on to bigger schools in the hill station. I am told that today it has a beautiful well-stocked library, but that the children are not allowed to use the books lest they soil them; everything remains as tidy and spotless as the nuns' habits.

One day in mid-term my mother turned up unexpectedly and withdrew me from the school. I was overjoyed but also a little puzzled by this sudden departure. After all, no one had really taken me seriously when I'd said I hated the place.

Oddly enough, we did not stop in Dehra Dun at my grandmother's place. Instead my mother took me straight to the railway station and put me on the night train to Delhi. I don't remember if anyone accompanied me—I must have been too young to travel alone—but remember being met at the Delhi station by my father in full uniform. It was early summer, and he was in khakis, but the blue RAF cap took my fancy. Come winter, he'd be wearing a dark blue uniform with a different kind of cap, and by then he'd be a flying officer and getting saluted by juniors. Being wartime, everyone was saluting madly, and I soon developed the habit, saluting everyone in sight.

An uncle on my mother's side, Fred Clark, was then the station superintendent at Delhi railway station, and he took us home for breakfast to his bungalow, not far from the station. From the conversation that took place during the meal I gathered that my parents had separated, that my mother was remaining in Dehra Dun, and that henceforth I would be in my father's custody. My sister Ellen was to stay with 'Calcutta Granny'—my father's seventy-year-old mother. The arrangement pleased me, I must admit.

~

The two years I spent with my father were probably the happiest of my childhood—although, for him, they must have been a period of trial and tribulation. Frequent bouts of malaria had undermined his constitution; the separation from my mother weighed heavily on him, and it could not be reversed; and at the age of eight I was self-willed and demanding.

He did his best for me, dear man. He gave me his time, his companionship, his complete attention.

A year was to pass before I was re-admitted to a boarding school, and I would have been quite happy never to have gone to school again. My year in the convent had been sufficient punishment for uncommitted sins. I felt that I had earned a year's holiday.

It was a glorious year, during which we changed our residence at least four times—from a tent on a flat treeless plain outside Delhi, to a hutment near Humayun's tomb; to a couple of rooms on Atul Grove Road; to a small flat on Hailey Road; and finally to an apartment in Scindia House, facing the Connaught Circus.

We were not very long in the tent and hutment—but long enough for me to remember the scorching winds of June, and the *bhisti's* hourly visit to douse the *khas-khas* matting with water. This turned a hot breeze into a refreshing, fragrant zephyr—for about half an hour. And then the dust and the prickly heat took over again. A small table fan was the only luxury.

Except for Sundays, I was alone during most of the day; my father's office in Air Headquarters was somewhere near India Gate. He'd return at about six, tired but happy to find me in good spirits. For although I had no friends during that period, I found plenty to keep me occupied—books, stamps, the old gramophone, hundreds of postcards which he'd collected during his years in England, a scrapbook, albums of photographs . . . And sometimes I'd explore the jungle behind the tents; but I did not go very far, because of the snakes that proliferated there.

I would have my lunch with a family living in a neighbouring tent, but at night my father and I would eat together. I forget who did the cooking. But he made the breakfast, getting up early to whip up some fresh butter (he loved doing this) and then laying the table with cornflakes or grapenuts, and eggs poached or fried.

The gramophone was a great companion when my father was away. He had kept all the records he had collected in Jamnagar, and these were added to from time to time. There were operatic arias and duets from *La Bohème* and *Madame Butterfly*; ballads and traditional airs rendered by Paul Robeson, Peter Dawson,

Richard Crooks, Webster Booth, Nelson Eddy and other tenors and baritones, and of course the great Russian bass, Chaliapin. And there were lighter, music-hall songs and comic relief provided by Gracie Fields (the 'Lancashire Lass'), George Formby with his ukelele, Arthur Askey ('big-hearted' Arthur—he was a tiny chap,) Flanagan and Allan, and a host of other recording artistes. You couldn't just put on some music and lie back and enjoy it. That was the day of the wind-up gramophone, and it had to be wound up fairly vigorously before a 75 rmp record could be played. I enjoyed this chore. The needle, too, had to be changed after almost every record, if you wanted to keep them in decent condition. And the records had to be packed flat, otherwise, in the heat and humidity they were inclined to assume weird shapes and become unplayable.

It was always a delight to accompany my father to one of the record shops in Connaught Place, and come home with a new record by one of our favourite singers.

After a few torrid months in the tent-house and then in a brick hutment, which was even hotter, my father was permitted to rent rooms of his own on Atul Grove Road, a tree-lined lane not far from Connaught Place, which was then the hub and business centre of New Delhi. Keeping me with him had been quite unofficial; his superiors were always wanting to know why my mother wasn't around to look after me. He was really hoping that the war would end soon, so that he could take me to England and put me in a good school there. He had been selling some of his more valuable stamps and had put quite a bit in the bank.

One evening he came home with a bottle of Scotch whisky. This was most unusual, because I had never seen him drinking—not even beer. Had he suddenly decided to hit the bottle?

The mystery was solved when an American officer dropped in to have dinner with us (having a guest for dinner was a very rare event), and our cook excelled himself by producing succulent pork chops, other viands and vegetables, and my favourite chocolate pudding. Before we sat down to dinner, our guest polished off several pegs of whisky (my father had a drink too), and after dinner they sat down to go through some of my father's stamp albums. The American collector bought several stamps, and we went to bed richer by a couple of thousand rupees.

That it was possible to make money out of one's hobby was something I was to remember when writing became my passion.

When my father had a bad bout of malaria and was admitted to the Military Hospital, I was on my own for about ten days. Our immediate neighbours, an elderly Anglo-Indian couple, kept an eye on me, only complaining that I went through a tin of guava jam in one sitting. This tendency to over-indulge has been with me all my life.

Those stringy convent meals must have had something to do with it.

I made one friend during the Atul Grove days. He was a boy called Joseph—from South India, I think—who lived next door. In the evenings we would meet on a strip of grassland across the road and engage in wrestling bouts which were watched by an admiring group of servants' children from a nearby hostelry. We also had a great deal of fun in the trenches that had been dug along the road in case of possible Japanese air raids (there had been one on Calcutta). During the monsoon they filled with rain-water, much to the delight of the local children, who used them as miniature swimming pools. They were then quite impracticable as air raid shelters.

Of course, the real war was being fought in Burma and the Far East, but Delhi was full of men in uniform. When winter came, my father's khakis were changed for dark blue RAF caps and uniforms, which suited him nicely. He was a good-looking man, always neatly dressed; on the short side but quite sturdy. He was over forty when he had joined up—hence the office job, deciphering (or helping to create) codes and ciphers. He was quite secretive about it all (as indeed he was supposed to be), and as he confided in me on almost every subject but his work, he was obviously a reliable Intelligence officer.

He did not have many friends in Delhi. There was the occasional visit to Uncle Fred near the railway station, and sometimes he'd spend a half-hour with Mr Rankin, who owned a large drapery shop at Connaught Circus, where officers' uniforms were tailored. Mr Rankin was another enthusiastic stamp collector, and the two of them would get together in Mr Rankin's back office and exchange stamps or discuss new issues. I think the drapery establishment closed down after the War. Mr Rankin was always extremely well dressed, as though he had stepped straight out of Saville Row and on to the steamy streets of Delhi.

My father and I explored old tombs and monuments, but going to the pictures was what we did most, if he was back from work fairly early.

Connaught Place was well served with cinemas—the Regal, Rivoli, Odeon and Plaza, all very new and shiny—and they exhibited the latest Hollywood and British productions. It was in these cinemas that I discovered the beautiful Sonja Henie, making love on skates and even getting married on ice; Nelson and Jeanette making love in duets; Errol Flynn making love on the high seas; and Gary Cooper and Claudette Colbert making love in the bedroom (*Bluebeard's Eighth Wife*). I made careful listings of all the films I saw, including their casts, and to this day I can give you the main performers in almost any film made in the 1940s. And I still think it was cinema's greatest decade, with the stress on good story, clever and economical direction (films seldom exceeded 120-minutes running time), superb black and white photography, and actors and actresses who were also personalities in their own right. The era of sadistic thrills, gore, and psychopathic killers was still far away. The accent was on entertainment—naturally enough, when the worst war in history had spread across Europe, Asia and the Pacific.

~

When my father broached the subject of sending me to a boarding school, I used every argument I could think of to dissuade him. The convent school was still fresh in my memory and I had no wish to return to any institution remotely resembling it—certainly not after almost a year of untrammelled freedom and my father's companionship.

'Why do you want to send me to school again?' I asked. 'I can learn more at home. I can read books, I can write letters, I can even do sums!'

'Not bad for a boy of nine,' said my father. 'But I can't teach you algebra, physics and chemistry.'

'I don't want to be a chemist.'

'Well, what would you like to be when you grow up?'

'A tap-dancer.'

'We've been seeing too many pictures. Everyone says I spoil you.'

I tried another argument. 'You'll have to live on your own again. You'll feel lonely.'

'That can't be helped, son. But I'll come to see you as often as I can. You see, they're posting me to Karachi for some time, and then I'll be moved again—they won't allow me to keep you with me at some of these places. Would you like to stay with your mother?'

I shook my head.

'With Calcutta Granny?'

'I don't know her.'

'When the War's over I'll take you with me to England. But for the next year or two we must stay here. I've found a nice school for you.'

'Another convent?'

'No, it's a prep school for boys in Simla. And I may be able to get posted there during the summer.'

'I want to see it first,' I said.

'We'll go up to Simla together. Not now—in April or May, before it gets too hot. It doesn't matter if you join school a bit later—I know you'll soon catch up with the others.'

There was a brief trip to Dehra Dun. I think my father felt that there was still a chance of a reconciliation with my mother. But her affair with the businessman was too far gone. His own wife had been practically abandoned and left to look after the photography shop she'd brought along with her dowry. She was a stout lady with high blood pressure, who once went in search of my mother and stepfather with an axe. Fortunately, they were not at home that day and she had to vent her fury on the furniture.

In later years, when I got to know her quite well, she told me that my father was a very decent man, who treated her with great courtesy and kindness on the one occasion they met.

I remember we stayed in a little hotel or boarding house just off the Eastern Canal Road.

Dehra was a green and leafy place. The houses were separated by hedges, not walls, and the residential areas were criss-crossed by little lanes bordered by hibiscus or oleander shrubs.

We were soon back in Delhi.

My parents' separation was final and it was to be almost two years before I saw my mother again.

SIMLA *and*
DELHI, 1943

We took the railcar to Simla. It was the nicest way of travelling through the mountains. The narrow-gauge train took twice as long and left you covered in soot. Going up in a motor car made you nauseous. The railcar glided smoothly round and up gradients, slipping through the 103 tunnels without subjecting the passengers to blasts of hot black smoke.

We stopped at Barog, a pretty little wayside station, famous for its breakfasts and in winter, for its mistletoe. We got into Simla at lunch-time and dined at Davico's. Simla was well-served by restaurants. Davico's was famous for its meringues, and I experienced one for the first time. Then we trudged off to a lodging house called Craig Dhu, which was to be another of our temporary homes.

The Bishop Cotton Prep School was situated in Chotta Simla, at some distance from the Senior School. The boys were at play when I first saw them from the road above the playing field.

'You can see they're a happy lot,' said my father.

They certainly seemed a good deal noisier (and less inhibited) than their counterparts at the Mussoorie convent. Some spun tops; others wrestled with each other; several boys were dashing about with butterfly nets, chasing a large blue butterfly. Three or four sat quietly on the steps, perusing comics. In those days you had story comics or papers, such as *Hotspur, Wizard* or *Champion*, and you had actually to read them.

It was to be a month before I joined the school (admission took time), and in the interim I enjoyed an idyllic holiday with my father. If Davico's had its meringues, Wenger's had its pastries and chocolate cakes, while at Kwality the curry puffs and ice creams were superb. The reader will consider me to have been a spoilt brat, and so I was for a time; but there was always the nagging fear that my father would be posted to some inaccessible corner of the country, and I would be left to rot in boarding school for the rest of my days.

During a rickshaw ride around Elysium Hill, my father told me Kipling's story of the phantom rickshaw— my first encounter with hill-station lore. He also showed me the shop where Kim got his training as a spy from the mysterious Lurgan Sahib. I had not read Kipling at the time, but through my father's retellings I was already familiar with many of his characters and settings. The same Lurgan Sahib (I learnt later) had inspired another novel, F. Marion Crawford's *Mr Isaacs*. A Bishop Cotton's boy, Richard Blaker, had written a novel called *Scabby Dixon*, which had depicted life in the school at the turn of the century. And Bishop Cotton, our founder, had himself been a young master at Rugby under the famous Dr Arnold who was to write *Tom Brown's Schooldays*. Cotton became the first headmaster at Marlborough before coming out to India.

All these literary traditions were beginning to crowd upon me. And of course there was the strange fact that my father had named me Ruskin, after the Victorian essayist and guru of art and architecture. Had my father been an admirer of Mr Ruskin? I did not ask him, because at that time I thought I was the *only* Ruskin. At some point during my schooldays I discovered John Ruskin's fairy story, *The King of the Golden River*, and thought it rather good. And years later, my mother was to confirm that my father had indeed named me after the Victorian writer. My other Christian name, Owen, was seldom used, and I have never really bothered with it. An extra Christian name seems quite superfluous. And besides, Owen (in Welsh) means 'brave', and I am not a brave person. I have done some foolhardy things, but more out of ignorance than bravery.

I settled down in the prep school without any fuss. Compared to the Mussoorie convent it was luxury. For lunch there was usually curry and rice (as compared to the spartan meat boiled with pumpkin, the convent speciality); for dinner there would be cutlets or a chop. There was a wartime shortage of eggs, but the school kitchen managed to make some fairly edible omelettes out of egg powder. Occasionally there were sausages, although no one could say with any certainty what was in them. On my questioning our housemaster as to their contents, he smiled mysteriously and sang the first line of a Nelson Eddy favourite—'Ah, sweet mystery of life!'

Our sausages came to be known as 'Sweet Mysteries.' This was 1943, and the end of the War was still two years away.

Flying heroes were the order of the day. There were the *Biggles* books, with a daredevil pilot as hero. And *Champion* comic books featured Rockfist Rogan of the RAF, another flying ace who, whenever he was shot down in enemy territory, took on the Nazis in the boxing ring before escaping in one of their aircraft.

Having a father in the RAF was very prestigious and I asked my father to wear his uniform whenever he came to see me. This he did, and to good effect.

'Bond's father is in the RAF,' word went round, and other boys looked at me with renewed respect. 'Does he fly bombers or fighter planes?' they asked me.

'Both,' I lied. After all, there wasn't much glamour in codes and ciphers, although they were probably just as important.

My own comic-book hero was Flying O'Flynn, an acrobatic goalkeeper who made some breathtaking saves in every issue, and kept his otherwise humble team at the top of the football league. I was soon emulating him, on our stony football field, and it wasn't long before I was the prep school goalkeeper.

Quite a few of the boys read books, the general favourites being the *William* stories, R.M. Ballantyne's adventure novels, Capt. W.E. Johns (Biggles), and any sort of spy or murder mystery. There was one boy, about my age, who was actually writing a detective story. As there was a paper shortage, he wrote in a small hand on slips of toilet paper, and stored these away in his locker. I can't remember his name, so have no idea if he grew up to become a professional writer. He left the following year, when most of the British boys began leaving India. Some had grown up in India; others had been sent out as evacuees during the Blitz.

I don't remember any special friend during the first year at the prep school, but I got on quite well with teachers and classmates. As I'd joined in mid-term, the rest of the year seemed to pass quickly. And when the Kalka-Delhi Express drew into Delhi, there was my father on the platform, wearing his uniform and looking quite spry and of course happy to see me.

He had now taken a flat in Scindia House, an apartment building facing Connaught Circus. This suited me perfectly, as it was only a few minutes from cinemas, bookshops and restaurants. Just across the road was the newly opened Milk Bar, and while my father was away at his office, I would occasionally slip out to have a milkshake—strawberry, chocolate or vanilla—and dart back home with a comic paper purchased at one of the newsstands.

All those splendid new cinemas were within easy reach too, and my father and I soon became regular cinegoers; we must have seen at least three films a week on an average. I again took to making lists of all the films I saw, including the casts as far as I could remember them. Even today, to reiterate, I can rattle off the cast of almost any Hollywood or British production of the 1940s. The films I enjoyed most that winter were *Yankee Doodle Dandy* (with James Cagney quite electric as George M. Cohan); and *This Above All*, a drama of wartime London.

When I asked my father how the film had got its title, he wrote down the lines from Shakespeare that had inspired it:

This above all, to thine own self be true,
And it must follow, as the night the day,
Thou can'st not then be false to any man.

I kept that piece of paper for many years, losing it only when I went to England.

Helping my father with his stamp collection, accompanying him to the pictures, dropping in at Wenger's for tea and muffins, bringing home a book or record—what more could a small boy of eight have asked for?

And then there were the walks.

In those days, you had only to walk a short distance to be out of New Delhi and into the surrounding fields or scrub forest. Humayun's Tomb was surrounded by a wilderness of babul and keekar trees, and so were other old tombs and monuments on the periphery of the new capital. Today they have all been swallowed up by new housing estates and government colonies, and the snarl of traffic is wonderful to behold.

New Delhi was still a small place in 1943. The big hotels (Maidens, the Swiss) were in Old Delhi. Only a few cars could be seen on the streets. Most people, including service personnel, travelled by pony-drawn tongas. When we went to the station to catch a train, we took a tonga. Otherwise we walked.

In the deserted Purana Kila my father showed me the narrow steps leading down from Humayun's library. Here the Emperor slipped and fell to his death. Not far away was Humayun's tomb. These places had few visitors then, and we could relax on the grass without being disturbed by hordes of tourists, guides, vagrants and health freaks. New Delhi still has its parks and tree-lined avenues—but oh, the press of people! Who could have imagined then that within forty years' time, the city would have swallowed huge tracts of land way beyond Ghaziabad, Faridabad, Gurgaon, Najafgarh, Tughlaqabad, small towns, villages, fields, most of the Ridge and all that grew upon it!

Change and prosperity have come to Delhi, but its citizens are paying a high price for the privilege of living in the capital. Too late to do anything about it now. Spread on, great octopus—your tentacles have yet to be fully extended.

~

If, in writing this memoir, I appear to be taking my father's side, I suppose it is only human nature for a boy to be loyal to the parent who stands by him, no matter how difficult the circumstances. An eight-year-old is bound to resent his mother's liaison with another man. Looking back on my boyhood, I feel sure that my mother must have had her own compulsions, her own views on life and how it should be lived. After all, she had only been eighteen when she had married my father, who was about fifteen years her senior. She and her sisters had been a fun-loving set; they enjoyed going to dances, picnics, parties. She must have found my father too serious, too much of a stay-at-home, happy making the morning butter or sorting through his stamps in the evening. My mother told me later that he was very jealous, keeping her away from other men. And who wouldn't have been jealous? She was young, pretty, vivacious—everyone looked twice at her!

They were obviously incompatible. They should never have married, I suppose. In which case, of course, I would not be here, penning these memoirs.

MY FATHER'S
LAST LETTER

1944. The war dragged on. No sooner was I back in prep school than my father was transferred to Calcutta. In some ways this was a good thing because my sister Ellen was there, living with 'Calcutta Granny,' and my father could live in his own home for a change. Granny had been living on Park Lane ever since Grandfather had died.

It meant, of course, that my father couldn't come to see me in Simla during my mid-term holidays. But he wrote regularly—once a week, on an average. The War was coming to an end, peace was in the air, but there was also talk of the British leaving India as soon as the war was over. In his letters my father spoke of the preparations he was making towards that end. Obviously he saw no future for us in a free India. He was not an advocate of Empire but he took a pragmatic approach to the problems of the day. There would be a new school for me in England, he said, and meanwhile he was selling off large segments of his stamp collection so that we'd have some money to start life afresh when he left the RAF. There was also his old mother to look after, and my sister Ellen and a baby brother, William, who was to be caught in no-man's land.

I did not concern myself too much with the future. Scout camps at Tara Devi and picnics at the Brockhurst tennis courts were diversions in a round of classes, games, dormitory inspections and evening homework. We could shower in the evenings, a welcome change from the tubs of my former school; and we did not have to cover our nudity—there were no nuns in attendance, only our prefects, who were there to see that we didn't scream the place down.

Did we have sexual adventures? Of course we did. It would have been unreasonable to expect a horde of eight to twelve-year-olds to take no interest in those parts of their anatomy which were undergoing constant change during puberty. But it did not go any further than a little clandestine masturbation in the dormitories late at night. There were no scandals, no passionate affairs, at least none that I can recall. We were at the age of inquisitive and innocent enquiry; not (as yet) the age of emotional attachment or experimentation.

Sex was far down our list of priorities; far behind the exploits of the new comic-book heroes—Captain Marvel, Superman, the Green Lantern and others of their ilk.

They had come into the country in the wake of the American troops, and looked like they would stay after everyone had gone. We modelled ourselves on our favourite heroes, giving each other names like Bulletman or Wonderman.

Our exploits, however, did not go far beyond the spectacular pillow-fights that erupted every now and then between the lower and upper dormitories, or one section of a dormitory and another. Those fluffy feather pillows, lovingly stitched together by fond mothers (or the darzi sitting on the verandah), would sometimes come apart, resulting in a storm of feathers sweeping across the dorm. On one occasion, the headmaster's wife, alerted by all the noise, rushed into the dorm, only to be greeted by a feather pillow full in the bosom. Mrs Priestley was a large-bosomed woman—we called her breasts 'nutcrackers'—and the pillow burst against them. She slid to the ground, buried in down. As punishment we all received the flat of her hairbrush on our posteriors. Canings were given only in the senior school.

Mrs Priestley played the piano, her husband the violin. They practised together in the assembly hall every evening. They had no children and were not particularly fond of children, as far as I could tell. In fact, Mrs Priestley had a positive antipathy for certain boys and lost no opportunity in using her brush on them. Mr Priestley showed a marked preference for upper-class English boys, of whom there were a few. He was lower middle class himself (as I discovered later).

Some good friends and companions during my two-and-a-half prep school years were Peter Blake, who did his hair in a puff like Alan Ladd; Brian Abbott, a quiet boy who boasted only of his father's hunting exploits—Abbott was a precursor to Jim Corbett, but never wrote anything; Riaz Khan, a good-natured, fun-loving boy; and Bimal Mirchandani, who grew up to become a Bombay industrialist. I don't know what happened to the others.

As I have said, I kept my father's letters, but the only one that I was able to retain (apart from some of the postcards) was the last one, which I reproduce here.

It is a good example of the sort of letter he wrote to me, and you can see why I hung on to it.

> AA Bond 108485 (RAF)
> c/o 231 Group
> Rafpost
> Calcutta 20/8/44

My dear Ruskin,

Thank you very much for your letter received a few days ago. I was pleased to hear that you were quite well and learning hard. We are all quite O.K. here, but I am still not strong enough to go to work after the recent attack of malaria I had. I was in hospital for a long time and that is the reason why you did not get a letter from me for several weeks.

I have now to wear glasses for reading, but I do not use them for ordinary wear—but only when I read or do book work. Ellen does not wear glasses at all now.

Do you need any new warm clothes? Your warm suits must be getting too small. I am glad to hear the rains are practically over in the hills where you are. It will be nice to have sunny days in September when your holidays are on. Do the holidays begin from the 9th of Sept? What will you do? Is there to be a Scouts Camp at Taradevi? Or will you catch butterflies on sunny days on the school Cricket Ground? I am glad to hear you have lots of friends. Next year you will be in the top class of the Prep. School. You only have 3½ months more for the Xmas holidays to come round, when you will be glad to come home, I am sure, to do more Stamp work and Library Study. The New Market is full of book shops here. Ellen loves the market.

I wanted to write before about your writing Ruskin, but forgot. Sometimes I get letters from you written in very small handwriting, as if you wanted to squeeze a lot of news into one sheet of letter paper. It is not good for you or for your eyes, to get into the habit of writing small. I know your handwriting is good and that you came 1st in class for handwriting, but try and form a larger style of writing and do not worry if you can't get all your news into one sheet of paper—but stick to big letters.

We have had a very wet month just passed. It is still cloudy, at night we have to use fans, but during the cold weather it is nice—not too cold like Delhi and not too warm either—but just moderate. Granny is quite well. She and Ellen send you their fond love. The last I heard a week ago, that William and all at Dehra were well also.

We have been without a cook for the past few days. I hope we find a good one before long. There are not many. I wish I could get our Delhi cook, the old man now famous for his 'Black Puddings' which Ellen hasn't seen since we arrived in Calcutta 4 months ago.

I have still got the Records and Gramophone and most of the best books, but as they are all getting old and some not suited to you which are only for children under 8 yrs old—I will give some to William, and Ellen and you can buy some new ones when you come home for Xmas. I am re-arranging all the stamps that became loose and topsy-turvy after people came and went through the collections to buy stamps. A good many got sold, the rest got mixed up a bit and it is now taking up all my time putting the balance of the collection in order. But as I am at home all day, unable to go to work as yet, I have lots of time to finish the work of re-arranging the Collection. Ellen loves drawing. I give her paper and a pencil and let her draw for herself without any help, to get her used to holding paper and pencil. She has got expert at using her pencil now and draws some wonderful animals like camels, elephants, dragons with many heads—cobras—rain clouds shedding buckets of water—tigers with long grass around them—horses with manes and wolves and foxes with bushy hair. Sometimes you can't see much of the animals because there is too much grass covering them or two much hair on the foxes and wolves and too much mane on the horses' necks—or too much rain from the clouds. All this decoration is made up by a sort of heavy scribbling of lines, but through it all one can see some very good shapes of animals, elephants and ostriches and other things. I will send you some.

Well, Ruskin, I hope this finds you well. With fond love from us all. Write again soon, Ever your loving daddy . . .

~

It was about two weeks after receiving this letter that I was given the news of my father's death. Those frequent bouts of malaria had undermined his health, and a severe attack of jaundice did the rest. A kind but inept teacher, Mr Murtough, was given the unenviable task of breaking the news to me. He mumbled something about God needing my father more than I did, and of course I knew what had happened and broke down and had to be taken to the infirmary, where I remained for a couple of days. It never made any sense to me why God should have needed my father more than I did, unless of course He envied my father's stamp collection. If God was Love, why did He have to break up the only loving relationship I'd known so far? What would happen to me now, I wondered . . . would I live with Calcutta Granny or some other relative or be put away in an orphanage?

Mr Priestley saw me in his office and said I'd be going to my mother when school closed. He said he'd been told that I had kept my father's letters and that if I wished to put them in his safe keeping he'd see that they were not lost. I handed them over—all except the one I've reproduced here.

The day before we broke up for the school holidays, I went to Mr Priestley and asked for my letters. 'What letters?' He looked bemused, irritated. He'd had a trying day. 'My father's letters,' I told him. 'You said you'd keep them for me.' 'Did I? Don't remember. Why should I want to keep your father's letters?' 'I don't know, sir. You put them in your drawer.' He opened the drawer, shut it. 'None of your letters here. I'm very busy now, Bond. If I find any of your letters, I'll give them to you.' I was dismissed from his presence.

I never saw those letters again. And I'm glad to say I did not see Mr Priestley again. All he'd given me was a lifelong aversion to violin players.

DEHRA *in* MY
TEENS

THE
SKELETON *in*
the CUPBOARD

Yes, there was skeleton in the cupboard, and although I never saw it, I played a small part in the events that followed its discovery.

I was fifteen that year, and I was back in my boarding school in Simla after spending the long winter holidays in Dehradun. My mother was still managing the old Green's Hotel in Dehra—a hotel that was soon to disappear and become part of Dehra's unrecorded history. It was called Green's not because it purported to spread any greenery (its neglected garden was choked with lantana), but because it had been started by an Englishman, Mr Green, back in 1920, just after the Great War had ended in Europe. Mr Green had died at the outset of the Second World War. He had just sold the hotel and was on his way back to England when the ship on which he was travelling was torpedoed by a German submarine.

Mr Green went down with the ship.

The hotel had already been in decline, and the new owner, a Sikh businessman from Ludhiana, had done his best to keep it going. But in the wake of the War and India's newly won Independence, Dehra was going through a lean period. My stepfather's motor workshop was also going through a lean period—a crisis, in fact—and my mother was glad to take the job of running the small hotel, while he took a job in Delhi.

She wrote to me about once a month, giving me news of the hotel, some of its more interesting guests, and the pictures that were showing in town.

'I know you're interested in detective stories,' she wrote during the summer term,

and that you fancy yourself a Sherlock Holmes or Ellery Queen. So what do you make of this strange happening? Last week we decided to clear out an old storeroom that hadn't been opened for years. The keys were missing, so we had to break open the lock. Inside there was a lot of old furniture, rotting carpets, dusty files, broken flowerpots, even a mounted tiger's head. There were two or three locked cupboards which had to be forced open. Nothing much in the first two, but the third cupboard gave everyone a fright. As Tirloki, our billiard marker, pulled open the door, a skeleton tumbled out! I mean a complete human skeleton! It must have been there for twenty years or more. How did it get there, and why? If you were here, you could do some detective work, but you'll have to wait for the winter holidays. Of course, we had to inform the police, and they took the skeleton away, saying they'd have it examined. But I doubt if they'll do much about it. It's obviously someone who died long ago—perhaps a hotel guest!—and someone here decided to hush it up. Suicide? Murder? Accident? Probably we'll never know . . .

Well, boy-detective that I fancied myself, I wrote back to my mother and said, 'I'll solve the case when I come home. But was it a man's skeleton, or a woman's? And did you find anything else in the cupboard?' A week later my mother wrote back:

I didn't look too closely at the skeleton—I like bones to be fully-fleshed if possible—but the police did say it was a woman. Not an old woman, and not too young either . . . There was nothing else in the cupboard except for some chipped or cracked plates and dishes, which have now been thrown away. The shelves were covered with sheets of old newspapers. I've kept these for you.

The newspapers excited me, and I wrote and asked my mother for some details.

She wrote back:

I hope you're preparing for your exams. After all, there's not much we can do about a skeleton that's been hidden away for fifteen or twenty years. Anyway, there were two newspapers in the cupboard. *The Daily Chronicle*, published from Delhi on 18 January 1930, is complete. That was four years before you were born.

The main headline refers to the 'Bareilly Train Disaster' in which thirteen passengers were killed and nineteen seriously injured. There are also two pages of book reviews, including a review of *The Glenlitten Murder* by E. Phillips Oppenheim. I think you may have read some of his books. He wrote that story *Crooks in the Sunshine*, if you remember.

The other book is about the spirit world, and the possibility of communicating with those who have passed from this material world. Perhaps we can summon up the spirit of the person who inhabited the skeleton? She could tell us how she met her end. Old Miss Kellner holds séances and table-rappings. But how would she summon up a spirit if she doesn't know who it was in the first place?

The second newspaper—incomplete—is *The Civil and Military Gazette* of 2 March 1930. This was published from Lahore, and as you know, Mr Kipling worked on it a few years earlier. The front page is missing, but page

5 carries an ad for a film called *The Awakening of Love* starring Vilma Banky. Vilma was a popular heroine when I was a girl. Nothing much else of interest except for a small item under the headline, 'Elder Murder Sequel':

Patna, Feb. 28: The Chief Justice and Mr Justice Scroope have dismissed the appeal of O.W. Harrison, who was charged with the murder of Mr. W.P. Elder in July and confirmed the sentence of death passed on him by the Sessions Judge of Manbhum.

Nothing to do with our skeleton, of course, because Mr Elder was buried at Jamshedpur, while Harrison occupies an unknown grave. And in any case our skeleton is a woman's. But I remember the case. Harrison was having an affair with Mr Elder's wife. When confronted by the outraged husband, Harrison took out his revolver and shot the poor man. All very sordid. No mystery there for you. Concentrate on your studies. Second-term exams must be near. I am sending you a parcel of socks. I know they don't last very long on you.

Two weeks later I wrote:

Dear Mum,

Thanks for the socks. But I wish you had sent me a food parcel instead. How about some guava cheese? And some mango pickle. They don't give us pickle in school. Headmaster's wife says it heats the blood.

About that skeleton. If a dead body was hidden in that cupboard after 1930—must have been, if the newspapers of that year were under the skeleton—it must have been someone who disappeared around that time or a little later. Must have been before Tirloki joined the hotel, or he'd remember. What about the hotel registers—would they give us a clue?

I soon received a parcel containing guava cheese, strawberry jam, and mango pickle. Headmaster confiscated the pickle. Maybe he needed it to heat his blood.

A note enclosed with the parcel read:

Old hotel registers missing. Must have been thrown out. Or perhaps Mr Green took them away when he left. Tirloki says a German spy stayed in the hotel just before the War broke out. The spy used to visit the Gurkha lines and the armaments factory. He was passing information on to a dentist who visited Germany every year. When the War broke out, the dentist was kept in a prisoner-of-war camp. The spy disappeared—some say to Tibet. Could the spy have been silenced and put away in the cupboard? But I keep forgetting it was a woman's skeleton. Tirloki says the spy was a man. But a clever spy may have been a woman dressed as a man. What do you think?

It was the football season, and I wasn't doing much thinking. Chasing a football in the monsoon mist and slush called for single-minded endurance, especially when we were being beaten 5-0 by the Simla Youngs, a team of junior clerks from the government offices. Not the ideal training for a boy-detective. The winter holidays were still four months distant, and the case of the unidentified skeleton appeared to be resolving itself with a little help from my mother and her friends.

'Well, I went to see Miss Kellner,' wrote my mother a few weeks later,

You know, the crippled old lady who used to be your Granny's tenant. She had me over for tea, and we talked about the old days, and what a good place Green's Hotel used to be, famous for its food and service and flower garden. Mr Green was a great one for the ladies. Very dapper and handsome. Women couldn't resist his charm, his polished manner, and he could dance! A great dancer, like Fred Astaire. Ballroom dancing, of course. None of your rumbas or sambas or jitterbugging.

'And what of Mrs Green,' I asked. 'He was married, wasn't he?'

'Poor Mrs Green,' said Miss Kellner, 'she had to put up with his amours and affairs. A quiet person, she came from a good English family. He'd married her for her money, of course. Her father owned hotels in Brighton. Green talked him into financing a couple of hotels in India. One in Poona, one in Dehra. This was a promising place then. Europeans wanted to settle here. But once married, Green neglected his wife. He fancied himself a Don Juan, and carried on with several women.'

'So did she leave him?' I asked.

'No one really knew what happened,' said Miss Kellner. 'Mrs Green just disappeared. It was all a great mystery, and of course there were all sorts of rumours. You see, if she'd just walked out on him she'd have told someone, confided in a friend. She did have a few friends. I like to think I was one of them. We were all expecting her to leave Green, but no one knew where she went or when. There were no letters, no postcards. Green gave out that she'd gone to stay with friends in Bombay, but after a six-month absence, speculation was rife. And no one believed she'd taken off with another man—she wasn't the sort.'

'And what about her father,' I asked Miss Kellner. 'Didn't he come looking for her?'

'Indeed, he did,' said Miss Kellner. 'She hadn't been in touch with him, and she hadn't returned to England as far as he knew.'

Apparently, he made inquiries all over India—no one had seen her or heard from her. So he spoke to the few friends she had in Dehra, including Miss Kellner. They only confirmed his suspicions, that she had been done away with—but how and where? He reported her disappearance to the police, but there was little they could do except question Mr Green, who maintained that he was just as mystified as anyone else and offered a large reward to anyone who could locate her! By then, of course, everyone was convinced that she was dead, and that Green had done away with her—or paid someone to do the dirty work.

Several years passed, and then Green sold up and went away. 'And deserved to go down with the ship,' added Miss Kellner. 'That was the general opinion.'

When I told Miss Kellner about the skeleton in the cupboard, she was certain that it was Miss Green's.

He must have strangled her or poisoned her, and then locked the body in that cupboard in the storeroom. Only he had the key to the stores.

I've spoken to Padre Dutt and one or two others who were here at the time, and they are all convinced that the skeleton is Mrs Green's. What can we do about it now? So many years have passed, and her old father is long dead. She did not have any children. If there were distant relatives it would be almost impossible to trace them after all this time. Padre Dutt thinks we should give the skeleton a Christian burial, on the strong assumption that it's Mrs Green.''

The mystery of the skeleton in the cupboard appeared to have been solved without the assistance of boy-detective Ruskin. I tried to forget it and concentrate on chemistry and mathematics, but I'm afraid I was spending more and more time perusing the works of Agatha Christie, Rex Stout and Raymond Chandler—and trying to write a detective story in which our Headmaster was found bludgeoned to death in the science lab.

My mother brought me up to date on events in Dehra.

Padre Dutt managed to retrieve the skeleton from police custody, and it was interred in a corner of the cemetery, not far from your grandfather's grave. I attended the funeral with two or three other old-timers who had known the Greens. Miss Kellner is bedridden now and could not come. Padre Dutt is getting on too, and is a little absent-minded.

It was raining heavily during the funeral service and by mistake he read out the 'Burial at Sea'. Not that anyone seemed to notice. Anyway, he had arranged for a decent coffin, and there's to be a tombstone too, paid for out of church funds and with a contribution from our Sardarji, the present owner of the hotel. So poor Mrs Green has found a final resting place. May she rest in peace!

And there the matter rested until the school term ended and I came home for my holidays.

~

My mother was still managing Green's, even though its days were numbered. The day after my return I joined her in the small office, where she sat behind her over-large desk, telephone on her right, a tin of Gold Flakes (her favourite cigarette) on her left, and the latest paperback western before her, ready to be taken up when nothing much was happening—which was fairly often. My mother enjoyed reading westerns—particularly Luke Short, Max Brand, and Clarence E. Mulford—much in the same way that I enjoyed detective fiction. Both genres were freely available in cheap Collins White Circle editions published during and just after the War.

We discussed the affair of the skeleton in the cupboard, but as there was no longer any mystery about it, there was nothing for me to investigate. However, armed with the keys to the storeroom, I went down to the basement on my own and made a thorough search of all the old furniture, on the off-chance that another skeleton might tumble out of a cupboard or be found jammed into a drawer or trunk. I did find some old tennis rackets, back numbers of Punch, a cracked china chamberpot, some old postcards of Darjeeling and Simla, and a framed photograph of King Edward VII. I took the copies of *Punch* to my room, and read the reviews of all the plays that had been running in London between 1926 and 1930, thus becoming an authority on the theatre in England of that period.

'No more skeletons,' I remarked to my mother in the office, two or three days later.

'How disappointing,' she said. 'And the one we did find is not only dead, it's buried. Why don't you join a cricket team?'

'Snooker is more exciting. Tirloki is teaching me.'

'I hope he isn't teaching you to smoke and drink.'

'When did you start smoking, Mum?'

'None of your business.'

Someone was standing in the doorway. An elderly woman, very fluffy, very pink. Her cheeks were pink, her dress was pink, her hair was bunched up and white. She was straight out of Agatha Christie.

'Miss Marple!' I exclaimed.

'May I come in?' asked the pink lady.

'Please come in,' said my mother. 'Do sit down. Do you require a room?'

'Not today, thank you. I'm staying with Padre Dutt. He insisted on putting me up. But I may want a room for a day or two—just for old time's sake.'

'You've stayed here before?'

'A long time ago. I'm Mrs Green, you know. The missing Mrs Green. The one for whom you put up that handsome tombstone in the cemetery. I was very touched by it. And I'm glad you didn't add 'Beloved Wife of Henry Green', because I didn't love him any more than he loved me.'

'Then—then—you aren't the skeleton?' stammered my mother.

'Do I look like a skeleton?'

'No!' we said together.

'But we heard you disappeared,' I said, 'and when we found that skeleton—'

'You put two and two together.'

'Well, it was Miss Kellner who convinced us,' said my mother. 'And you did disappear mysteriously. You were missing for years. And everyone knew Mr Green was a philanderer.'

'Couldn't wait to get away from him,' said the pink lady. 'Couldn't stand him any more. He was a lady killer, but not a real killer.'

'But your father came looking for you. Didn't you get in touch with him?'

'My father and I were never very close. Mother died when I was very young, and the only relative I had was a cousin in West Africa. So that's where I went—Sierra Leone!'

'How romantic!' said my mother.

'It's hot and steamy in Sierra Leone,' said Mrs Green. 'But the climate does wonders for your libido. I lived in sin with a wonderful black man for several years.'

'What happened to him?' I asked, conjuring up a picture of a small pink woman and a large black man having sex together. At fifteen, the imagination is swamped by erotic images.

'He was killed in a tribal war,' said Mrs Green without any show of emotion. 'It was a long time ago.'

'And that skeleton,' I asked. 'What about the skeleton in the cupboard? Did you know about it?'

'Yes, I knew about it. But I have no idea whose skeleton it was. You see, back in the 1920s, when Green took over this hotel, he had one of his sudden enthusiasms and was convinced this town needed a medical school or college, and he set about preparing the ground for one. He was ready to finance the project, or part of it. And of course medical students need a skeleton. So he acquired one from the Lady Hardinge Medical College in New Delhi. It was a medical-school skeleton you found. And if you'd looked closely, you'd have noticed that it was varnished.'

'Why was it varnished?' I asked.

'To help preserve it, of course. It was also articulated.'

'Articulated?'

'That means the joints were connected up, so that the whole thing wouldn't fall apart. Want to be a doctor, young man?'

'No,' I said. 'A detective.'

'Well, you didn't solve this case.'

'I wasn't here. And now we'll never be able to identify the skeleton.'

'Some poor woman of the streets, no doubt. Unclaimed, unwanted. But in the end you gave her a decent burial—even if she wasn't a Christian. Padre Dutt is a bit embarrassed, but I've told him I don't mind my name on the tombstone. I'll be returning to Africa shortly, and when I die I shall have another tombstone there. Not everyone is lucky enough to have two tombstones!'

And with that she made a graceful exit from our lives.

AT GREEN'S
HOTEL

'That Daryaganj Strangler has been at it again,' said my mother, looking up from her newspaper in the tiny office of Dehra's old Green's Hotel, where she had taken on the job of manager. 'The Delhi police say they have a good idea of the killer's identity. Maybe they'll catch him soon.'

'Where's Daryaganj?' I asked. 'And why does he strangle people?'

It was 1949. Iwas fourteen, and back once again for the winter holidays. And once again, our residence had changed. Times were hard. My stepfather, riddled by debts, had disappeared for a few months. My mother had taken up a job. It wasn't heavy work, as hardly anyone came to Green's, a small hotel that had seen better days. Dehra too had seen better days. The town was going through a slump, business was poor, and there were few visitors.

The hotel, a bungalow-type single-storey building, stood in fairly extensive grounds, with a neglected garden and a tennis court overrun by dandelions, thistles, and marigolds gone wild. Over the years I had developed a liking for neglected gardens and patches of wilderness. They were full of mystery, homes to snakes, mongooses, huge lizards, bandicoots, hedgehogs, butterflies . . . If you want to discover nature, start with a garden gone wild. And if you want to study human nature, stay in a small hotel that has seen better days.

There was a bar of sorts, attached to the billiard room, and both bar and billiard room were attended to by the 'marker', an attenuated individual of indeterminate age, who lived off the tips he occasionally received, his salary being two or three years in arrears. My mother received four hundred rupees a month for sitting in the office, ordering supplies, and making out bills for the few customers who came and went. There was also a cook, who was usually drunk. The hotel did not provide lunch or dinner, only breakfast, which consisted of an anaemic-looking omelette (or, if you preferred, an overdone fried egg), with a couple of cold, thinly buttered toasts. Those guests who were familiar with the place always ordered boiled eggs.

The owner, who ran a more profitable concern in Delhi, took little or no interest in Green's. It was up for sale, but offers were slow in coming in.

My mother and the family had quarters behind the hotel. But as there were plenty of vacant rooms in the hotel itself, I was permitted to use one of them. It was separated from the next room by a closed door, in front of which a cupboard had been placed. But this was far from being soundproof. If there were guests in the adjoining room, I could hear every word that was spoken, whether I wanted to or not.

Every morning, at around ten, I joined my mother in the office, supposedly to help her with some of the paperwork, but really to help myself to the coffee and pakoras that were brought to her. I would also share the newspaper with her.

Our newspapers were very dull in those days, just covering the activities of national leaders, but the Daryaganj Strangler was vying with them for space, thanks to the frequency and daring of his crimes.

'They say he's killed over a dozen women so far,' said my mother.

'Why?' I asked her again.

'For their jewellery, it seems. He strangles them, then rips off their rings, earrings, necklaces, bangles, brooches . . . He must have a good collection by now.'

'Are they young or old women?'

'He isn't fussy about their age. And he isn't interested in sex. But he leaves a little note behind—like a visiting card.'

'And what does it say?'

'"Die in a ditch, you rich bitch." Sometimes it's in Hindi. The bodies are usually found in a ditch.'

'Is Daryaganj a rich area?'

'It's a crowded part of Old Delhi. Narrow streets. That's why he likes it. But he operates elsewhere too.'

'Well, he won't come here,' I said. 'You haven't any jewellery. And Mrs Deeds just pawned her diamond ring.'

'How do you know?'

'Well, she and her son are in the next room, and I can't help hearing them. They quarrel most of the time. Yesterday he was demanding money for new clothes. She's waiting for a money order that doesn't come. They are really hard up. Won't be able to pay the hotel bill.'

'You shouldn't be listening, Ruskin.'

'Then put them in another room. Or put me in another room. There's just a door separating us.'

'I can't give you one of the better rooms. You'll have to stay where you are or come down to our quarters and share a room with your brothers.'

I had two half-brothers and one real brother, all much younger than me, and very noisy. Mrs Deeds and her son couldn't match them.

'I'll stay where I am,' I said.

Actually, I felt sorry for Mrs Deeds. She had seen better days. Her husband, a car salesman, had died a few years previously, leaving her nothing. She had worked as a dormitory matron in one of the hill schools, in order to see her son through school. Now they were waiting for an assisted passage to England. And a mysterious money order that was always overdue. Her son, Ronald, was always in need of pocket money, and gave her a hard time. To make matters worse, she was hitting the bottle. When the bar stopped giving her credit, she bought some cheap stuff in the bazaar.

There were a few non-resident regulars who patronized the bar and the billiard room. Resident guests seldom stayed long at the hotel. They were usually people in transit—medical salesmen, tourists on their way to Mussoorie, parents of children being admitted to boarding schools. The regulars were local lawyers like Suresh Mathur, or garage owners like Brij Lal, or property agents like Jugal Kishore. None of them were doing particularly well at the time, and they spent a lot of time on their bar stools discussing their and the town's future prospects.

Prospects in general brightened up by the arrival one day of a very rich lady in a posh new De Soto limousine, an American car that was gorgeous to look at but a great guzzler of petrol.

Not that the expense would have bothered Mrs Gupta, whose husband had made a fortune running Army canteens during the War (1939– 45). She moved into the hotel's only luxury suite and announced that she was thinking of buying the hotel and turning it into a private hospital.

'What kind of hospital?' I asked my mother.

'A mental hospital, she says. Apparently, there isn't one between here and Agra.'

'There aren't many mad people around,' I remarked.
'Not if they have to pay.'

'She'll probably bring them in from elsewhere. Anyway, let's humour her. The boss has promised me a commission if I help to swing the deal.'

'But then you'll be out of a job.'

'I'll be out of a job anyway. The hotel can't stay open much longer. There's hardly any income.'

So I was very polite to Mrs Gupta whenever I passed her, and she would respond by patting me on the head or giving me sweets. She was a large, pear-shaped woman, who waddled about like Donald Duck, rings flashing on her fingers, her throat encased in pearls. She had a maidservant who stayed with her and brought her meals from Kwality's down the road. She wouldn't touch the hotel food. She complained that the beds were full of bugs (which was true) and that the curtains hadn't been changed for years (also true), that the commode in the bathroom was rickety (it had, in fact, developed a list from the moment she'd sat on it), and that there were pigeons living in the skylight.

'They've been there for years,' said my mother.

'Well, hunt them away. They won't let me sleep in the afternoon, with their constant cooing and gurgling.'

So I hunted them away and earned a ten-rupee tip. They settled down in another skylight.

~

Sometimes, I wandered into the bar or billiard room to chat with old Tirloki, the marker, and occasionally I would have a lemonade (nothing stronger) with one of the players or drinkers. Suresh Mathur was a P.G. Wodehouse fan, and this gave us something in common. I had read all the Jeeves stories, Ukridge, and Blandings Castle novels—all easily available at a little lending library down the road. I do believe Suresh modelled himself on Bertie Wooster. He got up late, failed to keep appointments, lost clients, and even wore socks that did not match. The trouble was, Suresh did not have a Jeeves to sort his life out for him, and he was not in great demand as an income tax lawyer. And besides, there weren't many tax-payers around. There wasn't much income being generated in the Dehra of 1949.

Tirloki had been with the hotel since 1932, two years before I was born. He told us that it had been a busy little hotel in the 1930s, with a bandstand in the garden, and a dance floor in a recessed verandah-lounge.

'Was it for Europeans only?' asked a young man, who was visiting the bar for the first time.

'Most of the guests were European,' said Tirloki. 'But there were also well-to-do Indians—zamindars,

Rai Bahadurs, members of royal families. This was the place to be. But times change, customs change. It's all history now.'

The young man turned his attention to me. 'Do you stay here too?'

'My mother's the manager.'

'I see. Yes, I met her when I arrived. Would you like a drink?'

'Not allowed,' I said.

'Good boy. So have a Tepto Orange.'

I'd already had two Tepto Oranges, but I had a third. The range of soft drinks was rather limited in those days.

'So where do you go to school?' he asked.

'In Simla. I'm on holiday.'

'Good. Perhaps you can show me around. I've never been in this town before.'

'There's not much to see,' I said.

'I've heard there's a racecourse.'

'It closed down after the War.'

'So how do you spend your time?'

'I read, or go to the pictures. There are six cinemas in Dehra. Three show English films.'

'Well, then, I'll take you to the pictures. I'm on leave. Captain Ramesh.' And he extended his hand.

I didn't know what to make of Captain Ramesh—it was the first time a stranger had invited me to the pictures—but I shook his hand and had some difficulty in releasing it, his grip was so firm and strong. I supposed his Army training had something to do with it.

'I'll try to come,' I said. Finishing my Tepto Orange, I made my way back to my room.

Mrs Deeds and son were going at it hammer and tongs, and it was impossible to sleep. And just as impossible to read. What I needed was a bedside radio!

Next morning, dropping in at the office, I said, 'Mum, I want a radio.'

'There's a radiogram at home,' she said.

'It's too big. And it's out of order. And there are mice nesting inside.'

'Well, a new radio will be expensive. You'll have to wait until I get my salary. It's three months overdue!'

We were beginning to sound like Mrs Deeds and son. I changed the subject.

'Captain Ramesh is taking me to the pictures this evening.'

'He's the new guest, isn't he? Nice man, very polite. Don't give him any trouble.'

'Am I a troublesome boy?'

'Sometimes.'

~

I did not give Captain Ramesh any trouble. I was on my best behaviour. Who wouldn't be, if he was being plied with patties and ice-cream sodas? Captain Ramesh was generous and undemanding. All he wanted was a little company. He was on his way to a border posting, he told me, and he missed his parents, his sister, and his younger brother. I reminded him of his brother.

We sat in the most expensive seats, at the back of the hall, and laughed at the antics of Abbot and Costello, the favourite comedians of that era. Halfway through the film Captain Ramesh got up, saying he'd be back in five minutes. But he returned only as the picture was finishing—he'd been out for about half an hour.

'I get very restless if I'm sitting in one place for too long,' he explained, as we walked back to the hotel.

'You missed the best part,' I said

'Never mind,' he said. 'It's your company I enjoy. Would you like to see a Hindi film?'

'Last year I saw *Tansen* with my mother and stepfather. It was very long.'

'The public likes to get its money's worth of song and dance. Tomorrow let's see the latest hit—*Nadiya Ke Paar*. Dilip Kumar and Kamini Kaushal. We'll go to the night show.'

I had never been to a night show before. My mother would not have allowed it, as it meant getting home at midnight. But such was Captain Ramesh's charm and good looks that he soon overcame her objections. She was confident that I was in good hands. And I was comfortable in the captain's company. He was far from being the 'fond uncle'; just a friendly young man trying to pass the time in a small town that offered little by way of entertainment.

Well, *Nadiya Ke Paar* was memorable in more ways than one. It put me to sleep about halfway through. And when I woke up, Captain Ramesh was missing! Kamini Kaushal's beauty and Dilip Kumar's charm could not hold him to his seat any more than they could keep me from nodding off.

I got up and went into the foyer. It was raining outside. Where on earth could the captain have gone? Surely he did not fancy a walk in the rain? It was February, still quite cold in Dehra.

Presently he arrived, rather breathless after running across the road that separated the cinema from the shops on the other side. He wasn't too wet, so he must have been sheltering somewhere. Most of the shops were in darkness, having closed at eight or nine. A couple of tea-stalls were open, as well as a paan-shop.

Captain Ramesh seemed pleased with himself.

'Had a good walk,' he said. 'Did you enjoy the film?'

'It's still showing,' I said. 'But I fell asleep.'

'We'll go home, then.'

The rain had stopped, and we took a leisurely walk back to the hotel. Captain Ramesh kept whistling rather tunelessly. It was a habit of his when he was on the road.

~

Dehradun did not have a local newspaper in those days. It was still a very small town. This meant that news of a crime was spread by word of mouth. And it had to be a serious crime for it to merit wide attention.

I was sitting in the office with my mother when the dhobi walked in with a bundle of freshly pressed linen— bed sheets and tablecloths. He placed his bundle in a corner and said, 'A woman was murdered last night.'

'In your mohalla?'

'No, not one of us. A rich lady. She was driving home after visiting the jewellers, just before the shops closed. Someone must have been hiding in the back seat. She drove up to her gate, but she was killed before she could get out. Strangled. All her jewellery missing—what she was wearing, what she bought. They say it's that strangler from Delhi. Our streets aren't safe any more.'

'They never were. Did he leave a note?'

'What note? Money, you mean?'

'No, a written note?'

'Why should he do that?'

'The Delhi strangler does it. Just a custom.'

'Then this is another killer.'

'A copycat,' said my mother, and gave her attention to the dhobi's accounts.

Shortly after he left, Captain Ramesh walked in. At eleven in the morning there was always more socializing taking place in my mother's office than in the hotel.

Captain Ramesh had a parcel under his arm. He put it in my hands and said, 'Here's something for you. I heard you wanted one!'

Undoing the parcel, I disclosed a small Murphy radio. 'Oh, thanks, sir.' I was really pleased. 'You're spoiling the boy,' said my mother. 'Well, I'll be off soon. Consider it a farewell

present.' 'Will you come this way again?' 'Who knows? A soldier's life is uncertain.' 'But there is no war on, thank goodness.' A shadow fell across the doorway, and Mrs Gupta's head appeared in the opening.

'I have to complain about the cook,' she said, her several chins wobbling as though they had a life of their own. 'He was drunk at ten in the morning.

You know I don't trust the hotel's food. But I felt like a cup of tea, and I rang for the room-boy and he said he'd fetch it for me. Instead, the cook brings it, pours it all over the table, and then has the effrontery to ask me for a loan!'

'How much did he want?' asked my mother.

'Five hundred rupees. The cheek of it!'

'He usually asks for two. But he could see that you're well-to-do—must have heard that you're thinking of buying the hotel.'

'Well, I've changed my mind about that. The Royal Hotel is more suitable for my project.' She turned to Captain

Ramesh and beamed at him. 'I'm thinking of opening a mental hospital. We don't have one north of Delhi.'

Captain Ramesh was staring at her gold locket and pearl necklace. Diamonds glittered on her fingers.

He gave a start, smiled and said, 'I'm sure we need one, madam. Lots of crazy people around.'

'Schizophrenics. Split personalities. Jekyll-and-Hyde cases. They are roaming all over the place. A menace to society. Like this strangler in Delhi.'

'We have one here too,' said my mother.

'In Dehra? I don't believe it. What would bring him to such a dead end?' And with a shake of her head, and a jangle of bangles and bracelets, she marched off.

'Well, what would you rather have here?' asked Captain Ramesh, turning to me. 'This quiet little hotel, or a noisy mental hospital?'

'A cinema hall,' I said, and everyone laughed.

~

Mrs Deeds and son could well have been the first candidates for a mental asylum, the way they went on, constantly badgering each other. She accused him of having pawned her rings; he accused her of losing them when drunk. They had no specific plans for the future. Getting to England was the main priority.

'And there you'll have to go to work,' said Mrs Deeds. 'I won't be cooking and slaving for you.'

'I don't see you doing any cooking or slaving,' said the young man. 'Just cadging drinks at the bar. You were drinking with the marker yesterday.'

'He was good enough to buy me a drink.'

'Next thing you'll be sleeping with him.'

There was the sound of a slap. And then another. They were coming to blows.

I turned on my radio. Captain Ramesh had fixed it up for me. I found some music and turned up the volume, drowning out the sounds of battle in the next room. I started exploring. It was a good short-wave set, and I was able to tune in to the rest of the world. The Overseas Service of the BBC, Radio Hilversum, Radio Ceylon, Radio Vienna. All this, long before television arrived. I found a comedy show on the BBC—'Much-Binding-in-the-Marsh'—and listened, entranced. I was no longer alone.

Next morning Mrs Deeds was in the office, complaining that I had the radio on so loud that she couldn't sleep.

'We'll give you another room,' said my mother. 'Captain Ramesh will be leaving today.'

'Any letter for me?' asked Mrs Deeds. 'Any money orders?'

'Nothing, dear. And you're two weeks behind with the room-rent. The owner is getting fidgety.'

'What a nightmare!' exclaimed Mrs Deeds, turning to leave just as Captain Ramesh came in. 'I'll have to look for a job. Only there aren't any in this one-horse town.'

When she had left the room, Captain Ramesh sat down to settle his bill. 'Is the radio all right?' he asked.

'It's fine, thanks. I stayed up till twelve. Better than the cinema. If you're leaving today, I'll come and see you off.'

'I'm taking the night train to Amritsar. It leaves at eleven. Isn't that too late for you?'

'It's just a twenty-minute walk from the station. Can I go, Mum?'

'I'll arrange with Bansi to bring his tonga,' she said. 'You can come back with him.'

That was still the tonga era in Dehra. You don't see them around any more, except in the countryside. The one-pony carriage proceeds at a leisurely pace. One passenger can sit beside the driver, two in the sloping seat at the back. If you're in the back seat you have to make sure you don't slip off. If you're in the front seat, you have to put up with the pony raising his tail from time to time and farting in your face. And they could defecate while on the trot. Dehra had more than three hundred tongas, so there was always work for the street-cleaners.

There were just a few cars in Dehra then. No complaints about petrol or diesel fumes. But the smell of horse-dung can be equally stupefying. Sometimes nostalgia can be too selective.

~

Captain Ramesh gave me tea at Kwality's, along with chicken patties, pastries, lemon tarts—anything I wanted.

'When will you come again?' I asked, my mouth full of pastry.

'Can't say,' he said. 'Depends on where I'm posted.'

'But you will come again?' I said anxiously.

'Surely, surely. You've been a friend. Great company. And I like your mother and the hotel and this town. Small towns suit me when I want a change.'

That evening the Captain stood everyone drinks and presented Mrs Deeds with a bottle of Carew's gin. Tirloki received a handsome tip. Things were looking up at Green's Hotel!

Bansi arrived in his tonga at 10 p.m., and I helped Captain Ramesh carry his suitcase and travelling bag. The suitcase was pretty heavy.

'I'll take the suitcase,' said the Captain. 'It's too heavy for you.' And at the station he wouldn't let the coolies touch it.

When he had settled down in his first-class compartment, I stood on the platform and wished him luck.

'I'll need it,' he said.

As the train began moving, he put out his hand and took mine. His grasp was gentle, but he had a large hand, capable of exerting considerable pressure.

Bansi chattered away as he took me home. He was in a good mood. Captain Ramesh had given him a hundred-rupee note—more than a week's income!

When we reached the hotel, all the lights were on and people were running about. A police jeep stood in the driveway. My mother was in her dressing gown, standing outside the office.

'Looks like trouble,' said Bansi, as he helped me down from the front seat.

It was trouble.

While I was at the station, seeing off Captain Ramesh, Mrs Deeds had taken a stroll in the wilderness that passed for a garden, and had fallen over a body that lay sprawled on the grassy verge. The light from the hotel verandah's single bulb was just bright enough for her to make out the features of Mrs Gupta. Eyes bulging, tongue protruding, throat lacerated—it was the face of someone whose life had been choked out of her by powerful, practised hands. Necklaces had been torn from her throat, rings from her fingers, earrings from her ears, bracelets from her wrists. She had been stripped of every gem, every precious metal on her person.

Mrs Deeds staggered to her feet, ran indoors, and had a hysterical fit. The occupants of the bar poured brandy down her throat. Revived, she pointed to the garden. Everyone went out and gaped at the body.

More lights came on, my mother was roused, and the police sent for. Soon a small crowd had collected in front of Green's Hotel. That was when I returned from the station.

'You'd better go to bed, Ruskin,' said my mother.

But I had no intention of going to bed. Nor did anyone else retire for the night—not until 2 a.m., by which time the body had been taken away.

And next morning the police were all over the place, searching the rooms, the grounds; questioning guests and staff. And of course they finally got around to discovering the absent Captain Ramesh; but by then he would have alighted in Amritsar or at some station en route.

Over the next few days inquiries were set afoot, and policemen were in and out of the hotel and office throughout the day.

The Inspector in charge of the case, sitting opposite my mother and drinking innumerable cups of tea, finally stated: 'There is no Captain Ramesh. It was just an alias. There is no one in the Army who goes by that name or description.'

'That makes it difficult to find him,' said my mother. 'But are you sure he's the man who killed Mrs Gupta—and possibly others?'

The Inspector produced a photograph from a folder and handed it to my mother. I peered at it from over her shoulder. It wasn't a good photograph—it was a copy of a photo that had appeared in the Delhi papers—but it bore a faint resemblance to our 'Captain Ramesh' and possibly thousands like him.

'A lot of people come and go,' said my mother. 'It's difficult to recall some of them. The young man in this picture has a moustache. The captain was clean-shaven.'

'May have shaved it off,' said the Inspector. 'But there's a resemblance.'

'A slight resemblance. Who is he—the man in the photo?'

'The Daryaganj Strangler. Taken some time ago.'

We were silent for a minute or two, my mother and I pondering on the fact that we had been on friendly terms with a serial killer.

'Well, I hope you catch him,' she said at last.

'With all the loot he's got from his victims he'll be far away by now—'

'But if it's a habit or compulsion, he'll do it again.'

The Inspector got up to leave. 'Just let us know if you hear anything—if he tries to get in touch with anyone he met here.'

After he had gone I sat in the chair he had occupied and said, 'Not a real Captain . . . But I can't believe he strangled all those women. He was so friendly and generous.'

'Even paid Mrs Deeds's bill before he left. Didn't tell her. Just settled her account . . .'

As we spoke, Bansi's tonga drew up. Presently, Mrs Deeds and son climbed into it, followed by suitcases and bedding-rolls.

'The hotel must be empty,' I said.

'Almost.'

It took a few weeks for the hotel to recover from the trauma of Mrs Gupta's murder, and by that time I was back in my boarding school in Simla.

THE
LATE NIGHT
SHOW

According to the crime novels I used to read, there are four principal reasons for committing murder:

1. Money
2. Property
3. Revenge
4. Insanity, temporary or otherwise

In that order of priority.

But according to the crime movies I used to see, the priorities were a little different:

1. Passion (hate/jealousy)
2. Insanity (serial killing)
3. Money (bank hold-ups)
4. Espionage

Having grown up on crime fiction (both in literature and on film) I think my assessments are not far off the mark. When I put it to my friend Inspector Keemat Lal a few years ago, he said 50 per cent of murders were the result of greed—for money, property or another person's possessions. He was right, of course, but something as mundane as that doesn't make for great films or novels.

~

In the year I finished school, I was still staying with my mother in the old Green's Hotel in Dehradun. Just across the road was the Odeon, a small cinema showing English and American films. Every winter, during the school holidays, I had been a regular picture-goer. Now that I had finished school, I was still a patron of the cinema, but preferred going to the night shows, from nine thirty to twelve. At night, the hall was usually half-empty, and the usher-cum-ticket-collector, who had become a friend of mine, would let me in without a ticket—provided I occupied one of the cheaper seats. As pocket money was in short supply (my mother's salary was both poor and irregular), I readily accepted my friend's assistance. In this way I saw almost every Hollywood or British film made around that period.

Just as much of my reading was centred around Agatha Christie, Ellery Queen, and Edgar Wallace, so did my taste in films veer towards the slick thrillers in which stars such as James Cagney, Humphrey Bogart and Edward G. Robinson portrayed various colourful characters from the underworld. Back then, I remember how strange it felt watching these actors transition from their roles as gangsters or outlaws to portraying detective-heroes (as Bogart did in *The Maltese Falcon*) or even appearing in musicals (like Cagney in *Yankee Doodle Dandy*).

If today I have an almost encyclopaedic knowledge of films made in the 1940s and 1950s, it is due largely to my usher friend who allowed me into the Odeon night after night, putting his job at some risk in doing so. I reciprocated by bringing him the occasional bottle of beer from the Green's bar. The barman, too, was a friend of mine.

There were other regulars who came to the night shows—salesmen, shopkeepers, waiters, those who did not get much time off during the day. And some old characters too—like the retired postmaster who never missed a film but always fell asleep after a couple of reels and whose snoring drowned out the sound from the projection room; or the hunchback who always sat in the front row because he couldn't see anything from the back; or the man who drank endless cups of tea throughout the show. Mostly menfolk. Women seldom came to the night show, unless escorted by husbands or family.

One regular always intrigued me. He was a man in his thirties who sat through the show without ever removing his hat. Presumably he was bald and felt the cold draught that ran through the hall whenever one of the doors were opened. In January the hall could be cold. He wore an overcoat too, which also served as a receptacle for packets of channa which he munched assiduously during the film. Those were the days before fast foods of various descriptions took over. You had a choice between peanuts and channa. And apart from tea, there was a crimson-coloured cold drink called Vimto, which had a raspberry flavour. The gentleman with the hat always drank Vimto.

There was no social intercourse during the film. Either you saw the picture or you left the hall. The hatted gentleman almost always took the same seat, not far from one of the exit doors. Occasionally he would have a companion, but not for long. Mr Hat watched the film in its entirety, but the companions came and went. Sometimes he would offer them something from the folds of his overcoat. They would pocket the offering and leave after a few minutes.

One night there was a little more activity than usual in the row where Mr Hat was sitting. He came with a companion, who left after a few minutes. A little later he was joined by another person. I did not pay much attention to them. I was engrossed in *The Third Man*, Anton Karas's haunting zither music building up to the chase in the sewers of Vienna, with Joseph Cotten hunting down his black-marketeer friend Orson Welles. Cotten, not Welles, was my favourite actor.

The activity around Mr Hat was something of a distraction, and one or two in the hall shouted to them to shut up or go home. One of his companions, a tall individual, got up suddenly and walked towards the exit. He passed in front of me. And when he pushed open the door, the light from the foyer fell on his face and I caught a glimpse of narrow eyes, a large hooked nose, and a jutting chin. Then the door closed and I was back in the world of post-war Vienna. Ten minutes later the film was over and the lights came on. We began moving slowly out of the theatre—reluctantly, as it was freezing outside.

Mr Hat hadn't moved. He was hunched forward, his hat tilted over his head. I thought he'd fallen asleep. Curious as ever, I took a few steps down the central aisle and looked down at him. At first I thought he'd spilled a bottle of Vimto over his unbuttoned coat and shirt front. Then I realized that it was blood, not Vimto, that had gushed out of his torn and still bleeding throat. I cried out, and my usher friend came running. Then the manager. Then the tea-stall owner. Then those who were still in the hall.

'His throat's been cut,' said someone. 'He's dead or dying.'

And by the time a policeman and a doctor arrived, Mr Hat's life-blood had seeped away.

~

It was two or three weeks before I visited the Odeon again, and then too only for a matinée.

'No more night shows,' said my mother. 'You must be in the hotel by nine, and preferably in your bed.'

'But it had nothing to do with me,' I protested.

'He was just another film-goer.'

'No ordinary film-goer gets stabbed to death in the middle of a picture. Wasn't someone with him?'

'Sometimes. I didn't really notice.'

But I had noticed the tall, hawk-nosed man who had left before the show ended. I would recognize him again. But I did not tell my mother this.

With nothing much to do late in the evening I began hanging around the Green's Hotel bar, where the bartender, Melaram, often chatted to me if he wasn't too busy. I sat by myself in a corner of the large, dimly lit room, watching the customers and sipping a shandy. I would have preferred a beer, but my mother had given Melaram instructions to serve me with nothing stronger than shandy.

'A pity you can't go to the Odeon any more,' he said sympathetically. 'Not at night, anyway. Why don't you go to the afternoon shows?'

'The free pass was only for the night shows,' I told him. 'The hall is practically empty at night.'

'Not surprising, with people getting murdered in their seats.'

'It only happened once.'

'True . . . So how would you like to see a Hindi movie?
You can come with me. We'll go to the Filmistan. Your
mother won't mind.'

So Melaram took me to see an extravaganza called
Ali Baba aur Chalees Chor, which was the sort of film
Melaram enjoyed. All I remember is that it had a nifty little
heroine called Shakeela, who was easy on the eye.

The following week we saw another film, and this time
we were accompanied by my friend Sitaram, one of the
room boys. We sat in the cheaper seats and clapped with
the tonga-wallas and labourers whenever the dashing hero
(Dilip Kumar) rescued the coy heroine (Nalini Jaywant)
from the menacing villain (Pran, as usual).

As we left the cinema and were about to cross the road,
I thought I saw the man who had passed me in the Odeon
the night Mr Hat had been killed. He looked at me, hesitated
for a moment, and then passed on. Had he recognized me?

'Someone you know?' asked Melaram at my side.

'That fellow who just passed,' I said. 'I think he was
with the man who got killed that night.'

'Well, better keep quiet about it,' said Melaram. 'I think
he's from one of the drug gangs. If you see him again, don't
let him think you recognize him.'

~

To my suprise, the next time I saw him was in the Green's bar. He strode in as though looking for someone, then shrugged, sat down on a bar stool and ordered a beer. I was in my dark corner and probably he would not have noticed me just then, had I not got up and left the room by the service door. I felt his eyes on me. I thought it best not to hang around, so went to my room (my mother had allowed me to use one of the smaller hotel rooms), locked the door, switched on the bed-light, and immersed myself in Wuthering Heights.

It was the right sort of book for such a night. Outside, a storm had broken, thunder rolled across the heavens, and the rain came rattling down on the corrugated tin roof. I read for an hour or two, then looked at my watch—given to me recently for having passed out of school. It was only eleven o'clock. I switched off the light and tried to sleep. Presently the thunder grew more distant, the rain lessened. A breeze sprang up, and a bunch of bougainvillea kept tapping against the window panes.

And then someone was tapping on my door.

A light tap to begin with, and then louder, more insistent.

'Who's there?' I called, but no one answered.

Had it been the night-watchman, or Sitaram at a loose end, they would have said something. Perhaps Sitaram up to tricks?

'Go to bed,' I called out. 'I'm sleepy.'

No answer. But after a little while, more knocking. Then silence. Then footsteps receding.

I switched on my bedside radio and lay awake, listening to popular songs that held no special meaning for me. But at least the radio was company. Finally I fell asleep, the music still playing.

It must have been towards dawn that I woke again. The radio was still on, but the station had gone off the air and there was a lot of static coming over the airwaves. I switched it off.

That tapping again. But now it came from the window, not the door.

I got up on my knees and drew aside the window curtain. There was a face pressed against the glass. An outside light fell upon it and made it look more hideous than it really was. The slit eyes, hooked nose and wide sensual mouth seemed more sinister than ever. Boris Karloff as Frankenstein couldn't have been more frightening.

The apparition smiled at me, and I let the curtain fall.

And then I did a foolish thing. I leapt out of bed, opened my door, and ran barefoot down the corridor, calling for Sitaram, Melaram, the chowkidar, anyone!

But no one came. It was the hour before dawn, and no one stirred.

I ran out on to the back verandah, and he was waiting there—Hook Nose was waiting. In his right hand he held a kukri, its blade shining in the lamplight.

I turned and ran into the wilderness behind the hotel. A path ran down the slope and into a tangle of jungle. I knew it well.

He was running after me, crashing clumsily through the lantana, but I was faster than him, and I kept running until I came to an abandoned cowshed that stood at the edge of the jungle.

I did not enter it. He would have caught me there. Instead I crouched behind some bushes—and waited.

He was not long in coming. He stopped in front of the open door—the shed's only door—then stepped inside. I could hear him stumbling around in the dark.

I crept up to the door, pulled it shut, and slid the bolt in. It was an old door, but strong, made of deodar wood. There were no windows in the shed, just a small slit high up on the wall. Mr Hook Nose would have to break the door down in order to get out. He'd need an axe to do that. Already he was hammering away with his fists and cursing.

I left him to it, and returned to the hotel.

Dawn was breaking. A cock crowed near the kitchen outhouse, while an early riser emerged from his room, yelling for his morning tea.

~

I went to Bareilly to spend a month with one of my aunts. There were no bookshops in Bareilly, and no English cinema, and I was soon restless and eager to return to Dehradun.

When I got down at the station, Sitaram was there to meet me.

He told me that Melaram had gone to a new and bigger hotel, and that Green's had a new but inexperienced bartender. He also brought me up to date on all the films that were running in town.

Was it fear, curiosity, a morbid fascination that took me down to the old cowshed that very afternoon? Somehow I had to know if Hook Nose had escaped, or if he was still there, now a bag of bones!

I had lunch with my mother, then said I was going for a walk—it was a bracing February afternoon in the Doon—and took the jungle path down to the shed.

It was still locked. Dared I open that door? Would the revenant of Hook Nose come rushing out at me? Worse still, would I find his remains putrefying in the dust?

Well, I had to find out.

I opened the door and stepped inside.

It was so dark I could hardly see anything. In the stale air there was the smell of muskrats and rotting vegetation. But nothing that I would describe as a human smell.

I looked around. Toadstools grew on the floor. There was a pile of wood in one corner. A large grey rat ran out from under the woodpile and out through the open door. No sign of Hook Nose anywhere. Either he'd escaped on his own or someone had set him free. I felt relieved, but also apprehensive. What if he came looking for me again?

That evening, as I emerged from my room, Sitaram took me by the hand and said, 'Come on, the bar's open. I'll get you a beer. No customers as yet.'

I was still a year under the legal limit for drinking in a bar, but that didn't stop me from perching on a bar stool while Sitaram went in search of something for me to eat.

The bartender had his back to me. When he turned, a bottle of Golden Eagle in his hands, I received the shock of my life. It was Hook Nose!

I almost fell off my stool. My first impulse was to get up and run. But his face was expressionless. All he did was open the bottle and top up a glass with beer, and place it before me. Was it possible that he did not recognize me?

Sitaram was beckoning me to a table in a dark alcove.

I hurried towards him.

'Who's the new bartender?' I asked urgently.

'Don't know his name,' said Sitaram, speaking rapidly in Hindustani. 'I don't think he knows it himself. Your mother felt sorry for him and gave him the job. Somehow he'd got locked into that old shed behind the hotel. Must have been there for several days before he was found, just by chance, when we went there for some firewood— he'd had nothing to eat and drink, and he'd hurt his head trying to get out. Lost his memory. Couldn't remember a thing. Had nowhere to go. So your mother gave him a job.

He goes about in a bit of a daze, but he's all right for serving drinks. Perhaps he'll start remembering things one of these days . . . Why are you looking worried? It's no concern of yours. Come on, finish your beer and we'll go to the pictures. I've got the night off. There's a new film with Nimmi in it. You like her, don't you?'

HIS
NEIGHBOUR'S
WIFE

No (said Arun, as we waited for dinner to be prepared), I did not fall in love with my neighbour's wife. It is not that kind of story.

Mind you, Leela was a most attractive woman. She was not beautiful or pretty but she was handsome. Hers was the firm, athletic body of a sixteen-year-old boy, free of any surplus flesh. She bathed morning and evening, oiling herself well, so that her skin glowed a golden-brown in the winter sunshine. Her lips were often coloured with paan juice, but her teeth were perfect. I was her junior by about five years, and she called me her 'younger brother'. Her husband, who was forty to her thirty-two, was an official in the Customs and Excise Department: an extrovert, a hard-drinking, backslapping man, who spent a great deal of time on tour. Leela knew that he was not always faithful to her during these frequent absences, but she found solace in her own loyalty and in the well-being of her only child, a boy called Chandu.

I did not care for the boy. He had been well spoilt, and took great delight in disturbing me whenever I was at work. He entered my rooms uninvited, knocked my books about, and, if guests were present, made insulting remarks about them to their faces.

Leela, during her lonely evenings, would often ask me to sit on her verandah and talk to her. The day's work done, she would relax with a hookah. Smoking a hookah was a habit she had brought with her from her village near Agra, and it was a habit she refused to give up. She liked to talk and, as I was a good listener, she soon grew fond of me. The fact that I was twenty-six years old and still a bachelor never failed to astonish her.

It was not long before she took upon herself the responsibility of getting me married. I found it useless to protest. She did not believe me when I told her that I could not afford to marry, that I preferred a bachelor's life. A wife, she insisted, was an asset to any man. A wife reduced expenses. Where did I eat? At a hotel, of course. That must cost me at least sixty rupees a month, even on a vegetarian diet. But if I had a simple homely wife to do the cooking, we could both eat well for less than that.

Leela fingered my shirt, observing that a button was missing and that the collar was frayed. She remarked on my pale face and general look of debility, and told me that I would fall victim to all kinds of diseases if I did not find someone to look after me. What I needed, she declared between puffs at the hookah, was a woman—a young, healthy, buxom woman, preferably from a village near Agra.

'If I could find someone like you,' I said slyly, 'I would not mind getting married.'

She appeared neither flattered nor offended by my remark.

'Don't marry an older woman,' she advised. 'Never take a wife who is more experienced in the ways of the world than you are. You just leave it to me, I'll find a suitable bride for you.'

To please Leela, I agreed to this arrangement, thinking she would not take it seriously. But, two days later, when she suggested that I accompany her to a certain distinguished home for orphan girls, I became alarmed. I refused to have anything to do with her project.

'Don't you have confidence in me?' she asked. 'You said you would like a girl who resembled me. I know one who looks just as I did ten years ago.'

'I like you as you are now,' I said. 'Not as you were ten years ago.'

'Of course. We shall arrange for you to see the girl first.'

'You don't understand,' I protested. 'It's not that I feel I have to be in love with someone before marrying her—I know you would choose a fine girl, and I would really prefer someone who is homely and simple to an MA with honours in psychology—it's just that I'm not ready for it. I want another year or two of freedom. I don't want to be chained down. To be frank, I don't want the responsibility.'

'A little responsibility will make a man of you,' said Leela; but she did not insist on my accompanying her to the orphanage, and the matter was allowed to rest for a few days.

I was beginning to hope that Leela had reconciled herself to allowing one man to remain single in a world full of husbands when, one morning, she accosted me on the verandah with an open newspaper, which she thrust in front of my nose.

'There!' she said triumphantly. 'What do you think of that? I did it to surprise you.'

She had certainly succeeded in surprising me. Her henna-stained forefinger rested on an advertisement in the matrimonial columns.

Bachelor journalist, age twenty-five, seeks attractive young wife well versed in household duties. Caste, religion no bar. Dowry optional.

I must admit that Leela had made a good job of it. In a few days the replies began to come in, usually from the parents of the girls concerned. Each applicant wanted to know how much money I was earning. At the same time, they took the trouble to list their own connections and the high positions occupied by relatives. Some parents enclosed their daughters' photographs. They were very good photographs, though there was a certain amount of touching-up employed.

I studied the pictures with interest. Perhaps marriage wasn't such a bad proposition, after all. I selected the photographs of the three girls I most fancied and showed them to Leela.

To my surprise, she disapproved of all three. One of the girls she said had a face like a hermaphrodite; another obviously suffered from tuberculosis; and the third was undoubtedly an adventuress. Leela decided that the whole idea of the advertisement had been a mistake. She was sorry she had inserted it; the only replies we were likely to get would be from fortune hunters. And I had no fortune.

So we destroyed the letters. I tried to keep some of the photographs, but Leela tore them up too.

And so, for some time, there were no more attempts at getting me married.

Leela and I met nearly every day, but we spoke of other things. Sometimes, in the evenings, she would make me sit on the charpoy opposite her, and then she would draw up her hookah and tell me stories about her village and her family. I was getting used to the boy, too, and even growing rather fond of him.

All this came to an end when Leela's husband went and got himself killed. He was shot by a bootlegger, who had decided to get rid of the excise man rather than pay him an exorbitant sum of money. It meant that Leela had to give up her quarters and return to her village near Agra. She waited until the boy's school term had finished, and then she packed their things and bought two tickets, third class to Agra.

Something, I could see, had been troubling her, and when I saw her off at the station, I realized what it was. She was having a fit of conscience about my continued bachelorhood.

'In my village,' she said confidently, leaning out from the carriage window, 'there is a very comely young girl, a distant relative of mine; I shall speak to the parents.'

And then I said something which I had not considered before; which had never, until that moment, entered my head. And I was no less surprised than Leela when the words came tumbling out of my mouth: 'Why don't you marry me now?'

Arun didn't have time to finish his story because, just at this interesting stage, the dinner arrived.

But the dinner brought with it the end of his story.

It was served by his wife, a magnificent woman, strong and handsome, who could only have been Leela. And a few minutes later, Chandu, Arun's stepson, charged into the house, complaining that he was famished.

Arun introduced me to his wife, and we exchanged the usual formalities.

'But why hasn't your friend brought his family with him?' she asked.

'Family? Because he's still a bachelor!'

And then as he watched his wife's expression change from a look of mild indifference to one of deep concern, he hurriedly changed the subject.

THE
WINDOW

I came in the spring, and took the room on the roof. It was a long, low building which housed several families; the roof was flat, except for my room and a chimney. I don't know whose room owned the chimney, but my room owned the roof. And from the window of my room I owned the world.

But only from the window.

The banyan tree, just opposite, was mine, and its inhabitants my subjects. They were two squirrels, a few mina, a crow and at night, a pair of flying foxes. The squirrels were busy in the afternoons, the birds in the mornings and evenings, the foxes at night. I wasn't very busy that year; not as busy as the inhabitants of the banyan tree.

There was also a mango tree but that came later, in the summer, when I met Koki and the mangoes were ripe.

At first, I was lonely in my room. But then I discovered the power of my window. I looked out on the banyan tree, on the garden, on the broad path that ran beside the building, and out over the roofs of other houses, over roads and fields, as far as the horizon. The path was not a very busy one but it held variety: an ayah, with a baby in a pram; the postman, an event in himself; the fruit seller, the toy seller, calling their wares in high-pitched familiar cries; the rent collector; a posse of cyclists; a long chain of schoolgirls; a lame beggar . . . all passed my way, the way of my window . . .

In the early summer, a tonga came rattling and jingling down the path and stopped in front of the house. A girl and an elderly lady climbed down, and a servant unloaded their baggage. They went into the house and the tonga moved off, the horse snorting a little.

The next morning the girl looked up from the garden and saw me at my window.

She had long black hair that fell to her waist, tied with a single red ribbon. Her eyes were black like her hair and just as shiny. She must have been about ten or eleven years old.

'Hello,' I said with a friendly smile.

She looked suspiciously at me. 'Who are you?' she asked.

'I'm a ghost.'

She laughed, and her laugh had a gay, mocking quality. 'You look like one!'

I didn't think her remark particularly flattering, but I had asked for it. I stopped smiling anyway. Most children don't like adults smiling at them all the time.

'What have you got up there?' she asked.

'Magic,' I said.

She laughed again but this time without mockery. 'I don't believe you,' she said.

'Why don't you come up and see for yourself?'

She hesitated a little but came round to the steps and began climbing them, slowly, cautiously. And when she entered the room, she brought a magic of her own.

'Where's your magic?' she asked, looking me in the eye.

'Come here,' I said, and I took her to the window and showed her the world.

She said nothing but stared out of the window uncomprehendingly at first, and then with increasing interest. And after some time she turned around and smiled at me, and we were friends.

I only knew that her name was Koki, and that she had come with her aunt for the summer months; I didn't need to know any more about her, and she didn't need to know anything about me except that I wasn't really a ghost—not the frightening sort anyway . . .

She came up my steps nearly every day and joined me at the window. There was a lot of excitement to be had in our world, especially when the rains broke.

At the first rumblings, women would rush outside to retrieve the washing from the clothesline and if there was a breeze, to chase a few garments across the compound. When the rains came, they came with a vengeance, making a bog of the garden and a river of the path. A cyclist would come riding furiously down the path, an elderly gentleman would be having difficulty with an umbrella, naked children would be frisking about in the rain. Sometimes Koki would run out to the roof, and shout and dance in the rain. And the rain would come through the open door and window of the room, flooding the floor and making an island of the bed.

But the window was more fun than anything else. It gave us the power of detachment: we were deeply interested in the life around us, but we were not involved in it.

'It is like a cinema,' said Koki. 'The window is the screen, the world is the picture.'

Soon the mangoes were ripe, and Koki was in the branches of the mango tree as often as she was in my room. From the window I had a good view of the tree, and we spoke to each other from the same height. We ate far too many mangoes, at least five a day.

'Let's make a garden on the roof,' suggested Koki. She was full of ideas like this.

'And how do you propose to do that?' I asked.

'It's easy. We bring up mud and bricks and make the flower beds. Then we plant the seeds. We'll grow all sorts of flowers.'

'The roof will fall in,' I predicted.

But it didn't. We spent two days carrying buckets of mud up the steps to the roof and laying out the flower beds. It was very hard work, but Koki did most of it. When the beds were ready, we had the opening ceremony. Apart from a few small plants collected from the garden below, we had only one species of seeds—pumpkin . . .

We planted the pumpkin seeds in the mud, and felt proud of ourselves.

But it rained heavily that night, and in the morning I discovered that everything—except the bricks—had been washed away.

So we returned to the window.

A mina had been in a fight—with a crow perhaps—and the feathers had been knocked off its head. A bougainvillea that had been climbing the wall had sent a long green shoot in through the window.

Koki said, 'Now we can't shut the window without spoiling the creeper.'

'Then we will never close the window,' I said.

And we let the creeper into the room.

The rains passed, and an autumn wind came whispering through the branches of the banyan tree. There were red leaves on the ground, and the wind picked them up and blew them about, so that they looked like butterflies. I would watch the sun rise in the morning; the sky all red until its first rays splashed the windowsill and crept up the walls of the room. And in the evening, Koki and I watched the sun go down in a sea of fluffy clouds; sometimes the clouds were pink and sometimes orange; they were always coloured clouds framed in the window.

'I'm going tomorrow,' said Koki one evening.

I was too surprised to say anything.

'You stay here for ever, don't you?' she said.

I remained silent.

'When I come again next year you will still be here, won't you?'

'I don't know,' I said. 'But the window will still be here.'

'Oh, do be here next year,' she said, 'or someone will close the window!'

In the morning the tonga was at the door, and the servant, the aunt and Koki were in it. Koki waved to me at my window. Then the driver flicked the reins, the wheels of the carriage creaked and rattled, the bell jingled. Down the path went the tonga, down the path and through the gate, and all the time Koki waved; and from the gate I must have looked like a ghost, standing alone at the high window, amongst the bougainvillea.

When the tonga was out of sight, I took the spray of bougainvillea in my hand and pushed it out of the room. Then I closed the window. It would be opened only when the spring and Koki came again.

JERSEY *and* LONDON

A FAR CRY
from INDIA

It was while I was living in Jersey, in the Channel Islands, that I really missed India.

Jersey was a very pretty island, with wide sandy bays and rocky inlets, but it was worlds away from the land in which I had grown up. You did not see an Indian or eastern face anywhere. It was not really an English place, either, except in parts of the capital, St Helier, where some of the business houses, hotels and law firms were British-owned. The majority of the population—farmers, fishermen, councillors—spoke a French *patois* which even a Frenchman would have disowned. The island, originally French, and then for a century British, had been briefly occupied by the Germans. Now it was British again, although it had its own legislative council and made its own laws. It exported tomatoes, shrimps and Jersey cows, and imported people looking for a tax haven.

During the summer months the island was flooded with English holidaymakers. During the long, cold winter, gale-force winds swept across the Channel and the island's waterfront had a forlorn look. I knew I did not belong there and I disliked the place intensely. Within days of my arrival I was longing for the languid, easy-going, mango-scented air of small-town India: the gul mohur trees in their fiery summer splendour; barefoot boys riding buffaloes and chewing on sticks of sugarcane; a hoopoe on the grass, bluejays performing aerial acrobatics; a girl's pink dupatta flying in the breeze; the scent of wet earth after the first rain; and most of all my Dehra friends.

So what on earth was I doing on an island, twelve by five miles in size, in the cold seas off Europe? Islands always sound as though they are romantic places, but take my advice, don't live on one—you'll feel deeply frustrated after a week.

I was in Jersey because my Aunt E (my mother's eldest sister) had, along with her husband and three sons, settled there a couple of years previously. So had a few other financially stable Anglo-Indian families, former residents of Poona or Bangalore; but it was not a place where young people could make a career, except perhaps in local government.

I had finished school at the end of 1950, and then for almost a year I had been loafing around in Dehra Dun, convinced that I was a writer on the strength of a couple of stories sold to *The Hindu's Sport and Pastime* (now *there* was a sports' magazine with a difference—it published my fiction!) and *The Tribune* of Ambala (Chandigarh did not exist then). My mother and stepfather finally decided to pack me off to the U.K., where, it was hoped, I would make my fortune or become Lord Mayor of London like Dick Whittington. There really wasn't much else I could have done at the time, except take a teacher's training and spend the rest of my life teaching *As You Like It* or *Far from the Madding Crowd* to schoolboys (in private schools) who would always have more money than I could earn.

Anyway, my aunt had written to say that I could stay with her in Jersey until I found my bearings, and so off I went, in my trunk a new tweed coat and two pairs of grey flannel trousers; also a packet of haldi powder, which my aunt had particularly requested. During the voyage the packet burst and most of my clothes were stained with haldi.

One fine day I found myself on Ballard Pier and there followed the long sea voyage on the P&O liner, *Strathnaver*. (Built in the 1920s, it had been used as a troopship during the War and was now a passenger liner again.) In the early 1950s, the big passenger ships were still the chief mode of international travel. A leisurely cruise through the Red Sea, with a call at Aden; then through Suez, stopping at Port Said (you had a choice between visiting the pyramids or having a sexual adventure in the port's back alleys); then across the Mediterranean, with a view of Vesuvius (or was it Stromboli?) erupting at night; a look-in at Marseilles, where you could try out your school French and buy naughty postcards; finally docking at Tilbury, on the Thames estuary, just a short train ride to the heart of London.

At Bombay, waiting for the ship's departure, I had spent two nights in a very seedy hotel on Lamington Road, and probably picked up the hepatitis virus there, although I did not break out in jaundice until I was in Jersey. Bombay never did agree with me. Now that it has been renamed Mumbai, maybe I'll be luckier.

I liked Aden. It was unsophisticated. And although I am a lover of trees and forests, there is something about the desert (a natural desert, not a man-made one) that appeals to my solitary instincts. I am not sure that I could take up an abode permanently surrounded by sand, date-palms and camels, but it would be preferable to living in a concrete jungle—or in Jersey, for that matter!

And camels do have character.

Have I told you the story of the camel fair in Rajasthan, India's desert state? Well, there was a brisk sale in camels and the best ones fetched good prices. An elderly dealer was having some difficulty in selling a camel which, like its owner, had seen better days. It was lean, scraggy, half-blind, and moved with such a heavy roll that people were thrown off before they had gone very far.

'Who'll buy your scruffy, lame old camel?' asked a rival dealer. 'Tell me just one advantage it has over other camels.'

The elderly camel owner drew himself up with great dignity and with true Rajput pride, replied: 'There is something to be said for *character*, isn't there?'

Did I have 'character' as a boy? Probably more than I have now. I was prepared to put up with discomfort, frugal meals and even the occasional nine to five job provided I could stay up at night in order to complete my book or write a new story. Almost fifty years on, I am still leading the simple life—a good, strong bed, a desk of reasonable proportions, a coat-hanger for my one suit and a comfortable chair by the window. The rest is superstition.

~

When that ship sailed out of Aden, my ambitions were tempered by the stirrings of hepatitis within my system. That common toilet in the Lamington Road hotel, with its ever-growing uncleared mountain of human excreta, probably had something to do with it. The day after arriving at my uncle's house in Jersey, I went down with jaundice and had to spend two or three weeks in bed. It was my second attack of jaundice—I'd been hospitalized with it in Simla four years earlier—and of course I remembered that it had contributed to my father's death when he was only forty-eight. But now rest and the right diet brought about a good recovery. And as soon as I was back on my feet, I began looking for a job.

I had only three or four pounds left from my travel money, and I did not like the idea of being totally dependent on my relatives. They were a little disapproving of my writing ambitions. And sometimes they spoke disapprovingly of my mother because of her second marriage (to an 'Indian') and they were sorry for me in the way one feels sorry for an unfortunate or poor relative—simply because he or she is a relative. They were doing their duty by me, and this was noble of them; but it made me uneasy.

St Helier, the capital town and port of Jersey, was full of solicitors' offices, and I am not sure what prompted me to do the rounds of all of them, asking for a job; I think I was under the impression that solicitors were always in need of clerical assistants. But I had no luck. At seventeen, I was too young and inexperienced. One firm offered me the job of tea-boy, but as I never could brew a decent cup of tea, I felt obliged to decline the offer. Finally I ended up working for a pittance in a large grocery store, Le Riche's, where I found myself sitting on a high stool at a high desk (like Herbert Pocket in *Great Expectations*), alongside a row of similarly positioned clerks, making up bills for despatch to the firm's regular clients.

By then it was mid-winter, and I found myself walking to work in the dark (7.30 a.m.) and walking home when it was darker still (6 p.m.)—they gave you long working hours in those days! So I did not get to see much of St Helier except at weekends.

Saturdays were half-holidays. Strolling home via a circuitous route through the old part of the town, I discovered a little cinema which ran reruns of old British comedies. And here, for a couple of bob, I made the acquaintance of performers who had come of age in the era of the music halls, and who brought to their work a broad, farcical humour that appealed to me. At school in Simla, some of them had been familiar through the pages of a favourite comic, *Film Fun*—George Formby, Sidney Howard, Max Miller ('The Cheeky Chappie', known for his double entendres), Tommy Trinder, Old Mother Riley (really a man dressed up as a woman), Laurel and Hardy and many others.

I disliked Le Riche's store. My fellow junior clerk was an egregious fellow who never stopped picking his nose. The senior clerk was interested only in the racing results from England. There were a couple of girls who drooled over the latest pop stars. I don't remember much about this period except that when King George VI died, we observed a minute's silence. Then back to our ledgers.

George VI was a popular monarch, a quiet self-effacing man, and much respected because he had stayed in London through the Blitz when, every night for months, bombs had rained on the city. I thought he deserved more than a minute's silence. In India we observed whole holidays when almost any sort of dignitary or potentate passed away. But here it was 'The King is dead. Long live the Queen!' And then, 'Stop dreaming, Bond. Get on with those bills.'

The sea itself was always comforting and on holidays or summer evenings I would walk along the seafront, watching familiar rocks being submerged or exposed, depending on whether the tide was coming in or going out. On Sundays I would occasionally go down to the beach (St Helier's was probably the least attractive of Jersey's beaches, but it was only a short walk from my aunt's house) and sometimes I'd walk out with the tide until I came to a group of prominent rocks, and there I'd sunbathe in solitary and naked splendour. Not since the year of my father's death had I been such a loner.

I could swim a little but I was no Johnny Weissmuller, and I took care to wade back to dry land once the tide started turning. Only recently a couple had been trapped on those rocks; their bodies had been washed ashore the next day. At high tide I loved to watch the sea rushing against the sea wall, sending sprays of salt water into my face. Winter gales were frequent and I liked walking into the wind, just leaning against it. Sometimes it was strong enough to support me and I fell into its arms. It wasn't as much fun with the wind behind you, for then it propelled you along the road in a most undignified fashion, so that you looked like Charlie Chaplin in full flight.

Back in the little attic room which I had to myself, I started putting together a novel of sorts, based on the diaries I had kept during that last year in Dehra Dun. It remained a journal but I began to fill in details, trying to capture the sights, sounds and smells of that little corner of India which I had known so well. And I tried to recreate the nature and character of some of my friends—Somi, Ranbir, Kishen—and the essence of that calf-love I'd felt for Kishen's mother. I could have left it as a journal, but in that case it would not have found a publisher. In the 1950s, no publisher would have been interested in the sentimental diaries of an unknown 17-year-old. So it had to be turned into a novel. I had no title for it then, but one day it would be called *The Room on the Roof.*

THREE
JOBS *in* JERSEY

I was fortunate to discover the Jersey Library, and at this time I went through almost everything of Tagore's that had been published in those early Macmillan editions—*The Crescent Moon*, *The Gardener* and most of the plays—as well as Rumer Godden's Indian novels—*The River, Black Narcissus, Breakfast at the Nickolides.* And there was a Bengali writer, Sudhin Ghosh, who'd written a couple of enchanting memoirs of his childhood in rural Bengal—*And Gazelles Leaping* and *Cradle in the Clouds*; it's hard to find them now.

Jean Renoir's film of *The River* was released in 1952, and as I sat watching it in a St Helier cinema, waves of nostalgia flowed over me. I went to see it about five times. After three months with Le Riche's I found a job as an assistant to a travel agent, a single woman in her mid-thirties, who was opening an office in Jersey for Thomas Cook and Sons, the famous travel agency for whom she had been working in London. She was an efficient woman but jumpy, and she smoked a lot to calm her nerves. Although I abhorred the smoking habit, I was always finding myself in the company of heavy smokers—first my mother and stepfather, now Miss Manning, and in later years it was to be friends like William Matheson, Ganesh Saili and Victor Banerjee.

Miss Manning did not remove the cigarette from her lips even when she was on the phone to her London office. Her end of the conversation went something like this: 'Puff-puff—A double-room at the Seaview, did you say?—puff, suck—Separate beds or twin beds?—draw, suck, puff—Separate. They've always had separate beds, you say. Okay, puff—They're from South Africa?—puff—This hotel has a colour bar. Oh, they're white—puff—white-white or off-white?'

Colour-conscious Jersey did not encourage dark-skinned tourists from the Asian, African or American continents. I don't think Thomas Cook had any policy on this matter, but we were constantly being told by Jersey hotels that they did not take people of 'colour'. Multi-cultural Britain was still some twenty-five years away.

Miss Manning wasn't bothered by these (to her) trifles. She was having an affair with a man who sold renovated fire extinguishers. They spent the afternoons together in his rooms, a time of day when the only fires he attempted to extinguish were those raging in Miss Manning's heaving bosom. Nor could he do anything to reduce her smoking. He came to the office on one or two occasions and tried to talk me into investing twenty-five pounds in his business. I'd be part-owner of ten fire extinguishers, he told me. He was quite persuasive, but as my savings did not exceed seven pounds at the time, I could not take up his offer. He bought discarded fire extinguishers and put new life into them, he told me. They were as good as new.

So was Miss Manning, after several afternoon sessions in his rooms.

But Thomas Cook weren't happy. For several hours every day I was left in sole charge of the office, taking calls from London and booking people into the island's hotels. I couldn't help but confuse twin beds with double-beds, and was frequently putting elderly couples who hadn't slept together for years into double-beds, while forcibly separating those who couldn't have enough of each other. Miss Manning did her best to educate me in this matter of beds but I was a slow learner.

Beds could be changed around, but when I booked a group of Brazilian samba dancers into a hotel meant for 'whites only', I was fired. Later I heard that Miss Manning had been recalled to London. And her gentleman friend ran foul of the local authorities for passing off his re-charged extinguishers under his own brand name.

My next job was a more congenial one. This was in the public health department. Situated near the St Helier docks, it was a twenty-minute walk from my aunt's house—over the brow of a sometimes gale-swept hill, and down to a broad esplanade in the port area. My fellow clerks, all older than me, were a friendly, good-humoured lot, and I was to work under them as a junior clerk for more than a year.

One of them, Mr Bromley, helped me buy a new typewriter—a small Royal portable, which we saw in a department store window in town. It was priced at nineteen pounds. I had only five pounds at the time, but Mr Bromley gave me the rest and I paid it back in instalments, one pound at a time. He was a Yorkshireman who had come to work in Jersey in order to improve his health; he had a weak chest, and the cold and damp of Yorkshire did not suit him. The Channel Islands were sunnier than England. But not sunny enough for me.

I found Jersey cold in the winter. It did not snow but those gales went right through you, and my sports coat (I had no overcoat) did not really keep the cold out.

Still, there was something quite stirring, electrifying about those gales. One evening, feeling moody and dissatisfied, I deliberately went for a walk in the thick of a gale, taking the road along the seafront. The wind howled about me, almost carrying me with it along the promenade; and as it was high tide, the waves came crashing over the sea wall, stinging my face with their cold spray. It was during the walk I resolved that I was going to be a writer, come hell or high water, and that in order to do so I would have to leave Jersey and live and work in London.

This resolve was further strengthened when, a few days later, I happened to quarrel with my uncle over an entry I had made in my diary.

Keeping a diary or journal is something that I have done fitfully over the years, and sometimes it is no more than a notebook of ideas and impressions which go into the making of essays or stories. But when I am lonely or troubled it takes the form of a confessional, and this is what it was at the time. My uncle happened to come across it among my books. I don't think he was deliberately prying but he glanced through it and came across a couple of entries in which I had expressed my resentment over the very colonial attitudes that still prevailed in my uncle's family. He was a South Indian Christian, my aunt an Anglo-Indian, and yet they were champions of Empire!

This was their own business, of course, and they had a right to their views—but what I did resent was their criticism of the fact that I had young Indian friends who wrote to me quite regularly. They wanted me to forget these ties and be more British in my preferences and attitudes. Their own children had acquired English accents while I still spoke *chi-chi!*

I forget the exact words of my diary entry (I threw it away afterwards); but my uncle was offended and took me to task. I accused him of going through my personal letters and papers. Although things quietened down the next day, I had resolved to make a move.

I had saved about twelve pounds from my salary, and after giving a week's notice to the public health department, I packed my rather battered suitcase and took the cross-Channel ferry to Plymouth. A few hours later I was in London.

The cheapest place to stay was a student's hostel and I spent a few nights in the cheapest one I could find. The day after my arrival I went to the employment exchange and took the first job that was offered. I had grown quite used to changing jobs—this was my fourth or fifth in eighteen months!—and it didn't seem to matter what I did, provided it gave me enough to pay for my board and lodging and left me free to write on holidays and in the evenings.

I was alone and I was lonely but I was not afraid.

AND ANOTHER
in LONDON

Looking back on the three years I spent in London, I realize that it must have been the most restless period of my life, judging from the number of lodging houses and residential districts I lived in—Belsize Park, Haverstock Hill, Swiss Cottage, Tooting and a couple of other places whose names I have forgotten. I don't quite know why but I was never long in any one boarding house. And unlike a Graham Greene character, I wasn't trying to escape from sinister pursuers. Unless you could call Nirdosh a sinister pursuer.

This good-hearted girl, the sister of a former schoolmate, took it into her head that I needed a sister, and fussed over me so much, and followed me about so relentlessly that I was forced to flee my Glenmore Road lodgings and move to south London (Tooting) for a month. I preferred north London because it was more cosmopolitan, with a growing population of Indian, African and continental students. I tried living in a students' hostel for a time but the food was awful and there was absolutely no privacy, so I moved back into a bedsitter and took my meals at various snack bars and small cafés. There was a nice place near Swiss Cottage where I could have a glass or two of sherry with a light supper, and after this I would walk back to my room and write a few pages of my novel.

My meals were not very substantial and I must have been suffering from some form of malnutrition because my right eye started clouding over and my sight was partially affected. I had to go into hospital for some time. The condition was diagnosed as Eale's Disease, a rare tubercular condition of the eye, and I felt quite thrilled that I could count myself among the 'greats' who had also suffered from this disease in some form or another—Keats, the Brontes, Stevenson, Katherine Mansfield, Ernest Dowson—and I thought, If only I could write like them, I'd be happy to live with a consumptive eye!

But the disease proved curable (for a time, anyway), and I went back to my job at Photax on Charlotte Street, totting up figures in heavy ledgers. Adding machines were just coming in but my employers were quite happy with their old ledgers—and so was I. I became quite good at adding pounds, shillings and pence, for hours, days, weeks, months on end. And quite contented too, provided I wasn't asked to enter the higher realms of mathematical endeavour. Maths was never my forte, although I kept reminding myself that Lewis Caroll, one of my all-time favourites, also wrote books on mathematics.

This mundane clerical job did not prevent me from pursuing the literary life, although for most of the time it was a solitary pursuit—wandering the streets of London and the East End in search of haunts associated with Dr Johnson, Dickens and his characters, W.W. Jacobs, Jerome K. Jerome, George and Weedon Grossmith—Barrie's Kensington Gardens; Dickens' dockland; Gissing's mean streets; Fleet Street; old music halls; Soho and its Greek and Italian restaurants.

In these latter I could picture the melancholic 1890s poets, especially Ernest Dowson writing love poems to the vivacious waitress who was probably unaware of his presence. For a time I went through my Dowson period—wistful, dreamy, wallowing in a sense of loss and failure. I had even memorized some of his verses, such as these lovely lines:

> They are not long, the days of wine and roses:
> Out of a misty dream
> Our path emerges for a while, then closes
> Within a dream.

Poor Dowson, destined to die young and unfulfilled. A minor poet, dismissed as inconsequential by the critics, and yet with us still, a singer of sad but exquisite songs.

~

Although for my first six months in London I did live in a garret and an unhealthy one at that, I did not really see myself in the role of the starving poet. The first thing I did was to look for a job, and I took the first that was offered—the office job at Photax, a small firm selling photographic components and accessories. A little way down the road was the Scala Theatre, and as soon as I had saved enough for a theatre ticket (theatre-going wasn't expensive in those days), I went to see the annual Christmas production of *Peter Pan,* which I'd read as a play when I was going through the works of Barrie in my school library. This production had Margaret Lockwood as Peter. She had been Britain's most popular film star in the forties and she was still pretty and vivacious. I think Captain Hook was played by Donald Wolfit, better known for his portrayal of Svengali.

My colleagues in Photax, though not in the least literary, were a friendly lot. There was my fellow clerk, Ken, who shared his marmite sandwiches with me. There was Maisie of the auburn hair, who was constantly being rung up by her boyfriends. And there was Clarence, who was slightly effeminate and known to frequent the gay bars in Soho. (Except that the term 'gay' hadn't been invented yet.) And there was our head clerk, Mr Smedly, who'd been in the Navy during the War, and was a musical-theatre buff. We would often discuss the latest musicals—*Guys and Dolls, South Pacific, Paint Your Wagon, Pal Joey*—big musicals which used to run for months, even years.

The window opposite my desk looked out on a huge cinema hoarding, and it was always an event when a new poster went up on it. Weeks before the film was released, there was a poster of Judy Garland in her comeback film, *A Star is Born*, and I can still remember the publicity headline: 'Judy, the world is waiting for your sunshine!' And, of course, there was Marilyn Monroe in *Niagara*, with Marilyn looking much bigger than the waterfall, and that fine actor, Joseph Cotten, nowhere in sight.

My heart, though, was not in the Photax office. I had no ambitions to become head clerk or even to learn the intricacies of the business. It was a nine-to-five job, giving me just enough money to live on (six pounds a week, in fact), while I scribbled away of an evening, working on my second (or was it third?) draft of my novel. The title was the only thing about it that did not change. It was *The Room on the Roof* from the beginning.

How I worked at that book! I was always being asked to put things in or take things out. At first the publishers suggested that it needed 'filling out'. When I filled it out, I was told that it was now a little too descriptive and would I prune it a bit? And what started out as a journal and then became a first-person narrative finally ended up in the third person. But editors only made suggestions; they did not tamper with your language or style. And the 'feel' of the story—my love for India and my friends in particular—was ever present, running through it like a vein of gold.

Much of the publishers' uncertain and contradictory suggestions stemmed from the fact they relied heavily on their readers' recommendations. A 'reader' was a well-known writer or critic who was asked (and paid) to give his opinion on a book. *The Room on the Roof* was sent to the celebrated literary critic, Walter Allen, who said I was a 'born writer' and likened me to Sterne, but also said I should wait a little longer before attempting a novel. Another reader, Laurie Lee (the author of *Cider with Rosie*), said he had enjoyed the story but that it would be a gamble to publish it.*

Fortunately, Andre Deutsch was the sort of publisher who was ready to take a risk with a new, young author; so instead of rejecting the book, he bought an option on it, which meant that he could sit on it for a couple of years until he had made up his mind!

My mentor at this time was Diana Athill, Deutsch's editor and junior partner. She was at least ten years older than me but we became good friends. She invited me to her flat for meals and sometimes accompanied me to the pictures or the theatre. She was tall, auburn-haired and attractive in a sort of angular English way, but our relationship was purely platonic. It hadn't occurred to me

---

* Some of the correspondence (or that which has survived) in connection with this first novel is given in *Notes and Letters.* It might be of interest to other budding authors.

to try and make love to an older woman. I saw her as a literary person (which she undoubtedly was) and not as a sex object. She was fond of me. She could see I was suffering from malnutrition and as she was a good cook (in addition to being a good editor), she shared her very pleasant and wholesome meals with me. There is nothing better than good English food, no matter what the French or Italians or Chinese may say. A lamb chop, a fish nicely fried, cold meat with salad, or shepherd's pie, or even an Irish stew, are infinitely more satisfying than most of the stuff served in continental or Far Eastern restaurants. I suppose it's really a matter of childhood preferences. I still fancy a kofta curry because koftas were what I enjoyed most in Granny's house. And oh, for one of Miss Kellner's meringues—but no one seems to make them any more:

I really neglected myself during those three years I spent in London. Never much of a cook, I was hard put to fry myself an egg every morning before rushing off to catch the tube for Tottenham Court Road, a journey of about twenty-five minutes. In the lunch break I would stroll across to a snack bar and have the inevitable baked beans-on-toast. There wasn't time for a more substantial meal, even if I could afford it. In the evenings I could indulge myself a little, with a decent meal in a quiet café; but most of the time I existed on snacks. No wonder I ended up with a debilitating disease!

Perhaps the most relaxing period of my London life was the month I spent in the Hampstead General Hospital, which turned out to be a friendly sort of place.

I was sent there for my Eale's disease, and the treatment consisted of occasional cortisone injections to my right eye. But I was allowed—even recommended—a full diet, supplemented by a bottle of Guinness with my lunch. They felt that I needed a little extra nourishment—wise doctors, those!

The bottle of Guinness made me the envy of the ward, but I made myself popular by sharing the drink with neighbouring patients when the nurses weren't looking. One nurse was a ravishing South American beauty, and half the ward fell in love with her.

It was a general ward and one ailing patient—a West Indian from Trinidad—felt that he was being singled out for experimentation by the doctors. He set up a commotion whenever he had to be given a rather painful lumbar puncture. I would sit on his bed and try to calm him down, and he became rather dependent on my moral support, insisting on my presence whenever he was being examined or treated.

While I was in hospital, I got in a lot of reading (with one eye), wrote a short story, and received visitors in style. They ranged from my colleagues at Photax, to Diana Athill, my would-be publisher, to some of my Indian friends in

Hampstead, to my latest landlady, a motherly sort who'd lost some of her children in Hitler's persecution of the Jews.

When I left the hospital I was richer by a few pounds, having saved my salary and been treated free on account of the National Health Scheme. The spots had cleared from my eyes and I'd put on some weight, thanks to the lamb chops and Guinness that had constituted my lunch.

I gave George, the West Indian, my home address, although I did not expect to see him again. A few months later I found him on my doorstep, fully recovered. We repaired to a nearby pub and drank rum. He invited me to a calypso party in Camden Town, and when I arrived I found I was the only 'white' in a gathering of some forty handsome black men and women, all determined to eat, drink and be merry into the early hours of the morning. I fell asleep on a settee halfway through the party. Someone fell asleep on top of me.

I met George occasionally (he worked for British Rail), and there were one or two more wild parties; but before I could become a part of the calypso scene I met Vu-Phuong, and once again my life took on a different direction.

Thanh, a Vietnamese part-time student, befriended me because he thought I could improve his English. Later, when he discovered that I spoke more like an Indian than an Englishman, he decided to drop me; but for a couple of months I received the benefits of his cooking, Vietnamese dishes coming to him quite naturally as his uncle owned a restaurant in Paris. I never could learn to use chopsticks, and to his disgust consumed my rice and noodles with spoon, fork or fingers.

It was Thanh who introduced me to a Vietnamese girl call Vu-Phuong, and I promptly fell in love with her.

At that age it did not take long for me to fall in love with anyone, and Vu was the sort of girl—pretty, soft-spoken, demure—who could enslave me without any apparent effort.

She was happy to accompany me on walks across Hampstead Heath and over Primrose Hill. It was summer time and the grass smelt sweet and was good to lie upon. We lay close to each other and watched boys flying kites. No one bothered us. She put her hand in mine. I walked her home and she made tea for me, and she told me my fortune with playing cards. I can't remember what the cards foretold; I wasn't paying much attention to them.

We went about together. She said she looked upon me as a friend, a brother (fatal word!), and would depend upon me for many things. When she went away for a fortnight, I was desolate. It was only as far as a farm in Berkshire where she had joined some other girl students picking strawberries. On a Sunday I took a train to Newbury and then a small branch line to the village of Kintbury—a pretty little place with an old inn, a couple of small shops and plenty of farmland. I had Vu's address, and after lunching at the inn, I set off for the farm where Vu and her friends were working. It was a lovely summer's day, and my first walk in the English countryside.

It took me back to a favourite story, H.E. Bates' *Alexander,* and some of his Uncle Silas tales. Although I had walked all over London, this was different, and I wish now that I had spent more time in the country and less in the city.

Vu seemed happy to see me but she was equally happy among her friends—those fresh-faced, healthy-looking English schoolgirls—and obviously enjoyed living on the farm and picking strawberries. I don't suppose there could have been a better way of earning enough money for college and hostel fees. I walked back to Kintbury alone and reached Charing Cross station late at night. I spent an hour in one of those little news theatres which interspersed newsreels with cartoon shows; supped off station coffee and sandwiches; and then took the last train to Swiss Cottage.

Two or three weeks later I asked Vu if she'd marry me. She didn't say yes and she didn't say no. Nor did she ask me if I had any prospects, because it was obvious I had none. But she did say she would have to talk to her parents about it and they were in Haiphong, in North Vietnam, and she hadn't heard from them for several months. The war in Vietnam had just started and it was to last a long time.

I had to be patient, it seemed, very patient.

Because the next I heard from Vu was through a postcard from Paris saying she was staying with her sister for a time and they would be returning to Vietnam together to see their parents.

I kept that postcard for a long time. The stamp bore a picture of Joan of Arc looking like Michele Morgan in one of her early films.

The day I received it I took a day off from the office and went to a pub and drank several large brandies. They didn't do me any good, so I switched to Jamaica rum and all that it did was make me think of Vu and, of course, I never saw her again.

RETURN
to DEHRA

After the insularity of Jersey, London was liberating. Theatres, cinemas, bookshops, museums, libraries helped further my self-education. Not once did I give serious thought to joining a college and picking up a degree. In any case, I did not have the funds, and there was no one to sponsor me. Instead, I had to join the vast legion of the world's workers. But Kensington Gardens, Regent's Park, Hampstead Heath and Primrose Hill gave me the green and open spaces that I needed in order to survive. In many respects London was a green city. My forays into the East End were really in search of literary landmarks.

And yet something was missing from my life. Vu-Phuong had come and gone like the breath of wind after which she had been named. And there was no one to take her place.

The affection, the camaraderie, the easy-going pleasures of my Dehra friendships; the colour and atmosphere of India; the feeling of *belonging*—these things I missed . . .

Even though I had grown up with a love for the English language and its literature, even though my forefathers were British, Britain was not really my place. I did not belong to the bright lights of Piccadilly and Leicester Square; or, for that matter, to the apple orchards of Kent or the strawberry fields of Berkshire. I belonged, very firmly, to peepul trees and mango groves; to sleepy little towns all over India; to hot sunshine, muddy canals, the pungent scent of marigolds; the hills of home; spicy odours, wet earth after summer rain, neem pods bursting; laughing brown faces; and the intimacy of human contact.

Human contact! That was what I missed most. It was not to be found in the office where I worked, or in my landlady's house, or in any of the learned societies which I had joined, or even in the pubs into which I sometimes wandered . . . The freedom to touch someone without being misunderstood. To take someone by the hand as a mark of affection rather than desire. Or even to know desire. And fulfilment. To be among strangers without feeling like an outsider. For, in India there are no strangers . . .

I had been away for over three years but the bonds were as strong as ever, the longing to return had never left me.

How I expected to make a living in India when I returned is still something of a mystery to me. You did not just walk into the nearest employment exchange to find a job waiting for you. I had no qualifications. All I could do was write and I was still a novice at that. If I set myself up as a freelance writer and bombarded every magazine in the country, I could probably eke out a livelihood. At that time there were only some half a dozen English language magazines in India and almost no book publishers (except for a handful of educational presses left over from British days). The possibilities were definitely limited; but this did not deter me. I had confidence in myself (too much, perhaps), plenty of guts (my motto being, 'Never despair. But if you do, work on in despair.'). And, of course, all the optimism of youth.

As Diana Athill and Andre Deutsch kept telling me they would publish *The Room* one day (I had finally put my foot, or rather, my pen, down and refused to do any more work on it), I wheedled a fifty-pound advance out of them, this being the standard advance against royalties in 1953. Out of this princely sum I bought a ticket for Bombay on the *S. S. Batory*, a Polish passenger liner which had seen better days. There was a fee for a story I'd sold to the BBC and some money saved from my Photax salary; and with these amounts I bought a decent-looking suitcase and a few presents to take home.

I did not say goodbye to many people—just my office colleagues who confessed that they would miss my imitations of Sir Harry Lauder; and my landlady, to whom

I gave my Eartha Kitt records—and walked up the gangway of the *Batory* on a chilly day early in March.

Soon we were in the warmer waters of the Mediterranean and a few days later in the even warmer Red Sea. It grew gloriously hot. But the *Batory* was a strange ship, said to be jinxed. A few months earlier, most of its Polish crew had sought political asylum in Britain. And now, as we passed through the Suez Canal, a crew member jumped overboard and was never seen again. Hopefully he'd swum ashore.

Then, when we were in the Arabian Sea, we had to get out of our bunks in the middle of the night for the ship's alarm bells were ringing and we thought the *Batory* was sinking. As there had been no lifeboat drill and no one had any idea of how a lifebelt should be worn, there was a certain amount of panic. Cries of 'Abandon ship!' mingled with shouts of 'Man overboard!' and 'Women and children first!'—although there were no signs of women and children being given that privilege. Finally it transpired that a passenger, tipsy on too much Polish vodka, had indeed fallen overboard. A lifeboat was lowered and the ship drifted around for some time; but whether or not the passenger was rescued, we were not told. Nor did I discover his (or her) identity. Whatever tragedy had occurred had been swallowed up in the immensity of the darkness and the sea.

The saga of the *Batory* was far from over.

No sooner had the ship docked at Bombay's Ballard Pier than a fire broke out in the hold. Most of the passengers lost their heavy luggage. Fortunately, my suitcase and typewriter were both with me and these I clung to all the way to the Victoria Terminus and all the way to Dehra Dun. I knew it would be some time before I could afford more clothes or another typewriter.

When the train drew into Delhi I found that my stepfather had come to meet me. This was decent of him and it was the beginning of a more understanding relationship. He told me that he and my mother were planning to move to Delhi.

He travelled with me to Dehra Dun, and on Dehra's small platform I found Dipi waiting to greet me. (Somi and Haripal were now in Calcutta.)

Dipi had come on his cycle.

I told my stepfather I'd join him at home and put my suitcase and typewriter into his latest second-hand car. Then I got up on the crossbar of Dipi's bike and he took me home in style, through the familiar streets of the town that had so shaped my life.

The Odeon was showing an old Bogart film; the small roadside cafés were open; the bougainvillaea were a mass of colour; the mango blossoms smelt sweet; Dipi chattered away; and the girls looked prettier than ever.

And I was twenty-one that year.

RETURN
to
INDIA

A HANDFUL
of NUTS

One

It wasn't the room on the roof, but it was a large room with a balcony in front and a small verandah at the back. On the first floor of an old shopping complex, still known as Astley Hall, it faced the town's main road, although a walled-in driveway separated it from the street pavement. A neem tree grew in front of the building, and during the early rains, when the neem-pods fell and were crushed underfoot, they gave off a rich, pungent odour which I can never forget.

I had taken the room at the very modest rent of thirty-five rupees a month, payable in advance to the stout Punjabi widow who ran the provisions store downstairs. Her provisions ran to rice, lentils, spices and condiments, but I wasn't doing any cooking then, there wasn't time, so for a quick snack I'd cross the road and consume a couple of samosas or vegetable patties. Whenever I received a decent fee for a story, I'd treat myself to some sliced ham and a loaf of bread, and make myself ham sandwiches. If any of my friends were around, like Jai Shankar or William Matheson, they'd make short work of the ham sandwiches.

I don't think I ever went hungry, but I was certainly underweight and and undernourished, eating irregularly in cheap restaurants and dhabas and suffering frequent stomach upheavals. My four years in England had done nothing to improve my constitution, as there, too, I had lived largely on what was sold over the counter in snack-bars—baked beans on toast being the standard fare.

At the corner of the block, near the Orient Cinema, was a little restaurant called Komal's, run by a rotund Sikh gentleman who seldom left his seat near the window. Here I had a reasonably good lunch of dal, rice and a vegetable curry, for two or three rupees.

There were a few other regulars—a college teacher, a couple of salesmen and occasionally someone waiting for a film show to begin. William and Jai did not trail me to this place, as it was a little lowbrow for them (William being Swiss and Jai being Doon School); nor was it frequented much by students or children. It was lower middle-class, really; professional men who were still single and forced to eat in the town. I wasn't bothered by anyone here. And it suited me in other ways, because there was a news-stand close by and I could buy a paper or a magazine and skim through it before or after my meal. Determined as I was to making a living by writing, I had made it my duty to study every English language publication that found its way to Dehra (most of them did), to see which of them published short fiction. A surprisingly large number of magazines did publish short stories; the trouble was, the rates of payment were not very high, the average being about twenty-five rupees a story.

Ten stories a month would therefore fetch me two hundred and fifty rupees—just enough for me to get by!

After eating at Komal's, I made my way to the up-market Indiana for a cup of coffee, which was all I could afford there. Indiana was for the smart set. In the evenings it boasted a three-piece band, and you could dance if you had a partner, although dancing cheek to cheek went out with World War Two. From noon to three, Larry Gomes, a Dehra boy of Goan origin, tinkled on the piano, playing old favourites or new hits.

That spring morning, only one or two tables were occupied—by business people, who weren't listening to music—so Larry went through a couple of old numbers for my benefit, 'September Song' and 'I'll See You Again'. At twenty, I was very old-fashioned. Larry received three hundred rupees a month and a free lunch, so he was slightly better off than me. Also, his father owned a small music and record shop a short distance away.

While I was sipping my coffee and pondering upon my financial affairs (which were non-existent, as I had no finances), in walked the rich and baggy-eyed Maharani of Magador with her daughter Indu. I stood up to greet her and she gave me a gracious smile.

She knew that some five years previously, when I was in my last year at school, I had been infatuated with her daughter. She had even intercepted one of my love letters, but she had been quite sporting about it, and had told me that I wrote a nice letter. Now she knew that I was writing stories for magazines, and she said, 'We read your story in the *Weekly* last week. It was quite charming, didn't I say you'd make a good writer?' I blushed and thanked her, while Indu gave me a mischievous smile. She was still at college.

'You must come and see us someday,' said the Maharani and moved on majestically. Indu, small-boned and petite and dressed in something blue, looked more than ever like a butterfly; soft, delicate, flitting away just as you thought you could touch her.

They sat at a table in a corner, and I returned to my contemplation of the coffee-stains on the table-cloth. I had, of course, splashed my coffee all over the place.

Larry had observed my confusion, and guessing its cause, now played a very old tune which only Indu's mother would have recognized: 'I kiss your little hands, madame, I long to kiss your lips . . .'

On my way out, Larry caught my eye and winked at me. 'Next time I'll give you a tip,' I said.

'Save it for the waiter,' said Larry.

It was hot in the April sunshine, and I headed for my room, wishing I had a fan.

Stripping to vest and underwear, I lay down on the bed and stared at the ceiling. The ceiling stared back at me. I turned on my side and looked across the balcony, at the leaves of the neem tree. They were absolutely still. There was not even the promise of a breeze.

I dozed off, and dreamt of my princess, her deep dark eyes and the tint of winter moonlight on her cheeks. I dreamt that I was bathing with her in a clear moonlit pool, while small fishes of gold and silver and mother-of-pearl slipped between our thighs. I laved her exquisite little body with the fresh spring water and placed a hibiscus flower between her golden breasts and another behind her ear. I was overcome with lust and threw myself upon her, only to discover that she had turned into a fish with silver scales.

I opened my eyes to find Sitaram, the washerman's son, sitting at the foot of my bed.

Sitaram must have been about sixteen, a skinny boy with large hands, large feet and large ears. He had loose sensual lips. An unprepossessing youth, whom I found irritating in the extreme; but as he lived with his parents in the quarters behind the flat, there was no avoiding him.

'How did you get in here?' I asked brusquely.

'The door was open.'

'That doesn't mean you can walk right in. What do you want?'

'Don't you have any clothes for washing? My father asked.'

'I wash my own clothes.'

'And sheets?' He studied the sheet I was lying on. 'Don't you wash your sheet? It is very dirty.'

'Well, it's the only one I've got. So buzz off.'

But he was already pulling the sheet out from under me. 'I'll wash it for you free. You are a nice man. My mother says you are seeda-saada, very innocent.'

'I am not innocent. And I need the sheet.'

'I will bring you another. I will lend it to you free. We get lots of sheets to wash. Yesterday six sheets came from the hospital. Some people were killed in a bus accident.'

'You mean the sheets came from the morgue—they were used to cover dead bodies? I don't want a sheet from the morgue.'

'But it is very clean. You know khatmals can't live on dead bodies. They like fresh blood.'

He went away with my sheet and came back five minutes later with a freshly-pressed bedsheet.

'Don't worry,' he said. 'It's not from the hospital.'

'Where is this one from?'

'Indiana Hotel. I will give them a hospital sheet in exchange.'

Two

The gardens were bathed in moonlight, as I walked down the narrow old roads of Dehra—I stopped near the Maharani's house and looked over the low wall. The lights were still on in some of the rooms. I waited for some time until I saw Indu come to a window. She had a book in her hand, so I guessed she'd been reading. Maybe if I sent her a poem, she'd read it. A poem about a small red virgin rose.

But it wouldn't bring me any money.

I walked back to the bazaar, to the bright lights of the cinemas and small eating houses. It was only eight o'clock. The street was still crowded. Nowadays it's traffic; then it was just full of people. And so you were constantly bumping into people you knew—or did not know ...

I was staring at a poster of Nimmi, sexiest of Indian actresses, when a hand descended on my shoulder, and I turned to see Jai Shankar, the genius from the Doon School, whose father owned the New Empire Cinema.

'Jalebis, Ruskin, jalebis,' he crooned. Although he was from a rich family, he never seemed to have any pocket money. And of course it's easier to borrow from a poor man than it is to borrow from a rich one! Why is that, I wonder? There was William Matheson, for instance, who lived in a posh boarding-house, but was always cadging small sums off me—to pay his laundry bill or assist in his consumption of Charminar cigarettes: without them he was a nervous wreck. And with Jai Shankar it was jalebis . . .

'I haven't had a cheque for weeks,' I told him.

'What about the story you were writing for the BBC?'

'Well, I've just sent it to them.'

'And the novel you were writing?'

'I'm still writing it.'

'Jalebis will cost only two rupees.'

'Oh, all right . . .'

Jai Shankar stuffed himself with jalebis while I contented myself with a samosa. Jai wished to be an artist, poet and diarist, somewhat in the manner of André Gide, and had even given me a copy of Gide's *Fruits of the Earth* in an endeavour to influence me in the same direction. It is still with me today, forty years later, his spidery writing scrawling a message across the dancing angel drawn on the title-page. Our favourite books outlast our dreams . . .

Of course, after the jalebis I had to see Jai home. If I hadn't met him, someone else would have had to walk home with him. He was terrified of walking down the narrow lane to his house once darkness had fallen. There were no lights and the overhanging mango, neem and peepul trees made it a place of Stygian gloom. It was said that a woman had hanged herself from a mango tree on this very lane, and Jai was always in a dither lest he should see the lady dangling in front of him.

He kept a small pocket torch handy, but after leaving him at his gate I would have to return sans torch, for nothing could persuade him to part with it. On the way back, I would bump into other pedestrians who would be stumbling along the lane, guided by slivers of moonlight or the pale glimmer from someone's window.

Only the blind man carried a lamp.

'And what need have you of a light?' we asked.

'So that fools do not stumble against me in the dark.'

But I did not care for torchlight. I had taught myself to use whatever the night offered—moonlight, full and partial; starlight; the light from street lamps, from windows, from half-open doors. The night is beautiful, made ugly only by the searing headlights of cars.

When I got back to my room, the shops had closed and only the lights in Sitaram's quarters were on. His parents were quarrelling, and the entire neighbourhood could hear them. It was always like that. The husband was drunk and abusive; she refused to open the door for him, told him to go and sleep with a whore or, better still, a donkey. After some time he retreated into the dark.

I had no lights, as my landlady had neglected to pay the electricity bill for the past six months. But I did not mind the absence of light, although at times I would have liked an electric fan.

It meant, of course, that I could not type or even write by hand except when the full moon poured over the balcony. But I could always manage a few lines of poetry on a large white sheet of paper.

> *This sheet of paper is my garden,*
> *These words my flowers.*
> *I do not ask a miracle this night,*
> *Other than you beside me in the bright moonlight.*
> *Naked, entwined like the flowering vine . . .*

And there I got stuck. The last lines always fox me, one reason why I shall never be a poet.

'And we cling to each other for a long, long time . . .' Shades of 'September Song'?

In any case, I couldn't send it to Indu, as her mother would be sure to intercept the letter and read it first. The idea of her daughter clinging to me like a vine would not have appealed to the Maharani.

I would have to think of a more mundane method of making my feelings known.

Three

There was some excitement, as Stewart Granger, the British film actor, was in town.

Stewart Granger in Dehradun? Occasionally, a Bombay film star passed through, but this was the first time we were going to see a foreign star. We all knew what he looked like, of course. The Odeon and Orient cinemas had been showing British and American films since the days of the silent movies. Occasionally, they still showed 'silents', as their sound systems were antiquated and the projectors rattled a good deal, drowning the dialogue. This did not matter if the star was John Wayne (or even Stewart Granger) as their lines were quite predictable, but it made a difference if you were trying to listen to Nelson Eddy sing 'At the Balalaika' or Hope and Crosby exchanging wisecracks.

We had assembled outside the Indiana and were discussing the phenomenon of having Stewart Granger in town. What was he doing here?

'Making a film, I suppose,' I ventured.

Suresh Mathur, the lawyer, demurred, 'What about? Nobody's written a book about Dehra, except you, Ruskin, and no one has read yours. Has someone bought the film rights?'

'No such luck. And besides, the hero is sixteen and Stewart Granger is thirty-six.'

'Doesn't matter. They'll change the story.'

'Not if I can help it.'

William Matheson had another theory.

'He's visiting his old aunt in Rajpur.'

'We never knew he had an aunt in Rajpur.'

'Nor did I. It's just a theory.'

'You and your theories. We'll ask the owner of Indiana. Stewart Granger is going to stay here, isn't he?'

Mr Kapoor of Indiana enlightened us. 'They're location-hunting for a shikar movie. It's called *Harry Black and the Tiger*.

'Stewart Granger is playing a black man?' asked William.

'No, no, that's an English surname.'

'English is a funny language,' said William, who believed in the superiority of the French tongue.

'We don't have any tigers left in these forests,' I said.

'They'll bring in a circus tiger and let it loose,' said Suresh.

'In the jungle, I hope,' said William. 'Or will they let it loose on Rajpur Road?'

'Preferably in the Town Hall,' said Suresh, who was having some trouble with the municipality over his house tax.

Stewart Granger did not disappoint.

At about two in the afternoon, the hottest part of the day, he arrived in an open Ford convertible, shirtless and vestless. He was in his prime then, in pretty good condition after playing opposite Ava Gardner in *Bhowani Junction*, and everyone remarked on his fine torso and general good looks. He made himself comfortable in a cool corner of the Indiana and proceeded to down several bottles of chilled beer, much to everyone's admiration. Larry Gomes, at the piano, started playing 'Sweet Rosie O'Grady' until Granger, who wasn't Irish, stopped him and asked for something more modern. Larry obliged with 'Goodnight Irene', and Stewart, now into his third bottle of beer, began singing the refrain. At the next table, William, Suresh and I, trying to keep pace with the star's consumption of beer, joined in the chorus, and before long there was a mad sing-song in the restaurant.

The editor of the local paper, *The Doon Chronicle*, tried interviewing the star, but made little progress. Someone gave him an information and publicity sheet which did the rounds. It said Stewart Granger was born in 1913, and that he had black hair and brown eyes. He still had them— unless the hair was a toupe. It said his height was 6 feet 2 inches, and that he weighed 196 lbs. He looked every pound of it. It also said his youthful ambition was to become a 'nerve specialist'. We looked at him with renewed respect, although none of us was quite sure what a 'nerve specialist' was supposed to do.

'We just get on your nerves,' said Mr Granger when asked, and everyone laughed.

He tucked into his curry and rice with relish, downed another beer and returned to his waiting car. A few good-natured jests, a wave and a smile, and the star and his entourage drove off into the foothills.

We heard, later, that they had decided to make the film in Mysore, in distant south India.

No wonder it turned out to be a flop. Sorry, Stewart.

Two months later, Yul Brynner passed through but he didn't cause the same excitement. We were getting used to film stars. His film wasn't made in Dehra, either. They did it in Spain. Another flop.

Four

Why have I chosen to write about the twenty-first year of my life?

Well, for one thing, it's often the most significant year in any young person's life. A time for falling in love; a time to set about making your dreams come true; a time to venture forth, to blaze new trails, take risks, do your own thing, follow your star . . . And so it was with me.

I was just back after four years of living in the West; I had found a publisher in London for my first novel; I was looking for fresh fields and new laurels; and I wanted to prove that I could succeed as a writer with my small home town in India as a base, without having to live in London or Paris or New York.

In a couple of weeks' time it would be my twenty-first birthday, and I was feeling good about it.

I had mentioned the date to someone—Suresh Mathur, I think—and before long I was being told by everyone I knew that I would have to celebrate the event in a big way, twenty-one being an age of great significance in a young man's life. To tell the truth I wasn't feeling very youthful. Komal's rich food, swimming in oil, was beginning to take its toll, and I spent a lot of time turning input into output, so to speak.

Finding me flat on my back, Sitaram sat down beside me on my bed and expressed his concern for my health. I was too weak to drive him away.

'Just a stomach upset,' I said. 'It will pass off. You can go.'

'I will bring you some curds—very good for the stomach when you have the dast—when you are in full flow.'

'I took some tablets.'

'Medicine no good. Take curds.'

Seeing that he was serious, I gave him two rupees and he went off somewhere and returned after ten minutes with a bowl of curds. I found it quite refreshing, and he promised to bring more that evening. Then he said: 'So you will be twenty-one soon. A big party.'

'How did you know?' I asked, for I certainly hadn't mentioned it to him.

'Sitaram knows everything!'

'How did you find out?'

'I heard them talking in the Indiana, as I collected the table-cloths for washing. Will you have the party in Indiana?'

'No, no, I can't afford it.'

'Have it here then. I will help you.'

'Let's see . . .'

'How many people will you call for the tea-party?'

'I don't know. Most of them are demanding beer—it's expensive.'

'Give them kachi, they make it in our village behind the police lines. I'll bring a jerry-can for you. It's very cheap and very strong. Big nasha!'

'How do you know? Do you drink it?'

'I never drink. My father drinks enough for everyone.'

'Well, I can't give it to my guests.'

'Who will come?'

I gave some consideration to my potential guest list. There'd be Jai Shankar demanding jalebis and beer, a sickening combination! And William Matheson wanting French toast, I supposed. (Was French toast eaten by the French? It seemed very English, somehow.) And Suresh Mathur wanting something stronger than beer. (After two whiskeys, he claimed that he had discovered the fourth dimension.) And there were my young Sikh friends from the Dilaram Bazaar, who would be happy with lots to eat. And perhaps Larry Gomes would drop in.

Dare I invite the Maharani and Indu? Would they fit in with the rest of the mob? Perhaps I could invite them to a separate tea-party at the Indiana. Cream-rolls and cucumber sandwiches.

And where would the money come from for all these celebrations? My bank balance stood at a little over three hundred rupees—enough to pay the rent and the food bill at Komal's and make myself a new pair of trousers. The pair I'd bought on the Mile End Road in London, two years previously, were now very baggy and had a shine on the seat. The other pair, made of non-shrink material, got smaller at every wash. I had given them to a tailor to turn into a pair of shorts.

Sitaram, of course, was willing to lend me any number of trousers provided I wasn't fussy about who the owners were, and gave them back in time for them to be washed and pressed again before being delivered to their rightful owners. I did, on an occasion, borrow a pair made of a nice checked material, and was standing outside the Indiana, chatting to the owner, when I realized that he was staring hard at the trousers.

'I have a pair just like yours,' he remarked.

'It shows you have good taste,' I said, and gave Sitaram an earful when I got back to the flat.

'I can't trust you with other people's trousers!' I shouted. 'Couldn't you have lent me a pair belonging to someone who lives far from here?'

He was genuinely contrite. 'I was looking for the right size,' he said. 'Would you like to try a dhoti? You will look good in a dhoti. Or a lungi. There's a purple lungi here, it belongs to a sub-inspector of police.'

'A purple lungi? The police are human, after all.'

Yes, money talks—and it's usually saying goodbye.

A freelance writer can't tell what he's going to make from one month to the next. This uncertainty is part of the charm of the writing life, but it can also make for some nail-biting finishes when it comes to paying the rent, the food bill at Komal's, postage on my articles and correspondence, typing paper, toothpaste, socks, shaving soap, candles (there was no light in my room) and other necessities. And friends like William Matheson and Suresh Mathur (the only out-of-work lawyer I have ever known) did not make it any easier for me.

William, though Swiss, had served in the French Foreign Legion, and had been on the run in Vietnam along with the French administration and army once the Vietnamese had decided they'd had enough of the Marseillaise. The French are not known for their military prowess, although they would like to think otherwise.

William had drifted into Dehra as the assistant to a German newspaper correspondent, Von Radloff, who based his dispatches on the Indian papers and sent them out with a New Delhi dateline. Dehra was a little cooler than Delhi, and it was still pretty in parts. You could lead a pleasant life there, if you had an income.

William and Radloff fell out, and William decided he'd set up on his own as a correspondent. But there weren't many takers for his articles in Europe, and his debts were mounting. He continued to live in an expensive guest house whose owner, an unusually tolerant landlord, reminded him one day that he was five months in arrears.

William took to turning up at my room around the same time as the postman, to see if I'd received any cheques or international money orders.

'Only pounds,' I told him one day. 'No French or Swiss francs. How could I possibly aspire to a French publisher?'

'Pounds will do. I owe my Sardarji about five thousand rupees.'

'Well, you'll have to keep owing him. My twelve pounds from *The Young Elizabethan* won't do much for you.'

The Young Elizabethan was a classy British children's magazine, edited by Kaye Webb and Pat Campbell. A number of my early stories found a home between its covers. Alas, like many other good things, it vanished a couple of years later. But in that golden year of my debut it was one of my mainstays.

'Why don't you look for cheaper accommodation?' I asked William.

'I have to keep up appearances. How can the correspondent of the Franco-German press live in a hovel like yours?'

'Well, suit yourself,' I said. 'I hope you get some money soon.'

All the same, I lent him two hundred rupees, and of course never saw it again. Would I have enough for my birthday party? That was now the burning question.

Five

Early one morning I decided I'd take a long cycle ride out of the town's precincts. I'd read all about the dawn coming up like thunder, but had never really got up early enough to witness it. I asked Sitaram to do me a favour and wake me at six. He woke me at five. It was just getting light. As I dressed, the colour of the sky changed from ultramarine to a clear shade of lavender, and then the sun came up gloriously naked.

I had borrowed a cycle from my landlady—it was occasionally used by her son or servant to deliver purchases to favoured customers—and I rode off down the Rajpur Road in a rather wobbly, zig-zag manner, as it was about five years since I had ridden a cycle. I was careful; I did not want to end up a cripple like Denton Welch, the sensitive author of *A Voice in the Clouds,* whose idyllic country cycle-ride had ended in disaster and tragedy.

Dehra's traffic is horrific today, but there was not much of it then, and at six in the morning the roads were deserted. In any case, I was soon out of the town and then I reached the tea-gardens. I stopped at a small wayside teashop for refreshment and while I was about to dip a hard bun in my tea, a familiar shadow fell across the table, and I looked up to see Sitaram grinning at me. I'd forgotten—he too had a cycle.

Dear friend and familiar! I did not know whether to be pleased or angry.

'My cycle is faster than yours,' he said.

'Well, then carry on riding it to Rishikesh. I'll try to keep up with you.'

He laughed. 'You can't escape me that way, writer-sahib. I'm hungry.'

'Have something, then.'

'We will practise for your birthday.' And he helped himself to a boiled egg, two buns and a sponge cake that looked as though it had been in the shop for a couple of years. If Sitaram can digest that, I thought, then he's a true survivor.

'Where are you going?' he asked, as I prepared to mount my cycle.

'Anywhere,' I said. 'As far as I feel like going.'

'Come, I will show you roads that you have never seen before.'

Were these prophetic words? Was I to discover new paths and new meanings courtesy the washerman's son?

'Lead on, light of my life,' I said, and he beamed and set off at a good speed so that I had trouble keeping up with him.

He left the main road, and took a bumpy, dusty path through a bamboo-grove. It was a fairly broad path and we could cycle side by side. It led out of the bamboo grove into an extensive tea-garden, then turned and twisted before petering out beside a small canal.

We rested our cycles against the trunk of a mango tree, and as we did so, a flock of green parrots, disturbed by our presence, flew out from the tree, circling the area and making a good deal of noise. In India, the land of the loudspeaker, even the birds have learnt to shout in order to be heard.

The parrots finally settled on another tree. The mangoes were beginning to form, but many would be bruised by the birds before they could fully ripen.

A kingfisher dived low over the canal and came up with a little gleaming fish.

'Too tiny for us,' I said, 'or we might have caught a few.'

'We'll eat fish tikkas in the bazaar on our way back,' said Sitaram, a pragmatic person.

While Sitaram went exploring the canal banks, I sat down and rested my back against the bole of the mango tree.

A sensation of great peace stole over me. I felt in complete empathy with my surroundings—the gurgle of the canal water, the trees, the parrots, the bark of the tree, the warmth of the sun, the softness of the faint breeze, the caterpillar on the grass near my feet, the grass itself, each blade ... And I knew that if I always remained close to these things, growing things, the natural world, life would come alive for me, and I would be able to write as long as I lived.

Optimism surged through me, and I began singing an old song of Nelson Eddy's, a Vincent Huyman composition:

When you are down and out,
Lift up your head and shout—
It's going to be a great day!

Across the canal, moving through some wild babul trees, a dim figure seemed to be approaching. It wasn't the boy, it wasn't a stranger, it was someone I knew. Though he remained dim, I was soon able to recognize my father's face and form.

He stood there, smiling, and the song died on my lips.

But perhaps it was the song that had brought him back for a few seconds. He had always liked Nelson Eddy, collected his records. Where were they now? Where were the songs of old? The past has served us well; we must preserve all that was good in it.

As I stood up and raised my hand in greeting, the figure faded away.

My dear, dear father. How much I had loved him. And I had been only ten when he had been snatched away. Now he had given me a sign that he was still with me, would always be with me . . .

There was a great splashing close by, and I looked down to see that Sitaram was in the water. I hadn't even noticed him slip off his clothes and jump into the canal.

He beckoned to me to join him, and after a moment's hesitation, I decided to do so. Sitaram and I romped around in the waist-deep water for quite some time. He was a beautiful glistening chocolate colour in the late morning sunshine. I would have to get into the open more often; I felt pale and washed out.

After some time I climbed the opposite bank and walked to the place where I had seen my father approaching. But there was no sign that anyone had been there. Not even a footprint.

Six

It was mid-afternoon when we cycled back to the town. Siesta-time for many, but some brave souls were playing cricket on a vacant lot. There were spacious bungalows in the Dalanwala area; they had lawns and well-kept gardens. Dehra's establishment lived here. As did the Maharani of Magador, whose name-plate caught my eye as we rode slowly past the gate. I got off my cycle and stood at the kerb, looking over the garden wall.

'What are you looking at?' asked Sitaram, dismounting beside me.

'I want to invite the Maharani's daughter to my birthday party. But I don't suppose her mother will allow her to come.'

'Invite the mother too,' said Sitaram.

'Brilliant!' I said. 'Hit two Ranis with one stone.'

'Two birds in hand!' added Sitaram, who remembered his English proverbs from Class Seven. 'And look, there is one in the bushes!'

He pointed towards a hedge of hibiscus, where Indu was at work pruning the branches. Our voices had carried across the garden, and she looked up and stared at us for a few seconds before recognizing me. She walked slowly across the grass and stopped on the other side of the low wall, smiling faintly, looking from me to Sitaram and back to me.

'Hello,' she said. 'Where have you been cycling?'

'Oh, all over the place. Across the canal and into the fields like Hemingway. Now we're on our way home. Sitaram lives next door to me. When I saw your place, I thought I'd stop and say hello. Is your mother at home?'

'Yes, she's resting. Do you want to see her?'

'Er, no. Well, sure, but I won't disturb her. What I wanted to say was—if you're free on the 19th, come and join me and my friends for tea. It's my birthday, my twenty-first.'

'How nice. But my mother won't let me go alone.'

'The invitation includes her. If she comes, will you?'

'I'll ask her.'

I looked into her eyes. Deep brown, rather mischievous eyes. Were they responding to my look of gentle adoration?

Or were they just amused because I was so self-conscious, so gauche? I could write stories, earn a living, converse with people from all walks of life, ride a bicycle, play football, climb trees, put back a few drinks, walk for miles without tiring, play with babies, charm grandmothers, impress fathers; but when it came to making an impression on the opposite sex, I was sadly out of depth, a complete dunce. It was I, not Indu, who had to hide the blushes . . .

Even in London, two years earlier, when I had tried to prove my manhood by going to a prostitute in Leicester Square, everything had gone wrong. She had looked quite attractive under the street light where she had accosted me—or had I accosted her? But when she took me up to her room and exposed her flabby legs and thighs, I was repelled, mainly because she was suffering badly from varicose veins. You linger over your *Playboy* centre spreads, and then you go out and find your first woman, and she has varicose veins! I gave the unfortunate lady her fee and fled. But the smell of her powder and paint wouldn't leave my coat—my only coat—and I had to live with this failure for days!

The experience convinced me that I was more suited to romantic dalliance than sexual conquests, and that the latter would follow naturally from the former. My intentions towards Indu were perfectly honourable, although I couldn't see her mother accepting me into the royal fold. But perhaps one day when fame and fortune were mine (soon, I hoped!) Indu would give up her protected existence and come and live with me in a house by the sea or a villa on some tropical isle. I made up these lines on the spot, but held back from reciting them:

> *With the bougainvillaea in her hair*
> *And blossoms on her breasts*
> *My lips would search between her thighs for*
> *honeydew's caress . . .*

As Indu gazed into my eyes, I said, quite boldly and to my own surprise, 'I have to kiss you one of these days, Indu.'

'Why not today?'

She was offering me her cheek, and that's where I started, but then she let me kiss her on her lips, and it was so sweet and intoxicating that when I felt someone pressing my hand I was sure it was Indu. I returned the pressure, then realized that Indu was on the other side of the wall, still holding the hedge-cutters. I'd quite forgotten Sitaram's presence. The pressure of his hand increased; I turned to look at him and he nodded approvingly. Indu had drawn away from the wall just as her mother's voice carried to us across the garden: 'Who are you talking to, Indu? Is it someone we know?'

'Just a college student!' Indu called back, and then, waving, walked slowly in the direction of the verandah. She turned once and said, 'I'll come to the party, mother too!'

And I was left with Sitaram holding my hand.

'Only one thing missing,' he said.

'What's that?'

'Filmi music.'

There was filmi music in full measure when we got to the Orient Cinema, where they were showing *Mr and Mrs 55* starring Madhubala, who was everybody's heart-throb that year. Sitaram insisted that I return my bicycle and join him in the cheap seats, which I did, almost passing out from the aromatic beedi smoke that filled the hall. The Orient had once shown English films, and I remembered seeing an early British comedy, *The Ghost of St. Michael's* (with Will Hay), when I was a boy. The front of the cinema, facing the parade-ground, was decorated with a bas-relief of dancers, designed by Sudhir Khastgir, art master at the Doon School, and they certainly lent character to the building—the rest of its character was fast disintegrating. But I enjoyed watching the crowd at the cinema. For me, the audience was always more interesting than the performers.

All I remember of the film was that Sitaram got very restless whenever Madhubala appeared on the screen. He would whistle along with the tongawallahs and squeeze my arm or other parts of my anatomy to indicate that he was really turned on by his favourite screen heroine. A good thing Madhubala wasn't coming to town, or there'd have been a riot; but for some time there had been a rumour that Prem Nath, a successful male star, would be visiting Dehra, and my landlady had been quite excited at the prospect. But Sitaram was not turned on by Prem Nath. It was Madhubala or nothing.

After the film, while wending our way through the bazaar, we were accosted by Jai Shankar, who walked with us to the Frontier Sweet Shop, where hot fresh jalebis were being dished out to the evening's first customers.

'Your turn to pay,' I said.

'Next time, next time,' promised the pride of the Doon School.

'I'm broke,' I said.

'Your friend must have some money.'

It turned out that Sitaram did possess a few crumpled notes, which he thrust into my hand.

'What does your friend do?' asked Jai.

'He's in the garment business,' I said.

Jai looked at Sitaram with renewed respect. When he'd had his fill of jalebis he insisted on showing us his new painting. So we walked home with him along his haunted alley, and he took us into his studio and proudly displayed a painting of a purple lady, very long in the arms and legs, and somewhat flat-chested.

'Well, what do you think?' asked Jai, standing back and looking at his bizarre creation with an affectionate eye.

'Are you doing it for your school founder's day?' I asked innocently.

'No, nudes aren't permitted. But you should see my study of angels in flight. It won the first prize!'

'Well, if you give this one a halo and wings, it could be an angel.'

Jai turned from me in disgust and asked Sitaram for his opinion.

Sitaram stared at the painting quizzically and said, 'She must have given all her clothes for washing.'

'There speaks the garment manufacturer,' I put in.

'The breasts could be bigger,' added Sitaram, as an afterthought.

'Maybe I will enlarge the breasts,' conceded Jai, with a thoughtful nod.

'Not too much,' I said. 'Large breasts are going out of fashion.'

'Why's that?'

'Too many males have them.'

Jai saw us to the door, but not down the dark alley; he never took it alone. All his life he was to be afraid of being alone in the dark. Well, we all have our phobias. To this day, I won't use a lift or escalator unless I have company.

Sitaram and I walked back quite comfortably in the dark. He linked his fingers with mine and broke into song, a little off-key; he was no Saigal or Rafi. We cut across the maidaan, and a quarter-moon kept us company. I was overcome by a feeling of tranquility, a love for all the world, and wondered if it had something to do with the vision of my father earlier in the day.

As we climbed the steps to the landing that separated my rooms from Sitaram's quarters, we could hear his parents' voices raised in their nightly recriminations. His mother was a virago, no doubt; and his father was a drunk who gambled away most of his earnings. For Sitaram it was a trap from which there was only one escape. And he voiced my thought.

'I'll leave home one of these days,' he said.

'Well, tonight you can stay with me.'

I'd said it without any forethought, simply on an impulse. He followed me into my room, without bothering to inform his parents that he was back.

My landlady's large double-bed provided plenty of space for both of us. She hadn't used it since her husband's death, some six or seven years previously. And it was unlikely that she would be using it again.

Seven

Someone was getting married, and the wedding band, brought up on military marches, unwittingly broke into the Funeral March. And they played loud enough to wake the dead.

After a medley of Souza marches, they switched to Hindi film tunes, and Sitaram came in, flung his arms around and shattered my ear-drums with Talat Mahmood latest love ballad. I responded with the 'Volga Boatmen' in my best Nelson Eddy manner, and my landlady came running out of her shop downstairs wanting to know if the washerman had strangled his wife or vice-versa.

Anyway, it was to be a week of celebrations . . .

When I opened my eyes next day, it was to find a bright red geranium staring me in the face, accompanied by the aromatic odour of a crushed geranium leaf. Sitaram was thrusting a potted geranium at me and wishing me a happy birthday. I brushed a caterpillar from my pillow and sat up. Wordsworthian though I was in principle, I wasn't prepared for nature red in tooth and claw.

I picked up the caterpillar on its leaf and dropped it outside.

'Come back when you're a butterfly,' I said.

Sitaram had taken his morning bath and looked very fresh and spry. Unfortunately, he had doused his head with some jasmine-scented hair oil, and the room was reeking of it. Already a bee was buzzing around him.

'Thank you for the present,' I said. 'I've always wanted a geranium.

'I wanted to bring a rose-bush but the pot was too heavy.'

'Never mind. Geraniums do better on verandahs.'

I placed the pot in a sunny corner of the small balcony, and it certainly did something for the place. There's nothing like a red geranium for bringing a balcony to life.

While we were about to plan the day's festivities, a stranger walked through my open door (one day, I'd have to shut it), and declared himself the inventor of a new flush-toilet which, he said, would revolutionize the sanitary habits of the town. We were still living in the thunderbox era, and only the very rich could afford Western-style lavatories. My visitor showed me diagrams of a seat which, he said, combined the best of East and West. You could squat on it, Indian-style, without putting too much strain on your abdominal muscles, and if you used water to wash your bottom, there was a little sprinkler attached which, correctly aimed, would do that job for you. It was comfortable, efficient, safe. Your effluent would be stored in a little tank, which could be detached when full, and emptied—where? He hadn't got around to that problem as yet, but he assured me that his invention had a great future.

'But why are you telling me all this?' I asked, 'I can't afford a fancy toilet-seat.'

'No, no, I don't expect you to buy one.'

'You mean I should demonstrate?'

'Not at all. But you are a writer, I hear. I want a name for my new toilet-seat. Can you help?'

'Why not call it the Sit-Safe?' I suggested.

'The Sit-Safe! How wonderful. Young Mr Bond, let me show my gratitude with a small present.' And he thrust a ten-rupee note into my hand and left the room before I could protest. 'It's definitely my birthday,' I said. 'Complete strangers walk in and give me money.'

'We can see three films with that,' said Sitaram.

'Or buy three bottles of beer,' I said.

But there were no more windfalls that morning, and I had to go to the old Allahabad Bank—where my grandmother had kept her savings until they had dwindled away—and withdraw one hundred rupees.

'Can you tell me my balance?' I asked Mr Jain, the elderly clerk who remembered my maternal grandmother.

'Two hundred and fifty rupees,' he said with a smile. 'Try to save something!'

I emerged into the hot sunshine and stood on the steps of the bank, where I had stood as a small boy some fifteen years back, waiting for Granny to finish her work—I think she had been the only one in the family to put some money by for a rainy day—but these had been rainy days for her son and daughters and various fickle relatives who were always battening off her. Her own needs were few. She lived in one room of her house, leaving the rest of it for the family to use. When she died, the house was sold so that her children could once more go their impecunious ways.

I had no relatives to support, but here was William Matheson waiting for me under the old peepul tree. His hands were shaking.

'What's wrong?' I asked.

'Haven't had a cigarette for a week. Come on, buy me a packet of Charminar.'

Sitaram went out and bought samosas and jalebis and little cakes with icing made from solidified ghee. I fetched a few bottles of beer, some orangeades and lemonades and a syrupy cold drink called Vimto which was all the rage then. My landlady, hearing that I was throwing a party, sent me pakoras made with green chillies.

The party, when it happened, was something of an anticlimax:

Jai Shankar turned up promptly and ate all the jalebis.

William arrived with Suresh Mathur, finished the beer and demanded more.

Nobody paid much attention to Sitaram, he seemed so much at home. Caste didn't count for much in a fairly modern town, as Dehra was in those days. In any case, from the way Sitaram was strutting around, acting as though he owned the place, it was generally presumed that he was the landlady's son. He brought up a second relay of the lady's pakoras, hotter than the first lot, and they arrived just as the Maharani and Indu appeared in the doorway.

'Happy birthday, dear boy,' boomed the Maharani and seized the largest chilli pakora. Indu appeared behind her and gave me a box wrapped in gold and silver cellophane. I put it on my desk and hoped it contained chocolates, not studs and a tie-pin.

The chilli pakoras did not take long to violate the Maharani's taste-buds.

'Water, water!' she cried, and seeing the bathroom door open, made a dash for the tap.

Alas, the bathroom was the least attractive aspect of my flat. It had yet to be equipped with anything resembling the newly-invented Sit-Safe. But the lid of the thunderbox was fortunately down, as this particular safe hadn't been emptied for a couple of days. It was crowned by a rusty old tin mug. On the wall hung a towel that had seen better days. The remnants of a cake of Lifebuoy soap stood near a cracked washbasin. A lonely cockroach gave the Maharani a welcoming genuflection.

Taking all this in at a glance, she backed out, holding her hand to her mouth.

'Try a Vimto,' said William, holding out a bottle gone warm and sticky.

'A glass of beer?' asked Jai Shankar.

The Maharani grabbed a glass of beer and swallowed it in one long gulp. She came up gasping, gave me a reproachful look—as though the chilli pakora had been intended for her—and said, 'Must go now. Just stopped by to greet you. Thank you very much—you must come to Indu's birthday party. Next year.'

Next year seemed a long way off.

'Thank you for the present,' I said.

And then they were gone, and I was left to entertain my cronies.

Suresh Mathur was demanding something stronger than beer, and as I felt that way myself, we trooped off to the Royal Cafe; all of us, except Sitaram, who had better things to do.

After two rounds of drinks, I'd gone through what remained of my money. And so I left William and Suresh to cadge drinks off one of the latter's clients, while I bid Jai Shankar goodbye on the edge of the parade-ground. As it was still light, I did not have to see him home.

Some workmen were out on the parade-ground, digging holes for tent-pegs.

Two children were discussing the coming attraction.

'The circus is coming!'

'Is it big?'

'It's the biggest! Tigers, elephants, horses, chimpanzees! Tight-rope walkers, acrobats, strong men . . .'

'Is there a clown?'

'There has to be a clown. How can you have a circus without a clown?'

I hurried home to tell Sitaram about the circus. It would make a change from the cinema. The room had been tidied up, and the Maharani's present stood on my desk, still in its wrapper.

'Let's see what's inside,' I said, tearing open the packet.

It was a small box of nuts—almonds, pistachios, cashew nuts, along with a few dried figs.

273

'Just a handful of nuts,' said Sitaram, sampling a fig and screwing up his face.

I tried an almond, found it was bitter and spat it out.

'Must have saved them from her wedding day,' said Sitaram.

'Appropriate in a way,' I said. 'Nuts for a bunch of nuts.'

Eight

Lines written on a hot summer's night:

On hot summer nights I dream
Of you beside me, near a mountain stream
Cool in our bed of ferns we lie,
Lost in our loving, as the world slips by.

I tried to picture Indu in my arms, the two of us watching the moon come over the mountains. But her face kept dissolving and turning into her mother's. This transition from dream to nightmare kept me from sleeping. Sitaram slept peacefully at the edge of the bed, immune to the mosquitoes that came in like squadrons of dive-bombers. It was much too hot for any body contact, but even then, the sheets were soaked with perspiration.

Tired of his parents' quarrels, and his father's constant threat of turning him out if he did not start contributing towards the family's earnings, Sitaram was practically living with me. I had been on my own for the past five years and had grown used to a form of solitary confinement. I don't think I could have shared my life with an intellectual companion. William and Jai Shankar were stimulating company in the Indiana or Royal Cafe, but I doubt if I would have enjoyed waking up to their argumentative presences first thing every morning. William disagreed with everything I wrote or said; I was too sentimental, too whimsical, too descriptive. He was probably right, but I preferred to write in the manner that gave me the maximum amount of enjoyment. There was more give and take with Jai, but I knew he'd be writing a thousand words to my hundred, and this would have been a little disconcerting to a lazy writer.

Sitaram made no demands on my intellect. He left me to my writing-pad and typewriter. As a physical presence, he was acceptable and grew more interesting by the day. He ran small errands for me, accompanied me on the bicycle-rides which often took us past the Maharani's house. And he took an interest in converting the small balcony into a garden—so much so, that my landlady began complaining that water was seeping through the floor and dripping on to the flour sacks in her ration shop.

The red geranium was joined by a cerise one, and I wondered where it had come from, until I heard the Indiana proprietor complaining that one of his pots was missing.

A potted rose-plant, neglected by Suresh Mathur (who neglected his clients with much the same single-minded carelessness) was appropriated and saved from a slow and lingering death. Subjected to cigarette butts, the remnants of drinks and half-eaten meals, it looked as though it would never produce a rose. So it made the journey from Suresh's verandah to mine without protest from its owner (since he was oblivious of its presence) and under Sitaram's ministrations soon perked up and put forth new leaves and a bud.

My landlady had thrown out a wounded succulent, and this too found a home on the balcony, along with a sickly asparagus-fern left with me by William.

A plant hospital, no less!

Coming up the steps one evening, I was struck by the sweet smell of raat-ki-rani, Queen of the Night, and I was puzzled by its presence because I knew there was none growing on our balcony or anywhere else in the vicinity. In front of the building stood a neem tree, and a mango tree, the last survivor of the mango grove that had occupied this area before it was cleared away for a shopping block. There were no shrubs around—they would not have survived the traffic or the press of people. Only potted plants occupied the shopfronts and verandah-spaces. And yet there was that distinct smell of raat-ki-rani, growing stronger all the time.

Halfway up the steps, I looked up, and saw my father standing at the top of the steps, in the half-light of a neighbouring window. He was looking at me the way he had done that day near the canal—with affection and a smile playing on his lips—and at first I stood still, surprised by happiness. Then, waves of love and the old companionship sweeping over me, I advanced up the steps; but when I reached the top, the vision faded and I stood there alone, the sweet smell of raat-ki-rani still with me, but no one else, no sound but the distant shunting of an engine.

This was the second time I'd seen my father, or rather his apparition, and I did not know if it portended anything, or if it was just that he wanted to see me again, was trying to cross the gulf between our different worlds, the worlds of yesterday, today and tomorrow.

Alone on the balcony, looking down at the badly-lit street, I indulged in a bout of nostalgia, recalling boyhood days when my father was my only companion—in the RAF tent outside Delhi, with the hot winds of May and June swirling outside; then the cool evening walks in Chotta Simla, on the road to Bishop Cotton School; and earlier, exploring the beach at Jamnagar, picking up and storing away different kinds of seashells.

I still had one with me—a smooth round shell which must have belonged to a periwinkle. I put it to my ear and heard the hum of the ocean, the siren song of the sea.

I knew that one day I would have to choose between the sea and the mountains, but for the moment it was this little sub-tropical valley, hot and humid, patiently waiting for the monsoon rains . . .

The mango trees were sweet with blossom. 'My love is like a red, red rose,' sang Robbie Burns, while John Clare, another poet of the countryside, declared: 'My love is like a bean-field in blossom.' In India, sweethearts used to meet in the mango-groves at blossom time. They don't do that any more. Mango-groves are no longer private places. Better a dark corner of the Indiana, with Larry Gomes playing old melodies on his piano . . .

I walked down to A.N. John's saloon for a haircut, but couldn't get anywhere near the entrance. An excited but good-natured crowd had taken up most of the narrow road as well as a resident's front garden.

'What's happening?' I asked a man who was selling candyfloss.

'Dilip Kumar is inside. He's having a haircut.'

Dilip Kumar! The most popular male star of the silver screen!

'But what's he doing in Dehra?' I asked.

The candyfloss-seller looked at me as though I was a cretin. 'I just told you—having a haircut.'

I moved on to where the owner of the bicycle-hire shop was standing. 'What's Dilip Kumar doing in town?' I asked.

He shrugged. 'Don't know. Must be something to do with the circus.'

'Is he the ringmaster for the circus?' asked a little boy in a pyjama suit.

'Of course not,' said the pigtailed girl beside him. 'The circus won't be able to pay him enough.'

'Maybe he owns the circus,' said the little boy.

'It belongs to a friend of his,' said a tongawallah with a knowing air. 'He's come for the opening night.'

Whatever the reasons for Dilip Kumar's presence in Dehra, it was agreed by all that he was in A.N. John's, having a haircut. There was only one way out of A.N. John's and that was by the front door. There were a couple of windows on either side, but the crowd had them well covered.

Finally the star emerged; beaming, waving to people, looking very handsome indeed in a white bush shirt and neatly pressed silvery grey trousers. There was a nice open look about him. No histrionics. No impatience to get away. He was the ordinary guy who'd made good.

Where was Sitaram? Why wasn't my star-struck friend in the crowd? I found him later, watching the circus tents go up, but by then Dilip Kumar was on his way to Delhi. He hadn't come for the circus at all. He'd been visiting his young friend Nandu Jauhar at the Savoy in neighbouring Mussoorie.

Nine

The circus opened on time, and the parade-ground became a fairy land of lights and music. This happened only once in every five years when the Great Gemini Circus came to town. This particular circus toured every town, large and small, throughout the length and breadth of India, so naturally it took some time for it to return to scenes of past triumphs; and by the time it did so, some of the acts had changed, younger performers had taken the place of some of the older ones, and a new generation of horses, tigers and elephants were on display. So, in effect, it was a brand new circus in Dehra, with only a few familiar faces in the ring or on the trapeze.

The senior clown was an old-timer who'd been to Dehra before, and he welcomed the audience with a flattering little speech which was cut short when one of the prancing ponies farted full in his face. Was this accident or design? We in the audience couldn't tell, but we laughed all the same.

A circus does bring all kinds of people together under the one tent-top. The popular stands were of course packed, but the more expensive seats were also occupied. I caught sight of Indu and her mother. They were accompanied by someone who looked like the Prince of Purkazi. I looked again, and came to the conclusion that it was indeed the Prince of Purkazi. A pang of jealously assailed me.

What was the eligible young prince doing in the company of my princess? Why wasn't he playing cricket for India or the minor counties, or preferably on some distant field in east UP where bottles and orange-peels would be showered down on the players? Could the Maharani be scheming to get him married to her daughter? The dreadful thought crossed my mind.

He was handsome, he was becoming famous, he was royalty. And he probably owned racehorses.

But not the ones in the circus-ring. They looked reasonably well-fed, and they were obedient; but they weren't of racing stock. A gentle canter around the ring had them snorting and heaving at the flanks as though they'd just finished running all the way from Meerut, their last stop.

Dear Nergis Dalal was watching them with her eagle eye. She was just starting out on her campaign for the SPCA, with particular reference to circus animals, and she had her notebook and fountain-pen poised and ready for action. Nergis, then in her thirties, had come into prominence after winning a newspaper short story contest, and her articles and middles were now appearing quite regularly in the national press. She knew William Matheson and disapproved of him, for he was known to move around in a pony trap. She knew Suresh Mathur and disapproved of him; he had shot his neighbour's Dobermann for howling beneath his window all night.

She disapproved of the Indiana owner for serving up partridges at Christmas. And did she disapprove of me? Not yet. But I could sense her looking my way to see if I was enjoying the show. That would have gone against me. So I pretended to look bored; then turned towards her with a resigned look and threw my arms up in the air in a sort of world-weary gesture. 'I'm here for the same reasons as you,' was what it meant, and I must have succeeded, because she gave me a friendly nod. Quite a decent sort, Nergis.

There were several other acquaintances strewn about the audience, including a pale straw-haired boy called Tom Alter, who had managed to secure Dilip Kumar's autograph earlier that day. Tom was the son of American missionaries, but his heart was in Hindi movies and already he was nursing an ambition to be a film star.

William and Jai were absent. They felt the circus was just a little below their intellectual brows. Jai said he had a painting to finish, and William was writing a long article on one of the country's Five-Year Plans—don't ask me which one . . . At the time a writer named Khushwant Singh was editing a magazine called *Yojana*, which was all about Five-Year Plans, and he had asked William to do the article. I'd offered the editor an article on punch and its five ingredients—spirit, lemon or lime juice, spice, sugar and rose water—but had been politely turned down. Mr Singh liked his Scotch, but punch was not within the purview of the Five-Year Plan.

To return to the circus . . . The trapeze artistes (from Kerala) were very good. The girl on the tight rope (from Andhra) was scintillating in her skin-tight, blue-sequinned costume. The lady lion-tamer (from Tamil Nadu) was daunting, although her lion did look a bit scruffy. The talent seemed to come largely from the south, so that it did not surprise me when the band broke into that lovely Strauss waltz, 'Roses of the South'.

The ringmaster came from Bengal. He had a snappy whip, and its sound, as it whistled through the air, was sufficient to command obedience from snarling tigers, prancing ponies and dancing bears. He did not actually touch anyone with it. The whistle of the whip was sufficient.

Sitaram, who sat beside me looking like Sabu in *The Thief of Baghdad*, was enthralled by all he saw. This was his first circus, and every single act and individual performance had his complete attention. His face was suffused with delighted anticipation. He gasped when the trapeze artistes flew through the air. He laughed at the clown's antics. He sang to the tunes the band played, and he whistled (along with the rowdier sections of the audience) when those alluring southern beauties stood upright on their cantering, wheeling ponies—oh, to be a pony!

Oh, to be a pony
With a girl upon my rump,
And I'll take you round the ring, my dear,
Without a single bump.

Not one of my best efforts, but it came to me on the spur of the moment and I said it out loud for the benefit of Sitaram.

'Nice song,' he said. 'I like the one on the second pony. Isn't she beautiful?'

'Stunning,' I agreed. 'I like the sparkle in her eyes.'

'Sparkling eyes are for the poets,' said Sitaram, always bringing me back to earth. 'I like her thighs. Say something about her thighs, poet.'

'Her thighs are like melons—' I began.

'Not melons! I hate melons. They grow all over the dhobi-ghat.'

'Sorry, friend. Like half-moons? You like moons?'

'Yes. And her lips?'

'Like rosebuds.'

'Rosebuds. Good. And her breasts?'

'Well, in the frilled costume she's wearing, they look like cabbages.'

Sitaram pinched my thigh, fiercely, so that it hurt. But he wasn't angry. His gaze followed the girl on the pony until she, along with the others in the act, made their exit from the ring.

There were a number of other interesting acts—a dare-devil motor-cyclist riding through a ring of fire, the lady-wrestler taking on a rather somnolent bear and three tigers forming a sort of pyramid atop a revolving platform—but Sitaram was only half-attentive, his thoughts still being with the beautiful, dark, pink-sequinned girl on her white pony.

On the way home he held my hand and sighed.

'I have to go again tomorrow,' he said. 'You'll lend me the money won't you? I have to see that girl again.'

Ten

For a couple of weeks Sitaram was busy with the circus, and I did not see much of him. When he wasn't watching the evening performance, he was there in the mornings, hanging round the circus tents, trying to strike up an acquaintance with the ring-hands or minor performers. Most of the artistes and performers were staying in cheap hotels near the railway station. Sitaram appointed himself an unofficial messenger boy, and as he was familiar with every corner of the town, the circus people found him quite useful. He told them where they could get their clothes stitched or repaired, dry-cleaned or laundered; he guided them to the best eating-places, cheap but substantial restaurants such as Komal's or Chacha-da-Hotel (no Indiana or Royal Cafe for the circus crew); posted their letters home; found them barbers and masseurs; brought them newspapers. He was even able to get a copy of the *Madras Mail* for the lady lion-tamer.

Late one night (it must have been after the night show was over) he woke me from a deep dreamless sleep and without any preamble stuffed a laddoo into my mouth. Laddoos are not my favourite sweetmeat, and certainly not in bed at midnight, when the crumbs on the bedsheet were likely to attract an army of ants. While I was still choking on the laddoo, he gave me his good news.

'I've got a job at the circus!'

'What, as assistant to the clown?'

'No, not yet. But the manager likes me. He's made me his office boy. Two hundred rupees a month!'

'Almost as much as I make—but I suppose you'll be running around at all hours. And have you met the girl you liked—the dark girl on the white pony?'

'I have spoken to her. She smiles whenever she sees me. I have spoken to all the girls. They are very nice—especially the ones from the south.'

'Well, you're luckier than I am with girls.'

'Would you like to meet the lady wrestler?'

'The one who wrestles with the bear every night? After that, would she have any time for mere men?'

'They say she's in love with the ringmaster, Mr Victor. He uses his whip if she gets too rough.'

'I don't want to have anything to do with lady wrestlers, lions, bears or whips. Now let me go to sleep. I have to write a story in the morning. Something romantic.'

'What are you calling it?'

'"The Night Train at Deoli." Now go to sleep.'

He leant over and gave me a quick sharp bite on the cheek. I yelped.

'What's that supposed to be?' I demanded.

'That's how tigers make love,' he said, and vanished into the night.

The monsoon was only a fortnight away, we were told, and we were all looking forward to some relief from the hot and dusty days of June. Sometimes the nights were even more unbearable, as squadrons of mosquitoes came zooming across the eastern Doon. In those days the eastern Doon was more malarious than the western, probably because it was low-lying in parts and there was more still water in drains and pools. Wild boar and swamp deer abounded.

But it was now mango-time, and this was one of the compensations of summer. I kept a bucket filled with mangoes and dipped into it frequently during the day. So did Jai Shankar, William, Suresh Mathur and others who came by.

One of my more interesting visitors was a writer called G.V. Desani who had, a few years earlier, written a comic novel called *All About H. Hatterr*. I suspect that the character of Hatterr was based on Desani himself, for he was an eccentric individual who told me that he slept in a coffin.

'Do you carry it around with you?' I asked, over a coffee at Indiana.

'No, hotels won't allow me to bring it into the lobby, let alone my room. Hotel managers have a morbid fear of death, haven't they?'

'A coffin should make a good coffee-table. We'll put it to the owner of the Indiana.' 'Trains are fussy too. You can't have it in your compartment, and in the brake-van it gets smashed. Mine's an expensive mahogany coffin, lined with velvet.'

'I wish you many comfortable years sleeping in it. Do you intend being buried in it too?'

'No, I shall be cremated like any other good Hindu. But I may will the coffin to a good Christian friend. Would you like it?'

'I rather fancy being cremated myself. I'm not a very successful Christian. A pagan all my life. Maybe I'll get religious when I'm older.'

Mr Desani then told me that he was nominating his own novel for the Nobel Prize, and would I sign a petition that was to be presented to the Nobel Prize Committee extolling the merits of his book? Gladly, I said; always ready to help a good cause. And did I know of any other authors or patrons of literature who might sign? I told him there was Nergis Dalal; and William Matheson, an eminent Swiss Journalist; and old Mrs D' Souza who did a gardening column for *Eve's Weekly*; and Holdsworth, at the Doon School—he'd climbed Kamet with Frank Smythe, and had written an account for the journal of the Bombay Natural

History Society—and of course there was Jai Shankar who was keeping a diary in the manner of Stendhal; and wasn't Suresh Mathur planning to write a Ph.D on P.G. Wodehouse? I gave their names and addresses to the celebrated author, and even added that of the inventor of the Sit-Safe. After all, hadn't he encouraged this young writer by commissioning him to write a brochure for his toilet-seat?

Mr Desani produced his own brochure, with quotes from reviewers and writers who had praised his work. I signed his petition and allowed him to pay for the coffee.

As I walked through the swing doors of the Indiana, Indu and her mother walked in. It was too late for me to turn back. I bowed like the gentleman my grandmother had always wanted me to be, and held the door for them, while they breezed in to the restaurant. Larry Gomes was playing 'Smoke Gets in Your Eyes' with a wistful expression.

Eleven

Lady Wart of Worcester, Lady Tryiton and the Earl of Stopwater, the Hon. Robin Crazier, Mr and Mrs Paddy Snott-Noble, the Earl and Countess of Lost Marbles and General Sir Peter de l'Orange-Peel . . .

These were only some of the gracious names that graced the pages of the Doon Club's guest and membership register at the turn of the century, when the town was the favourite retiring place for the English aristocracy. So well did the Club look after its members that most of them remained permanently in Dehra, to be buried in the Chandernagar cemetery just off the Hardwar Road.

My own ancestors were not aristocracy. Dad's father came to India as an eighteen-year-old soldier in a Scots Regiment, a contemporary of Kipling's 'Soldiers Three'— Privates Othenis, Mulvaney and Learoyd. He married an orphaned girl who had been brought up on an indigo plantation at Motihari in Bihar. My maternal grandfather worked in the Indian Railways, as a foreman in the railway workshops at some god-forsaken railway junction in central India. He married a statuesque, strong-willed lady who had also grown up in India. Dad was born in the Shahjahanpur military camp; my mother in Karachi. So although my forebears were, for the most part, European, I was third generation India-born. The expression, 'Anglo-Indian', has come to mean so many things—British settler, Old Koi-Hai, Colonel Curry or Captain Chapatti, or simply Eurasian—that I don't use it very often. Indian is good enough for me. I may have relatives scattered around the world, but I have no great interest in meeting them. My feet are firmly planted in Ganges soil.

Grandfather (of the Railways) retired in Dehradun (or Deyrah Dhoon, as it was spelt in the old days) and built a sturdy bungalow on the Old Survey Road. Sadly, it was sold at the time of Independence when most of his children decided to quit the country. After my father's death, my mother married a Punjabi gentleman and so I stayed on in India, except for that brief sojourn in England and the Channel Islands. I'd come back to Dehra to find that even mother and stepfather had left, but it was still home, and in the cemetery there were several relatives including Grandfather and Great-grandmother. If I sat on their graves, I felt I owned a bit of property. Not a bungalow or even a vegetable patch, but a few feet of well-nourished sod. There were even marigolds flowering at the edges of the graves. And a little blue everlasting that I have always associated with Dehra. It grows in ditches, on vacant plots, in neglected gardens, along footpaths, on the edges of fields, behind lime-kilns, wherever there is a bit of wasteland. Call it a weed if you like, but I have every respect for a plant that will survive the onslaught of brick, cement, petrol fumes, grazing cows and goats, heat and cold (for it flowers almost all the year round) and overflowing sewage. As long as that little flowering weed is still around, there is hope for both man and nature.

A feeling of tranquility and peace always pervaded my being when I entered the cemetery. Were my long-gone relatives pleased by my presence there? I did not see them in any form, but then, cemeteries are the last place for departed souls to hang around in. Given a chance, they would rather be among the living, near those they cared for or in places where they were happy. I have never been convinced by ghost stories in which the tormented spirit revisits the scene of some ghastly tragedy. Why on earth (or why in heaven) should they want to relive an unpleasant experience?

My maternal grandfather, by my mother's account, was a man with a sly sense of humour who often discomfited his relatives by introducing into their homes odd creatures who refused to go away. Hence the tiny Jharipani bat released into Aunt Mabel's bedroom, or the hedgehog slipped between his brother Major Clerke's bedsheets. A cousin, Mrs Blanchette, found her house swarming with white rats, while a neighbour received a gift of a parcel of papayas—and in their midst, a bright green and yellow chameleon.

And so, when I was within some fifty to sixty feet of Grandfather's grave, I was not in the least surprised to see a full-grown tiger stretched out on his tombstones apparently enjoying the shade of the magnolia tree which grew beside it.

Was this a manifestation of the tiger cub he'd kept when I was a child? Did the ghosts of long dead tigers enjoy visiting old haunts? Live tigers certainly did, and when this one stirred, yawned and twitched its tail, I decided I wouldn't stay to find out if it was a phantom tiger or a real one.

Beating a hasty retreat to the watchman's quarters near the lych-gate, I noticed that a large, well-fed and very real goat was tethered to one of the old tombstones (Colonel Ponsonby of Her Majesty's Dragoons), and I concluded that the tiger had already spotted it and was simply building up an appetite before lunch.

'There's a tiger on Grandfather's grave,' I called out to the watchman, who was checking out his cabbage patch. (And healthy cabbages they were, too.)

The watchman was a bit deaf and assumed that I was complaining about some member of his family, as they were in the habit of grinding their masalas on the smoother gravestones.

'It's that boy Masood,' he said. 'I'll get after him with a stick.' And picking up his lathi, he made for the grave.

A yell, a roar, and the watchman was back and out of the lych-gate before me.

'Send for the police, sahib,' he shouted. 'It's one of the circus tigers. It must have escaped!'

Twelve

Sincerely hoping that Sitaram had not been in the way of the escaping tiger, I made for the circus tents on the parade-ground. There was no show in progress. It was about noon, and everyone appeared to be resting. If a tiger was missing, no one seemed to be aware of it.

'Where's Sitaram?' I asked one of the hands.

'Helping to wash down the ponies,' he replied.

But he wasn't in the pony enclosure. So I made my way to the rear, where there was a cage housing a lion (looking rather sleepy, after its late-night bout with the lady lion-tamer), another cage housing a tiger (looking ready to bite my head off) and another cage with its door open—empty!

Someone came up behind me, whistling cheerfully. It was Sitaram.

'Do you like the tigers?' he asked.

'There's only one here. There are three in the show, aren't there?'

'Of course, I helped feed them this morning.'

'Well, one of them's gone for a walk. Someone must have unlocked the door. If it's the same tiger I saw in the cemetery, I think it's looking for another meal—or maybe just dessert!'

Sitaram ran back into the tent, yelling for the trainer and the ringmaster. And then, of course, there was commotion. For no one had noticed the tiger slipping away. It must have made off through the bamboo-grove at the edge of the parade-ground, through the Forest Rangers College (well-wooded then), circled the police lines and entered the cemetery. By now it could have been anywhere.

It was, in fact, walking right down the middle of Dehra's main road, causing the first hold-up in traffic since Pandit Nehru's last visit to the town. Mr Nehru would have fancied the notion; he was keen on tigers. But the citizens of Dehra took no chances. They scattered at the noble beast's approach. The Delhi bus came to a grinding halt, while tonga-ponies, never known to move faster than a brisk trot, broke into a gallop that would have done them proud at the Bangalore Races.

The only creature that failed to move was a large bull (the one that someimes blocked the approach to my steps) sitting in the middle of the road, forming a traffic island of its own. It did not move for cars, buses, tongas and trucks. Why budge for a mere tiger?

And the tiger, having been fed on butcher's meat for most of its life, now disdained the living thing (since the bull refused to be stalked) and headed instead for the back entrance to the Indiana's kitchens.

There was a general exodus from the Indiana. William Matheson, who had been regaling his friends with tales of his exploits in the Foreign Legion, did not hang around either; he made for the comparative safety of my flat. Larry Gomes stopped in the middle of playing the 'Anniversary Waltz', and fox-trotted out of the restaurant. The owner of the Indiana rushed into the street and collided with the owner of the Royal Cafe. Both swore at each other in choice Pashtu—they were originally from Peshawar. Swami Aiyar, a Doon School boy with ambitions of being a newspaper correspondent, buttonholed me near my landlady's shop and asked me if I knew Jim Corbett's telephone number in Haldwani.

'But he only shoots man-eaters,' I protested.

'Well, they're saying three people have already been eaten in the bazaar.'

'Ridiculous. No self-respecting tiger would go for a three-course meal.'

'All the same, people are in danger.'

'So, we'll send for Jim Corbett. Aurora of the Green Bookshop should have his number.'

Mr Aurora was better informed than either of us. He told us that Jim Corbett had settled in Kenya several years ago.

Swami looked dismayed. 'I thought he loved India so much that he refused to leave.'

'You're confusing him with Jack Gibson of the Mayo School,' I said.

At this point the tiger came through the swing doors of the Indiana and started crossing the road. Suresh Mathur was driving slowly down Rajpur Road in his 1936 Hillman. He'd been up half the night, drinking and playing cards, and he had a terrible hangover. He was now heading for the Royal Cafe, convinced that only a chilled beer could help him recover. When he saw the tiger, his reflexes—never very good—failed him completely, and he drove his car onto the pavement and into the plate-glass window of Bhai Dhian Singh's Wine and Liquor Shop. Suresh looked quite happy among the broken rum bottles. The heady aroma of XXX Rosa Rum, awash on the shopping verandah, was too much for a couple of old topers, who began to mop up the liquor with their handkerchiefs. Suresh would have done the same had he been conscious.

We carried him into the deserted Indiana and sent for Dr Sharma.

'Nothing much wrong with him,' said the doctor, 'but he looks anaemic,' and proceeded to give him an injection of vitamin B12. This was Dr Sharma's favourite remedy for anyone who was ailing. He was a great believer in vitamins.

I don't know if the B12 did Suresh any good, but the jab of the needle woke him up, and he looked around, blinked up at me and said, 'Thought I saw a tiger. Could do with a drink, old boy.'

'I'll stand you a beer,' I said. 'But you'll have to pay the bill at Bhai Dhian's. And your car needs repairs.'

'And this injection costs five rupees,' said Dr Sharma.

'Beer is the same price. I'll stand you one too.'

So we settled down in the Indiana and finished several bottles of beer, Dr Sharma expounding all the time on the miracle of Vitamin B12, while Suresh told me that he knew now what it felt like to enter the fourth dimension.

The tiger was soon forgotten, and when I walked back to my room a couple of hours later and found the postman waiting for me with a twenty-five rupee money-order from *Sainik Samachar* (the Armed Forces' weekly magazine), I tipped him five rupees and put the rest aside for a rainy day—which, hopefully, would be the morrow, as monsoon clouds had been advancing from the south.

They say that those with a clear conscience usually sleep well. I have always done a lot of sleeping, especially in the afternoons, and have never been unduly disturbed by pangs of conscience, for I haven't deprived any man of his money, his wife or his song.

I kicked off my chappals and lay down and allowed my mind to dwell on my favourite Mexican proverb: 'How sweet it is to do nothing, and afterwards to rest!'

I hoped the tiger had found a shady spot for his afternoon siesta. With goodwill towards one and all, I drifted into a deep sleep and woke only in the early evening, to the sound of distant thunder.

Thirteen

The tiger padded silently but purposefully past the Dilaram Bazaar, paying no attention to the screaming and shouting of the little gesticulating creatures who fled at his approach. He'd seen them every night at the circus—all in search of excitement, provided there was no risk attached to it!

Walking down from the other end of the Dilaram Road was a tiger of another sort—sub-Inspector Sher ('Tiger') Singh, in charge of the local police outpost. 'Tiger Singh' was feeling on the top of the world. His little thana was notorious for beating up suspected criminals, and he'd had a satisfying night supervising the third-degree interrogation of three young suspects in a case of theft. None of them had broken down and confessed, but 'Tiger' had the pleasure (and what was it if not a pleasure, an appeal to his senses?) of kicking one youth senseless, blackening the eyes of another and fracturing the ankle and shinbone of the third. The damage done, they had been ejected into the street with a warning to keep their noses clean in the future.

These young men could have saved themselves from physical injury had they disbursed a couple of hundred rupees to the sub-inspector and his cohorts, but they were unemployed and without friends of substance; so, beaten and humiliated, they crawled home as best they could. 'Tiger' Singh liked the money he sometimes picked up from suspects and the relatives of petty offenders; but many years in the service had brought out the sadistic side to his nature, and now he took a certain pleasure in seeing noses broken and teeth knocked out. He claimed that he could extract teeth without anaesthesia, and would do the job free for those who could not afford dentists' bills. There were no takers.

Today he strutted along the pavement, twirling his moustaches with one hand and pulling up his trousers with the other. For he was a well-fed gentleman, whose belly protruded above his belt. He had a constant struggle keeping his trousers, along with his heavy revolver holster, from slipping to the ground. Had he not been in the direct path of the tiger, he would have been ignored. But he chose to stand frozen to the ground, really too terrified to reach for his gun or even hitch up his trousers.

The tiger slapped him to the ground, picked him up by his fat neck and dragged him into the lantana bushes. Sher Singh let out one despairing cry, which turned into a gurgle as the blood spurted from his throat.

The tiger did not eat humans. Their flesh was unappetizing, acceptable only to the lame or ageing beasts who could no longer hunt. True, the circus tiger had almost forgotten how to hunt, but his instincts told him that more succulent repasts could be found in the depths of the forest. And the forest was close at hand (or so it was in those days), so he abandoned the dead policeman, who would have made a more suitable meal for vultures had not his colleagues come and taken him away.

The autopsy report said, 'Killed by wild tiger,' which was inaccurate in that the tiger was tame, but it was the only extenuating remark ever made about the sub-inspector. His family received a pension and lived fairly happily ever after.

Neither the tiger nor the S.I. was familiar with the Laws of Karma, or Emerson's Law of Compensation, but they appeared to have been working all the same.

As the tiger sought its freedom in the forest, the clouds that had gathered over the foothills finally gave way under their burden of moisture. The first rain of the monsoon descended upon the hills, the valley, the town. In minutes, a two-month layer of dust was washed away from trees, rooftops and pavements. The rain swept across the streets of Dehra, sending people scattering for shelter. Umbrellas unfolded for the first time in months. A gust of wind shook the circus tent. The old lion, scenting the rain on the wind, sat up in its cage and gave a great roar of delight. The ponies shook their manes, an elephant trumpeted. One of the dwarves, who had been making love to the lady-wrestler, now did so with greater abandon. The ravished lady squealed with pleasure; for it has to be said that the dwarf was undersized in every department but one, and in that one area few could surpass him.

The rain swept over the railway yards, washing the soot and dust from the carriages and engines. It brought freshness and new life to the tea-gardens and sugarcane fields. Even earthworms responded to the cool dampening of their environment and stretched sensuously in the soft mud.

Mud! Buffaloes wallowed in it; children romped in it; frogs broke into antiphonal chants. Glorious, squelchy mud. Hateful for the rest of the year, but wonderfully inviting on the first day of the monsoon. A large amount got washed down from the loose eroded soil of the foothills, so that the streams and canals were soon clogged, silted up and flooded their banks.

The mango and litchi trees were washed clean. Sal and shisham shook in the wind. Peepul leaves danced.

The roots of the banyan drank up the good rain. The neem gave out its heady fragrance. Squirrels ran for shelter into the embracing branches of Krishna's buttercup. Parrots made merry in the guava groves.

I walked home through the rain. Home, did I say? Yes, my small flat was becoming a home, what with Sitaram and his geraniums upstairs, my landlady below and other familiars in the neighbourhood. Even the geckos on the wall were now recognizable, each acquiring an identity and personality of its own. Sitaram had trained one of them to take food from his fingers. At first he had stuck a bit of meat at the end of a long thin stick. The lizard had snapped up this morsel. Then, every day, he had shortened the stick until the lizard, growing in confidence, took his snack from the short end of the stick and finally from the boy's fingers. I hadn't got around to feeding the wall lizards. One of them had fallen with a plop on my forehead in the middle of the night, and my landlady told me of how a whole family had been poisoned when a gecko had fallen into a cooking pot and been served up with a mixed vegetable curry.

A neighbour, who worked for Madras Coffee House, told me that down south there were a number of omens connected with the fall of the wall lizard, especially if it dropped on some part of your body. He told me that I'd been fortunate that the lizard fell on my forehead, but had it fallen on my tummy I'd have been in for a period of bad luck. But I wasn't taking any chances. The lizards could have all the snacks they wanted from Sitaram, but I wasn't going to encourage any familiarity.

Now, happy to get my clothes wet with the first monsoon shower, I ran up the steps to my rooms, but found them empty. Then Sitaram's voice, raised in song, wafted down to me from the rooftop. I climbed up to the roof by means of an old iron ladder that was always fixed there, and found him on the flat roof, prancing about in the nude.

'Come and join me,' he shouted. 'It is good to dance in the first monsoon shower.'

'You can be seen from the roofs across the road,' I said.

'Never mind. Don't you think I'm the sexiest man of 1955?'

'I shall look forward to seeing you in 1956,' I said, and retreated below.

Fourteen

It was still 1955, and the middle of the monsoon, when Sitaram decided to throw his lot in with the circus and leave Dehra. Those roses of the south had a lot to do with it. I wasn't sure if he was in love with one of the pony-riders, or with the girl on the flying trapeze.

Perhaps both of them; perhaps all of them. He was at an age when his sexual energies had to be directed somewhere, and those beautiful dusky circus girls were certainly more approachable, and more glamorous, than the coy college girls we saw every day.

'So you're going to desert me,' I said, when he told me of his plans.

'Only for a few months. I'll see the country this way.'

'Once with the circus, always with the circus.'

'Well, you have your Indu.'

'I don't. I hear she's getting engaged to that cricket-playing princeling. I hate all cricketers!'

'You're better-looking.'

'But I'm not a prince. I haven't any money, and I don't play cricket. Well, I played a little at school, but they always made me twelfth man, which meant carrying out the drinks like a waiter. What a stupid game!'

'I agree. Football is better.'

'More manly. But not as glamorous.'

Sitaram pondered a while, and then gave me the benefit of his wisdom.

'To win Indu you must win her mother.'

'And how do I do that? She's a dragon.'

'Well, you must pretend you like dragons.'

I was sitting in the Indiana, having my coffee, when Indu's mother walked in. She was alone. (Indu was probably with her prince, learning to bowl under-arm). I said good morning and asked her if she'd like to join me for a cup of coffee. To my surprise, she assented. Larry Gomes was playing 'Love is a Many-Splendoured

Thing', and the Maharani was just a bit dreamy-eyed and probably a little sloshed too. But she wasn't in any way attractive. Her eyes were baggy (did she drink?) and her skin was coarse (too many skin lotions?) and her chin was developing a dewlap. Would Indu look like her one day?

She drank her coffee and asked me if I would like a drive. On the assumption that she would be driving me to her house, I thanked her and followed her out of the restaurant, while Larry Gomes looked anxiously at me over his spectacles and broke into the 'Funeral March'.

Fifteen

Well, it was very nearly my funeral.

Have you ever made love to a dragon—and a scaly one at that? How could a monster like the Maharani have produced a beautiful, tender, vivacious, electrifying girl like Indu? It was like making a succulent dish from a pumpkin, a bitter gourd and a spent cucumber.

The Maharani had denied me the dish, but she was prepared to give me the ingredients.

She drove me to her home in her smart little Sunbeam-Talbot, and no sooner was I settled on her sofa, with a glass of Carew's Gin in my hand, than I found my free hand encased in a fold of crocodile skin—her hand!

A shudder ran down my spine. She mistook the shudder for a shiver of excitement, and started playing with the lobe of my ear. My ear got caught between two of her gold bangles and was almost wrenched off as I jerked my head away. Gin was spilt on my trousers, and I put the glass down on a sidetable. As I did so, the Maharani cuddled up to me, and I discovered that the sofa wasn't really large enough for both of us. Also, one was inclined to sink deeper into the upholstery, making a quick escape very difficult.

It had never occured to me that this badly-preserved Christmas pudding could be of an amorous disposition. I had always thought of middle-aged mothers as having gone beyond the pursuit of carnal pleasures. But not this one!

She tried to set me at my ease.

'I'm a child psychologist, you know.'

'But I'm twenty-one.'

'All the better to treat you, my dear.'

'Your Highness,' I began.

'Don't Highness me, darling. My pet name is Liz.'

'As in lizard?'

'Cheeky! After Queen Elizabeth.' And she gave me a sharp pinch on the thigh. 'You write poetry, don't you? Recite one of your poems.'

'You need moonlight and roses.'

'I prefer sunshine and cactii.'

'Well, here's a funny one.' I was anxious to please her without succumbing to her blandishments and advances. So I recited my latest limerick.

There was a fat man in Lucknow
Who swallowed six plates of pillau,
When his belly went bust
(As distended, it must)
His buttons rained down upon Mhow.

She clapped her hands and shrieked with delight. 'Buttons, buttons!' And she made a grab for mine. (We weren't using zips in those days.)

I tried to get up from the sofa, but she pulled me down again.

'You deserve a reward,' she said, producing a lump of barley-sugar from a box on the side-table. 'This came all the way from Calcutta. Open your mouth.'

Dutifully I opened my mouth. But instead of popping the sweet in, she planted her lips on mine, large lips like suction pumps, and thrust her long lizard-like tongue down my throat. Her crocodile fingers were all over me, and even if my buttons did not reach Mhow, they must have landed on Mussoorie.

What can you do in such a situation? Not much, really. You just let the more active partner take over—in this case, the rich Maharani of Magador. She certainly knew how to get you worked up. After a hesitant start, all I had to do was imagine that I was another crocodile. I slid into her quivering orifice, and my virginity was at an end.

Afterwards I was rewarded with more barley-sugar and Turkish coffee.

She offered to drop me home, but I said I would walk. Physically I felt great, but I wanted to put my head in order. My thoughts were in whirl. How could I be the Maharani's lover while I was in love with her daughter? Love lyrics for Indu, and limericks for her mother?

'There's no justice anywhere,' I said aloud, in my best William Brown manner. ''T'isn't fair.' And then, as Popeye would have said, 'It's disgustipating!'

And as I closed the gate and stepped onto the sidewalk, who should appear but Indu, riding pillion on her cricketing prince's Triumph motor-bike. At the sight of him my feelings of guilt evaporated. And looking at Indu, smiling insincerely at me, I began to see points of resemblance between her and her mother. Would she be like the Maharani in twenty years' time? I had never seen her father (the late deceased Maharaja of Magador) but fervently hoped that he had been as goodlooking as his portraits suggested and that Indu had taken after him.

I gave her and her escort a polite bow (part of my grandmother's influence, no doubt) and set off at a dignified pace in the direction of the bazaar. A car would never be mine, but at least my legs wouldn't atrophy from disuse. Hadn't this very cricketing legend suffered from several torn ligaments in the course of his short career? Chasing cricket balls is a certain way to get a hernia, I said to myself, and then turned my thoughts to the composition of a new limerick in honour of the lady who had just tormented me into becoming her lover. There was no Amnesty International in those days; I had to defend myself in my own way. So I composed the following lines:

> *They called her the Queen of the Nile,*
> *For she walked like a fat crocodile.*
> *But she said, 'You young bugger,*
> *I'll make you my mugger,'*
> *And took me to bed with a smile.*

Sixteen

We all need one friend in whom to confide—to whom we can confess our misdemeanours, look for sympathy in times of trouble. Sitaram was my only intimate, and he listened with bated breath while I gave him a hair-raising account of my seduction by royalty. But he wasn't sympathetic. His first response was the following succinct remark:

'Congratulations, *ullu ka pattha*.'

'Why the heady compliment?' I asked.

'Because you cannot escape her now. She'll suck you dry.'

'A succubus, forsooth!'

'Don't use fancy language—you know what I mean. When an older woman gets hold of a young man, she doesn't let him go until he's quite useless to her or anyone else! You'd better join the circus with me.'

'And what do I do in the circus? Feed the animals?'

'They need someone for giving massage.'

'I've always fancied myself as a masseur. Whom do I get to massage—the acrobats, the dancing-girls, the trapeze artistes?'

'The elephants. They lie down and you massage their legs. And backsides.'

'I'll stick to the Maharani,' I said. 'Her skin has the same sort of texture, but there's not so much of it.'

'Well, please yourself . . . See, I've brought you a pretty tree. Will you look after it while I'm away?'

It was a red oleander in a pot. It was just coming into flower. We placed it on the balcony beside the rose bush and the geraniums. There were several geraniums now—white, cerise, salmon-pink and bright red—and they were all in flower, making quite a display on the sunny verandah.

'I'll look after them,' I said. 'As long as the landlady doesn't turn me out. The rent is overdue.'

'Don't lend money to your friends. Especially that Swiss fellow. He owes money everywhere—hasn't even paid my parents for two months' washing. One of these days he'll just go away—and your money with him. There is nothing to keep him here.'

'There is nothing to keep me here.'

'This is where you belong, where you grew up. You will always be here.'

It was where I had grown up—my mother's, her parents' home—but I had always been happier with my father, sharing a wartime tent with him on the outskirts of Delhi or Karachi; visiting the ruins of Old Delhi—Humayun's Tomb, the Purana Killa, the Kashmiri Gate; going to the cinema with him to see the beautiful skating legend Sonja Henie in *Sun Valley Serenade*, Nelson Eddy singing 'Volga Boatmen' and 'Ride, Cossack, Ride' in Balalaika, Carmen Miranda swinging her hips *Down Argentine Way*, and Hope and Crosby *On the Road to Zanzibar* or Morocco or Singapore; rickshaw-rides in Simla; ice creams at Davico's; Comics—*Film Fun* and *Hotspur* . . . And those colourful postcards he used to send me once a week. At school, the distribution of the post was always something to look forward to.

But I must also have inherited a great deal of my mother's sensuality, her unconventional attitude to life, her stubborn insistence on doing things that respectable people did not approve of . . . Traits that she probably got from her father, a convivial character, who mingled with all and shocked not a few.

I'm sure my mother was quite a handful for my poor father, bookish and intellectual, who did so want her to be a 'lady'. But this was something that went against her nature. She liked to drink and swear a bit. The ladies of the Dehra

Benevolent Society did not approve. Nor did they approve of my mother going to church without a hat! This was considered the height of irreverence in those days. There were remonstrances and anguished letters of protest from other (always female) members of the Congregation.

As a result, my mother stopped going to church, and I never picked up the habit. Her sisters, with the exception of the eldest, Enid, were conventional types who found and kept conventional husbands. Aunt Enid, though married to a doctor, distributed her favours on a first-come, first-served basis; she wasn't particular about the cut of your trousers as long as there was something in them. She liked having a good time, and in those war years there was no shortage of Allied troops prepared to make her their mascot. She had a daughter, Sally, who was my age and a bit of a tomboy. Sally and I wrestled in Granny's flowerbeds and took a spirited interest in each other's anatomy. We were only six or seven, and it was all innocent play—or arrested foreplay, I suppose. We sucked each other's lollipops, and this gave us as great a thrill as anything else we did.

Growing up in fairly unfettered fashion, I was quite at ease with Sitaram, another free soul. I was not so sure about the Maharani, although I suspect Aunt Enid would have approved of her. Would she pursue me with relentless abandon, as Sitaram feared, or would she already be looking for other conquests? If she was anything like Aunt E, it would be the latter.

Seventeen

The circus tents were being dismantled and the parade-ground was comparatively silent again. Some boys kicked a football around. Others flew kites. The monsoon season is kite-flying time, for it's not too windy, and the moist aircurrents are just right for keeping a kite aloft.

In the old part of the Dhamawalla bazaar, there used to be a kite-shop (it was still there five years ago, when I revisited the area), and, taking a circuitous way home, I stopped at the shop and bought a large pink kite. I thought Sitaram would enjoy flying it from the rooftop when he wasn't dancing in the rain. But when I got home, I found he had gone. His parents told me he had left in a hurry, as most of the circus people had taken the afternoon train to Amritsar. He had taken his clothes and a cracked bathroom mirror, nothing else, and yet the flat seemed strangely empty and forlorn without him. The plants on the balcony were poignant reminders of his presence.

I thought of giving the kite to my landlady's son, but I knew him for a destructive brat who'd put his fist through it at the first opportunity, so I hung it on a nail on the bedroom wall, and thought it looked rather splendid there, better than a Picasso although perhaps not in the same class as one of Jai Shankar's angels.

As I stood back, admiring it, there was a loud knocking at my door (as in the knocking at the gate in *Macbeth*, portending deeds of darkness) and I turned to open it, wondering why I had bothered to close it in the first place (I seldom did), when something about the knocking—its tone, its texture—made me hesitate.

There are knocks of all kinds—hesitant knocks, confident knocks, friendly knocks, good-news knocks, bad-news knocks, tax-collector's knocks (exultant, these!), policemen's knocks (peremptory, business-like), drunkard's knocks (slow and deliberate), the landlady's knock (you could tell she owned the place) and children's knocks (loud thumps halfway down the door).

I had come to recognize different kinds of knocks, but this one, was unfamiliar. It was a possessive kind of knock, gloating, sensual, bold and arrogant. I stood a chair on a table, then balanced myself on the chair and peered down through the half-open skylight.

It was Indu's mother. Her perfume nearly knocked me off the chair. Her bosom heaved with passion and expectancy, her eyes glinted like a hyena's and her crocodile hands were encased in white gloves!

I withdrew quietly and tiptoed back across the room and out on the balcony. On the next balcony, my neighbour's maidservant was hanging out some washing.

'For God's sake,' I told her. 'That woman out front, banging on my door. Go and tell her I'm not at home!'

'Who is she?'

'A *rakshasni*, if you want to know.'

'Then I'm not going near her!'

'All right, can you let me out through your flat? Is there anyone at home?'

'No, but come quickly. Can you climb over the partition?'

The partition did not look as if it would take my weight, so I climbed over the balcony wall and, clinging to it, moved slowly along the ledge till I got to my neighbour's balcony. The maidservant helped me over. Such nice hands she had! How could a working girl have such lovely hands while a lady of royal lineage had crocodile-skin hands? It was the Law of Compensation, I suppose; Mother Nature looking after her own.

'What's your name?' I whispered, as she led me through her employer's flat and out to the back stairs.

'Radha,' she said, her smile lighting up the gloom.

'Rather you than that rakshasni outside!' I gave her hand a squeeze and said, 'I'll see you again,' then took off down the stairs as though a swarm of bees was after me.

My landlady's son's bicycle was standing in the verandah. I decided to borrow it for a couple of hours.

I rode vigorously until I was out of the town, and then I took a narrow unmetalled road through the sal forest on the Hardwar road. I thought I would be safe there, but it wasn't long before I heard the menacing purr of the Maharani's Sunbeam-Talbot. Looking over my shoulder, I saw it bumping along in a cloud of dust. It was like a chase-scene in a Hitchcock film, and I was Cary Grant about to be machinegunned from a low-flying aircraft. I saw another narrow trail to the right, and swerved off the road, only to find myself parting company with the bicycle and somersaulting into some lantana bushes. There was a screech of brakes, a car door shot open and the rich Maharani of Magador was bounding towards me like a man-eating tigress.

'Jim Corbett, where are you?' I called feebly.

'He's in Kenya, you fool,' said the tigress, as she engulfed me and swallowed me whole.

Eighteen

A change of air was needed. What with the attentions of the Maharani, the borrowings of William, the loss of Indu and the absence of Sitaram, I wasn't doing much writing. My bank balance was very low. I had also developed a throat infection, probably as a result of having that rasping lizard's tongue slide down my throat. Anyone else would have bitten it off!

There was the sum of two hundred and seventy rupees in the bank. Always prudent, I withdrew two hundred and fifty and left twenty rupees for my last supper. Then I packed a bag, and left my keys with the landlady with the entreaty that she tell no one in Dehra of my whereabouts and took the bus to Rishikesh.

Rishikesh was then little more than a village, scattered along the banks of the Ganga where it cut through the foothills. There were a few ashrams and temples, a tiny bazaar and a police outpost. The saffron-robed sadhus and ascetics outnumbered the rest of the population.

There had been a break in the rains, and I spent a night sleeping on the sands sloping down to the river. The next night it did rain, and I moved to a bench on the small railway platform. I could have stayed in one of the two ashrams, but I had no pretensions to religion of any kind, and was not inclined to become an acolyte to some holy man. Kim had his Lama, the braying Beatles had their Master and others have had their gurus and godmen, but I have always been stubborn and thick-headed enough to want to remain my own man—just myself, warts and all, singing my own song. Nobody's chela, nobody's camp-follower.

Let nature reign, let freedom sing! . . .

And, so, on the third morning of my voluntary exile from the fleshpots of Dehra, I strode up river, taking a well-worn path which led to the shrines in the higher mountains. I was not seeking salvation or enlightenment; I wished merely to come to terms with myself and my situation.

Should I stay on in Dehra, or should I strike out for richer pastures—Delhi or Bombay perhaps? Or should I return to London and my desk in the Thomas Cook office? Oh, for the life of a clerk! Or I could give English tuitions,

I supposed. Except that everyone seemed to know English. What about French? I'd picked up a French patois in the Channel Islands. It wasn't the real thing, but who would know the difference?

I practised a few lines, reciting aloud to myself:

Jeune femme au rendezvous.
(Waiting for her lover.)
Oh, Oui! Il va venir
(Oh, yes, he is coming!)
Enfin je le verrai!
(Finally I shall see him!)
Pourquoi je attends?
(What am I waiting for?)

Roll up, folks. Learn how to make love in French! I could see my flat overflowing with students from all over Dehra and beyond. But how was I to keep the Maharani from attending?

The future looked rather empty as I trudged forlornly up the mountain trail. What I really needed just then was a good companion—someone to confide in, someone with whom to share life's little problems. No wonder people get married! An admirable institution, marriage. But who'd marry an indigent writer, with twenty rupees in the bank and no prospects in a land where English was on the way out. (I was not to know that English would be 'in' again, thirty years later.) No self-respecting girl really wants to share the proverbial attic with a down-and-out writer; least of all the princess Indu from Magador. I was pretty sure her mother would let me stay in the garage—but for how long? She was the sort who tired pretty quickly of her playthings.

I should have taken my cricket more seriously, I told myself. Must dress better. Put on the old school tie.

This depressing thought in mind, I found myself standing on the middle of a small wooden bridge that crossed one of the swift mountain streams that fed the great river. No, I wasn't thinking of hurling myself on the rocks below. The thought would have terrified me! I'm the sort who clings to life no matter how strong the temptation is to leave it. But absent-mindedly I leant against the wooden railing of the bridge. The wood was rotten and gave way immediately.

I fell some thirty feet, fortunately into the middle of the stream where the water was fairly deep. I did not strike any rocks. But the current was swift and carried me along with it. I could swim a little (thank God for those two years in the Channel Islands), and as I'd lost my chappals in my fall, I swam and drifted with the current, even though my clothes were an encumbrance. The breast-stroke seemed the best in those turbulent waters, but ahead I saw a greater turbulence and knew I was approaching rapids and, possibly, a waterfall. That would have spelt the end of a promising young writer.

So I tried desperately to reach the river bank on my right. I got my hands on a smooth rock but was pulled away by the current. Then I clutched at the branch of a dead tree that had fallen into the stream. I held fast; but I did not have the strength to pull myself out of the water.

Looking up I saw my father standing on the grassy bank. He was smiling at me in the way he had done that lazy afternoon at the canal. Was he beckoning to me to join him in the next world, or urging me to make a bid to continue for a while in this one?

I made a special effort—yes, I was a stouthearted boy—heaved myself out of the water and climbed along the waterlogged tree-trunk until I sank into ferns and soft grass.

I looked up again, but the vision had gone. The air was scented with wild roses and magnolia.

> *You may break, you may shatter*
> *the vase if you will,*
> *But the scent of the roses will linger*
> *there still.*

Nineteen

Back to sleepy Dehra, somnolent in the hot afternoon sun and humid from the recent rain. Dragonflies hovered over the canals. Mosquitoes bred in still waters, multiplying their own species and putting a brake on ours. Someone at the bus stand told me that the Maharani was down with malaria; as a result I walked through the bazaar with a spring in my step, even though my cheap new chappals were cutting into the flesh between my toes. Underfoot, the neem-pods gave out their refreshing though pungent odour. This was home, even though it did not offer fame or riches.

As I approached Astley Hall, I saw a kite flying from the roof of my flat. The landlady's son had probably got hold of it. It darted about, pirouetted, made extravagant nose-dives, recovered and went through teasing little acrobatic sallies, as though it had a life of its own. A pink kite against a turquoise-blue sky.

It was definitely my kite. How dare my landlady presume I had no need for it! I hurried to the stairs, stepping into cowdung as I went and consoling myself with the thought that stepping into fresh cow-dung was considered lucky, at least according to Sitaram's mother.

And perhaps it was, because, as I took the narrow stairway to the flat roof, who should I find up there but Sitaram himself, flying my kite without a care in the world.

When he saw me, he tied the kite-string to a chimney-stack and ran up and gave me a tight hug and bit me on the cheek.

'Why aren't you with the circus?' I asked.

'Left the circus,' he said, and we sat down on the parapet and exchanged news.

'What made you leave so suddenly? You were ready to follow those circus-girls wherever they went.'

'They are all in Ambala. There's a big parade-ground there. But it was too hot. Much hotter than Dehra.'

'Is that why you left—because of the heat?'

'Well, there was also this tiger that escaped.'

'But it escaped in Dehra! Don't tell me it returned to the circus?'

'No, no! This was the other tiger. It got out of its cage, somehow.'

'Not again! Did you have anything to do with it?'

'Of course not. I hadn't been near it since early that morning.'

'Someone must have left the cage open. Or failed to close it properly.'

'Must have been Mr Victor, the ringmaster. Anyway, when he tried to drive it back into the cage, it sprang on him and took his arm off. He's in hospital.'

'And the tiger?'

'It ran into the sugarcane fields. No one saw it again.'

'So the circus has lost two tigers and the ringmaster his arm. Has the lion escaped too, since you've been there?'

'No, the lion's too old. Besides, it's deeply in love with the lady-wrestler.'

'I thought that was the dwarf.'

'They both love her.'

I gave up. I had a sneaking suspicion that he'd had something to do with the escape of the tiger, but he managed to convince me that he'd come back (a) because of the heat, and (b) because he missed me. In that order. Had it been the other way round, I wouldn't have believed him.

I collected my keys from the landlady (Sitaram had got into the flat through the skylight, anxious to find clues to my whereabouts), and she gave me a couple of letters. One of them contained a cheque from the *Weekly*, with a note from its editor, C.R. Mandy, saying he would be happy to serialize my novel, *The Room on the Roof*. The cheque was for seven hundred rupees.

'We're rich!' I shouted, showing Sitaram the cheque. 'Well, for two or three months, at least . . . See, I told you I'd be a successful writer some day!'

'Will there be more cheques?'

'As long as I keep writing.'

'Then sit down and write.' He pulled a chair up for me and forced me to sit in front of my desk.

'Not now, you ass. I'll start tomorrow.'

'No, today!'

And so, to make him happy, I wrote a new limerick:

There was a young fellow called Ram,
Who set up a frantic alarm,
For he'd let loose a tiger,

Two bears and a liger,
Who bit off the ringmaster's arm.

'What's a liger?'

    'A cross between a lion and a lady-wrestler.'

    'Write more about me.'

    'Tomorrow. Now let's go out and celebrate.'

We went to one of the sweetshops near the bazaar and ate jalebis. Jai Shankar found us there and we ate more jalebis.

Then, walking down Rajpur Road, we met William Matheson, who said he was badly in need of a drink. So we took him to the Royal Cafe, where we found Suresh Mathur expounding on the fourth dimension. There were a great many drinks, and everyone got drunk. Suresh Mathur so forgot himself that he signed the chit for the drinks.

It was late evening when we rolled into the Indiana for dinner. Larry Gomes played 'Roll Out the Barrel' and joined us for a beer.

I couldn't write the next day because I had a terrible hangover. But I started again the following day, and I have been writing ever since.

Epilogue

The friendly reader knows that I have continued scribbling away for forty years, but he (or she) might well be interested in knowing what happened to the other nuts described in the foregoing pages.

Unlike her mother, Indu grew old quite gracefully. She did not marry the Purkazi prince, as the Maharani had hoped; and this was just as well, for his nose was permanently disfigured by a bump-ball hurled at him by a West Indies paceman. He retired shortly afterward and became a sports journalist known for his bitter diatribes against his fellow cricketers and fast bowlers in particular. Indu married a hotelier in Mauritius where she spends most of her time.

The Maharani of Magador went quite potty in her declining years, took to the bottle and became convinced that she'd been Mae West in a previous incarnation. Whenever she saw a good-looking man approaching, she welcomed him with the line, 'Is that a gun in your pocket, or are you just happy to see me?'

I met her a few months before she died. She was sitting at the bar of a well-know club in New Delhi, and when I greeted her deferentially, she looked me up and down speculatively and said, 'You're that writer chap, Bunskin Ronde, aren't you? Tried to seduce me when I was a girl!'

William Matheson returned to Switzerland, where he inherited a fortune from his father and lived the good life for a number of years; but he never returned the money he'd borrowed from me.

Suresh Mathur went to practise law in the neighbouring hill station of Mussoorie, a resort that at close quarters looked as though it had been hammered out of old biscuit-tins. It is prettier at night when darkness hides the scars on its cardboard hillsides. Suresh had one too many Vodka Marys, and finally entered the fourth dimension.

Jai Shankar went to Oxford, where he painted a mural for his college dining-room. Apparently the boat-crew did not like it and dumped him in the Thames near Tilbury. He gave up art when one of his models sued him for exhibiting a painting in which he had shown her with three breasts. He now lives in Paris and writes poems in French.

And what of dear Sitaram?

No, he did not enter his father's profession. He remained with me for another year, and then, at the age of eighteen, decided to try his luck in Mumbai, then Bombay. He went to work for a well-known actress, who liked his winning ways and got him a small part in one of her films. After that, he went from strength to strength and by the time he was in his thirties he was one of the most popular stars of the Indian screen. He wrote to me a couple of times and asked me to come and stay with him; but I felt shy of his success and stayed away. The bright lights, whether in the circus or on the film-sets, were not for me. The writer's art is a lonely one.

Of course Sitaram became famous under another, assumed name, and I am sure, dear reader, that you would like to know his identity. But I have promised to keep it a secret, and so we must leave it at that. But I'll give you a few clues: he doesn't sing, though he dances; he can't act but he has a sexy smile; and although the hair on his head is jet-black, the hair on his torso is now quite grey. But most of them are a bit like that, aren't they?

SITA
and the
RIVER

The Island in the River

In the middle of the river, the river that began in the mountains of the Himalayas and ended in the Bay of Bengal, there was a small island. The river swept round the island, sometimes clawing at its banks but never going right over it. The river was still deep and swift at this point, because the foothills were only forty miles distant. More than twenty years had passed since the river had flooded the island, and at that time no one had lived there. But then years ago a small family had come to live on the island and now a small hut stood on it, a mud-walled hut with a sloping thatched roof. The hut had been built into a huge rock. Only three of its walls were mud, the fourth was rock.

A few goats grazed on the short grass and the prickly leaves of the thistle. Some hens followed them about. There was a melon patch and a vegetable patch and a small field of marigolds. The marigolds were sometimes made into garlands, and the garlands were sold during weddings or festivals in the nearby town.

In the middle of the island stood a peepul tree. It was the only tree on this tongue of land. But peepul trees will grow anywhere—through the walls of old temples, through gravestones, even from rooftops. It is usually the buildings, and not the trees, that give way!

Even during the great flood, which had occurred twenty years back, the peepul tree had stood firm.

It was an old tree, much older than the old man on the island, who was only seventy. The peepul was about three hundred. It provided shelter for the birds who sometimes visited it from the mainland.

Three hundred years ago, the land on which the peepul tree stood had been part of the mainland; but the river had changed its course and the bit of land with the tree on it had become an island. The tree had lived alone for many years. Now it gave shade and shelter to a small family who were grateful for its presence.

The people of India love peepul trees, especially during the hot summer months when the heart-shaped leaves catch the least breath of air and flutter eagerly, fanning those who sit beneath.

A sacred tree, the peepul, the abode of spirits, good and bad.

'Do not yawn when you are sitting beneath the tree,' Grandmother would warn Sita, her ten-year-old granddaughter. 'And if you must yawn, always snap your fingers in front of your mouth. If you forget to do that, a demon might jump down your throat!'

'And then what will happen?' asked Sita.

'He will probably ruin your digestion,' said Grandfather, who didn't take demons very seriously.

The peepul had beautiful leaves and Grandmother likened it to the body of the mighty God Krishna—broad at the shoulders, then tapering down to a very slim waist.

The tree attracted birds and insects from across the river. On some nights it was full of fireflies.

Whenever Grandmother saw the fireflies, she told her favourite story.

'When we first came here,' she said, 'we were greatly troubled by mosquitoes. One night your grandfather rolled himself up in his sheet so that they couldn't get at him. After a while he peeped out of his bedsheet to make sure they were gone. He saw a firefly and said, "You clever mosquito! You could not see in the dark, so you got a lantern!"'

Grandfather was mending a fishing net. He had fished in the river for ten years, and he was a good fisherman. He knew where to find the slim silver chilwa and the big, beautiful mahseer and the singhara with its long whiskers;

he knew where the river was deep and where it was shallow; he knew which baits to use—when to use worms and when to use gram. He had taught his son to fish, but his son had gone to work in a factory in a city nearly a hundred miles away. He had no grandson but he had a granddaughter, Sita, and she could do all the things a boy could do and sometimes she could do them better. She had lost her mother when she was two or three. Grandmother had taught her all that a girl should know—cooking, sewing, grinding spices, cleaning the house, feeding the birds— and Grandfather had taught her other things, like taking a small boat across the river, cleaning a fish, repairing a net, or catching a snake by the tail! And some things she had learnt by herself—like climbing the peepul tree, or leaping from rock to rock in shallow water, or swimming in an inlet where the water was calm.

Neither grandparent could read or write, and as a result Sita couldn't read or write.

There was a school in one of the villages across the river, but Sita had never seen it. She had never been further than Shahganj, the small market town near the river. She had never seen a city. She had never been in a train. The river cut her off from many things, but she could not miss what she had never known and, besides, she was much too busy.

While Grandfather mended his net, Sita was inside the hut, pressing her grandmother's forehead which was hot

331

with fever. Grandmother had been ill for three days and could not eat. She had been ill before but she had never been so bad. Grandfather had brought her some sweet oranges but she couldn't take anything else.

She was younger than Grandfather but, because she was sick, she looked much older. She had never been very strong. She coughed a lot and sometimes she had difficulty in breathing.

When Sita noticed that Grandmother was sleeping, she left the bedside and tiptoed out of the room on her bare feet.

Outside, she found the sky dark with monsoon clouds. It had rained all night and, in a few hours, it would rain again. The monsoon rains had come early at the end of June. Now it was the end of July and already the river was swollen. Its rushing sounds seemed nearer and more menacing than usual.

Sita went to her grandfather and sat down beside him.

'When you are hungry, tell me,' she said, 'and I will make the bread.'

'Is your grandmother asleep?'

'Yes. But she will wake soon. The pain is deep.'

The old man stared out across the river, at the dark green of the forest, at the leaden sky, and said, 'If she is not better by morning, I will take her to the hospital in Shahganj. They will know how to make her well. You may be on your own for two or three days. You have been on your own before.'

Sita nodded gravely—she had been alone before; but not in the middle of the rains with the river so high. But she knew that someone must stay behind. She wanted Grandmother to get well and she knew that only Grandfather could take the small boat across the river when the current was so strong.

Sita was not afraid of being left alone, but she did not like the look of the river. That morning, when she had been fetching water, she had noticed that the level had suddenly disappeared.

'Grandfather, if the river rises higher, what will I do?'

'You must keep to the high ground.'

'And if the water reaches the high ground?'

'Then go into the hut and take the hens with you.'

'And if the water comes into the hut?'

'Then climb into the peepul tree. It is a strong tree. It will not fall. And the water cannot rise higher than the tree.'

'And the goats, Grandfather?'

'I will be taking them with me. I may have to sell them, to pay for good food and medicine for your grandmother. As for the hens, you can put them on the roof if the water enters the hut. But do not worry too much,' and he patted Sita's head, 'the water will not rise so high. Has it ever done so? I will be back soon, remember that.'

'And won't Grandmother come back?'

'Yes—but they may keep her in the hospital for some time.'

The Sound of the River

That evening it began to rain again. Big pellets of rain, scarring the surface of the river. But it was warm rain and Sita could move about in it. She was not afraid of getting wet, she rather liked it. In the previous month, when the first monsoon shower had arrived, washing the dusty leaves of the tree and bringing up the good smell of the earth, she had exulted in it, had run about shouting for joy. She was used to it now, even a little tired of the rain, but she did not mind getting wet. It was steamy indoors and her thin dress would soon dry in the heat from the kitchen fire.

She walked about barefooted, barelegged. She was very sure on her feet. Her toes had grown accustomed to gripping all kinds of rocks, slippery or sharp, and though thin, she was surprisingly strong.

Black hair, streaming across her face. Black eyes. Slim brown arms. A scar on her thigh: when she was small, visiting her mother's village, a hyena had entered the house where she was sleeping, fastened on to her leg and tried to drag her away, but her screams had roused the villagers and the hyena had run off.

She moved about in the pouring rain, chasing the hens into a shelter behind the hut. A harmless brown snake, flooded out of its hole, was moving across the open ground. Sita took a stick, picked the snake up with it, and dropped it behind a cluster of rocks. She had no quarrel with snakes.

They kept down the rats and the frogs. She wondered how the rats had first come to the island—probably in someone's boat or in a sack of grain.

She disliked the huge black scorpions which left their waterlogged dwellings and tried to take shelter in the hut. It was so easy to step on one and the sting could be very painful. She had been bitten by a scorpion the previous monsoon, and for a day and a night she had known fever and great pain. Sita had never killed living creatures but now, whenever she found a scorpion, she crushed it with a rock! When, finally, she went indoors, she was hungry. She ate some parched gram and warmed up some goat's milk.

Grandmother woke once and asked for water, and Grandfather held the brass tumbler to her lips.

It rained all night.

The roof was leaking and a small puddle formed on the floor. Grandfather kept the kerosene lamps alight. They did not need the light but somehow it made them feel safer.

The sound of the river had always been with them, although they seldom noticed it. But that night they noticed a change in its sound. There was something like a moan, like a wind in the tops of tall trees, and a swift hiss as the water swept round the rocks and carried away pebbles. And sometimes there was a rumble as loose earth fell into the water. Sita could not sleep.

She had a rag doll made with Grandmother's help out of bits of old clothing. She kept it by her side every night.

The doll was someone to talk to when the nights were long and sleep, elusive. Her grandparents were often ready to talk but sometimes Sita wanted to have secrets, and though there were no special secrets in her life, she made up a few because it was fun to have them.

And if you have secrets, you must have a friend to share them with. Since there were no other children on the island, Sita shared her secrets with the rag doll whose name was Mumta.

Grandfather and Grandmother were asleep, though the sound of Grandmother's laboured breathing was almost as persistent as the sound of the river.

'Mumta,' whispered Sita in the dark, starting one of her private conversations, 'do you think Grandmother will get well again?'

Mumta always answered Sita's questions, even though the answers were really Sita's answers.

'She is very old,' said Mumta.

'Do you think the river will reach the hut?' asked Sita.

'If it keeps raining like this and the river keeps rising, it will reach the hut.'

'I am afraid of the river, Mumta. Aren't you afraid?'

'Don't be afraid. The river has always been good to us.'

'What will we do if it comes into the hut?'

'We will climb on the roof.'

'And if it reaches the roof?'

'We will climb the peepul tree. The river has never gone higher than the peepul tree.'

As soon as the first light showed through the little skylight, Sita got up and went outside. It wasn't raining hard, it was drizzling; but it was the sort of drizzle that could continue for days, and it probably meant that heavy rain was falling in the hills where the river began.

Sita went down to the water's edge. She couldn't find her favourite rock, the one on which she often sat dangling her feet in the water, watching the little chilwa fish swim by. It was still there, no doubt, but the river had gone over it.

She stood on the sand and she could feel the water oozing and bubbling beneath her feet.

The river was no longer green and blue and flecked with white. It was a muddy colour.

Sita milked the goat thinking that perhaps it was the last time she would be milking it. But she did not care for the goat in the same way that she cared for Mumta.

The sun was just coming up when Grandfather pushed off in the boat. Grandmother lay in the prow. She was staring hard at Sita, trying to speak, but the words would not come. She raised her hand in blessing.

Sita bent and touched her grandmother's feet and then Grandfather pushed off. The little boat—with its two old people and three goats—rode swiftly on the river, edging its way towards the opposite bank. The current was very swift and the boat would be carried about half a mile downstream before Grandfather would be able to get it to dry land.

It bobbed about on the water, getting small and smaller, until it was just a speck on the broad river.

And suddenly Sita was alone.

There was a wind, whipping the raindrops against her face; and there was the water, rushing past the island; and there was the distant shore, blurred by rain; and there was the small hut; and there was the tree.

Sita got busy. The hens had to be fed. They weren't concerned about anything except food. Sita threw them a handful of coarse grain, potato peels and peanut shells.

Then she took the broom and swept out the hut, lit the charcoal burner, warmed some milk, and thought, 'Tomorrow there will be no milk . . .' She began peeling onions. Soon her eyes started smarting, and pausing for a few moments and glancing round the quiet room, she became aware again that she was alone. Grandfather's hookah pipe stood by itself in one corner. It was a beautiful old hookah, which had belonged to Sita's great-grandfather. The bowl was made out of a coconut encased in silver. The long, winding stem was at least four feet long. It was their most treasured possession. Grandmother's sturdy shishamwood walking stick stood in another corner.

Sita looked around for Mumta, found the doll beneath the light wooden charpoy, and placed her within sight and hearing. Thunder rolled down from the hills. Boom—boom—boom . . .

'The gods of the mountains are angry,' said Sita. 'Do you think they are angry with me?'

'Why should they be angry with you?' asked Mumta.

'They don't need a reason for being angry. They are angry with everything and we are in the middle of everything. We are so small—do you think they know we are here?'

'Who knows what the gods think?'

'But I made you,' said Sita, 'and I know you are here.'

'And will you save me if the river rises?'

'Yes, of course. I won't go anywhere without you, Mumta.'

The Water Rises

Sita couldn't stay indoors for long. She went out, taking Mumta with her, and stared out across the river, to the safe land on the other side. But was it really safe there? The river looked much wider now. It had crept over its banks and spread far across the flat plain. Far away, people were driving their cattle through waterlogged, flooded fields, carrying their belongings in bundles on their heads or shoulders, leaving their homes, making for high land. It wasn't safe anywhere.

Sita wondered what had happened to Grandfather and Grandmother. If they had reached the shore safely,

Grandfather would have had to engage a bullock cart or a pony-drawn ekka to get Grandmother to the district hospital, five or six miles away. Shahganj had a market, a court, a jail, a cinema and a hospital.

She wondered if she would ever see Grandmother again. She had done her best to look after the old lady, remembering the times when Grandmother had looked after her, had gently touched her fevered brow, and had told her stories—stories about the gods—about the young Krishna, friend of birds and animals, so full of mischief, always causing confusion among the other gods. He made God Indra angry by shifting a mountain without permission. Indra was the god of the clouds, who made the thunder and lightning, and when he was angry he sent down a deluge such as this one.

The island looked much smaller now. Some of its mud banks had dissolved quickly, sinking into the river. But in the middle of the island there was rocky ground, and the rocks would never crumble, they could only be submerged.

Sita climbed into the tree to get a better view of the flood. She had climbed the tree many times, and it took her only a few seconds to reach the higher branches. She put her hand to her eyes as a shield from the rain and gazed upstream.

There was water everywhere. The world had become one vast river. Even the trees on the forested side of the river looked as though they had grown out of the water, like mangroves. The sky was banked with massive, moisture-laden clouds. Thunder rolled down from the hills, and the river seemed to take it up with a hollow booming sound.

Something was floating down the river, something big and bloated. It was closer now and Sita could make out its bulk—a drowned bullock being carried downstream.

So the water had already flooded the villages further upstream. Or perhaps, the bullock had strayed too close to the rising river.

Sita's worst fears were confirmed when, a little later, she saw planks of wood, small trees and bushes, and then a wooden bedstead, floating past the island.

As she climbed down from the tree, it began to rain more heavily. She ran indoors, shooing the hens before her. They flew into the hut and huddled under Grandmother's cot. Sita thought it would be best to keep them together now.

There were three hens and a cockbird. The river did not bother them. They were interested only in food, and Sita kept them content by throwing them a handful of onion skins.

She would have liked to close the door and shut out the swish of the rain and the boom of the river, but then she would have no way of knowing how fast the water rose.

She took Mumta in her arms, and began praying for the rain to stop and the river to fall. She prayed to God Indra, and just in case he was busy elsewhere, she prayed to other gods too. She prayed for the safety of her grandparents and for her own safety. She put herself last—but only after an effort!

Finally Sita decided to make herself a meal. So she chopped up some onions, fried them, then added turmeric and red chilli powder, salt and water, and stirred until she had everything sizzling; and then she added a cup of lentils and covered the pot.

Doing this took her about ten minutes. It would take about half an hour for the dish to cook.

When she looked outside, she saw pools of water among the rocks. She couldn't tell if it was rainwater or the overflow from the river.

She had an idea.

A big tin trunk stood in a corner of the room. In it Grandmother kept an old single-thread sewing machine. It had belonged once to an English lady, had found its way to a Shahganj junkyard, and had been rescued by Grandfather who had paid fifteen rupees for it. It was just over a hundred years old but it could still be used.

The trunk also contained an old sword. This had originally belonged to Sita's great-grandfather, who had used it to help defend his village against marauding Rohilla soldiers more than a century ago. Sita could tell that it had been used to fight with, because there were several small dents in the steel blade.

But there was no time for Sita to start admiring family heirlooms. She decided to stuff the trunk with everything useful or valuable. There was a chance that it wouldn't be carried away by the water.

Grandfather's hookah went into the trunk. Grandmother's walking stick went in, too. So did a number of small tins containing the spices used in cooking—nutmeg, caraway seed, cinnamon, coriander, pepper—also a big tin of flour and another of molasses. Even if she had to spend several hours in the tree, there would be something to eat when she came down again.

A clean white cotton dhoti of Grandfather's, and Grandmother's only spare sari also went into the trunk. Never mind if they got stained with curry powder! Never mind if they got the smell of salted fish—some of that went in, too.

Sita was so busy packing the trunk that she paid no attention to the lick of cold water at her heels. She locked the trunk, dropped the key into a crack in the rock wall and turned to give her attention to the food. It was only then that she discovered that she was walking about on a watery floor.

She stood still, horrified by what she saw. The water was oozing over the threshold, pushing its way into the room.

In her fright, Sita forgot about her meal and everything else. Darting out of the hut, she ran splashing through ankle-deep water towards the safety of the peepul tree.

If the tree hadn't been there, such a well-known landmark, she might have floundered into deep water, into the river.

She climbed swiftly into the strong arms of the tree, made herself comfortable on a familiar branch and thrust her wet hair away from her eyes.

The Tree

She was glad she had hurried. The hut was now surrounded by water. Only the higher parts of the island could still be seen—a few rocks, the big rock into which the hut was built, a hillock on which some brambles and thorn apples grew.

The hens hadn't bothered to leave the hut. Instead, they were perched on the wooden bedstead.

'Will the river rise still higher?' wondered Sita. She had never seen it like this before. With a deep, muffled roar it swirled around her, stretching away in all directions.

The most unusual things went by on the water—an aluminium kettle, a cane chair, a tin of tooth powder, an empty cigarette packet, a wooden slipper, a plastic doll . . .

A doll!

With a sinking feeling, Sita remembered Mumta.

Poor Mumta, she had been left behind in the hut. Sita, in her hurry, had forgotten her only companion.

She climbed down from the tree and ran splashing through the water towards the hut. Already the current was pulling at her legs. When she reached the hut, she found it full of water. The hens had gone and so had Mumta.

Sita struggled back to the tree. She was only just in time, for the waters were higher now, the island fast disappearing.

She crouched miserably in the fork of the tree, watching her world disappear.

She had always loved the river. Why was it threatening her now? She remembered the doll and thought, 'If I can be so careless with someone I have made, how can I expect the gods to notice me?'

Something went floating past the tree. Sita caught a glimpse of a stiff, upraised arm and long hair streaming behind on the water. The body of a drowned woman. It was soon gone but it made Sita feel very small and lonely, at the mercy of great and cruel forces. She began to shiver and then to cry.

She stopped crying when she saw an empty kerosene tin, with one of the hens perched on top. The tin came bobbing along on the water and sailed slowly past the tree. The hen looked a bit ruffled but seemed secure on its perch.

A little later, Sita saw the remaining hens fly up to the rock ledge to huddle there in a small recess.

The water was still rising. All that remained of the island was the big rock behind the hut and the top of the hut and the peepul tree.

She climbed a little higher into the crook of a branch. A jungle crow settled in the branches above her. Sita saw the nest, the crow's nest, an untidy platform of twigs wedged in the fork of a branch.

In the nest were four speckled eggs. The crow sat on them and cawed disconsolately. But though the bird sounded miserable, its presence brought some cheer to Sita. At least she was not alone. Better to have a crow for company than no one at all.

Other things came floating out of the hut—a large pumpkin; a red turban belonging to Grandfather, unwinding in the water like a long snake; and then— Mumta!

The doll, being filled with straw and wood shavings, moved quite swiftly on the water, too swiftly for Sita to do anything about rescuing it. Sita wanted to call out, to urge her friend to make for the tree, but she knew that Mumta could not swim—the doll could only float, travel with the river, and perhaps be washed ashore many miles downstream.

The trees shook in the wind and rain. The crow cawed and flew up, circled the tree a few times, then returned to the nest. Sita clung to the branch.

The tree trembled throughout its tall frame. To Sita it felt like an earthquake tremor. She felt the shudder of the tree in her own bones.

The river swirled all around her now. It was almost up to the roof of the hut. Soon the mud walls would crumble and vanish. Except for the big rock and some trees very far away, there was only water to be seen. Water and grey, weeping sky.

In the distance, a boat with several people in it moved sluggishly away from the ruins of a flooded village. Someone looked out across the flooded river and said, 'See, there is a tree right in the middle of the river! How could it have got there? Isn't someone moving in the tree?'

But the others thought he was imagining things. It was only a tree carried down by the flood, they said. In worrying about their own distress, they had forgotten about the island in the middle of the river.

The river was very angry now, rampaging down from the hills and thundering across the plain, bringing with it dead animals, uprooted trees, household goods and huge fish choked to death by the swirling mud.

The peepul tree groaned. Its long, winding roots still clung tenaciously to the earth from which it had sprung many, many years ago. But the earth was softening, the stones were being washed away. The roots of the tree were rapidly losing their hold.

The crow must have known that something was wrong, because it kept flying up and circling the tree, reluctant to settle in it, yet unwilling to fly away. As long as the nest was there, the crow would remain too.

Sita's wet cotton dress clung to her thin body. The rain streamed down from her long, black hair. It poured from every leaf of the tree. The crow, too, was drenched and groggy.

The tree groaned and moved again.

There was a flurry of leaves, then a surge of mud from below. To Sita it seemed as though the river was rising to meet the sky. The tree tilted, swinging Sita from side to side. Her feet were in the water but she clung tenaciously to her branch.

And then, she found the tree moving, moving with the river, rocking her about, dragging its roots along the ground as it set out on the first and last journey of its life.

And as the tree moved out on the river and the little island was lost in the swirling waters, Sita forgot her fear and her loneliness. The tree was taking her with it. She was not alone. It was as though one of the gods had remembered her after all.

Taken with the Flood

The branches swung Sita about, but she did not lose her grip. The tree was her friend. It had known her all these years and now it held her in its old and dying arms as though it was determined to keep her from the river.

The crow kept flying around the moving tree. The bird was in a great rage. Its nest was still up there—but not for long! The tree lurched and twisted and the nest fell into the water. Sita saw the eggs sink.

The crow swooped low over the water, but there was nothing it could do. In a few moments the nest had disappeared.

The bird followed the tree for sometime. Then, flapping its wings, it rose high into the air and flew across the river until it was out of sight.

Sita was alone once more. But there was no time for feeling lonely. Everything was in motion—up and down and sideways and forwards.

She saw a turtle swimming past—a great big river turtle, the kind that feeds on decaying flesh. Sita turned her face away. In the distance she saw a flooded village and people in flat-bottomed boats; but they were very far.

Because of its great size, the tree did not move very swiftly on the river. Sometimes, when it reached shallow water, it stopped, its roots catching in the rocks. But not for long, the river's momentum soon swept it on.

At one place, where there was a bend in the river, the tree struck a sandbank and was still. It would not move again.

Sita felt very tired. Her arms were aching and she had to cling tightly to her branch to avoid slipping into the water. The rain blurred her vision. She wondered if she should brave the current and try swimming to safety. But she did not want to leave the tree. It was all that was left to her now, and she felt safe in its branches.

Then, above the sound of the river, she heard someone calling. The voice was faint and seemed very far, but looking upriver through the curtain of rain, Sita was able to make out a small boat coming towards her.

There was a boy in the boat. He seemed quite at home in the turbulent river, and he was smiling at Sita as he guided his boat towards the tree. He held on to one of the branches to steady himself and gave his free hand to Sita.

She grasped the outstretched hand and slipped into the boat beside the boy.

He placed his bare foot against the trunk of the tree and pushed away.

The little boat moved swiftly down the river. Sita looked back and saw the big tree lying on its side on the sandbank, while the river swirled round it and pulled at its branches, carrying away its beautiful, slender leaves.

And then the tree grew smaller and was left far behind. A new journey had begun.

The Boy in the Boat

She lay stretched out in the boat, too tired to talk, too tired to move. The boy looked at her but did not say anything. He just kept smiling. He leant on his two small oars, stroking smoothly, rhythmically, trying to keep from going into the middle of the river. He wasn't strong enough to get the boat right out of the swift current, but he kept trying.

A small boat on a big river—a river that had broken its bounds and reached across the plains in every direction—the boat moved swiftly on the wild brown water, and the girl's home and the boy's home were both left far behind.

The boy wore only a loincloth. He was a slim, wiry boy, with a hard, flat belly. He had high cheekbones and strong white teeth. He was a little darker than Sita.

He did not speak until they reached a broader, smoother stretch of river, and then, resting on his oars and allowing the boat to drift a little, he said, 'You live on the island. I have seen you sometimes from my boat. But where are the others?'

'My grandmother was sick,' said Sita. 'Grandfather took her to the hospital in Shahganj.'

'When did they leave?'

'Early this morning.'

Early that morning—and already Sita felt as though it had been many mornings ago!

'Where are you from?' she asked.

'I am from a village near the foothills. About six miles from your home. I was in my boat, trying to get across the river with the news that our village was badly flooded. The current was too strong. I was swept down and past your island. We cannot fight the river when it is like this, we must go where it takes us.'

'You must be tired,' said Sita. 'Give me the oars.'

'No. There is not much to do now. The river has gone wherever it wanted to go—it will not drive us before it any more.'

He brought in one oar, and with his free hand felt under the seat where there was a small basket. He produced two mangoes and gave one to Sita.

'I was supposed to sell these in Shahganj,' he said. 'My father is very strict. Even if I return home safely, he will ask me what I got for the mangoes!'

'And what will you tell him?'

'I will say they are at the bottom of the river!'

They bit deep into the ripe fleshy mangoes, using their teeth to tear the skin away. The sweet juice trickled down their skins. The good smell—like the smell of the leaves of the cosmos flower when crushed between the palms—helped to revive Sita. The flavour of the fruit was heavenly—truly the nectar of the gods!

Sita hadn't tasted a mango for over a year. For a few moments she forgot about everything else. All that mattered was the sweet, dizzy flavour of the mango.

The boat drifted, but slowly now, for as they went further downstream, the river gradually lost its power and fury. It was late afternoon when the rain stopped, but the clouds did not break up.

'My father has many buffaloes,' said the boy, 'but several have been lost in the flood.'

'Do you go to school?' asked Sita.

'Yes, I am supposed to go to school. I don't always go. At least not when the weather is fine! There is a school near our village. I don't think you go to school?'

'No. There is too much work at home.'

'Can you read and write?'

'Only a little . . .'

'Then you should go to a school.'

'It is too far away.'

'True. But you should know how to read and write. Otherwise, you will be stuck on your island for the rest of your life—that is, if your island is still there!'

'But I like the island,' protested Sita.

'Because you are with people you love,' said the boy. 'But your grandparents, they are old, they must die some day—and then you will be alone, and will you like the island then?'

Sita did not answer. She was trying to think of what life would be like without her grandparents. It would be an empty island, that was true. She would be imprisoned by the river.

'I can help you,' said the boy. 'When we get back—if we get back—I will come to see you sometimes and I will teach you to read and write. All right?'

'Yes,' said Sita, nodding thoughtfully. When we get back . . .

The boy smiled.

'My name is Vijay,' he said.

Towards evening the river changed colour. The sun, low in the sky, broke through a rift in the clouds, and the river changed slowly from grey to gold, from gold to a deep orange, and then, as the sun went down, all these colours were drowned in the river, and the river took the colour of night.

The moon was almost at the full, and they could see a belt of forest along the line of the river.

'I will try to reach the trees,' said Vijay.

He pulled for the trees, and after ten minutes of strenuous rowing reached a bend in the river and was able to escape the pull of the main current.

Soon they were in a forest, rowing between tall trees, sal and shisham.

The boat moved slowly as Vijay took it in and out of the trees, while the moonlight made a crooked silver path over the water.

'We will tie the boat to a tree,' he said. 'Then we can rest. Tomorrow, we will have to find a way out of the forest.'

He produced a length of rope from the bottom of the boat, tied one end to the boat's stem, and threw the other end over a stout branch which hung only a few feet above the water. The boat came to rest against the trunk of the tree.

It was a tall, sturdy tree, the Indian mahogany. It was a safe place, for there was no rush of water in the forest and the trees grew close together, making the earth firm and unyielding.

But those who lived in the forest were on the move. The animals had been flooded out of their homes, caves and lairs, and were looking for shelter and high ground.

Sita and Vijay had just finished tying the boat to the tree, when they saw a huge python gliding over the water towards them.

'Do you think it will try to get into the boat?' asked Sita.

'I don't think so,' said Vijay, although he took the precaution of holding an oar ready to fend off the snake.

But the python went past them, its head above water, its great length trailing behind, until it was lost in the shadows.

Vijay had more mangoes in the basket, and he and Sita sucked hungrily on them while they sat in the boat.

A big sambhar stag came threshing through the water. He did not have to swim. He was so tall that his head and shoulders remained well above the water. His antlers were big and beautiful.

'There will be other animals,' said Sita. 'Should we climb on to the tree?'

'We are quite safe in the boat,' said Vijay. 'The animals will not be dangerous tonight. They will not even hunt each other. They are only interested in reaching dry land. For once, the deer are safe from the tiger and the leopard. You lie down and sleep. I will keep watch.'

Sita stretched herself out in the boat and closed her eyes. She was very tired and the sound of the water lapping against the side of the boat soon lulled her to sleep.

She woke once, when a strange bird called overhead. She raised herself on one elbow but Vijay was awake, sitting beside her, his legs drawn up and his chin resting on his knees. He was gazing out across the water. He looked blue in the moonlight, the colour of the young God Krishna, and for a few moments Sita was confused and wondered if the boy was actually Krishna. But when she thought about it, she decided that it wasn't possible; he was just a village boy and she had seen hundreds like him—well, not exactly like him, he was a little different . . .

And when she slept again, she dreamt that the boy and Krishna were one, and that she was sitting beside him on a great white bird, which flew over the mountains, over the snow peaks of the Himalayas, into the cloud-land of the gods. And there was a great rumbling sound, as though the gods were angry about the whole thing, and she woke up to this terrible sound and looked about her, and there in the moonlit glade, up to his belly in water, stood a young elephant, his trunk raised as he trumpeted his predicament to the forest— for he was a young elephant, and he was lost, and was looking for his mother.

He trumpeted again, then lowered his head and listened. And presently, from far away, came the shrill trumpeting of another elephant. It must have been the young one's mother, because he gave several excited trumpet calls, and then went stamping and churning through the water towards a gap in the trees. The boat rocked in the waves made by his passing.

'It is all right,' said Vijay. 'You can go to sleep again.'

'I don't think I will sleep now,' said Sita.

'Then I will play my flute for you and the time will pass quickly.'

He produced a flute from under the seat and putting it to his lips began to play. And the sweetest music that Sita had ever heard came pouring from the little flute, and it seemed to fill the forest with its beautiful sound. And the music carried her away again, into the land of dreams, and they were riding on the bird once more, Sita and the blue god. And they were passing through cloud and mist, until suddenly the sun shot through the clouds. And at that moment Sita opened her eyes and saw the sky through the branches of the mahogany tree, the shiny green leaves making a bold pattern against the blinding blue of an open sky.

The forest was drenched with sunshine. Clouds were gathering again, but for an hour or so there would be hot sun on a steamy river.

Vijay was fast asleep in the bottom of the boat. His flute lay in the palm of his half-open hand. The sun came slanting across his bare brown legs. A leaf had fallen on his face, but it had not woken him. It lay on his cheek as though it had grown there.

Sita did not move about as she did not want to wake the boy. Instead she looked around her, and she thought the water level had fallen in the night, but she couldn't be sure.

Vijay woke at last. He yawned, stretched his limbs and sat up beside Sita.

'I am hungry,' he said.

'So am I,' said Sita.

'The last mangoes,' he said, emptying the basket of its last two mangoes.

After they had finished the fruit, they sucked the big seeds until they were quite dry. The discarded seeds floated well on the water. Sita had always preferred them to paper boats.

'We had better move on,' said Vijay.

He rowed the boat through the trees, and then for about an hour they were passing through the flooded forest, under the dripping branches of rain-washed trees. Sometimes, they had to use the oars to push away vines and creepers. Sometimes, submerged bushes hampered them. But they were out of the forest before ten o'clock.

The water was no longer very deep and they were soon gliding over flooded fields. In the distance they saw a village standing on high ground. In the old days, people had built their villages on hill tops as a better defence against bandits and the soldiers of invading armies. This was an old village, and though its inhabitants had long ago exchanged their swords for pruning forks, the hill on which it stood gave it protection from the flood waters.

A Bullock Cart Ride

The people of the village were at first reluctant to help Sita and Vijay.

'They are strangers,' said an old woman. 'They are not of our people.'

'They are of low caste,' said another. 'They cannot remain with us.'

'Nonsense!' said a tall, turbaned farmer, twirling his long, white moustache. 'They are children, not robbers. They will come into my house.'

The people of the village—long-limbed, sturdy men and women of the Jat race—were generous by nature, and once the elderly farmer had given them the lead they were friendly and helpful.

Sita was anxious to get to her grandparents, and the farmer, who had business to transact at a village fair some twenty miles distant, offered to take Sita and Vijay with him.

The fair was being held at a place called Karauli, and at Karauli there was a railway station from which a train went to Shahganj.

It was a journey that Sita would always remember. The bullock cart was so slow on the waterlogged roads that there was plenty of time in which to see things, to notice one another, to talk, to think, to dream.

Vijay couldn't sit still in the cart. He was used to the swift, gliding movements of his boat (which he had had to leave behind in the village), and every now and then he would jump off the cart and walk beside it, often ankle-deep in water.

There were four of them in the cart. Sita and Vijay, Hukam Singh, the Jat farmer and his son, Phambiri, a mountain of a man who was going to take part in the wrestling matches at the fair.

Hukam Singh, who drove the bullocks, liked to talk. He had been a soldier in the British Indian army during the First World War, and had been with his regiment to Italy and Mesopotamia.

'There is nothing to compare with soldiering,' he said, 'except, of course, farming. If you can't be a farmer, be a soldier. Are you listening, boy? Which will you be—farmer or soldier?'

'Neither,' said Vijay. 'I shall be an engineer!'

Hukam Singh's long moustache seemed almost to bristle with indignation.

'An engineer! What next! What does your father do, boy?'

'He keeps buffaloes.'

'Ah! And his son would be an engineer? . . . Well, well, the world isn't what it used to be! No one knows his rightful place any more. Men send their children to schools and what is the result? Engineers! And who will look after the buffaloes while you are engineering?'

'I will sell the buffaloes,' said Vijay, adding rather cheekily, 'Perhaps you will buy one of them, Subedar Sahib!'

He took the cheek out of his remark by adding 'Subedar Sahib', the rank of a non-commissioned officer in the old army. Hukam Singh, who had never reached this rank, was naturally flattered.

'Fortunately, Phambiri hasn't been to school. He'll be a farmer and a fine one, too.'

Phambiri simply grunted, which could have meant anything. He hadn't studied further than class 6, which was just as well, as he was a man of muscle, not brain.

Phambiri loved putting his strength to some practical and useful purpose. Whenever the cart wheels got stuck in the mud, he would get off, remove his shirt and put his shoulder to the side of the cart, while his muscles bulged and the sweat glistened on his broad back.

'Phambiri is the strongest man in our district,' said Hukam Singh proudly. 'And clever, too! It takes quick thinking to win a wrestling match.'

'I have never seen one,' said Sita.

'Then stay with us tomorrow morning, and you will see Phambiri wrestle. He has been challenged by the Karauli champion. It will be a great fight!'

'We must see Phambiri win,' said Vijay.

'Will there be time?' asked Sita.

'Why not? The train for Shahganj won't come in till evening. The fair goes on all day and the wrestling bouts will take place in the morning.'

'Yes, you must see me win!' exclaimed Phambiri, thumping himself on the chest as he climbed back on to the cart after freeing the wheels. 'No one can defeat me!'

'How can you be so certain?' asked Vijay.

'He has to be certain,' said Hukam Singh. 'I have taught him to be certain! You can't win anything if you are uncertain . . . Isn't that right, Phambiri? You know you are going to win!'

'I know,' said Phambiri with a grunt of confidence.

'Well, someone has to lose,' said Vijay.

'Very true,' said Hukam Singh smugly. 'After all, what would we do without losers? But for Phambiri, it is win, win, all the time!'

'And if he loses?' persisted Vijay.

'Then he will just forget that it happened and will go on to win his next fight!'

Vijay found Hukam Singh's logic almost unanswerable, but Sita, who had been puzzled by the argument, now saw everything very clearly and said, 'Perhaps he hasn't won any fights as yet. Did he lose the last one?'

'Hush!' said Hukam Singh looking alarmed. 'You must not let him remember. You do not remember losing a fight, do you, my son?'

'I have never lost a fight,' said Phambiri with great simplicity and confidence.

'How strange,' said Sita. 'If you lose, how can you win?'

'Only a soldier can explain that,' said Hukam Singh. 'For a man who fights, there is no such thing as defeat. You fought against the river, did you not?'

'I went with the river,' said Sita. 'I went where it took me.'

'Yes, and you would have gone to the bottom if the boy had not come along to help you. He fought the river, didn't he?'

'Yes, he fought the river,' said Sita.

'You helped me to fight it,' said Vijay.

'So you both fought,' said the old man with a nod of satisfaction. 'You did not go with the river. You did not leave everything to the gods.'

'The gods were with us,' said Sita.

And so they talked, while the bullock cart trundled along the muddy village roads. Both bullocks were white, and were decked out for the fair with coloured bead necklaces and bells hanging from their necks. They were patient, docile beasts. But the cartwheels which were badly in need of oiling, protested loudly, creaking and groaning as though all the demons in the world had been trapped within them.

Sita noticed a number of birds in the paddy fields. There were black-and-white curlews and cranes with pink coat-tails. A good monsoon means plenty of birds. But Hukam Singh was not happy about the cranes.

'They do great damage in the wheat fields,' he said. Lighting up a small, hand-held hookah pipe, he puffed at it and became philosophical again: 'Life is one long struggle for the farmer. When he has overcome the drought, survived the flood, hunted off the pig, killed the crane and reaped the crop, then comes that blood-sucking ghoul, the moneylender. There is no escaping him! Is your father in debt to a moneylender, boy?'

'No,' said Vijay.

'That is because he doesn't have daughters who must be married! I have two. As they resemble Phambiri, they will need generous dowries.'

In spite of his grumbling, Hukam Singh seemed fairly content with his lot. He'd had a good maize crop, and the front of his cart was piled high with corn. He would sell the crop at the fair, along with some cucumbers, eggplants and melons.

The bad road had slowed them down so much that when darkness came, they were still far from Karauli. In India there is hardly any twilight. Within a short time of the sun's going down, the stars come out.

'Six miles to go,' said Hukam Singh. 'In the dark our wheels may get stuck again. Let us spend the night here. If it rains, we can pull an old tarpaulin over the cart.'

Vijay made a fire in the charcoal burner which Hukam Singh had brought along, and they had a simple meal, roasting the corn over the fire and flavouring it with salt and spices and a squeeze of lemon. There was some milk, but not enough for everyone because Phambiri drank three tumblers by himself.

'If I win tomorrow,' he said, 'I will give all of you a feast!'

They settled down to sleep in the bullock cart, and Phambiri and his father were soon snoring. Vijay lay awake, his arms crossed behind his head, staring up at the stars. Sita was very tired but she couldn't sleep. She was worrying about her grandparents and wondering when she would see them again.

The night was full of sounds. The loud snoring that came from Phambiri and his father seemed to be taken up by invisible sleepers all around them, and Sita, becoming alarmed, turned to Vijay and asked, 'What is that strange noise?'

He smiled in the darkness, and she could see his white teeth and the glint of laughter in his eyes.

'Only the spirits of lost demons,' he said, and then laughed. 'Can't you recognize the music of the frogs?'

And that was what they heard—a sound more hideous than the wail of demons, a rising crescendo of noise— wurrk, wurrk, wurrk—coming from the flooded ditches on either side of the road. All the frogs in the jungle seemed to have gathered at that one spot, and each one appeared to have something to say for himself. The speeches continued for about an hour. Then the meeting broke up and silence returned to the forest.

A jackal slunk across the road. A puff of wind brushed through the trees. The bullocks, freed from the cart, were asleep beside it. The men's snores were softer now. Vijay slept, a half-smile on his face. Only Sita lay awake, worried and waiting for the dawn.

At the Fair

Already, at nine o'clock, the fairground was crowded. Cattle were being sold or auctioned. Stalls had opened, selling everything from pins to ploughs. Foodstuffs were on sale—hot food, spicy food, sweets and ices. A merry-go-round, badly oiled, was squeaking and groaning, while a loudspeaker blared popular film music across the grounds.

While Phambiri was preparing for his wrestling match, Hukam Singh was busy haggling over the price of pumpkins. Sita and Vijay wandered on their own among the stalls, gazing at toys and kites and bangles and clothing, at brightly coloured, syrupy sweets. Some of the rural people had transistor radios dangling by straps from their shoulders, the radio music competing with the loudspeaker. Occasionally a buffalo bellowed, drowning all other sounds.

Various people were engaged in roadside professions. There was the fortune teller. He had slips of paper, each of them covered with writing, which he kept in little trays along with some grain. He had a tame sparrow. When you gave the fortune teller your money, he allowed the little bird to hop in and out among the trays until it stopped at one and started pecking at the grain. From this tray the fortune teller took the slip of paper and presented it to his client. The writing told you what to expect over the next few months or years.

A harassed, middle-aged man, who was surrounded by six noisy sons and daughters, was looking a little concerned, because his slip of paper said: 'Do not lose hope. You will have a child soon.'

Some distance away sat a barber, and near him a professional ear cleaner. Several children clustered around a peepshow, which was built into an old gramophone cabinet. While one man wound up the gramophone and placed a well-worn record on the turntable, his partner pushed coloured pictures through a slide viewer.

A young man walked energetically up and down the fairground, beating a drum and announcing the day's attractions. The wrestling bouts were about to start. The main attraction was going to be the fight between Phambiri, described as a man 'whose thighs had the thickness of an elephant's trunk', and the local champion, Sher Dil (tiger's heart)—a wild-looking man, with hairy chest and beetling brow. He was heavier than Phambiri but not so tall.

Sita and Vijay joined Hukam Singh at one corner of the akhara, the wrestling pit. Hukam Singh was massaging his son's famous thighs.

A gong sounded and Sher Dil entered the ring, slapping himself on the chest and grunting like a wild boar. Phambiri advanced slowly to meet him.

They came to grips immediately, and stood swaying from side to side, two giants pitting their strength against each other. The sweat glistened on their well-oiled bodies.

Sher Dil got his arms round Phambiri's waist and tried to lift him off his feet, but Phambiri had twined one powerful leg around his opponent's thigh, and they both came down together with a loud squelch, churning up the soft mud of the wrestling pit. But neither wrestler had been pinned down.

Soon they were so covered with mud that it was difficult to distinguish one from the other. There was a flurry of arms and legs. The crowd was cheering and Sita and Vijay were cheering too, but the wrestlers were too absorbed in their struggle to be aware of their supporters. Each sought to turn the other on to his back. That was all that mattered. There was no count.

For a few moments Sher Dil had Phambiri almost helpless, but Phambiri wriggled out of a crushing grip, and using his legs once again, sent Sher Dil rocketing across the akhara. But Sher Dil landed on his belly, and even with Phambiri on top of him, it wasn't victory.

Nothing happened for several minutes, and the crowd became restless and shouted for more action. Phambiri thought of twisting his opponent's ear but he realized that he might get disqualified for doing that, so he restrained himself. He relaxed his grip slightly, and this gave Sher Dil a chance to heave himself up and send Phambiri spinning across the akhara. Phambiri was still in a sitting position when the other took a flying leap at him. But Phambiri dived forward, taking his opponent between the legs, and then rising, flung him backwards with a resounding thud. Sher Dil was helpless, and Phambiri sat on his opponent's chest to remove all doubts as to who was the winner. Only when the applause of the spectators told him that he had won did he rise and leave the ring.

Accompanied by his proud father, Phambiri accepted the prize money, thirty rupees, and then went in search of a tap. After he had washed the oil and mud from his body, he put on fresh clothes. Then, putting his arms around Vijay and Sita, he said, 'You have brought me luck, both of you. Now let us celebrate!' And he led the way to the sweet shops.

They ate syrupy rasgollas (made from milk and sugar) and almond-filled fudge, and little pies filled with minced meat, and washed everything down with a fizzy orange drink.

'Now I will buy each of you a small present,' said Phambiri.

He bought a bright blue sports shirt for Vijay. He bought a new hookah bowl for his father. And he took Sita to a stall where dolls were sold, and asked her to choose one.

There were all kinds of dolls—cheap plastic dolls, and beautiful dolls made by hand, dressed in the traditional costumes of different regions of the country. Sita was immediately reminded of Mumta, her own rag doll, who had been made at home with Grandmother's help. And she remembered Grandmother, and Grandmother's sewing machine, and the home that had been swept away, and the tears started to her eyes.

The dolls seemed to smile at Sita. The shopkeeper held them up one by one, and they appeared to dance, to twirl their wide skirts, to stamp their jingling feet on the counter. Each doll made her own special appeal to Sita. Each one wanted her love.

'Which one will you have?' asked Phambiri. 'Choose the prettiest, never mind the price!'

But Sita could say nothing. She could only shake her head. No doll, no matter how beautiful, could replace Mumta. She would never keep a doll again. That part of her life was over.

So instead of a doll Phambiri bought her bangles— coloured glass bangles which slipped easily on Sita's thin wrists. And then he took them into a temporary cinema, a large shed made of corrugated tin sheets.

Vijay had been to a cinema before—the towns were full of cinemas—but for Sita it was another new experience. Many things that were common enough for other boys and girls were strange and new for a girl who had spent nearly all her life on a small island in the middle of a big river.

As they found seats, a curtain rolled up and a white sheet came into view. The babble of talk dwindled into silence. Sita became aware of a whirring noise somewhere not far behind her. But, before she could turn her head to see what it was, the sheet became a rectangle of light and colour. It came to life. People moved and spoke. A story unfolded.

But, long afterwards, all that Sita could remember of her first film was a jumble of images and incidents. A train in danger, the audience murmuring with anxiety, a bridge over a river (but smaller than hers), the bridge being blown to pieces, the engine plunging into the river, people struggling in the water, a woman rescued by a man who immediately embraced her, the lights coming on again, and the audience rising slowly and drifting out of the theatre, looking quite unconcerned and even satisfied. All those people struggling in the water were now quite safe, back in the little black box in the projection room.

Catching the Train

And now a real engine, a steam engine belching smoke and fire, was on its way towards Sita.

She stood with Vijay on the station platform along with over a hundred other people waiting for the Shahganj train.

The platform was littered with the familiar bedrolls (or holdalls) without which few people in India ever travel. On these rolls sat women, children, great-aunts and great-uncles, grandfathers, grandmothers and grandchildren, while the more active adults hovered at the edge of the platform, ready to leap on to the train as soon as it arrived and reserve a space for the family. In India, people do not travel alone if they can help it. The whole family must be taken along—especially if the reason for the journey is a marriage, a pilgrimage, or simply a visit to friends or relations.

Moving among the piles of bedding and luggage were coolies; vendors of magazines, sweetmeats, tea and betel-leaf preparations; also stray dogs, stray people and sometimes a stray stationmaster. The cries of the vendors mingled with the general clamour of the station and the shunting of a steam engine in the yard. 'Tea, hot tea!', 'Fresh limes!' Sweets, papads, hot stuff, cold drinks, mangoes, toothpowder, photos of film stars, bananas, balloons, wooden toys! The platform had become a bazaar. What a blessing for those vendors that trains ran late and that people had to wait, and waiting, drank milky tea, bought toys for children, cracked peanut shells, munched bananas and chose little presents for the friends or relations on whom they were going to descend very shortly.

But there came the train!

The signal was down. The crowd surged forward, swamping an assistant stationmaster. Vijay took Sita by the hand and led her forward. If they were too slow, they would not get a place on the crowded train. In front of them was a tall, burly, bearded Sikh from the Punjab. Vijay decided it would be a wise move to stand behind him and move forward at the same time.

The station bell clanged and a big, puffing, black steam engine appeared in the distance. A stray dog, with a lifetime's experience of trains, darted away across the railway lines. As the train came alongside the platform, doors opened, window shutters fell, eager faces appeared in the openings, and even before the train had come to a stop, people were trying to get in or out.

For a few moments there was chaos. The crowd surged backwards and forwards. No one could get out. No one could get in! Fifty people were leaving the train, a hundred were catching it! No one wanted to give way. But every problem has a solution somewhere, provided one looks for it. And this particular problem was solved by a man climbing out of a window. Others followed his example. The pressure at the doors eased and people started squeezing into the compartments.

Vijay stayed close to the Sikh who forged a way through the throng. The Sikh reached an open doorway and was through. Vijay and Sita were through! They found somewhere to sit and were then able to look down at the platform, into the whirlpool and enjoy themselves a little. The vendors had abandoned the people on the platform and had started selling their wares at the windows. Hukam Singh, after buying their tickets, had given Vijay and Sita a rupee to spend on the way. Vijay bought a freshly split coconut, and Sita bought a comb for her hair. She had never bothered with her hair before.

They saw a worried man rushing along the platform searching for his family; but they were already in the compartment, having beaten him to it, and eagerly helped him in at the door. A whistle shrilled and they were off! A couple of vendors made last-minute transactions, then jumped from the slow-moving train. One man did this expertly with a tray of teacups balanced on one hand.

The train gathered speed.

'What will happen to all those people still on the platform?' asked Sita anxiously. 'Will they all be left behind?'

She put her head out of the window and looked back at the receding platform. It was strangely empty. Only the vendors and the coolies and the stray dogs and the dishevelled railway staff were in evidence. A miracle had happened. No one—absolutely no one—had been left behind!

Then the train was rushing through the night, the engine throwing out bright sparks that danced away like fireflies. Sometimes the train had to slow down, as flood water had weakened the embankments. Sometimes it stopped at brightly lit stations.

When the train started again and moved on into the dark countryside, Sita would stare through the glass of the window, at the bright lights of a town or the quiet glow of village lamps. She thought of Phambiri and Hukam Singh, and wondered if she would ever see them again. Already they were like people in a fairy tale, met briefly on the road and never seen again.

There was no room in the compartment in which to lie down; but Sita soon fell asleep, her head resting against Vijay's shoulder.

A Meeting and a Parting

Sita did not know where to look for her grandfather. For an hour she and Vijay wandered through the Shahganj bazaar, growing hungrier all the time. They had no money left and they were hot and thirsty.

Outside the bazaar, near a small temple, they saw a tree in which several small boys were helping themselves to the sour, purple fruit.

It did not take Vijay long to join the boys in the tree. They did not object to his joining them. It wasn't their tree, anyway.

Sita stood beneath the tree while Vijay threw the jamuns down to her. They soon had a small pile of the fruit. They were on the road again, their faces stained with purple juice.

They were asking the way to the Shahganj hospital, when Sita caught a glimpse of her grandfather on the road.

At first the old man did not recognize her. He was walking stiffly down the road, looking straight ahead, and would have walked right past the dusty, dishevelled girl, had she not charged straight at his thin, shaky legs and clasped him round the waist.

'Sita!' he cried, when he had recovered his wind and his balance. 'Why are you here? How did you get off the island? I have been very worried—it has been bad, these last two days . . .'

'Is Grandmother all right?' asked Sita.

But even as she spoke, she knew that Grandmother was no longer with them. The dazed look in the old man's eyes told her as much. She wanted to cry—not for Grandmother, who could suffer no more, but for Grandfather, who looked so helpless and bewildered. She did not want him to be unhappy. She forced back her tears and took his gnarled and trembling hand, and with Vijay walking beside her, led the old man down the crowded street.

She knew, then, that it would be on her shoulder that Grandfather would lean in the years to come.

They decided to remain in Shahganj for a couple of days, staying at a dharamsala—a wayside rest house—until the flood waters subsided. Grandfather still had two of the goats—it had not been necessary to sell more than one—but he did not want to take the risk of rowing a crowded boat across to the island. The river was still fast and dangerous.

But Vijay could not stay with Sita any longer.

'I must go now,' he said. 'My father and mother will be very worried and they will not know where to look for me. In a day or two the water will go down, and you will be able to go back to your home.'

'Perhaps the island has gone forever,' said Sita.

'It will be there,' said Vijay. 'It is a rocky island. Bad for crops but good for a house!'

'Will you come?' asked Sita.

What she really wanted to say was, 'Will you come to see me?' but she was too shy to say it; and besides, she wasn't sure if Vijay would want to see her again.

'I will come,' said Vijay. 'That is, if my father gets me another boat!'

As he turned to go, he gave her his flute.

'Keep it for me,' he said. 'I will come for it one day.' When he saw her hesitate, he smiled and said, 'It is a good flute!'

The Return

There was more rain, but the worst was over, and when Grandfather and Sita returned to the island, the river was no longer in spate.

Grandfather could hardly believe his eyes when he saw that the tree had disappeared—the tree that had seemed as permanent as the island, as much a part of his life as the river itself had been. He marvelled at Sita's escape.

'It was the tree that saved you,' he said.

'And the boy,' said Sita.

'Yes, and the boy.'

She thought about Vijay and wondered if she would ever see him again. Would he, like Phambiri and Hukam Singh, be one of those people who arrived as though out of a fairy tale and then disappeared silently and mysteriously? She did not know it then, but some of the moving forces of our lives are meant to touch us briefly and go their way . . .

And because Grandmother was no longer with them, life on the island was quite different. The evenings were sad and lonely.

But there was a lot of work to be done, and Sita did not have much time to think of Grandmother or Vijay or the world she had glimpsed during her journey.

For three nights they slept under a crude shelter made out of gunny bags. During the day, Sita helped Grandfather rebuild the mud hut. Once again they used the big rock for support.

The trunk which Sita had packed so carefully had not been swept off the island, but water had got into it and the food and clothing had been spoilt. But Grandfather's hookah had been saved, and in the evenings, after work was done and they had eaten their light meal which Sita prepared, he would smoke with a little of his old contentment and tell Sita about other floods which he had experienced as a boy. And he would tell her about the wrestling matches he had won, and the kites he had flown.

Sita planted a mango seed in the same spot where the peepul tree had stood. It would be many years before it grew into a big tree, but Sita liked to imagine herself sitting in the branches, picking the mangoes straight from the tree and feasting on them all day.

Grandfather was more particular about making a vegetable garden, putting down peas, carrots, gram and mustard.

One day, when most of the hard work had been done and the new hut was ready, Sita took the flute which had been given to her by Vijay, and walked down to the water's edge and tried to play it. But all she could produce were a few broken notes, and even the goats paid no attention to her music.

Sometimes Sita thought she saw a boat coming down the river, and she would run to meet it; but usually there was no boat, or if there was, it belonged to a stranger or to another fisherman. And so she stopped looking out for boats.

Slowly, the rains came to an end. The flood waters had receded, and in the villages people were beginning to till the land again and sow crops for the winter months. There were more cattle fairs and wrestling matches. The days were warm and sultry. The water in the river was no longer muddy, and one evening Grandfather brought home a huge mahseer, and Sita made it into a delicious curry.

Deep River

Grandfather sat outside the hut, smoking his hookah. Sita was at the far end of the island, spreading clothes on the rocks to dry. One of the goats had followed her. It was the friendlier of the two, and often followed Sita about the island. She had made it a necklace of coloured beads.

She sat down on a smooth rock, and as she did so, she noticed a small bright object in the sand near her feet. She picked it up. It was a little wooden toy—a coloured peacock, God Krishna's favourite bird—it must have come down on the river and been swept ashore on the island. Some of the paint had been rubbed off; but for Sita, who had no toys, it was a great find.

There was a soft footfall behind her. She looked round, and there was Vijay, barefoot, standing over her and smiling.

'I thought you wouldn't come,' said Sita.

'There was much work in my village. Did you keep my flute?'

'Yes, but I cannot play it properly.'

'I will teach you,' said Vijay.

He sat down beside her and they cooled their feet in the water, which was clear now, taking in the blue of the sky. They could see the sand and the pebbles of the riverbed.

'Sometimes the river is angry and sometimes it is kind,' said Sita.

'We are part of the river,' said Vijay.

It was a good river, deep and strong, beginning in the mountains and ending in the sea.

Along its banks, for hundreds of miles, lived millions of people, and Sita was only one small girl among them, and no one had ever heard of her, no one knew her—except for the old man, and the boy, and the water that was blue and white and wonderful.

THE
TUNNEL

It was almost noon, and the jungle was very still, very silent. Heat waves shimmered along the railway embankment where it cut a path through the tall evergreen trees. The railway lines were two straight black serpents disappearing into the tunnel in the hillside.

Ranji stood near the cutting, waiting for the midday train. It wasn't a station and he wasn't catching a train. He was waiting so he could watch the steam engine come roaring out of the tunnel.

He had cycled out of town and taken the jungle path until he had come to a small village. He had left the cycle there, and walked over a low, scrub-covered hill and down to the tunnel exit.

Now he looked up. He had heard, in the distance, the shrill whistle of the engine. He couldn't see anything, because the train was approaching from the other side of the hill, but presently a sound like distant thunder came from the tunnel, and he knew the train was coming through.

A second or two later the steam engine shot out of the tunnel, snorting and puffing like some green, black and gold dragon, some beautiful monster out of Ranji's dreams. Showering sparks right and left, it roared a challenge to the jungle.

Instinctively Ranji stepped back a few paces. Waves of hot steam struck him in the face. Even the trees seemed to flinch from the noise and heat. And then the train had gone, leaving only a plume of smoke to drift lazily over the tall shisham trees.

The jungle was still again. No one moved.

Ranji turned from watching the drifting smoke and began walking along the embankment towards the tunnel. It grew darker the further he walked, and when he had gone about twenty yards, it became pitch black. He had to turn and look back at the opening to make sure that there was a speck of daylight in the distance.

Ahead of him, the tunnel's other opening was also a small round circle of light.

The walls of the tunnel were damp and sticky. A bat flew past. A lizard scuttled between the lines. Coming straight from the darkness into the light, Ranji was dazzled by the sudden glare. He put a hand up to shade his eyes and looked up at the scrub-covered hillside, and he thought he saw something moving between the trees.

It was just a flash of gold and black, and a long swishing tail. It was there between the trees for a second or two, and then it was gone.

About fifty feet from the entrance to the tunnel stood the watchman's hut. Marigolds grew in front of the hut, and at the back there was a small vegetable patch. It was the watchman's duty to inspect the tunnel and keep it clear of obstacles.

Every day, before the train came through, he would walk the length of the tunnel. If all was well, he would return to his hut and take a nap. If something was wrong, he would walk back up the line and wave a red flag and the engine driver would slow down.

At night, the watchman lit an oil lamp and made a similar inspection. If there was any danger to the train, he'd go back up the line and wave his lamp to the approaching engine. If all was well, he'd hang his lamp at the door of his hut and go to sleep.

He was just settling down on his cot for an afternoon nap when he saw the boy come out of the tunnel. He waited until the boy was only a few feet away and then said, 'Welcome, welcome. I don't often get visitors. Sit down for a while, and tell me why you were inspecting my tunnel.'

'Is it your tunnel?' asked Ranji.

'It is,' said the watchman. 'It is truly my tunnel, since no one else will have anything to do with it. I have only lent it to the government.'

Ranji sat down on the edge of the cot.

'I wanted to see the train come through,' he said. 'And then, when it had gone, I decided to walk through the tunnel.'

'And what did you find in it?'

'Nothing. It was very dark. But when I came out, I thought I saw an animal—up on the hill—but I'm not sure, it moved off very quickly.'

'It was a leopard you saw,' said the watchman. 'My leopard.'

'Do you own a leopard, too?'

'I do.'

'And do you lend it to the government?'

'I do not.'

'Is it dangerous?'

'Not if you leave it alone. It comes this way for a few days every month, because there are still deer in this jungle, and the deer is its natural prey. It keeps away from people.'

'Have you been here a long time?' asked Ranji.

'Many years. My name is Kishan Singh.'

'Mine is Ranji.'

'There is one train during the day. And there is one train during the night. Have you seen the Night Mail come through the tunnel?'

'No. At what time does it come?'

'About nine o'clock, if it isn't late. You could come and sit here with me, if you like. And, after it has gone, I will take you home.'

'I'll ask my parents,' said Ranji. 'Will it be safe?'

'It is safer in the jungle than in the town. No rascals out here. Only last week, when I went into the town, I had my pocket picked! Leopards don't pick pockets.'

Kishan Singh stretched himself out on his cot. 'And now I am going to take a nap, my friend. It is too hot to be up and about in the afternoon.'

'Everyone goes to sleep in the afternoon,' complained Ranji. 'My father lies down as soon as he's had his lunch.'

'Well, the animals also rest in the heat of the day. It is only the tribe of boys who cannot, or will not, rest.'

Kishan Singh placed a large banana leaf over his face to keep away the flies, and was soon snoring gently. Ranji stood up, looking up and down the railway tracks. Then he began walking back to the village.

The following evening, towards dusk, as the flying foxes swooped silently out of the trees, Ranji made his way to the watchman's hut.

It had been a long hot day, but now the earth was cooling and a light breeze was moving through the trees. It carried with it the scent of mango blossom, the promise of rain.

Kishan Singh was waiting for Ranji. He had watered his small garden and the flowers looked cool and fresh. A kettle was boiling on an oil stove.

'I am making tea,' he said. 'There is nothing like a glass of hot sweet tea while waiting for a train.'

They drank their tea, listening to the sharp notes of the tailor bird and the noisy, chatter of the seven sisters. As the brief twilight faded, most of the birds fell silent. Kishan lit his oil lamp and said it was time for him to inspect the tunnel. He moved off towards the dark entrance, while Ranji sat on the cot, sipping tea.

In the dark, the trees seemed to move closer. And the night life of the forest was conveyed on the breeze—the sharp call of a barking deer, the cry of a fox, the quaint tonk-tonk of a nightjar.

There were some sounds that Ranji would not recognize—sounds that came from the trees. Creakings, and whisperings, as though the trees were coming alive, stretching their limbs in the dark, shifting a little, flexing their fingers.

Kishan Singh stood outside the tunnel, trimming his lamp. The night sounds were familiar to him and he did not give them much thought; but something else—a padded footfall, a rustle of dry leaves—made him stand still for a few seconds, peering into the darkness. Then, humming softly, he returned to where Ranji was waiting. Ten minutes remained for the Night Mail to arrive.

As the watchman sat down on the cot beside Ranji, a new sound reached both of them quite distinctly—a rhythmic sawing sound, as of someone cutting through the branch of a tree.

'What's that?' whispered Ranji.

'It's the leopard,' said Kishan Singh. 'I think it's in the tunnel.'

'The train will soon be here.'

'Yes, my friend. And if we don't drive the leopard out of the tunnel, it will be run over by the engine.'

'But won't it attack us if we try to drive it out?' asked Ranji, beginning to share the watchman's concern.

'It knows me well. We have seen each other many times. I don't think it will attack. Even so, I will take my axe along. You had better stay here, Ranji.'

'No, I'll come too. It will be better than sitting here alone in the dark.'

'All right, but stay close behind me. And remember, there is nothing to fear.'

Raising his lamp, Kishan Singh walked into the tunnel, shouting at the top of his voice to try and scare away the animal. Ranji followed close behind. But he found he was unable to do any shouting; his throat had gone quite dry.

They had gone about twenty paces into the tunnel when the light from the lamp fell upon the leopard. It was crouching between the tracks, only fifteen feet away from them. Baring its teeth and snarling, it went down on its belly, tail twitching. Ranji felt sure it was going to spring at them.

Kishan Singh and Ranji both shouted together. Their voices rang through the tunnel. And the leopard, uncertain as to how many terrifying humans were there in front of him, turned swiftly and disappeared into the darkness.

To make sure it had gone, Ranji and the watchman walked the length of the tunnel. When they returned to the entrance, the rails were beginning to hum. They knew the train was coming.

Ranji put his hand to one of the rails and felt its tremor. He heard the distant rumble of the train. And then the engine came round the bend, hissing at them, scattering sparks into the darkness, defying the jungle as it roared through the steep sides of the cutting. It charged straight into the tunnel, thundering past Ranji like the beautiful dragon of his dreams.

And when it had gone, the silence returned and the forest seemed to breathe, to live again. Only the rails still trembled with the passing of the train.

They trembled again to the passing of the same train, almost a week later, when Ranji and his father were both travelling in it.

Ranji's father was scribbling in a notebook, doing his accounts. How boring of him, thought Ranji as he sat near an open window staring out at the darkness. His father was going to Delhi on a business trip and had decided to take the boy along.

'It's time you learnt something about the business,' he had said, to Ranji's dismay.

The Night Mail rushed through the forest with its hundreds of passengers. The carriage wheels beat out a steady rhythm on the rails. Tiny flickering lights came and went, as they passed small villages on the fringe of the jungle.

Ranji heard the rumble as the train passed over a small bridge. It was too dark to see the hut near the cutting, but he knew they must be approaching the tunnel. He strained his eyes, looking out into the night; and then, just as the engine let out a shrill whistle, Ranji saw the lamp.

He couldn't see Kishan Singh, but he saw the lamp, and he knew that his friend was out there.

The train went into the tunnel and out again, it left the jungle behind and thundered across the endless plains. And Ranji stared out at the darkness, thinking of the lonely cutting in the forest, and the watchman with the lamp who would always remain a firefly for those travelling thousands, as he lit up the darkness for steam engines and leopards.

SUSANNA'S
SEVEN HUSBANDS

Locally the tomb was known as 'the grave of the seven times married one'.

You'd be forgiven for thinking it was Bluebeard's grave; he was reputed to have killed several wives in turn because they showed undue curiosity about a locked room. But this was the tomb of Susanna Anna-Maria Yeates, and the inscription (most of it in Latin) stated that she was mourned by all who had benefited from her generosity, her beneficiaries having included various schools, orphanages and the church across the road. There was no sign of any other grave in the vicinity and presumably her husbands had been interred in the old Rajpur graveyard, below the Delhi Ridge.

I was still in my teens when I first saw the ruins of what had once been a spacious and handsome mansion. Desolate and silent, its well-laid paths were overgrown with weeds, and its flower beds had disappeared under a growth of thorny jungle. The two-storeyed house had looked across the Grand Trunk Road. Now abandoned, feared and shunned, it stood encircled in mystery, reputedly the home of evil spirits.

Outside the gate, along the Grand Trunk Road, thousands of vehicles sped by—cars, trucks, buses, tractors, bullock carts—but few noticed the old mansion or its mausoleum, set back as they were from the main road, hidden by mango, neem and peepul trees. One old and massive peepul tree grew out of the ruins of the house, strangling it much as its owner was said to have strangled one of her dispensable paramours.

As a much-married person with a quaint habit of disposing of her husbands whenever she tired of them, Susanna's malignant spirit was said to haunt the deserted garden. I had examined the tomb, I had gazed upon the ruins, I had scrambled through shrubbery and overgrown rose bushes, but I had not encountered the spirit of this mysterious woman. Perhaps, at the time, I was too pure and innocent to be targeted by malignant spirits. For malignant she must have been, if the stories about her were true.

The vaults of the ruined mansion were rumoured to contain a buried treasure—the amassed wealth of the lady Susanna. But no one dared go down there, for the vaults were said to be occupied by a family of cobras, traditional guardians of buried treasure. Had she really been a woman of great wealth, and could treasure still be buried there? I put these questions to Naushad, the furniture maker, who had lived in the vicinity all his life, and whose father had made the furniture and fittings for this and other great houses in Old Delhi.

'Lady Susanna, as she was known, was much sought after for her wealth,' recalled Naushad. 'She was no miser, either. She spent freely, reigning in state in her palatial home, with many horses and carriages at her disposal. Every evening she rode through the Roshanara Gardens, the cynosure of all eyes, for she was beautiful as well as wealthy. Yes, all men sought her favours, and she could choose from the best of them. Many were fortune hunters. She did not discourage them. Some found favour for a time, but she soon tired of them. None of her husbands enjoyed her wealth for very long!

'Today no one enters those ruins, where once there was mirth and laughter. She was a zamindari lady, the owner of much land, and she administered her estate with a strong hand. She was kind if rents were paid when they fell due, but terrible if someone failed to pay.

'Well, over fifty years have gone by since she was laid to rest, but still men speak of her with awe. Her spirit is restless, and it is said that she often visits the scenes of her former splendour. She has been seen walking through this gate, or riding in the gardens, or driving in her phaeton down the Rajpur road.'

'And what happened to all those husbands?' I asked.

'Most of them died mysterious deaths. Even the doctors were baffled. Tomkins Sahib drank too much. The lady soon tired of him. A drunken husband is a burdensome creature, she was heard to say. He would eventually have drunk himself to death, but she was an impatient woman and was anxious to replace him. You see those datura bushes growing wild in the grounds? They have always done well here.'

'Belladonna?' I suggested.

'That's right, huzoor. Introduced in the whisky-soda, it put him to sleep forever.'

'She was quite humane in her way.'

'Oh, very humane, sir. She hated to see anyone suffer. One sahib, I don't know his name, drowned in the tank behind the house, where the water lilies grew. But she made sure he was half-dead before he fell in. She had large, powerful hands, they said.'

'Why did she bother to marry them? Couldn't she just have had men friends?'

'Not in those days, huzoor. Respectable society would not have tolerated it. Neither in India nor in the West would it have been permitted.'

'She was born out of her time,' I remarked.

'True, sir. And remember, most of them were fortune hunters. So we need not waste too much pity on them.'

'She did not waste any.'

'She was without pity. Especially when she found out what they were really after. Snakes had a better chance of survival.'

'How did the other husbands take their leave of this world?'

'Well, the Colonel Sahib shot himself while cleaning his rifle. Purely an accident, huzoor. Although some say she had loaded his gun without his knowledge. Such was her reputation by now that she was suspected even when innocent. But she bought her way out of trouble. It was easy enough, if you were wealthy.'

'And the fourth husband?'

'Oh, he died a natural death. There was a cholera epidemic that year, and he was carried off by the haija. Although, again, there were some who said that a good dose of arsenic produced the same symptoms! Anyway, it was cholera on the death certificate. And the doctor who signed it was the next to marry her.'

'Being a doctor, he was probably quite careful about what he ate and drank.'

'He lasted about a year.'

'What happened?'

'He was bitten by a cobra.'

'Well, that was just bad luck, wasn't it? You could hardly blame it on Susanna.'

'No, huzoor, but the cobra was in his bedroom. It was coiled around the bedpost. And when he undressed for the night, it struck! He was dead when Susanna came into the room an hour later. She had a way with snakes. She did not harm them and they never attacked her.'

'And there were no antidotes in those days. Exit the doctor. Who was the sixth husband?'

'A handsome man. An indigo planter. He had gone bankrupt when the indigo trade came to an end. He was hoping to recover his fortune with the good lady's help. But our Susanna mem, she did not believe in sharing her fortune with anyone.'

'How did she remove the indigo planter?'

'It was said that she lavished strong drink upon him, and when he lay helpless, she assisted him on the road we all have to take by pouring molten lead in his ears.'

'A painless death, I'm told.'

'But a terrible price to pay, huzoor, simply because one is no longer needed . . .'

We walked along the dusty highway, enjoying the evening breeze, and some time later we entered the Roshanara Gardens, in those days Delhi's most popular and fashionable meeting place.

'You have told me how six of her husbands died, Naushad. I thought there were seven?'

'Ah, the seventh was a gallant young magistrate who perished right here, huzoor. They were driving through the park after dark when the lady's carriage was attacked by brigands. In defending her, the young man received a fatal sword wound.'

'Not the lady's fault, Naushad.'

'No, huzoor. But he was a magistrate, remember, and the assailants, one of whose relatives had been convicted by him, were out for revenge. Oddly enough, though, two of the men were given employment by the lady Susanna at a later date. You may draw your own conclusions.'

'And were there others?'

'Not husbands. But an adventurer, a soldier of fortune came along. He found her treasure, they say. And he lies buried with it, in the cellars of the ruined house. His bones lie scattered there, among gold and silver and precious jewels. The cobras guard them still! But how he perished was a mystery, and remains so till this day.'

'And Susanna? What happened to her?'

'She lived to a ripe old age. If she paid for her crimes, it wasn't in this life! She had no children, but she started an orphanage and gave generously to the poor and to various schools and institutions, including a home for widows. She died peacefully in her sleep.'

'A merry widow,' I remarked. 'The Black Widow spider!'

Don't go looking for Susanna's tomb. It vanished some years ago, along with the ruins of her mansion. A smart new housing estate has come up on the site, but not before several workmen and a contractor succumbed to snake bite! Occasionally, residents complain of a malignant ghost in their midst, who is given to flagging down cars, especially those driven by single men. There have also been one or two mysterious disappearances.

And after dusk, an old-fashioned horse and carriage can sometimes be seen driving through the Roshanara Gardens. If you chance upon it, ignore it, my friend. Don't stop to answer any questions from the beautiful fair lady who smiles at you from behind lace curtains. She's still looking for her final victim.

BHABIJI'S
HOUSE*

At first light there is a tremendous burst of birdsong from the guava tree in the little garden. Over a hundred sparrows wake up all at once and give tongue to whatever it is that sparrows have to say to each other at five o'clock on a foggy winter's morning in Delhi.

In the small house, people sleep on; that is, everyone except Bhabiji—Granny—the head of the lively Punjabi middle-class family with whom I nearly always stay when I am in Delhi.

She coughs, stirs, groans, grumbles and gets out of bed. The fire has to be lit, and food prepared for two of her sons to take to work. There is a daughter-in-law, Shobha, to

---

* My neighbours in Rajouri Garden back in the 1960s were the Kamal family. This entry from my journal, which I wrote on one of my later visits, describes a typical day in that household.

help her; but the girl is not very bright at getting up in the morning. Actually, it is this way: Bhabiji wants to show up her daughter-in-law; so, no matter how hard Shobha tries to be up first, Bhabiji forestalls her. The old lady does not sleep well, anyway; her eyes are open long before the first sparrow chirps, and as soon as she sees her daughter-in-law stirring, she scrambles out of bed and hurries to the kitchen. This gives her the opportunity to say: 'What good is a daughter-in-law when I have to get up to prepare her husband's food?'

The truth is that Bhabiji does not like anyone else preparing her sons' food.

She looks no older than when I first saw her ten years ago. She still has complete control over a large family and, with tremendous confidence and enthusiasm, presides over the lives of three sons, a daughter, two daughters-in-law and fourteen grandchildren. This is a joint family (there are not many left in a big city like Delhi), in which the sons and their families all live together as one unit under their mother's benevolent (and sometimes slightly malevolent) autocracy. Even when her husband was alive, Bhabiji dominated the household.

The eldest son, Shiv, has a separate kitchen, but his wife and children participate in all the family celebrations and quarrels. It is a small miracle how everyone (including myself when I visit) manages to fit into the house; and a stranger might be forgiven for wondering where everyone sleeps, for no beds are visible during the day. That is because the beds—light wooden frames with rough strings across—are brought in only at night, and are taken out first thing in the morning and kept in the garden shed.

As Bhabiji lights the kitchen fire, the household begins to stir, and Shobha joins her mother-in-law in the kitchen. As a guest I am privileged and may get up last. But my bed soon becomes an island battered by waves of scurrying, shouting children, eager to bathe, dress, eat and find their school books. Before I can get up, someone brings me a tumbler of hot sweet tea. It is a brass tumbler and burns my fingers; I have yet to learn how to hold one properly. Punjabis like their tea with lots of milk and sugar—so much so that I often wonder why they bother to add any tea.

Ten years ago, 'bed tea' was unheard of in Bhabiji's house. Then, the first time I came to stay, Kamal, the youngest son, told Bhabiji: 'My friend is Angrez. He must have tea in bed.' He forgot to mention that I usually took my morning cup at seven; they gave it to me at five. I gulped it down and went to sleep again. Then, slowly, others in the household began indulging in morning cups of tea. Now everyone, including the older children, has 'bed tea'. They bless my English forebears for instituting the custom; I bless the Punjabis for perpetuating it.

Breakfast is by rota, in the kitchen. It is a tiny room and accommodates only four adults at a time. The children have eaten first; but the smallest children, Shobha's toddlers, keep coming in and climbing over us. Says Bhabiji of the youngest and most mischievous: 'He lives only because God keeps a special eye on him.'

Kamal, his elder brother, Arun, and I sit crosslegged and barefooted on the floor, while Bhabiji serves us hot parathas stuffed with potatoes and onions, along with omelettes—an excellent dish. Arun then goes to work on his scooter, while Kamal catches a bus for the city, where he attends an art college. After they have gone, Bhabiji and Shobha have their breakfast.

By nine o'clock everyone who is still in the house is busy doing something. Shobha is washing clothes. Bhabiji has settled down on a cot with a huge pile of spinach, which she methodically cleans and chops up. Madhu, her fourteen-year-old granddaughter, who attends school only in the afternoons, is washing down the sitting room floor. Madhu's mother is a teacher in a primary school in Delhi, and earns a pittance of Rs 150 a month. Her husband went to England ten years ago, and never returned; he does not send any money home.

Madhu is made attractive by the gravity of her countenance. She is always thoughtful, reflective; seldom speaks, smiles rarely (but looks very pretty when she does). I wonder what she thinks about as she scrubs floors, prepares meals with Bhabiji, washes dishes and even finds a few hard-pressed moments for her school work. She is the Cinderella of the house. Not that she has to put up with anything like a cruel stepmother; Madhu is Bhabiji's favourite. She has made herself so useful that she is above all reproach. Apart from that, there is a certain measure of aloofness about her—she does not get involved in domestic squabbles—and this is foreign to a household in which everyone has something to say for himself or herself. Her two young brothers are constantly being reprimanded; but no one says anything to Madhu. Only yesterday morning, when clothes were being washed and Madhu was scrubbing the floor, the following dialogue took place.

Madhu's mother (picking up a school book left in the courtyard): 'Where's that boy Popat? See how careless he is with his books! Popat! He's run off. Just wait till he gets back. I'll give him a good beating.'

Vinod's mother: 'It's not Popat's book. It's Vinod's. Where's Vinod?'

Vinod (grumpily): 'It's Madhu's book.'

Silence for a minute or two. Madhu continues scrubbing the floor; she does not bother to look up. Vinod picks up the book and takes it indoors. The women return to their chores.

Manju, daughter of Shiv and sister of Vinod, is averse to housework and, as a result, is always being scolded—by her parents, grandmother, uncles and aunts.

Now, she is engaged in the unwelcome chore of sweeping the front yard. She does this with a sulky look, ignoring my cheerful remarks. I have been sitting under the guava tree, but Manju soon sweeps me away from this spot. She creates a drifting cloud of dust, and seems satisfied only when the dust settles on the clothes that have just been hung up to dry. Manju is a sensuous creature and, like most sensuous people, is lazy by nature. She does not like sweeping because the boy next door can see her at it, and she wants to appear before him in a more glamorous light. Her first action every morning is to turn to the cinema advertisements in the newspaper. Bombay's movie moguls cater for girls like Manju who long to be tragic heroines. Life is so very dull for middle-class teenagers in Delhi, that it is only natural that they should lean so heavily on escapist entertainment. Every residential area has a cinema. But there is not a single bookshop in this particular suburb, although it has a population of over twenty thousand literate people. Few children read books; but they are adept at swotting up examination 'guides'; and students of, say, Hardy or Dickens read the guides and not the novels.

Bhabiji is now grinding onions and chillies in a mortar. Her eyes are watering but she is in a good mood. Shobha sits quietly in the kitchen. A little while ago she was complaining to me of a backache. I am the only one who lends a sympathetic ear to complaints of aches and pains. But since last night, my sympathies have been under severe strain. When I got into bed at about ten o'clock, I found the sheets wet. Apparently Shobha had put her baby to sleep in my bed during the afternoon.

While the housework is still in progress, cousin Kishore arrives. He is an itinerant musician who makes a living by arranging performances at marriages. He visits Bhabiji's house frequently and at odd hours, often a little tipsy, always brimming over with goodwill and grandiose plans for the future. It was once his ambition to be a film producer, and some years back he lost a lot of Bhabiji's money in producing a film that was never completed. He still talks of finishing it.

'Brother,' he says, taking me into his confidence for the hundredth time, 'do you know anyone who has a movie camera?'

'No,' I say, knowing only too well how these admissions can lead me into a morass of complicated manoeuvres. But Kishore is not easily put off, especially when he has been fortified with country liquor.

'But you knew someone with a movie camera?' he asks.

'That was long ago.'

'How long ago?' (I have got him going now.)

'About five years back.'

'Only five years? Find him, find him!'

'It's no use. He doesn't have the movie camera any more. He sold it.'

'Sold it!' Kishore looks at me as though I have done him an injury. 'But why didn't you buy it? All we need is a movie camera, and our fortune is made. I will produce the film, I will direct it, I will write the music. Two in one,

Charlie Chaplin and Raj Kapoor. Why didn't you buy the camera?'

'Because I didn't have the money.'

'But we could have borrowed the money.'

'If you are in a position to borrow money, you can go out and buy another movie camera.'

'We could have borrowed the camera. Do you know anyone else who has one?'

'Not a soul.' I am firm this time; I will not be led into another maze.

'Very sad, very sad,' mutters Kishore. And with a dejected, hangdog expression designed to make me feel that I am responsible for all his failures, he moves off.

Bhabiji had expressed some annoyance at his arrival, but he softens her up by leaving behind an invitation to a marriage party this evening. No one in the house knows the bride's or bridegroom's family, but that does not matter; knowing one of the musicians is just as good. Almost everyone will go.

While Bhabiji, Shobha and Madhu are preparing lunch, Bhabiji engages in one of her favourite subjects of conversation, Kamal's marriage, which she hopes she will be able to arrange in the near future. She freely acknowledges that she made grave blunders in selecting wives for her other sons—this is meant to be heard by Shobha—and promises not to repeat her mistakes. According to Bhabiji,

Kamal's bride should be both educated and domesticated; and, of course, she must be fair.

'What if he likes a dark girl?' I ask teasingly.

Bhabiji looks horrified. 'He cannot marry a dark girl,' she declares.

'But dark girls are beautiful,' I tell her.

'Impossible!'

'Do you want him to marry a European girl?'

'No foreigners! I know them, they'll take my son away. He shall have a good Punjabi girl, with a complexion the colour of wheat.'

Noon. The shadows shift and cross the road. I sit beneath the guava tree and watch the women at work. They will not let me do anything, but they like talking to me and they love to hear my broken Punjabi. Sparrows flit about at their feet, snapping up the gram that runs away from their busy fingers. A crow looks speculatively at the empty kitchen, sidles towards the open door; but Bhabiji has only to glance up and the experienced crow flies away. He knows he will not be able to make off with anything from this house.

One by one the children come home, demanding food. Now it is Madhu's turn to go to school. Her younger brother Popat, an intelligent but undersized boy of thirteen, appears in the doorway and asks for lunch.

'Be off!' says Bhabiji. 'It isn't ready yet.'

Actually the food is ready and only the chapattis remain to be made. Shobha will attend to them. Bhabiji lies down on her cot in the sun, complaining of a pain in her back and ringing noises in her ears.

'I'll press your back,' says Popat. He has been out of Bhabiji's favour lately, and is looking for an opportunity to be rehabilitated.

Barefooted, he stands on Bhabiji's back and treads her weary flesh and bones with a gentle walking-in-one-spot movement. Bhabiji grunts with relief. Every day she has new pains in new places. Her age, and the daily business of feeding the family and running everyone's affairs, are beginning to tell on her. But she would sooner die than give up her position of dominance in the house. Her working sons still hand over their pay to her, and she dispenses the money as she sees fit.

The pummelling she gets from Popat puts her in a better mood, and she holds forth on another favourite subject, the respective merits of various dowries. Shiv's wife (according to Bhabiji) brought nothing with her but a string cot; Kishore's wife brought only a sharp and clever tongue; Shobha brought a wonderful steel cupboard, fully expecting that it would do all the housework for her.

This last observation upsets Shobha, and a little later I find her under the guava tree weeping profusely. I give her the comforting words she obviously expects, but it is her husband Arun who will have to bear the brunt of her outraged feelings when he comes home this evening. He is rather nervous of his wife. Last night he wanted to eat out, at a restaurant, but did not want to be accused of wasting money; so he stuffed fifteen rupees into my pocket and asked me to invite both him and Shobha to dinner, which I did. We had a good dinner. Such unexpected hospitality on my part has further improved my standing with Shobha. Now, in spite of other chores, she sees that I get cups of tea and coffee at odd hours of the day.

Bhabiji knows Arun is soft with his wife, and taunts him about it. She was saying this morning that whenever there is any work to be done, Shobha retires to bed with a headache (partly true). She says even Manju does more housework (not true). Bhabiji has certain talents as an actress, and does a good take-off of Shobha sulking and grumbling at having too much to do.

While Bhabiji talks, Popat sneaks off and goes for a ride on the bicycle. It is a very old bicycle and is constantly undergoing repairs. 'The soul has gone out of it,' says Vinod philosophically and makes his way on to the roof, where he keeps a store of pornographic literature. Up there, he cannot be seen and cannot be remembered, and so avoids being sent out on errands.

One of the boys is bathing at the hand pump. Manju, who should have gone to school with Madhu, is stretched out on a cot, complaining of fever. But she will be up in time to attend the marriage party . . .

Towards evening, as the birds return to roost in the guava tree, their chatter is challenged by the tumult of people in the house getting ready for the marriage party.

Manju presses her tight pyjamas but neglects to darn them. She wears a loose-fitting, diaphanous shirt. She keeps flitting in and out of the front room so that I can admire the way she glitters. Shobha has used too much powder and lipstick in an effort to look like the femme fatale which she indubitably is not. Shiv's more conservative wife floats around in loose, old-fashioned pyjamas. Bhabiji is sober and austere in a white sari. Madhu looks neat. The men wear their suits.

Popat is holding up a mirror for his Uncle Kishore, who is combing his long hair. (Kishore kept his hair long, like a court musician at the time of Akbar, before the hippies had been heard of.) He is nodding benevolently, having fortified himself from a bottle labelled 'Som Ras' ('nectar of the gods'), obtained cheaply from an illicit still.

Kishore: 'Don't shake the mirror, boy!'

Popat: 'Uncle, it's your head that's shaking.'

Shobha is happy. She loves going out, especially to marriages, and she always takes her two small boys with her, although they invariably spoil the carpets.

Only Kamal, Popat and I remain behind. I have had more than my share of marriage parties.

The house is strangely quiet. It does not seem so small now, with only three people left in it. The kitchen has been locked (Bhabiji will not leave it open while Popat is still in the house), so we visit the dhaba, the wayside restaurant near the main road, and this time I pay the bill with my own money. We have kababs and chicken curry.

Yesterday, Kamal and I took our lunch on the grass of the Buddha Jayanti Gardens (Buddha's Birthday Gardens). There was no college for Kamal, as the majority of Delhi's students had hijacked a number of corporation buses and headed for the Pakistan high commission, with every intention of levelling it to the ground if possible, as a protest against the hijacking of an Indian plane from Srinagar to Lahore. The students were met by the Delhi police in full strength, and a pitched battle took place, in which stones from the students and tear gas shells from the police were the favoured missiles. There were two shells fired every minute, according to a newspaper report. And this went on all day. A number of students and policemen were injured, but by some miracle no one was killed. The police held their ground, and the Pakistan High Commission remained inviolate. But the Australian High Commission, situated to the rear of the student brigade, received most of the tear gas shells, and had to close down for the day.

Kamal and I attended the siege for about an hour, before retiring to the Gardens with our ham sandwiches.

A couple of friendly squirrels came up to investigate, and were soon taking bread from our hands. We could hear the chanting of the students in the distance. I lay back on the grass and opened my copy of *Barchester Towers*. Whenever life in Delhi, or in Bhabiji's house (or anywhere, for that matter), becomes too tumultuous, I turn to Trollope. Nothing could be further removed from the turmoil of our times than an English cathedral town in the nineteenth century. But I think Jane Austen would have appreciated life in Bhabiji's house.

By ten o'clock, everyone is back from the marriage. (They had gone for the feast, and not for the ceremonies, which continue into the early hours of the morning.) Shobha is full of praise for the bridegroom's good looks and fair complexion. She describes him as being gora chitta—very white! She does not have a high opinion of the bride.

Shiv, in a happy and reflective mood, extols the qualities of his own wife, referring to her as The Barrel. He tells us how, shortly after their marriage, she had threatened to throw a brick at the next-door girl. This little incident remains fresh in Shiv's mind, after eighteen years of marriage.

He says: 'When the neighbours came and complained, I told them, "It is quite possible that my wife will throw a brick at your daughter. She is in the habit of throwing bricks." The neighbours held their peace.'

I think Shiv is rather proud of his wife's militancy when it comes to taking on neighbours; recently she vanquished the woman next door (a formidable Sikh lady) after a verbal battle that lasted three hours. But in arguments or quarrels with Bhabiji, Shiv's wife always loses, because Shiv takes his mother's side.

Arun, on the other hand, is afraid of both wife and mother, and simply makes himself scarce when a quarrel develops. Or he tells his mother she is right, and then, to placate Shobha, takes her to the pictures.

Kishore turns up just as everyone is about to go to bed. Bhabiji is annoyed at first, because he has been drinking too much; but when he produces a bunch of cinema tickets, she is mollified and asks him to stay the night. Not even Bhabiji likes missing a new picture. Kishore is urging me to write his life story.

'Your life would make a most interesting story,' I tell him. 'But it will be interesting only if I put in everything—your successes and your failures.'

'No, no, only successes,' exhorts Kishore. 'I want you to describe me as a popular music director.'

'But you have yet to become popular.'

'I will be popular if you write about me.'

Fortunately we are interrupted by the cots being brought in. Then Bhabiji and Shiv go into a huddle, discussing plans for building an extra room. After all, Kamal may be married soon.

One by one, the children get under their quilts. Popat starts massaging Bhabiji's back. She gives him her favourite blessing: 'God protect you and give you lots of children.' If God listens to all Bhabiji's prayers and blessings, there will never be a fall in the population.

The lights are off and Bhabiji settles down for the night. She is almost asleep when a small voice pipes up: 'Bhabiji, tell us a story.'

At first Bhabiji pretends not to hear; then, when the request is repeated, she says: 'You'll keep Aunty Shobha awake, and then she'll have an excuse for getting up late in the morning.' But the children know Bhabiji's one great weakness, and they renew their demand.

'Your grandmother is tired,' says Arun. 'Let her sleep.'

But Bhabiji's eyes are open. Her mind is going back over the crowded years, and she remembers something very interesting that happened when her younger brother's wife's sister married the eldest son of her third cousin . . .

Before long, the children are asleep, and I am wondering if I will ever sleep, for Bhabiji's voice drones on, into the darker reaches of the night.

TO *the*
HILLS

BINYA
PASSES BY

While I was walking home one day, along the path through the pines, I heard a girl singing.

It was summer in the hills, and the trees were in new leaf. The walnuts and cherries were just beginning to form between the leaves.

The wind was still and the trees were hushed, and the song came to me clearly; but it was not the words—which I could not follow—or the rise and fall of the melody which held me in thrall, but the voice itself, which was a young and tender voice.

I left the path and scrambled down the slope, slipping on fallen pine needles. But when I came to the bottom of the slope the singing had stopped and there was no one there. 'I'm sure I heard someone singing,' I said to myself and then thought I might have been wrong. In the hills it is always possible to be wrong.

So I walked on home, and presently I heard another song, but this time it was the whistling thrush rendering a broken melody, singing a dark, sweet secret in the depths of the forest.

I had little to sing about myself. The electricity bill hadn't been paid, and there was nothing in the bank, and my second novel had just been turned down by another publisher. Still, it was summer and men and animals were drowsy, and so, too, were my creditors. The distant mountains loomed purple in the shimmering dust haze.

I walked through the pines again, but I did not hear the singing. And then for a week I did not leave the cottage, as the novel had to be rewritten, and I worked hard at it, pausing only to eat and sleep and take note of the leaves turning a darker green.

The window opened on to the forest. Trees reached up to the window. Oak, maple, walnut. Higher up the hill, the pines started, and further on, armies of deodars marched over the mountains.

And the mountains rose higher, and the trees grew stunted until they finally disappeared and only the black spirit-haunted rocks rose up to meet the everlasting snows. Those peaks cradled the sky. I could not see them from my windows. But on clear mornings they could be seen from the pass on the Tehri road.

There was a stream at the bottom of the hill. One morning, quite early, I went down to the stream, and using the boulders as stepping stones, moved downstream for about half a mile. Then I lay down to rest on a flat rock in the shade of a wild cherry tree and watched the sun shifting through the branches as it rose over the hill called Pari Tibba (Fairy Hill) and slid down the steep slope into the valley. The air was very still and already the birds were silent. The only sound came from the water running over the stony bed of the stream. I had lain there ten, perhaps fifteen, minutes, when I began to feel that someone was watching me.

Someone in the trees, in the shadows, still and watchful. Nothing moved; not a stone shifted, not a twig broke. But someone was watching me. I felt terribly exposed; not to danger, but to the scrutiny of unknown eyes. So I left the rock and, finding a path through the trees, began climbing the hill again.

It was warm work. The sun was up, and there was no breeze. I was perspiring profusely by the time I got to the top of the hill. There was no sign of my unseen watcher. Two lean cows grazed on the short grass; the tinkling of their bells was the only sound in the sultry summer air.

That song again! The same song, the same singer. I heard her from my window. And putting aside the book I was reading, I leant out of the window and started down through the trees. But the foliage was too heavy and the singer too far away for me to be able to make her out. 'Should I go and look for her?' I wondered. 'Or is it better this way—heard but not seen? For, having fallen in love with a song, must it follow that I will fall in love with the singer? No. But surely it is the voice and not the song that has touched me . . .' Presently the singing ended, and I turned away from the window.

A girl was gathering bilberries on the hillside. She was fresh-faced, honey-coloured. Her lips were stained with purple juice. She smiled at me. 'Are they good to eat?' I asked.

She opened her fist and thrust out her hand, which was full of berries, bruised and crushed. I took one and put it in my mouth.

It had a sharp, sour taste. 'It is good,' I said. Finding that I could speak haltingly in her language, she came nearer, said, 'Take more then,' and filled my hand with bilberries. Her fingers touched mine. The sensation was almost unique, for it was nine or ten years since my hand had touched a girl's.

'Where do you live?' I asked. She pointed across the valley to where a small village straddled the slopes of a terraced hill.

'It's quite far,' I said. 'Do you always come so far from home?'

'I go further than this,' she said. 'The cows must find fresh grass. And there is wood to gather and grass to cut.' She showed me the sickle held by the cloth tied firmly about her waist. 'Sometimes I go to the top of Pari Tibba, sometimes to the valley beyond. Have you been there?'

'No. But I will go some day.'

'It is always windy on Pari Tibba.'

'Is it true that there are fairies there?'

She laughed. 'That is what people say. But those are people who have never been there. I do not see fairies on Pari Tibba. It is said that there are ghosts in the ruins on the hill. But I do not see any ghosts.'

'I have heard of the ghosts,' I said. 'Two lovers who ran away and took shelter in a ruined cottage. At night there was a storm, and they were killed by lightning. Is it true, this story?'

'It happened many years ago, before I was born. I have heard the story. But there are no ghosts on Pari Tibba.'

'How old are you?' I asked.

'Fifteen, sixteen, I do not know for sure.'

'Doesn't your mother know?'

'She is dead. And my grandmother has forgotten. And my brother, he is younger than me and he's forgotten his own age. Is it important to remember?'

'No, it is not important. Not here, anyway. Not in the hills. To a mountain, a hundred years are but as a day.'

'Are you very old?' she asked.

'I hope not. Do I look very old?'

'Only a hundred,' she said, and laughed, and the silver bangles on her wrists tinkled as she put her hands up to her laughing face.

'Why do you laugh?' I asked.

'Because you looked as though you believed me. How old are you?'

'Thirty-five, thirty-six, I do not remember.'

'Ah, it is better to forget!'

'That's true,' I said, 'but sometimes one has to fill in forms and things like that, and then one has to state one's age.'

'I have never filled a form. I have never seen one.'

'And I hope you never will. It is a piece of paper covered with useless information. It is all a part of human progress.'

'Progress?'

'Yes. Are you unhappy?'

'No.'

'Do you go hungry?'

'No.'

'Then you don't need progress. Wild bilberries are better.'

She went away without saying goodbye. The cows had strayed and she ran after them, calling them by name: 'Neelu, Neelu!' (Blue) and 'Bhuri!' (Old One). Her bare feet moved swiftly over the rocks and dry grass.

Early May. The cicadas were singing in the forest; or rather, orchestrating, since they make the sound with their legs. The whistling thrushes pursued each other over the treetops in acrobatic love flights. Sometimes the langoors visited the oak trees to feed on the leaves. As I moved down the path to the stream, I heard the same singing, and coming suddenly upon the clearing near the water's edge I saw the girl sitting on a rock, her feet in the rushing water—the same girl who had given me bilberries. Strangely enough, I had not guessed that she was the singer. Unseen voices conjure up fanciful images. I had imagined a woodland nymph, a graceful, delicate, beautiful, goddess-like creature, not a mischievous-eyed, round-faced, juice-stained, slightly ragged pixie. Her dhoti—a rough, homespun sari—was faded and torn; an impractical garment, I thought, for running about on the hillside, but the village folk put their girls into dhotis before they are twelve. She'd compromised by hitching it up and by strengthening the waist with a length of cloth bound tightly about her, but she'd have been more at ease in the long, flounced skirt worn in the hills further away.

But I was not disillusioned. I had clearly taken a fancy to her cherubic, open countenance; and the sweetness of her voice added to her charms.

I watched her from the banks of the stream, and presently she looked up, grinned, and stuck her tongue out at me.

'That's a nice way to greet me,' I said. 'Have I offended you?'

'You surprised me. Why did you not call out?'

'Because I was listening to your singing. I did not wish to speak until you had finished.'

'It was only a song.'

'But you sang it sweetly.'

She smiled. 'Have you brought anything to eat?'

'No. Are you hungry?'

'At this time I get hungry. When you come to meet me you must always bring something to eat.'

'But I didn't come to meet you. I didn't know you would be here.'

'You do not wish to meet me?'

'I didn't mean that. It is nice to meet you.'

'You will meet me if you keep coming into the forest. So always bring something to eat.'

'I will do so next time. Shall I pick you some berries?'

'You will have to go to the top of the hill again to find the kingora bushes.'

'I don't mind. If you are hungry, I will bring some.'

'All right,' she said, and looked down at her feet, which were still in the water.

Like some knight errant of old, I toiled up the hill again until I found the bilberry bushes, and stuffing my pockets with berries I returned to the stream. But when I got there I found she'd slipped away. The cowbells tinkled on the far hill.

Glow-worms shone fitfully in the dark. The night was full of sounds—the tonk-tonk of a nightjar, the cry of a barking deer, the shuffling of porcupines, the soft flip-fop of moths beating against the windowpanes. On the hill across the valley, lights flickered in the small village—the dim lights of kerosene lamps swinging in the dark.

'What is your name?' I asked, when we met again on the path through the pine forest.

'Binya,' she said. 'What is yours?'

'I've no name.'

'All right, Mr No-name.'

'I mean I haven't made a name for myself. We must make our own names, don't you think?'

'Binya is my name. I do not wish to have any other. Where are you going?'

'Nowhere.'

'No-name goes nowhere! Then you cannot come with me, because I am going home and my grandmother will set the village dogs on you if you follow me.' And laughing, she ran down the path to the stream; she knew I could not catch up with her.

Her face streamed summer rain as she climbed the steep hill, calling the white cow home. She seemed very tiny on the windswept mountainside. A twist of hair lay flat against her forehead and her torn blue dhoti clung to her firm round thighs. I went to her with an umbrella to give her shelter. She stood with me beneath the umbrella and let me put my arm around her. Then she turned her face up to mine, wanderingly, and I kissed her quickly, softly on the lips. Her lips tasted of raindrops and mint. And then she left me there, so gallant in the blistering rain. She ran home laughing. But it was worth the drenching.

Another day I heard her calling to me—'No-name, Mister No-name!'—but I couldn't see her, and it was some time before I found her, halfway up a cherry tree, her feet pressed firmly against the bark, her dhoti tucked up between her thighs—fair, rounded thighs, and legs that were strong and vigorous.

'The cherries are not ripe,' I said.

'They are never ripe. But I like them green and sour. Will you come on to the tree?'

'If I can still climb a tree,' I said.

'My grandmother is over sixty, and she can climb trees.'

'Well, I wouldn't mind being more adventurous at sixty. There's not so much to lose then.' I climbed on to the tree without much difficulty, but I did not think the higher branches would take my weight, so I remained standing in the fork of the tree, my face on a level with Binya's breasts. I put my hand against her waist, and kissed her on the soft inside of her arm. She did not say anything. But she took me by the hand and helped me to climb a little higher, and I put my arm around her, as much to support myself as to be close to her.

The full moon rides high, shining through the tall oak trees near the window. The night is full of sounds—crickets, the tonk-tonk of a nightjar, and floating across the valley from your village the sound of drums beating and people singing. It is a festival day, and there will be feasting in your home. Are you singing too, tonight? And are you thinking of me, as you sing, as you laugh, as you dance with your friends? I am sitting here alone, and so I have no one to think of but you.

Binya . . . I take your name again and again—as though by taking it I can make you hear me, and come to me, walking over the moonlit mountain . . .

There are spirits abroad tonight. They move silently in the trees; they hover about the window at which I sit; they take up with the wind and rush about the house. Spirits of the trees, spirits of the old house. An old lady died here last year. She'd lived in the house for over thirty years; something of her personality surely dwells here still. When I look into the tall, old mirror which was hers, I sometimes catch a glimpse of her pale face and long, golden hair. She likes me, I think, and the house is kind to me. Would she be jealous of you, Binya?

The music and singing grows louder. I can imagine your face glowing in the firelight. Your eyes shine with laughter. You have all those people near you and I have only the stars, and the nightjar, and the ghost in the mirror.

I woke early, while the dew was still fresh on the grass, and walked down the hill to the stream, and then up to a little knoll where a pine tree grew in solitary splendour, the wind going hoo-hoo in its slender branches. This was my favourite place, my place of power, where I came to renew myself from time to time. I lay on the grass, dreaming. The sky in its blueness swung round above me. An eagle soared in the distance. I heard her voice down among the trees; or I thought I heard it. But when I went to look, I could not find her.

I'd always prided myself on my rationality, had taught myself to be wary of emotional states, like 'falling in love', which turned out to be ephemeral and illusory. And although I told myself again and again that the attraction was purely physical, on my part as well as hers, I had to admit to myself that my feelings towards Binya differed from the feelings I'd had for others; and that while sex had often been for me a celebration, it had, like any other feast, resulted in satiety, a need for change, a desire to forget . . .

Binya represented something else—something wild, dream-like, fairy-like. She moved close to the spirit-haunted rocks, the old trees, the young grass. She had absorbed something from them—a primeval innocence, an unconcern with the passing of time and events, an affinity with the forest and the mountains, and this made her special and magical.

And so, when three, four, five days went by, and I did not find her on the hillside, I went through all the pangs of frustrated love: had she forgotten me and gone elsewhere? Had we been seen together, and was she being kept at home? Was she ill? Or had she been spirited away?

I could hardly go and ask for her. I would probably be driven from the village. It straddled the opposite hill, a cluster of slate-roof houses, a pattern of little terraced fields. I could see figures in the fields, but they were too far away, too tiny, for me to be able to recognize anyone.

She had gone to her mother's village a hundred miles away, or so, a small boy told me.

And so I brooded; walked disconsolately through the oak forest, hardly listening to the birds—the sweet-throated whistling thrush; the shrill barbet; the mellow-voiced doves. Happiness had always made me more responsive to nature. Feeling miserable, my thoughts turned inward. I brooded upon the trickery of time and circumstance; I felt the years were passing by, had passed by, like waves on a receding tide, leaving me washed up like a bit of flotsam on a lonely beach. But at the same time, the whistling thrush seemed to mock at me, calling tantalizingly from the shadows of the ravine: 'It isn't time that's passing by, it is you and I, it is you and I . . .'

Then I forced myself to snap out of my melancholy. I kept away from the hillside and the forest. I did not look towards the village. I buried myself in my work, tried to think objectively, and wrote an article on 'The Inscriptions on the Iron Pillar at Kalsi'; very learned, very dry, very sensible.

But at night I was assailed by thoughts of Binya. I could not sleep. I switched on the light, and there she was, smiling at me from the looking glass, replacing the image of the old lady who had watched over me for so long.

WILSON'S
BRIDGE

The old wooden bridge has gone, and today an iron suspension bridge straddles the Bhagirathi as it rushes down the gorge below Gangotri. But villagers will tell you that you can still hear the hooves of Wilson's horse as he gallops across the bridge he had built a hundred and fifty years ago. At the time people were sceptical of its safety, and so, to prove its sturdiness, he rode across it again and again. Parts of the old bridge can still be seen on the far bank of the river. And the legend of Wilson and his pretty hill bride, Gulabi, is still well known in this region.

I had joined some friends in the old forest rest house near the river. There were the Rays, recently married, and the Duttas, married many years. The younger Rays quarrelled frequently; the older Duttas looked on with more amusement than concern. I was a part of their group and yet something of an outsider. As a single man, I was a person of no importance. And as a marriage counsellor, I wouldn't have been of any use to them.

I spent most of my time wandering along the river banks or exploring the thick deodar and oak forests that covered the slopes. It was these trees that had made a fortune for Wilson and his patron, the raja of Tehri. They had exploited the great forests to the full, floating huge logs downstream to the timber yards in the plains.

Returning to the rest house late one evening, I was halfway across the bridge when I saw a figure at the other end, emerging from the mist. Presently I made out a woman, wearing the plain dhoti of the hills; her hair fell loose over her shoulders. She appeared not to see me, and reclined against the railing of the bridge, looking down at the rushing waters far below. And then, to my amazement and horror, she climbed over the railing and threw herself into the river.

I ran forward, calling out, but I reached the railing only to see her fall into the foaming waters below, where she was carried swiftly downstream.

The watchman's cabin stood a little way off. The door was open. The watchman, Ram Singh, was reclining on his bed, smoking a hookah.

'Someone just jumped off the bridge,' I said breathlessly. 'She's been swept down the river!'

The watchman was unperturbed. 'Gulabi again,' he said, almost to himself; and then to me, 'Did you see her clearly?'

'Yes, a woman with long loose hair—but I didn't see her face very clearly.'

'It must have been Gulabi. Only a ghost, my dear sir. Nothing to be alarmed about. Every now and then someone sees her throw herself into the river. Sit down,' he said, gesturing towards a battered old armchair, 'be comfortable and I'll tell you all about it.'

I was far from comfortable, but I listened to Ram Singh tell me the tale of Gulabi's suicide. After making me a glass of hot sweet tea, he launched into a long, rambling account of how Wilson, a British adventurer seeking his fortune, had been hunting musk deer when he encountered Gulabi on the path from her village. The girl's grey-green eyes and peach-blossom complexion enchanted him, and he went out of his way to get to know her people. Was he in love with her, or did he simply find her beautiful and desirable? We shall never really know. In the course of his travels and adventures he had known many women, but Gulabi was different, childlike and ingenuous, and he decided he would marry her. The humble family to which she belonged had no objection. Hunting had its limitations, and Wilson found it more profitable to trap the region's great forest wealth. In a few years he had made a fortune. He built a large timbered house at Harsil, another in Dehra Dun and a third at Mussoorie. Gulabi had all she could have wanted, including two robust little sons. When he was away on work, she looked after their children and their large apple orchard at Harsil.

And then came the evil day when Wilson met the Englishwoman, Ruth, on the Mussoorie Mall, and decided that she should have a share of his affections and his wealth. A fine house was provided for her, too. The time he spent at Harsil with Gulabi and his children dwindled. 'Business affairs'—he was now one of the owners of a bank—kept him in the fashionable hill resort. He was a popular host and took his friends and associates on shikar parties in the Doon.

Gulabi brought up her children in village style. She heard stories of Wilson's dalliance with the Mussoorie woman and, on one of his rare visits, she confronted him and voiced her resentment, demanding that he leave the other woman. He brushed her aside and told her not to listen to idle gossip. When he turned away from her, she picked up the flintlock pistol that lay on the gun table and fired one shot at him. The bullet missed him and shattered her looking glass. Gulabi ran out of the house, through the orchard and into the forest, then down the steep path to the bridge built by Wilson only two or three years before. When he had recovered his composure, he mounted his horse and came looking for her. It was too late. She had already thrown herself off the bridge into the swirling waters far below. Her body was found a mile or two downstream, caught between some rocks.

This was the tale that Ram Singh told me, with various flourishes and interpolations of his own. I thought it would make a good story to tell my friends that evening, before the fireside in the rest house. They found the story fascinating, but when I told them I had seen Gulabi's ghost, they thought I was doing a little embroidering of my own. Mrs Dutta thought it was a tragic tale. Young Mrs Ray thought Gulabi had been very silly. 'She was a simple girl,' opined Mr Dutta. 'She responded in the only way she knew . . .'; 'Money can't buy happiness,' said Mr Ray. 'No,' said Mrs Dutta, 'but it can buy you a great many comforts.' Mrs Ray wanted to talk of other things, so I changed the subject. It can get a little confusing for a bachelor who must spend the evening with two married couples. There are undercurrents which he is aware of but not equipped to deal with.

I would walk across the bridge quite often after that. It was busy with traffic during the day, but after dusk there were only a few vehicles on the road and seldom any pedestrians. A mist rose from the gorge below and obscured the far end of the bridge. I preferred walking there in the evening, half-expecting, half-hoping to see Gulabi's ghost again. It was her face that I really wanted to see. Would she still be as beautiful as she was fabled to be?

It was on the evening before our departure that something happened that would haunt me for a long time afterwards.

There was a feeling of restiveness as our days there drew to a close. The Rays had apparently made up their differences, although they weren't talking very much. Mr Dutta was anxious to get back to his office in Delhi and Mrs Dutta's rheumatism was playing up. I was restless too, wanting to return to my writing desk in Mussoorie.

That evening I decided to take one last stroll across the bridge to enjoy the cool breeze of a summer's night in the mountains. The moon hadn't come up, and it was really quite dark, although there were lamps at either end of the bridge providing sufficient light for those who wished to cross over.

I was standing in the middle of the bridge, in the darkest part, listening to the river thundering down the gorge, when I saw the sari-draped figure emerging from the lamplight and making towards the railings.

Instinctively I called out, 'Gulabi!'

She half-turned towards me, but I could not see her clearly. The wind had blown her hair across her face and all I saw was wildly staring eyes. She raised herself over the railing and threw herself off the bridge. I heard the splash as her body struck the water far below.

Once again I found myself running towards the part of the railing where she had jumped. And then someone was running towards the same spot, from the direction of the rest house. It was young Mr Ray.

'My wife!' he cried out. 'Did you see my wife?'

He rushed to the railing and stared down at the swirling waters of the river.

'Look! There she is!' He pointed at a helpless figure bobbing about in the water.

We ran down the steep bank to the river but the current had swept her on. Scrambling over rocks and bushes, we made frantic efforts to catch up with the drowning woman. But the river in that defile is a roaring torrent, and it was over an hour before we were able to retrieve poor Mrs Ray's body, caught in driftwood about a mile downstream.

She was cremated not far from where we found her and we returned to our various homes in gloom and grief, chastened but none the wiser for the experience.

If you happen to be in that area and decide to cross the bridge late in the evening, you might see Gulabi's ghost or hear the hoofbeats of Wilson's horse as he canters across the old wooden bridge looking for her. Or you might see the ghost of Mrs Ray and hear her husband's anguished cry. Or there might be others. Who knows?

THE
MONKEYS

I couldn't be sure, next morning, if I had been dreaming or if I had really heard dogs barking in the night and had seen them scampering about on the hillside below the cottage. There had been a golden Cocker, a Retriever, a Peke, a Dachshund, a black Labrador and one or two nondescripts. They had woken me with their barking shortly after midnight, and had made so much noise that I had got out of bed and looked out of the open window. I saw them quite plainly in the moonlight, five or six dogs rushing excitedly through the bracket and long monsoon grass.

It was only because there had been so many breeds among the dogs that I felt a little confused. I had been in the cottage only a week, and I was already on nodding or speaking terms with most of my neighbours. Colonel Fanshawe, retired from the Indian army, was my immediate neighbour. He did keep a Cocker, but it was black. The elderly Anglo-Indian spinsters who lived beyond the deodars kept only cats. (Though why cats should be the prerogative of spinsters, I have never been able to understand.) The milkman kept a couple of mongrels. And the Punjabi industrialist who had bought a former prince's palace—without ever occupying it—left the property in charge of a watchman who kept a huge Tibetan mastiff.

None of these dogs looked like the ones I had seen in the night.

'Does anyone here keep a Retriever?' I asked Colonel Fanshawe, when I met him taking his evening walk.

'No one that I know of,' he said and gave me a swift, penetrating look from under his bushy eyebrows. 'Why, have you seen one around?'

'No, I just wondered. There are a lot of dogs in the area, aren't there?'

'Oh, yes. Nearly everyone keeps a dog here. Of course, every now and then a panther carries one off. Lost a lovely little terrier myself only last winter.'

Colonel Fanshawe, tall and red-faced, seemed to be waiting for me to tell him something more—or was he just taking time to recover his breath after a stiff uphill climb?

That night I heard the dogs again. I went to the window and looked out. The moon was at the full, silvering the leaves of the oak trees.

The dogs were looking up into the trees and barking. But I could see nothing in the trees, not even an owl.

I gave a shout, and the dogs disappeared into the forest.

Colonel Fanshawe looked at me expectantly when I met him the following day. He knew something about those dogs, of that I was certain; but he was waiting to hear what I had to say. I decided to oblige him.

'I saw at least six dogs in the middle of the night,' I said. 'A Cocker, a Retriever, a Peke, a Dachshund and two mongrels. Now, Colonel, I'm sure you must know whose they are.'

The colonel was delighted. I could tell by the way his eyes glinted that he was going to enjoy himself at my expense.

'You've been seeing Miss Fairchild's dogs,' he said with smug satisfaction.

'Oh, and where does she live?'

'She doesn't, my boy. Died fifteen years ago.'

'Then what are her dogs doing here?'

'Looking for monkeys,' said the colonel. And he stood back to watch my reaction.

'I'm afraid I don't understand,' I said.

'Let me put it this way,' said the colonel. 'Do you believe in ghosts?'

'I've never seen any,' I said.

'But you have, my boy, you have. Miss Fairchild's dogs died years ago—a Cocker, a Retriever, a Dachshund, a Peke and two mongrels. They were buried on a little knoll under the oaks. Nothing odd about their deaths, mind you.

They were all quite old, and didn't survive their mistress very long. Neighbours looked after them until they died.'

'And Miss Fairchild lived in the cottage where I stay? Was she young?'

'She was in her mid-forties, an athletic sort of woman, fond of the outdoors. Didn't care much for men. I thought you knew about her.'

'No, I haven't been here very long, you know. But what was it you said about monkeys? Why were the dogs looking for monkeys?'

'Ah, that's the interesting part of the story. Have you seen the langoor monkeys that sometimes come to eat oak leaves?'

'No.'

'You will, sooner or later. There has always been a band of them roaming these forests. They're quite harmless really, except that they'll ruin a garden if given half a chance . . . Well, Miss Fairchild fairly loathed those monkeys. She was very keen on her dahlias—grew some prize specimens—but the monkeys would come at night, dig up the plants and eat the dahlia bulbs. Apparently they found the bulbs much to their liking. Miss Fairchild would be furious. People who are passionately fond of gardening often go off balance when their best plants are ruined—that's only human, I suppose. Miss Fairchild set her dogs on the monkeys whenever she could, even if it was in the middle of the night. But the monkeys simply took to the trees and left the dogs barking.

'Then one day—or rather one night—Miss Fairchild took desperate measures. She borrowed a shotgun and sat up near a window. And when the monkeys arrived, she shot one of them dead.'

The colonel paused and looked out over the oak trees which were shimmering in the warm afternoon sun.

'She shouldn't have done that,' he said.

'Never shoot a monkey. It's not only that they're sacred to Hindus—but they are rather human, you know. Well, I must be getting on. Good day!' And the colonel, having ended his story rather abruptly, set off at a brisk pace through the deodars.

I didn't hear the dogs that night. But the next day I saw the monkeys—the real ones, not ghosts. There were about twenty of them, young and old, sitting in the trees munching oak leaves. They didn't pay much attention to me, and I watched them for some time.

They were handsome creatures, their fur a silver-grey, their tails long and sinuous. They leapt gracefully from tree to tree, and were very polite and dignified in their behaviour towards each other—unlike the bold, rather crude red monkeys of the plains. Some of the younger ones scampered about on the hillside, playing and wrestling with each other like schoolboys.

There were no dogs to molest them—and no dahlias to tempt them into the garden.

But that night, I heard the dogs again. They were barking more furiously than ever.

'Well, I'm not getting up for them this time,' I mumbled, and pulled the blanket over my ears.

But the barking grew louder, and was joined by other sounds, a squealing and a scuffling.

Then suddenly, the piercing shriek of a woman rang through the forest. It was an unearthly sound, and it made my hair stand up.

I leapt out of bed and dashed to the window.

A woman was lying on the ground, three or four huge monkeys were on top of her, biting her arms and pulling at her throat. The dogs were yelping and trying to drag the monkeys off, but they were being harried from behind by others. The woman gave another bloodcurdling shriek, and I dashed back into the room, grabbed hold of a small axe and ran into the garden.

But everyone—dogs, monkeys and shrieking woman— had disappeared, and I stood alone on the hillside in my pyjamas, clutching an axe and feeling very foolish.

The colonel greeted me effusively the following day.

'Still seeing those dogs?' he asked in a bantering tone.

'I've seen the monkeys too,' I said.

'Oh, yes, they've come around again. But they're real enough, and quite harmless.'

'I know—but I saw them last night with the dogs.'

'Oh, did you really? That's strange, very strange.'

The colonel tried to avoid my eye, but I hadn't quite finished with him.

'Colonel,' I said. 'You never did get around to telling me how Miss Fairchild died.'

'Oh, didn't I? Must have slipped my memory. I'm getting old, don't remember people as well as I used to. But, of course, I remember about Miss Fairchild, poor lady. The monkeys killed her. Didn't you know? They simply tore her to pieces . . .'

His voice trailed of, and he looked thoughtfully at a caterpillar that was making its way up his walking stick.

'She shouldn't have shot one of them,' he said. 'Never shoot a monkey—they're rather human, you know . . .'

THE PROSPECT
of FLOWERS

Fern Hill, The Oaks, Hunter's Lodge, The Parsonage, The Pines, Dumbarnie, Mackinnon's Hall and Windermere. These are the names of some of the old houses that still stand on the outskirts of one of the smaller Indian hill stations. Most of them have fallen into decay and ruin. They are very old, of course—built over a hundred years ago by Britishers who sought relief from the searing heat of the plains. Today's visitors to the hill stations prefer to live near the markets and cinemas, and many of the old houses, set amidst oak and maple and deodar, are inhabited by wild cats, bandicoots, owls, goats and the occasional charcoal burner or mule driver.

But amongst these neglected mansions stands a neat, whitewashed cottage called Mulberry Lodge. And in it, up to a short time ago, lived an elderly English spinster named Miss Mackenzie.

In years Miss Mackenzie was more than 'elderly', being well over eighty. But no one would have guessed it. She was clean, sprightly, and wore old-fashioned but well-preserved dresses. Once a week, she walked the two miles to town to buy butter and jam and soap and sometimes a small bottle of eau de cologne.

She had lived in the hill station since she had been a girl in her teens, and that had been before the First World War. Though she had never married, she had experienced a few love affairs and was far from being the typical frustrated spinster of fiction. Her parents had been dead thirty years; her brother and sister were also dead. She had no relatives in India, and she lived on a small pension of forty rupees a month and the gift parcels that were sent out to her from New Zealand by a friend of her youth.

Like other lonely old people, she kept a pet—a large black cat with bright yellow eyes. In her small garden she grew dahlias, chrysanthemums, gladioli and a few rare orchids. She knew a great deal about plants and about wild flowers, trees, birds and insects. She had never made a serious study of these things, but having lived with them for so many years had developed an intimacy with all that grew and flourished around her.

She had few visitors. Occasionally, the padre from the local church called on her, and once a month the postman came with a letter from New Zealand or her pension papers.

The milkman called every second day with a litre of milk for the lady and her cat. And sometimes she received a couple of eggs free, for the egg seller remembered a time when Miss Mackenzie, in her earlier prosperity, had bought eggs from him in large quantities. He was a sentimental man. He remembered her as a ravishing beauty in her twenties when he had gazed at her in round-eyed, nine-year-old wonder and consternation.

Now it was September and the rains were nearly over, and Miss Mackenzie's chrysanthemums were coming into their own. She hoped the coming winter wouldn't be too severe because she found it increasingly difficult to bear the cold.

One day, as she was pottering about in her garden, she saw a schoolboy plucking wild flowers on the slope about the cottage.

'Who's that?' she called. 'What are you up to, young man?'

The boy was alarmed and tried to dash up the hillside, but he slipped on pine needles and came slithering down the slope on to Miss Mackenzie's nasturtium bed.

When he found there was no escape, he gave a bright disarming smile and said, 'Good morning, miss.'

He belonged to the local English-medium school and wore a bright red blazer and a red and black striped tie. Like most polite Indian schoolboys, he called every woman 'miss'.

'Good morning,' said Miss Mackenzie severely. 'Would you mind moving out of my flower bed?'

The boy stepped gingerly over the nasturtiums and looked up at Miss Mackenzie with dimpled cheeks and appealing eyes. It was impossible to be angry with him.

'You're trespassing,' said Miss Mackenzie.

'Yes, miss.'

'And you ought to be in school at this hour.'

'Yes, miss.'

'Then what are you doing here?'

'Picking flowers, miss.' And he held up a bunch of ferns and wild flowers.

'Oh,' Miss Mackenzie was disarmed. It was a long time since she had seen a boy taking an interest in flowers, and, what was more, playing truant from school in order to gather them.

'Do you like flowers?' she asked.

'Yes, miss. I'm going to be a botan—a botantist?'

'You mean a botanist.'

'Yes, miss.'

'Well, that's unusual. Most boys at your age want to be pilots or soldiers or perhaps engineers. But you want to be a botanist. Well, well. There's still hope for the world, I see. And do you know the names of these flowers?'

'This is a bukhilo flower,' he said, showing her a small golden flower. 'That's a Pahari name. It means puja or prayer. The flower is offered during prayers. But I don't know what this is . . .'

He held out a pale pink flower with a soft, heart-shaped leaf.

'It's a wild begonia,' said Miss Mackenzie. 'And that purple stuff is salvia, but it isn't wild. It's a plant that escaped from my garden. Don't you have any books on flowers?'

'No, miss.'

'All right, come in and I'll show you a book.'

She led the boy into a small front room, which was crowded with furniture and books and vases and jam jars, and offered him a chair. He sat awkwardly on its edge. The black cat immediately leapt on to his knees, and settled down on them, purring loudly.

'What's your name?' asked Miss Mackenzie, as she rummaged through her books.

'Anil, miss.'

'And where do you live?'

'When school closes, I go to Delhi. My father has a business.'

'Oh, and what's that?'

'Bulbs, miss.'

'Flower bulbs?'

'No, electric bulbs.'

'Electric bulbs! You might send me a few, when you get home. Mine are always fusing, and they're so expensive, like everything else these days. Ah, here we are!' She pulled a heavy volume down from the shelf and laid it on the table. '*Flora Himaliensis*, published in 1892, and probably the only copy in India. This is a very valuable book, Anil. No other naturalist has recorded so many wild Himalayan flowers. And let me tell you this, there are many flowers and plants which are still unknown to the fancy botanists who spend all their time with microscopes instead of in the mountains. But perhaps, you'll do something about that, one day.'

'Yes, miss.'

They went through the book together, and Miss Mackenzie pointed out many flowers that grew in and around the hill station, while the boy made notes of their names and seasons. She lit a stove, and put the kettle on for tea. And then the old English lady and the small Indian boy sat side by side over cups of hot sweet tea, absorbed in a book on wild flowers.

'May I come again?' asked Anil, when finally he rose to go.

'If you like,' said Miss Mackenzie. 'But not during school hours. You mustn't miss your classes.'

After that, Anil visited Miss Mackenzie about once a week, and nearly always brought a wild flower for her to identify. She found herself looking forward to the boy's visits—and sometimes, when more than a week passed and he didn't come, she was disappointed and lonely and would grumble at the black cat.

Anil reminded her of her brother, when the latter had been a boy. There was no physical resemblance. Andrew had been fair-haired and blue-eyed. But it was Anil's eagerness, his alert, bright look and the way he stood— legs apart, hands on hips, a picture of confidence—that reminded her of the boy who had shared her own youth in these same hills.

And why did Anil come to see her so often?

Partly because she knew about wild flowers, and he really did want to become a botanist. And partly because she smelt of freshly baked bread, and that was a smell his own grandmother had possessed. And partly because she was lonely and sometimes a boy of twelve can sense loneliness better than an adult. And partly because he was a little different from other children.

By the middle of October, when there was only a fortnight left for the school to close, the first snow had fallen on the distant mountains. One peak stood high above the rest, a white pinnacle against the azure-blue sky. When the sun set, this peak turned from orange to gold to pink to red.

'How high is that mountain?' asked Anil.

'It must be over twelve thousand feet,' said Miss Mackenzie. 'About thirty miles from here, as the crow flies. I always wanted to go there, but there was no proper road. At that height, there'll be flowers that you don't get here— the blue gentian and the purple columbine, the anemone and the edelweiss.'

'I'll go there one day,' said Anil.

'I'm sure you will, if you really want to.'

The day before his school closed, Anil came to say goodbye to Miss Mackenzie.

'I don't suppose you'll be able to find many wild flowers in Delhi,' she said. 'But have a good holiday.'

'Thank you, miss.'

As he was about to leave, Miss Mackenzie, on an impulse, thrust the *Flora Himaliensis* into his hands.

'You keep it,' she said. 'It's a present for you.'

'But I'll be back next year, and I'll be able to look at it then. It's so valuable.'

'I know it's valuable and that's why I've given it to you. Otherwise it will only fall into the hands of the junk dealers.'

'But, miss . . .'

'Don't argue. Besides, I may not be here next year.'

'Are you going away?'

'I'm not sure. I may go to England.'

She had no intention of going to England; she had not seen the country since she was a child, and she knew she would not fit in with the life of post-war Britain. Her home was in these hills, among the oaks and maples and deodars. It was lonely, but at her age it would be lonely anywhere.

The boy tucked the book under his arm, straightened his tie, stood stiffly to attention and said, 'Goodbye, Miss Mackenzie.'

It was the first time he had spoken her name.

Winter set in early and strong winds brought rain and sleet, and soon there were no flowers in the garden or on the hillside. The cat stayed indoors, curled up at the foot of Miss Mackenzie's bed.

Miss Mackenzie wrapped herself up in all her old shawls and mufflers, but still she felt the cold. Her fingers grew so stiff that she took almost an hour to open a can of baked beans. And then it snowed and for several days the milkman did not come. The postman arrived with her pension papers, but she felt too tired to take them up to town to the bank.

She spent most of the time in bed. It was the warmest place. She kept a hot-water bottle at her back, and the cat kept her feet warm. She lay in bed, dreaming of the spring and summer months. In three months' time the primroses would be out, and with the coming of spring the boy would return.

One night the hot-water bottle burst and the bedding was soaked through. As there was no sun for several days, the blanket remained damp. Miss Mackenzie caught a chill and had to keep to her cold, uncomfortable bed. She knew she had a fever but there was no thermometer with which to take her temperature. She had difficulty in breathing.

A strong wind sprang up one night, and the window flew open and kept banging all night. Miss Mackenzie was too weak to get up and close it, and the wind swept the rain and sleet into the room. The cat crept into the bed and snuggled close to its mistress's warm body. But towards morning that body had lost its warmth and the cat left the bed and started scratching about on the floor.

As a shaft of sunlight streamed through the open window, the milkman arrived. He poured some milk into the cat's saucer on the doorstep, and the cat leapt down from the windowsill and made for the milk.

The milkman called a greeting to Miss Mackenzie, but received no answer. Her window was open and he had always known her to be up before sunrise. So he put his head in at the window and called again. But Miss Mackenzie did not answer. She had gone away to the mountain where the blue gentian and purple columbine grew.

WHEN
DARKNESS FALLS

Markham had, for many years, lived alone in a small room adjoining the disused cellars of the old Empire Hotel in one of our hill stations. His army pension gave him enough money to pay for his room rent and his basic needs, but he shunned the outside world—by daylight, anyway—partly because of a natural reticence and partly because he wasn't very nice to look at.

While Markham was serving in Burma during the War, a shell had exploded near his dugout, tearing away most of his face. Plastic surgery was then in its infancy, and although the doctors had done their best, even going to the extent of giving Markham a false nose, his features were permanently ravaged. On the few occasions that he had walked abroad by day, he had been mistaken for someone in the final stages of leprosy and been given a wide berth.

He had been given the basement room by the hotel's elderly estate manager, Negi, who had known Markham in the years before the War, when Negi was just a room-boy. Markham had himself been a youthful assistant manager at the time, and he had helped the eager young Negi advance from room-boy to bartender to office clerk. When Markham took up a wartime commission, Negi rose even further. Now Markham was well into his late sixties, with Negi not very far behind. After a post-War, post-Independence slump, the hill station was thriving again; but both Negi and Markham belonged to another era, another time and place. So did the old hotel, now going to seed, but clinging to its name and surviving on its reputation.

'We're dead, but we won't lie down,' joked Markham, but he didn't find it very funny.

Day after day, alone in the stark simplicity of his room, there was little he could do except read or listen to his short-wave transistor radio; but he would emerge at night to prowl about the vast hotel grounds and occasionally take a midnight stroll along the deserted Mall.

During these forays into the outer world, he wore an old felt hat, which hid part of his face. He had tried wearing a mask, but that had been even more frightening for those who saw it, especially under a street lamp. A couple of honeymooners, walking back to the hotel late at night, had come face to face with Markham and had fled the hill station

455

the next day. Dogs did not like the mask, either. They set up a furious barking at Markham's approach, stopping only when he removed the mask; they did not seem to mind his face. A policeman returning home late had accosted Markham, suspecting him of being a burglar, and snatched off the mask. Markham, sans nose, jaw and one eye, had smiled a crooked smile, and the policeman had taken to his heels. Thieves and goondas he could handle; not ghostly apparitions straight out of hell.

Apart from Negi, only a few knew of Markham's existence. These were the lower-paid employees who had grown used to him over the years, as one gets used to a lame dog or a crippled cow. The gardener, the sweeper, the dhobi, the night chowkidar, all knew him as a sort of presence. They did not look at him. A man with one eye is said to have the evil eye; and one baleful glance from Markham's single eye was enough to upset anyone with a superstitious nature. He had no problems with the menial staff, and he wisely kept away from the hotel lobby, bar, dining room and corridors—he did not want to frighten the customers away; that would have spelt an end to his own liberty. The owner, who was away most of the time, did not know of his existence; nor did his wife, who lived in the east wing of the hotel, where Markham had never ventured.

The hotel covered a vast area, which included several unused buildings and decaying outhouses. There was a beer garden, no longer frequented, overgrown with weeds and untamed shrubbery. There were tennis courts, rarely used; a squash court, inhabited by a family of goats; a children's playground with a broken see-saw; a ballroom which hadn't seen a ball in fifty years; cellars which were never opened; and a billiard room, said to be haunted.

As his name implied, Markham's forebears were English, with a bit of Allahabad thrown in. It was said that he was related to Kipling on his mother's side; but he never made this claim himself. He had fair hair and one grey-blue eye. The other, of course, was missing.

His artificial nose could be removed whenever he wished, and as he found it a little uncomfortable he usually took it off when he was alone in his room. It rested on his bedside table, staring at the ceiling. Over the years it had acquired a character of its own, and those (like Negi) who had seen it looked upon it with a certain amount of awe. Markham avoided looking at himself in the mirror, but sometimes he had to shave one side of his face, which included a few surviving teeth. There was a gaping hole in his left cheek. And after all these years, it still looked raw.

When it was past midnight, Markham emerged from his lair and prowled the grounds of the old hotel. They belonged to him, really, as no one else patrolled them at that hour—not even the night chowkidar, who was usually to be found asleep on a tattered sofa outside the lounge.

Wearing his old hat and cape, Markham did his rounds.

He was a ghostly figure, no doubt, and the few who had glimpsed him in those late hours had taken him for a supernatural visitor. In this way the hotel had acquired a reputation of being haunted. Some guests liked the idea of having a resident ghost; others stayed away.

On this particular night Markham was more restless than usual, more discontented with himself in particular and with the world in general; he wanted a little change— and who wouldn't in similar circumstances?

He had promised Negi that he would avoid the interior of the hotel as far as possible; but it was midsummer—the days were warm and languid, the nights cool and balmy— and he felt like being in the proximity of other humans even if he could not socialize with them.

And so, late at night, he slipped out of the passage to his cellar room and ascended the steps that led to the old banquet hall, now just a huge dining room. A single light was burning at the end of the hall. Beneath it stood an old piano.

Markham lifted the lid and ran his fingers over the keys. He could still pick out a tune, although it was many years since he had played for anyone or even for himself. Now at least he could indulge himself a little. An old song came back to him, and he played it softly, hesitantly, recalling a few words:

> But it's a long, long time, from May to December,
> And the days grow short when we reach September . . .

458

He couldn't remember all the words, so he just hummed a little as he played. Suddenly, something came down with a crash at the other end of the room. Markham looked up, startled. The hotel cat had knocked over a soup tureen that had been left on one of the tables. Seeing Markham's tall, shifting shadow on the wall, its hair stood on end. And with a long, low wail it fled the banquet room.

Markham left too, and made his way up the carpeted staircase to the first-floor corridor.

Not all the rooms were occupied. They seldom were these days. He tried one or two doors, but they were locked. He walked to the end of the passage and tried the last door. It was open.

Assuming the room was unoccupied, he entered it quietly. The lights were off, but there was sufficient moonlight coming through the large bay window with its view of the mountains. Markham looked towards the large double bed and saw that it was occupied. A young couple lay there, fast asleep, wrapped in each other's arms. A touching sight! Markham smiled bitterly. It was over forty years since anyone had lain in his arms.

There were footsteps in the passage. Someone stood outside the closed door. Had Markham been seen prowling about the corridors? He moved swiftly to the window, unlatched it, and stepped quickly out on to the landing abutting the roof. Quietly he closed the window and moved away.

Outside, on the roof, he felt an overwhelming sense of freedom. No one would find him there. He wondered why he hadn't thought of the roof before. Being on it gave him a feeling of ownership. The hotel, and all who lived in it, belonged to him.

The lights, from a few skylights and the moon above, helped him to move unhindered over the sloping, corrugated old tin roof.

He looked out at the mountains, striding away into the heavens. He felt at one with them.

The owner, Mr Khanna, was away on one of his extended trips abroad. Known to his friends as the Playboy of the Western World, he spent a great deal of his time and money in foreign capitals: London, Paris, New York, Amsterdam. Mr Khanna's wife had health problems (mostly in her mind) and seldom travelled, except to visit godmen and faith healers. At this point in time she was suffering from insomnia, and was pacing about her room in her dressing gown, a loose-fitting garment that did little to conceal her overblown figure; for inspite of her many ailments, her appetite for everything on the menu card was undiminished. Right now she was looking for her sleeping tablets. Where on earth had she put them? They were not on her bedside table; not on the dressing table; not on the bathroom shelf. Perhaps they were in her handbag. She rummaged through a drawer, found and opened the bag, and extracted a strip of Valium. Pouring herself a glass of water from the bedside carafe, she tossed her head back, revealing several layers of chin. Before she could swallow the tablet, she saw a face at the skylight. Not really a face. Not a human face, that is. An empty eye socket, a wicked grin and a nose that wasn't a nose, pressed flat against the glass.

Mrs Khanna sank to the floor and passed out. She had no need of the sleeping tablet that night.

For the next couple of days Mrs Khanna was quite hysterical and spoke wildly of a wolf-man or rakshas who was pursuing her. But no one—not even Negi—attributed the apparition to Markham, who had always avoided the guests' rooms.

The daylight hours he passed in his cellar room, which received only a dapple of late afternoon sunlight through a narrow aperture that passed for a window. For about ten minutes the sun rested on a framed picture of Markham's mother, a severe-looking but handsome woman who must have been in her forties when the picture was taken. His father, an army captain, had been killed in the trenches at Mons during the First World War. His picture stood there, too; a dashing figure in uniform. Sometimes Markham wished that he, too, had died from his wounds; but he had been kept alive, and then he had stayed dead-alive all these years, a punishment maybe for sins and excesses committed in some former existence. Perhaps there was something in the theory or belief in karma, although he wished that things would even out a little more in this life—why did we have to wait for the next time around? Markham had read Emerson's essay on the law of compensation, but that didn't seem to work either. He had often thought of suicide as a way of cheating the fates that had made him, the child of handsome parents, no better than a hideous gargoyle; but he had thrust the thought aside, hoping (as most of us do) that things would change for the better.

His room was tidy—it had the bare necessities—and those pictures were the only mementoes of a past he couldn't forget. He had his books, too, for he considered them necessities—the Greek philosophers, Epicurus, Epictetus, Marcus Aurelius, Seneca. When Seneca had nothing left to live for, he had cut his wrists in his bathtub and bled slowly to death. Not a bad way to go, thought Markham; except that he didn't have a bathtub, only a rusty iron bucket.

Food was left outside his door, as per instructions; sometimes fresh fruit and vegetables, sometimes a cooked meal. If there was a wedding banquet in the hotel, Negi would remember to send Markham some roast chicken or pilaf. Markham looked forward to the marriage season with its lavish wedding parties. He was a permanent though unknown wedding guest.

After discovering the freedom of the Empire's roof, Markham's nocturnal excursions seldom went beyond the hotel's sprawling estate. As sure-footed as when he was a soldier, he had no difficulty in scrambling over the decaying rooftops, moving along narrow window ledges, and leaping from one landing or balcony to another. It was late summer, and guests often left their windows open to enjoy the pine-scented breeze that drifted over the hillside. Markham was no voyeur, he was really too insular and subjective a person for that form of indulgence; nevertheless, he found it fascinating to observe people in their unguarded moments: how they preened in front of mirrors, or talked to themselves, or attended to their little vanities, or sang or scratched or made love (or tried to), or drank themselves into a stupor. There were many men (and a few women) who preferred drinking in their rooms to drinking in the bar—it was cheaper, and they could get drunk and stupid without making fools of themselves in public.

· One of those who enjoyed a quiet tipple in her room was Mrs Khanna. A vodka with tomato juice was her favourite drink. Markham was watching her soak up her third Bloody Mary when the room telephone rang and Mrs Khanna, receiving some urgent message, left her room and went swaying down the corridor like a battleship of yore.

On an impulse, Markham slipped in through the open window and crossed the room to the table where the bottles were arranged. He felt like having a Bloody Mary himself. It was years since he'd had one; not since that evening at New Delhi's Imperial, when he was on his first leave. Now a little rum during the winter months was his only indulgence.

Taking a clean glass, he poured himself three fingers of vodka and drank it neat. He was about to pour himself another drink when Mrs Khanna entered the room. She stood frozen in her tracks. For there stood the creature of her previous nightmare, the half-face wolf-demon, helping himself to her vodka!

Mrs Khanna screamed. And screamed again.

Markham made a quick exit through the window and vanished into the night. But Mrs Khanna would not stop screaming—not until Negi, half the staff and several guests had entered the room to try and calm her down.

Commotion reigned for a couple of days. Doctors came and went. Policemen came and went. So did Mrs Khanna's palpitations. She insisted that the hotel be searched for the maniac who was in hiding somewhere, only emerging from his lair to single her out for attention. Negi kept the searchers away from the cellar, but he went down himself and confronted Markham.

'Mr Markham, sir, you must keep away from the rooms and the main hotel. Mrs Khanna is very upset. She's called in the police and she's having the hotel searched.'

'I'm sorry, Mr Negi, I did not mean to frighten anyone. It's just that I get restless down here.'

'If she finds out you're living here, you'll have to go. She gives the orders when Mr Khanna is away.'

'This is my only home. Where would I go?'

'I know, Mr Markham, I know. I understand. But do others? It unnerves them, coming upon you without any warning. Stories are going around . . . Business is bad enough without the hotel getting a reputation for strange goings-on. If you must go out at night, use the rear gate and stick to the forest path. Avoid the Mall road. Times have changed, Mr Markham. There are no private places any more. If you have to leave, you will be in the public eye—and I know you don't want that . . .'

'No, I can't leave this place. I'll stick to my room. You've been good to me, Mr Negi.'

'That's all right. I'll see that you get what you need. Just keep out of sight.'

So Markham confined himself to his room for a week, two weeks, three, while the monsoon rains swept across the hills, and a clinging mist gave everything a musty, rotting smell. By mid-August, life in a hill station can become quite depressing for its residents. The absence of sunshine has something to do with it, Even strolling along the Mall is not much fun when a thin, cloying drizzle is drifting into your face. No wonder some take to drink. The hotel bar had a few more customers than usual, although the carpet stank of mildew and rats' urine.

Markham made friends with a shrew that used to visit his room. Shrews have poor eyesight and are easily caught and killed. But as they are supposed to bring good fortune, they were left alone by the hotel staff. Markham was grateful for a little company, and fed his shrew biscuits and dry bread. It moved about his room quite freely and slept in the bottom drawer of his dressing table. Unlike the cat, it had no objection to Markham's face or lack of it.

Towards the end of August, when there was still no relief from the endless rain and cloying mist, Markham grew restless again. He made one brief, nocturnal visit to the park behind the hotel, and came back soaked to the skin. It seemed a pointless exercise, tramping through the long, leech-infested grass. What he really longed for was to touch that piano again. Bits of old music ran through his head. He wanted to pick out a few tunes on that cracked old instrument in the deserted ballroom.

The rain was thundering down on the corrugated tin roofs. There had been a power failure—common enough on nights like this—and most of the town, including the hotel, had been plunged into darkness. There was no need of mask or cape. No need for his false nose, either. Only in the occasional flashes of lightning could you see his torn and ravaged countenance.

Markham slipped out of his room and made his way through the cellars beneath the ballroom. It was a veritable jungle down there. No longer used as a wine cellar, the complex was really a storeroom for old and rotting furniture, rusty old boilers from another age, broken garden urns, even a chipped and mutilated statue of Cupid. It had stood in the garden in former times; but recently the town municipal committee had objected to it as being un-Indian and obscene, and so it had been banished to the cellar.

That had been several years ago, and since then no one had been down into the cellars. It was Markham's short cut to the living world above.

It had stopped raining, and a sliver of moon shone through the clouds. There were still no lights in the hotel. But Markham was used to darkness. He slipped into the ballroom and approached the old piano.

He sat there for half an hour, strumming out old tunes.

There was one old favourite that kept coming back to him, and he played it again and again, recalling the words as he went along.

> *Oh, pale dispenser of my joys and pains,*
> *Holding the doors of Heaven and of Hell,*
> *How the hot blood rushed wildly through the veins*
> *Beneath your touch, until you waved farewell.*

The words of Laurence Hope's 'Kashmiri Love Song' took him back to happier times when life seemed full of possibilities. And when he came to the end of the song, he felt his loss even more passionately:

Pale hands, pink-tipped, like lotus buds that float
On these cool waters where we used to dwell,
I would rather have felt you round my throat
Crushing out life, than waving me farewell!

He had loved and been loved once. But that had been a long, long time ago. Pale hands he'd loved, beside the Shalimar . . .

He stopped playing. All was still.

Should he return to his room now, and keep his promise to Negi? But then again, no one was likely to be around on a night like this, reasoned Markham; and he had no intention of entering any of the rooms. Through the glass doors at the other end of the ballroom he could see a faint glow, as of a firefly in the darkness. He moved towards the light, as a moth to a flame. It was the chowkidar's lantern. He lay asleep on an old sofa, from which the stuffing was protruding.

Markham's was a normal mind handicapped by a physical abnormality. But how long can a mind remain normal in such circumstances?

Markham took the chowkidar's lamp and advanced into the lobby. Moth-eaten stag heads stared down at him from the walls. They had been shot about a hundred years ago, when the hunting of animals had been in fashion. The taxidermist's art had given them a semblance of their former nobility; but time had taken its toll. A mounted panther's head had lost its glass eyes. Even so, thought Markham wryly, its head is in better shape than mine!

The door of the barroom opened to a gentle pressure. The bartender had been tippling on the quiet and had neglected to close the door properly. Markham placed the lamp on a table and looked up at the bottles arrayed in front of him. Some foreign wines, sherries and vermouth. Rum, gin and vodka. He'd never been much of a drinker; drink went to his head rather too quickly, he'd always know that. But the bottles certainly looked attractive and he felt in need of some sustenance, so he poured himself a generous peg of whisky and drank it neat. A warm glow spread through his body. He felt a little better about himself. Life could be made tolerable if he had more frequent access to the bar!

Pacing about in her room on the floor above, Mrs Khanna heard a noise downstairs. She had always suspected the bartender, Ram Lal, of helping himself to liquor on the quiet. After ten o'clock, his gait was unsteady, and in the mornings he often turned up rather groggy and unshaven. Well, she was going to catch him red-handed tonight!

Markham sat on a bar stool with his back to the swing doors. Mrs Khanna, entering on tiptoe, could only make out the outline of a man's figure pouring himself a drink.

The wind in the passage muffled the sound of Mrs Khanna's approach. And anyway, Markham's mind was far away, in the distant Shalimar Bagh where hands, pink-tipped, touched his lips and cheeks, his face yet undespoiled.

'Ram Lal!' hissed Mrs Khanna, intent on scaring the bartender out of his wits. 'Having a good time again?'

Markham was startled, but he did not lose his head. He did not turn immediately.

'I'm not Ram Lal, Mrs Khanna,' said Markham quietly. 'Just one of your guests. An old resident, in fact. You've seen me around before. My face was badly injured a long time ago. I'm not very nice to look at. But there's nothing to be afraid of. I'm quite normal, you know.'

Markham got up slowly. He held his cape up to his face and began moving slowly towards the swing doors. But Mrs Khanna was having none of it. She reached out and snatched at the cape. In the flickering lamplight she stared into that dreadful face. She opened her mouth to scream.

But Markham did not want to hear her screams again. They shattered the stillness and beauty of the night. There was nothing beautiful about a woman's screams—especially Mrs Khanna's.

He reached out for his tormentor and grabbed her by the throat. He wanted to stop her screaming, that was all. But he had strong hands. Struggling, the pair of them knocked over a chair and fell against the table.

'Quite normal, Mrs Khanna,' he said, again and again, his voice ascending. 'I'm quite normal!'

Her legs slid down beneath a bar stool. Still he held on, squeezing, pressing. All those years of frustration were in that grip. Crushing out life and waving it farewell!

Involuntarily, she flung out an arm and knocked over the lamp. Markham released his grip; she fell heavily to the carpet. A rivulet of burning oil sped across the floor and set fire to the hem of her nightgown. But Mrs Khanna was now oblivious to what was happening. The flames took hold of a curtain and ran up towards the wooden ceiling.

Markham picked up a jug of water and threw it on the flames. It made no difference. Horrified, he dashed through the swing doors and called for help. The chowkidar stirred sluggishly and called out: 'Khabardar! Who goes there?' He saw a red glow in the bar, rubbed his eyes in consternation and began looking for his lamp. He did not really need one. Bright flames were leaping out of the French windows.

'Fire!' shouted the chowkidar, and ran for help.

The old hotel, with its timbered floors and ceilings, oaken beams and staircases, mahogany and rosewood furniture, was a veritable tinderbox. By the time the chowkidar could summon help, the fire had spread to the dining room and was licking its way up the stairs to the first-floor rooms.

Markham had already ascended the staircase and was pounding on doors, shouting, 'Get up, get up! Fire below!' He ran to the far end of the corridor, where Negi had his room, and pounded on the door with his fists until Negi woke up.

'The hotel's on fire!' shouted Markham, and ran back the way he had come. There was little more that he could do.

Some of the hotel staff were now rushing about with buckets of water, but the stairs and landing were ablaze, and those living on the first floor had to retreat to the servants' entrance, where a flight of stone steps led down to the tennis courts. Here they gathered, looking on in awe and consternation as the fire spread rapidly through the main building, showing itself at the windows as it went along. The small group on the tennis courts was soon joined by outsiders, for bad news spreads as fast as a good fire, and the townsfolk were not long in turning up.

Markham emerged on the roof and stood there for some time, while the fire ran through the Empire Hotel, crackling vigorously and lighting up the sky. The people below spotted him on the roof, and waved and shouted to him to come down. Smoke billowed around him, and then he disappeared from view.

It was a fire to remember. The town hadn't seen anything like it since the Abbey School had gone up in flames forty years earlier, and only the older residents could remember that one. Negi and the hotel staff could only watch helplessly as the fire raged through the old timbered building, consuming all that stood in its way. Everyone was out of the building except Mrs Khanna, and as yet no one had any idea as to what had happened to her.

Towards morning it began raining heavily again, and this finally quenched the fire; but by then the buildings had been gutted, and the Empire Hotel, that had stood protectively over the town for over a hundred years, was no more.

Mrs Khanna's charred body was recovered from the ruins. A telegram was sent to Mr Khanna in Geneva, and phone calls were made to sundry relatives and insurance offices. Negi was very much in charge.

When the initial confusion was over, Negi remembered Markham and walked around to the rear of the gutted building and down the cellar steps. The basement and the cellar had escaped the worst of the fire, but they were still full of smoke. Negi found Markham's door open.

Markham was stretched out on his bed. The empty bottle of sleeping tablets on the bedside table told its own story; but it was more likely that he had suffocated from the smoke.

Markham's artificial nose lay on the dressing table. Negi picked it up and placed it on the dead man's poor face.

The hotel had gone, and with it Negi's livelihood. An old friend had gone too. An era had passed. But Negi was the sort who liked to tidy up afterwards.

DUST *on the* MOUNTAIN

I

Winter came and went, without so much as a drizzle. The hillside was brown all summer and the fields were bare. The old plough that was dragged over the hard ground by Bisnu's lean oxen made hardly any impression. Still, Bisnu kept his seeds ready for sowing. A good monsoon, and there would be plenty of maize and rice to see the family through the next winter.

Summer went its scorching way, and a few clouds gathered on the south-western horizon.

'The monsoon is coming,' announced Bisnu.

His sister Puja was at the small stream, washing clothes. 'If it doesn't come soon, the stream will dry up,' she said. 'See, it's only a trickle this year. Remember when there were so many different flowers growing here on the banks of the stream? This year there isn't one.'

'The winter was dry. It did not even snow,' said Bisnu.

'I cannot remember another winter when there was no snow,' said his mother. 'The year your father died, there was so much snow the villagers could not light his funeral pyre for hours . . . And now there are fires everywhere.' She pointed to the next mountain, half-hidden by the smoke from a forest fire.

At night they sat outside their small house, watching the fire spread. A red line stretched right across the mountain. Thousands of Himalayan trees were perishing in the flames. Oaks, deodars, maples, pines; trees that had taken hundreds of years to grow. And now a fire started carelessly by some campers had been carried up the mountain with the help of the dry grass and strong breeze. There was no one to put it out. It would take days to die down by itself.

'If the monsoon arrives tomorrow, the fire will go out,' said Bisnu, ever the optimist. He was only twelve, but he was the man in the house; he had to see that there was enough food for the family and for the oxen, for the big black dog and the hens.

There were clouds the next day but they brought only a drizzle.

'It's just the beginning,' said Bisnu as he placed a bucket of muddy water on the steps.

'It usually starts with a heavy downpour,' said his mother.

But there were to be no downpours that year. Clouds gathered on the horizon but they were white and puffy and soon disappeared. True monsoon clouds would have been dark and heavy with moisture. There were other signs— or lack of them—that warned of a long dry summer. The birds were silent, or simply absent. The Himalayan barbet, who usually heralded the approach of the monsoon with strident calls from the top of a spruce tree, hadn't been seen or heard. And the cicadas, who played a deafening overture in the oaks at the first hint of rain, seemed to be missing altogether.

Puja's apricot tree usually gave them a basket full of fruit every summer. This year it produced barely a handful of apricots, lacking juice and flavour. The tree looked ready to die, its leaves curled up in despair. Fortunately there was a store of walnuts, and a binful of wheat grain and another of rice stored from the previous year, so they would not be entirely without food; but it looked as though there would be no fresh fruit or vegetables. And there would be nothing to store away for the following winter. Money would be needed to buy supplies in Tehri, some thirty miles distant. And there was no money to be earned in the village.

'I will go to Mussoorie and find work,' announced Bisnu.

'But Mussoorie is a two-day journey by bus,' said his mother. 'There is no one there who can help you. And you may not get any work.'

'In Mussoorie there is plenty of work during the summer. Rich people come up from the plains for their holidays. It is full of hotels and shops and places where they can spend their money.'

'But they won't spend any money on you.'

'There is money to be made there. And if not, I will come home. I can walk back over the Nag Tibba mountain. It will take only two and a half days and I will save the bus fare!'

'Don't go, Bhai,' pleaded Puja. 'There will be no one to prepare your food—you will only get sick.'

But Bisnu had made up his mind so he put a few belongings in a cloth shoulder bag, while his mother prised several rupee coins out of a cache in the wall of their living room. Puja prepared a special breakfast of parathas and an egg scrambled with onions, the hen having laid just one for the occasion. Bisnu put some of the parathas in his bag. Then, waving goodbye to his mother and sister, he set off down the road from the village.

After walking for a mile, he reached the highway where there was a hamlet with a bus stop. A number of villagers were waiting patiently for a bus. It was an hour late but they were used to that. As long as it arrived safely and got them to their destination, they would be content.

They were patient people. And although Bisnu wasn't quite so patient, he too had learnt how to wait—for late buses and late monsoons.

II

Along the valley and over the mountains went the little bus with its load of frail humans. A little misjudgement on the part of the driver, and they would all be dashed to pieces on the rocks far below.

'How tiny we are,' thought Bisnu, looking up at the towering peaks and the immensity of the sky. 'Each of us no more than a raindrop . . . And I wish we had a few raindrops!'

There were still fires burning to the north but the road went south, where there were no forests anyway, just bare brown hillsides. Down near the river there were small paddy fields but unfortunately rivers ran downhill and not uphill, and there was no inexpensive way in which the water could be brought up the steep slopes to the fields that depended on rainfall.

Bisnu stared out of the bus window at the river running far below. On either bank huge boulders lay exposed, for the level of the water had fallen considerably during the past few months.

'Why are there no trees here?' he asked aloud, and received the attention of a fellow passenger, an old man in the next seat who had been keeping up a relentless dry coughing. Even though it was a warm day, he wore a woollen cap and had an old muffler wrapped about his neck.

'There were trees here once,' he said. 'But the contractors took the deodars for furniture and houses. And the pines were tapped to death for resin. And the oaks were stripped of their leaves to feed the cattle—you can still see a few tree skeletons if you look hard—and the bushes that remained were finished off by the goats!'

'When did all this happen?' asked Bisnu.

'A few years ago. And it's still happening in other areas, although it's forbidden now to cut trees. The only forests that remain are in remote places where there are no roads.' A fit of coughing came over him, but he had found a good listener and was eager to continue. 'The road helps you and me to get about but it also makes it easier for others to do mischief. Rich men from the cities come here and buy up what they want—land, trees, people!'

'What takes you to Mussoorie, Uncle?' asked Bisnu politely. He always addressed elderly people as uncle or aunt.

'I have a cough that won't go away. Perhaps they can do something for it at the hospital in Mussoorie. Doctors don't like coming to villages, you know—there's no money to be made in villages. So we must go to the doctors in the towns. I had a brother who could not be cured in Mussoorie.

They told him to go to Delhi. He sold his buffaloes and went to Delhi, but there they told him it was too late to do anything. He died on the way back. I won't go to Delhi. I don't wish to die amongst strangers.'

'You'll get well, Uncle,' said Bisnu.

'Bless you for saying so. And you—what takes you to the big town?'

'Looking for work—we need money at home.'

'It is always the same. There are many like you who must go out in search of work. But don't be led astray. Don't let your friends persuade you to go to Bombay to become a film star! It is better to be hungry in your village than to be hungry on the streets of Bombay. I had a nephew who went to Bombay. The smugglers put him to work selling afeem (opium) and now he is in jail. Keep away from the big cities, boy. Earn your money and go home.'

'I'll do that, Uncle. My mother and sister will expect me to return before the summer season is over.'

The old man nodded vigorously and began coughing again. Presently he dozed off. The interior of the bus smelt of tobacco smoke and petrol fumes and as a result Bisnu had a headache. He kept his face near the open window to get as much fresh air as possible, but the dust kept getting into his mouth and eyes.

Several dusty hours later the bus got into Mussoorie, honking its horn furiously at everything in sight.

The passengers, looking dazed, got down and went their different ways. The old man trudged off to the hospital.

Bisnu had to start looking for a job straightaway. He needed a lodging for the night and he could not afford even the cheapest of hotels. So he went from one shop to another, and to all the little restaurants and eating places, asking for work—anything in exchange for a bed, a meal, and a minimum wage. A boy at one of the sweet shops told him there was a job at the Picture Palace, one of the town's three cinemas. The hill station's main road was crowded with people, for the season was just starting. Most of them were tourists who had come up from Delhi and other large towns.

The street lights had come on, and the shops were lighting up, when Bisnu presented himself at the Picture Palace.

III

The man who ran the cinema's tea stall had just sacked the previous helper for his general clumsiness. Whenever he engaged a new boy (which was fairly often) he started him off with the warning: 'I will be keeping a record of all the cups and plates you break, and their cost will be deducted from your salary at the end of the month.'

As Bisnu's salary had been fixed at fifty rupees a month, he would have to be very careful if he was going to receive any of it.

'In my first month,' said Chittru, one of the three tea stall boys, 'I broke six cups and five saucers, and my pay came to three rupees! Better be careful!'

Bisnu's job was to help prepare the tea and samosas, serve these refreshments to the public during intervals in the film, and later wash up the dishes. In addition to his salary, he was allowed to drink as much tea as he wanted or could hold in his stomach. But the sugar supply was kept to a minimum.

Bisnu went to work immediately and it was not long before he was as well-versed in his duties as the other two tea boys, Chittru and Bali. Chittru was an easy-going, lazy boy who always tried to place the brunt of his work on someone else's shoulders. But he was generous and lent Bisnu five rupees during the first week. Bali, besides being a tea boy, had the enviable job of being the poster boy. As the cinema was closed during the mornings, Bali would be busy either pushing the big poster board around Mussoorie, or sticking posters on convenient walls.

'Posters are very useful,' he claimed. 'They prevent old walls from falling down.'

Chittru had relatives in Mussoorie and slept at their house. But both Bisnu and Bali were on their own and had to sleep at the cinema. After the last show the hall was locked up, so they could not settle down in the expensive seats as they would have liked! They had to sleep on a dirty mattress in the foyer, near the ticket office, where they were often at the mercy of icy Himalayan winds.

Bali made things more comfortable by setting his posterboard at an angle to the wall, which gave them a little alcove where they could sleep protected from the wind. As they had only one blanket each, they placed their blankets together and rolled themselves into a tight warm ball.

During shows, when Bisnu took the tea around, there was nearly always someone who would be rude and offensive. Once when he spilt some tea on a college student's shoes, he received a hard kick on the shin. He complained to the tea stall owner, but his employer said, 'The customer is always right. You should have got out of the way in time!'

As he began to get used to this life, Bisnu found himself taking an interest in some of the regular customers.

There was, for instance, the large gentleman with the soup-strainer moustache, who drank his tea from the saucer. As he drank, his lips worked like a suction pump, and the tea, after a brief agitation in the saucer, would disappear in a matter of seconds. Bisnu often wondered if there was something lurking in the forests of that gentleman's upper lip, something that would suddenly spring out and fall upon him! The boys took great pleasure in exchanging anecdotes about the peculiarities of some of the customers.

Bisnu had never seen such bright, painted women before. The girls in his village, including his sister Puja, were good-looking and often sturdy; but they did not use perfumes or make-up like these more prosperous women from the towns of the plains. Wearing expensive clothes and jewellery, they never gave Bisnu more than a brief, bored glance. Other women were more inclined to notice him, favouring him with kind words and a small tip when he took away the cups and plates. He found he could make a few rupees a month in tips; and when he received his first month's pay, he was able to send some of it home.

Chittru accompanied him to the post office and helped him to fill in the money order form. Bisnu had been to the village school, but be wasn't used to forms and official paperwork. Chittru, a town boy, knew all about them, even though he could just about read and write.

Walking back to the cinema, Chittru said, 'We can make more money at the limestone quarries.'

'All right, let's try them,' said Bisnu.

'Not now,' said Chittru, who enjoyed the busy season in the hill station. 'After the season—after the monsoon.'

But there was still no monsoon to speak of, just an occasional drizzle which did little to clear the air of the dust that blew up from the plains. Bisnu wondered how his mother and sister were faring at home. A wave of homesickness swept over him. The hill station, with all its glitter, was just a pretty gift box with nothing inside.

One day in the cinema Bisnu saw the old man who had been with him on the bus. He greeted him like a long lost friend. At first the old man did not recognize the boy, but when Bisnu asked him if he had recovered from his illness, the old man remembered and said, 'So you are still in Mussoorie, boy. That is good. I thought you might have gone down to Delhi to make more money.' He added that he was a little better and that he was undergoing a course of treatment at the hospital. Bisnu brought him a cup of tea and refused to take any money for it; it could be included in his own quota of free tea. When the show was over, the old man went his way and Bisnu did not see him again.

In September the town began to empty. The taps were running dry or giving out just a trickle of muddy water. A thick mist lay over the mountain for days on end, but there was no rain. When the mists cleared, an autumn wind came whispering through the deodars.

At the end of the month the manager of the Picture Palace gave everyone a week's notice, a week's pay, and announced that the cinema would be closing for the winter.

IV

Bali said, 'I'm going to Delhi to find work. I'll come back next summer. What about you, Bisnu, why don't you come with me? It's easier to find work in Delhi.'

'I'm staying with Chittru,' said Bisnu. 'We may work at the quarries.'

'I like the big towns,' said Bali. 'I like shops and people and lots of noise. I will never go back to my village. There is no money there, no fun.'

Bali made a bundle of his things and set out for the bus stand. Bisnu bought himself a pair of cheap shoes, for his old ones had fallen to pieces. With what was left of his money, he sent another money order home. Then he and Chittru set out for the limestone quarries, an eight-mile walk from Mussoorie.

They knew they were nearing the quarries when they saw clouds of limestone dust hanging in the air. The dust hid the next mountain from view. When they did see the mountain, they found that the top of it was missing— blasted away by dynamite to enable the quarries to get at the rich strata of limestone rock below the surface.

The skeletons of a few trees remained on the lower slopes. Almost everything else had gone—grass, flowers, shrubs, birds, butterflies, grasshoppers, ladybirds . . . A rock lizard popped its head out of a crevice to look at the intruders. Then, like some prehistoric survivor, it scuttled back into its underground shelter.

'I used to come here when I was small,' announced Chittru cheerfully.

'Were the quarries here then?'

'Oh, no. My friends and I—we used to come for the strawberries. They grew all over this mountain. Wild strawberries, but very tasty.'

'Where are they now?' asked Bisnu, looking around at the devastated hillside.

'All gone,' said Chittru. 'Maybe there are some on the next mountain.'

Even as they approached the quarries, a blast shook the hillside. Chittru pulled Bisnu under an overhanging rock to avoid the shower of stones that pelted down on the road. As the dust enveloped them, Bisnu had a fit of coughing. When the air cleared a little, they saw the limestone dump ahead of them.

Chittru, who was older and bigger than Bisnu, was immediately taken on as a labourer; but the quarry foreman took one look at Bisnu and said, 'You're too small. You won't be able to break stones or lift those heavy rocks and load them into the trucks. Be off, boy. Find something else to do.'

He was offered a job in the labourers' canteen, but he'd had enough of making tea and washing dishes. He was about to turn round and walk back to Mussoorie when he felt a heavy hand descend on his shoulder. He looked up to find a grey-bearded, turbanned Sikh looking down at him in some amusement.

'I need a cleaner for my truck,' he said. 'The work is easy, but the hours are long!'

Bisnu responded immediately to the man's gruff but jovial manner.

'What will you pay?' he asked.

'Fifteen rupees a day, and you'll get food and a bed at the depot.'

'As long as I don't have to cook the food,' said Bisnu.

The truck driver laughed. 'You might prefer to do so, once you've tasted the depot food. Are you coming on my truck? Make up your mind.'

'I'm your man,' said Bisnu; and waving goodbye to Chittru, he followed the Sikh to his truck.

V

A horn blared, shattering the silence of the mountains, and the truck came round a bend in the road. A herd of goats scattered to left and right.

The goatherds cursed as a cloud of dust enveloped them, and then the truck had left them behind and was rattling along the bumpy, unmetalled road to the quarries.

At the wheel of the truck, stroking his grey moustache with one hand, sat Pritam Singh. It was his own truck. He had never allowed anyone else to drive it. Every day he made two trips to the quarries, carrying truckloads of limestone back to the depot at the bottom of the hill. He was paid by the trip and he was always anxious to get in two trips every day.

Sitting beside him was Bisnu, his new cleaner. In less than a month Bisnu had become an experienced hand at looking after trucks, riding in them, and even sleeping in them. He got on well with Pritam, the grizzled, fifty-year-old Sikh, who boasted of two well-off sons—one a farmer in Punjab, the other a wine merchant in far-off London. He could have gone to live with either of them, but his sturdy independence kept him on the road in his battered old truck.

Pritam pressed hard on his horn. Now there was no one on the road—neither beast nor man—but Pritam was fond of the sound of his horn and liked blowing it. He boasted that it was the loudest horn in northern India. Although it struck terror into the hearts of all who heard it—for it was louder than the trumpeting of an elephant—it was music to Pritam's ears.

Pritam treated Bisnu as an equal and a friendly banter had grown between them during their many trips together.

'One more year on this bone-breaking road,' said Pritam, 'and then I'll sell my truck and retire.'

'But who will buy such a shaky old truck?' asked Bisnu. 'It will retire before you do!'

'Now don't be insulting, boy. She's only twenty years old—there are still a few years left in her!' And as though to prove it he blew the horn again. Its strident sound echoed and re-echoed down the mountain gorge. A pair of wildfowl burst from the bushes and fled to more silent regions.

Pritam's thoughts went to his dinner.

'Haven't had a good meal for days.'

'Haven't had a good meal for weeks,' said Bisnu, although in fact he looked much healthier than when he had worked at the cinema's tea stall.

'Tonight I'll give you a dinner in a good hotel. Tandoori chicken and rice pilaf.'

He sounded his horn again as though to put a seal on his promise. Then he slowed down, because the road had become narrow and precipitous, and trotting ahead of them was a train of mules.

As the horn blared, one mule ran forward, another ran backward. One went uphill, another went downhill. Soon there were mules all over the place. Pritam cursed the mules and the mule drivers cursed Pritam; but he had soon left them far behind.

Along this range, all the hills were bare and dry. Most of the forest had long since disappeared.

'Are your hills as bare as these?' asked Pritam.

'No, we still have some trees,' said Bisnu. 'Nobody has started blasting the hills as yet. In front of our house there is a walnut tree which gives us two baskets of walnuts every year. And there is an apricot tree. But it was a bad year for fruit. There was no rain. And the stream is too far away.'

'It will rain soon,' said Pritam. 'I can smell rain. It is coming from the north. The winter will be early.'

'It will settle the dust.'

Dust was everywhere. The truck was full of it. The leaves of the shrubs and the few trees were thick with it. Bisnu could feel the dust under his eyelids and in his mouth. And as they approached the quarries, the dust increased. But it was a different kind of dust now—whiter, stinging the eyes, irritating the nostrils.

They had been blasting all morning.

'Let's wait here,' said Pritam, bringing the truck to a halt.

They sat in silence, staring through the windscreen at the scarred cliffs a little distance down the road. There was a sharp crack of explosives and the hillside blossomed outwards. Earth and rocks hurtled down the mountain.

Bisnu watched in awe as shrubs and small trees were flung into the air. It always frightened him—not so much the sight of the rocks bursting asunder, as the trees being flung aside and destroyed. He thought of the trees at home—the walnut, the chestnuts, the pines—and wondered if one day they would suffer the same fate, and whether the mountains would all become a desert like this particular range. No trees, no grass, no water—only the choking dust of mines and quarries.

VI

Pritam pressed hard on his horn again, to let the people at the site know that he was approaching. He parked outside a small shed where the contractor and the foreman were sipping cups of tea. A short distance away, some labourers, Chittru among them, were hammering at chunks of rock, breaking them up into manageable pieces. A pile of stones stood ready for loading, while the rock that had just been blasted lay scattered about the hillside.

'Come and have a cup of tea,' called out the contractor.

'I can't hang about all day,' said Pritam. 'There's another trip to make—and the days are getting shorter. I don't want to be driving by night.'

But he sat down on a bench and ordered two cups of tea from the stall. The foreman strolled over to the group of labourers and told them to start loading. Bisnu let down the grid at the back of the truck. Then, to keep himself warm, he began helping Chittru and the men with the loading.

'Don't expect to be paid for helping,' said Sharma, the contractor, for whom every rupee spent was a rupee off his profits.

'Don't worry,' said Bisnu. 'I don't work for contractors, I work for friends.'

'That's right,' called out Pritam. 'Mind what you say to Bisnu—he's no one's servant!'

Sharma wasn't happy until there was no space left for a single stone. Then Bisnu had his cup of tea and three of the men climbed on the pile of stones in the open truck.

'All right, let's go!' said Pritam. 'I want to finish early today—Bisnu and I are having a big dinner!'

Bisnu jumped in beside Pritam, banging the door shut. It never closed properly unless it was slammed really hard. But it opened at a touch.

'This truck is held together with sticking plaster,' joked Pritam. He was in good spirits. He started the engine, and blew his horn just as he passed the foreman and the contractor.

'They are deaf in one ear from the blasting,' said Pritam. 'I'll make them deaf in the other ear!'

The labourers were singing as the truck swung round the sharp bends of the winding road. The door beside Bisnu rattled on its hinges. He was feeling quite dizzy.

'Not too fast,' he said.

'Oh,' said Pritam. 'And since when did you become nervous about my driving?'

'It's just today,' said Bisnu uneasily. 'It's a feeling, that's all.'

'You're getting old,' said Pritam. 'That's your trouble.'

'I suppose so,' said Bisnu.

Pritam was feeling young, exhilarated. He drove faster.

As they swung round a bend, Bisnu looked out of his window. All he saw was the sky above and the valley below. They were very near the edge; but it was usually like that on this narrow mountain road.

After a few more hairpin bends, the road descended steeply to the valley. Just then a stray mule ran into the middle of the road. Pritam swung the steering wheel over to the right to avoid the mule, but here the road turned sharply to the left. The truck went over the edge.

As it tipped over, hanging for a few seconds on the edge of the cliff, the labourers leapt from the back of the truck. It pitched forward, and as it struck a rock outcrop, the loose door burst open. Bisnu was thrown out.

The truck hurtled forward, bouncing over the rocks, turning over on its side and rolling over twice before coming to rest against the trunk of a scraggly old oak tree. But for the tree, the truck would have plunged several hundred feet down to the bottom of the gorge.

Two of the labourers sat on the hillside, stunned and badly shaken. The third man had picked himself up and was running back to the quarry for help.

Bisnu had landed in a bed of nettles. He was smarting all over, but he wasn't really hurt; the nettles had broken his fall.

His first impulse was to get up and run back to the road. Then he realized that Pritam was still in the truck.

Bisnu skidded down the steep slope, calling out, 'Pritam Uncle, are you all right?'

There was no answer.

VII

When Bisnu saw Pritam's arm and half his body jutting out of the open door of the truck, he feared the worst. It was a strange position, half in and half out. Bisnu was about to turn away and climb back up the hill, when he noticed that

Pritam had opened a bloodied and swollen eye. It looked straight up at Bisnu.

'Are you alive?' whispered Bisnu, terrified.

'What do you think?' muttered Pritam. He closed his eye again.

When the contractor and his men arrived, it took them almost an hour to get Pritam Singh out of the wreckage of the truck, and another hour to get him to the hospital in the next big town. He had broken bones and fractured ribs and a dislocated shoulder. But the doctors said he was repairable— which was more than could be said for the truck.

'So the truck's finished,' said Pritam, between groans when Bisnu came to see him after a couple of days. 'Now I'll have to go home and live with my son. And what about you, boy? I can get you a job on a friend's truck.'

'No,' said Bisnu, 'I'll be going home soon.'

'And what will you do at home?'

'I'll work on my land. It's better to grow things on the land, than to blast things out of it.'

They were silent for some time.

'There is something to be said for growing things,' said Pritam. 'But for that tree, the truck would have finished up at the foot of the mountain, and I wouldn't be here, all bandaged up and talking to you. It was the tree that saved me. Remember that, boy.'

'I'll remember, and I won't forget the dinner you promised me, either.'

It snowed during Bisnu's last night at the quarries. He slept on the floor with Chittru, in a large shed meant for the labourers. The wind blew the snowflakes in at the entrance; it whistled down the deserted mountain pass. In the morning Bisnu opened his eyes to a world of dazzling whiteness. The snow was piled high against the walls of the shed, and they had some difficulty getting out.

Bisnu joined Chittru at the tea stall, drank a glass of hot sweet tea, and ate two stale buns. He said goodbye to Chittru and set out on the long march home. The road would be closed to traffic because of the heavy snow, and he would have to walk all the way.

He trudged over the hills all day, stopping only at small villages to take refreshment. By nightfall he was still ten miles from home. But he had fallen in with other travellers, and with them he took shelter at a small inn. They built a fire and crowded round it, and each man spoke of his home and fields and all were of the opinion that the snow and rain had come just in time to save the winter crops. Someone sang, and another told a ghost story. Feeling at home already, Bisnu fell asleep listening to their tales. In the morning they parted and went their different ways.

It was almost noon when Bisnu reached his village.

The fields were covered with snow and the mountain stream was in spate. As he climbed the terraced fields to his house, he heard the sound of barking, and his mother's big black mastiff came bounding towards him over the snow.

The dog jumped on him and licked his arms and then went bounding back to the house to tell the others.

Puja saw him from the courtyard and ran indoors shouting, 'Bisnu has come, my brother has come!'

His mother ran out of the house, calling, 'Bisnu, Bisnu!'

Bisnu came walking through the fields, and he did not hurry, he did not run; he wanted to savour the moment of his return, with his mother and sister smiling, waiting for him in front of the house.

There was no need to hurry now. He would be with them for a long time, and the manager of the Picture Palace would have to find someone else for the summer season . . . It was his home, and these were his fields! Even the snow was his. When the snow melted he would clear the fields, and nourish them, and make them rich.

He felt very big and very strong as he came striding over the land he loved.

THE
RIPLEY-BEAN
MYSTERIES

BORN
EVIL

'Can someone be born evil?' asked Mr Lobo, handing Miss Ripley-Bean a glass of nimbu paani as they sat on the sunny verandah lounge of the Royal. 'Be totally evil, that is—from birth through manhood and into old age. Someone without a conscience, someone who inflicts cruelty without a qualm, who cares a damn for what the world would think of him. Someone like Hitler, perhaps?'

'Hitler was vegetarian,' said Miss Ripley-Bean, helping herself to a cracker and giving it to her Tibetan terrier, Fluff, who gobbled it up. A notice in the hotel lobby said 'No dogs allowed', but this was blissfully ignored by Miss Ripley-Bean. After all, Fluff was no ordinary dog.

'What has that to do with it?' asked Mr Lobo, curious. 'Being a vegetarian?'

'Well, presumably he was kind to animals. Didn't approve of killing and eating them. But of course he hated Jews—and Russians—and gypsies—and black people.'

'And killed them without compunction, or had his lackeys do the job for him. He thought that was his duty. Or rather, his policy.'

'And he was driven by hatred. Don't forget that.'

'So would you say he was born evil?'

'I think the evil grew in him,' said Miss Ripley-Bean, giving Fluff another cracker. The plate of crackers would soon be empty.

Neither Miss Ripley-Bean nor Mr Lobo were hotel guests. Miss Ripley-Bean's father had sold the hotel to Nandu's father at the time of Independence, on condition that she, May Ripley-Bean, could continue to live there for the rest of her days. He had died shortly afterwards. And Mr Lobo was the hotel pianist. He had been there for a couple of years. Every evening he would sit at the piano in the lounge, strumming out old favourites or popular film tunes for the benefit of a dwindling clientele. In the late 1960s hill stations were going through a slump, and classier hotels like the Royal were feeling the pinch.

Miss Ripley-Bean and Mr Lobo had struck up a quaint friendship. She was almost seventy and he was just forty. Neither had ever been married. Mr Lobo enjoyed listening to Miss Ripley-Bean's tales of old Mussoorie and the Doon valley, and she enjoyed listening to him play

Viennese waltzes and romantic ballads from old movies. Miss Ripley-Bean had been quite a movie buff once—a fan of Eddie Cantor, Al Jolson, Fred Astaire, Nelson Eddy and of course Greta Garbo, but that had been back in the thirties and forties, when the cinemas had been flooded with Hollywood's best. But over the years her eyesight had deteriorated, and now, unless she sat in the front row with the rickshaw boys and shop assistants she couldn't see very much. Also, she couldn't take Fluff into a cinema hall; he might want to pee on people's legs.

'I have never known anyone who was completely evil,' said Mr Lobo reflectively. 'Even Hitler had his softer side. He could love Eva Braun—and die beside her. Have you known anyone who was completely evil? Born evil—evil to the end of his days?'

'Evil is an aberration of personality, often ingrained in the mind at birth,' said Miss Ripley-Bean.

'You mean it's in the genes—it can't be helped?'

'I am not sure. I knew a couple who were both very good people. And yet they had a son who took to crime like a duck to water.'

'It could go far back, to earlier forebears—that propensity for crime.'

'Quite possibly. You see, this young man—or rather boy, as he was when I knew him—had the most charming and innocent-looking face that you could imagine. It was almost angelic. Everyone fell for him—old ladies, young women, strict headmasters, peppery old colonels, older boys, younger boys, schoolgirls. And he smiled at everyone and was oh-so-polite and well mannered. But he hated all of them—he hated everyone!'

'But why—was there any reason for it?'

'None at all. He was just made that way. The rest of humanity meant absolutely nothing to him. They were just his playthings, his toys. He played with them and then threw them away. But not before damaging them a little— sometimes more than a little.'

'And who was this paragon of evil? You seem to have known him well.'

Miss Ripley-Bean gave Fluff another cracker. 'Young Alexander. Yes, I knew him. But I did not really know him. No one did. In a way he lived in a world of his own making—he made things happen. Like dropping a lighted match in the petrol tank of a motorcycle and watching it go up in flames. Or firing Diwali rockets through the open window of the headmaster's bedroom and destroying all the bed linen.'

'He must have been crackers,' said Mr Lobo.

'Yes, but not this sort of cracker'—and Miss Ripley-Bean slipped another Royal cracker to Fluff, who accepted graciously. 'He was cracked in the head all right, but in an evil way—like Emperor Nero, who loved to watch his slaves being torn apart by lions. It was fire that excited Alexander. Conflagrations! If he heard that there was a building on

504

fire, in Mussoorie or Dehradun or wherever his family happened to be staying, he'd rush to watch. Sometimes he'd pretend to help the firefighters, get involved in what was happening, but it was the spreading fire that he really enjoyed—and the screams of people who were trapped inside or running about on the roof or jumping from windows.

'There was this big fire at Green's Hotel back in the late forties. The ballroom went up in flames. Alexander was just a boy then, home from school; his family lived in one wing of the hotel. Out front was a ballroom that had come up during the war. American and British soldiers would come over in the evenings—Dehra was a recreation centre for Allied soldiers—and dance with the Anglo-Indian girls. They were great dancers, those girls, and so pretty. Fights broke out over them. Of course the Americans had more money to spend and that was part of the trouble.

'Alexander was fourteen at the time, too young to be familiar with that lot, but he liked listening to the band— Jimmy Cotton and his Band, they came from the Imperial in Delhi, just to play at Green's.

'No one knows how the fire started. And no one believed Alexander had anything to do with it—he looked so charming, so cute, just sitting there behind the band, his eyes sparkling with excitement as he tapped his feet to a tango or swayed to the rhythms of a rumba. The air was full of cigarette smoke, so at first no one noticed the smoke rising from an alcove near the bar. Had someone thrown a lighted cigarette on to a rug? Very careless but common enough at these dance parties. Rugs were always being ruined. Only this time the rug was already soaked in kerosene—a spill from an oil lamp, probably—and in no time at all the rug caught fire and the ballroom was full of smoke.

'"Fire! Fire!" It was Alexander shouting.

'And sure enough, the curtains were on fire, and the dancing stopped and the band stopped playing. Yes, the dancing had stopped, but now Alexander was dancing, doing a tap dance of his own, as he grew more and more excited.

'There was panic in the ballroom. Girls, soldiers, musicians, waiters, everyone rushed for the exit. There was only one exit, and in the melee two of the girls fell to the ground and were crushed to death. By the time a fire engine arrived, the flames were out of control. Young Alexander made a big show of helping the firefighters—giving instructions, directing the water hoses, dashing about with a fire extinguisher—oh, he was quite the hero. Later, everyone commended him for his efforts. It was all an act of course. No one had any idea that he was the real culprit.'

'Diabolical,' said Mr Lobo.

'Exactly. The face of an angel and the mind of the devil. You know, the world is full of criminals and many end up behind bars so that society is protected from them. But they are, for the most part, ordinary people—people like you and me—who have transgressed, crossed the line of decency, given in to their animal instincts or succumbed to human greed and paid the price for it. But Alexander was consistently evil. He went from one brazen act of evil to another—and got away with it, time after time.'

'What happened next?'

'There were minor incidents—a fire in a cinema, at a railway station—but these were detected in time and brought under control. Alexander's school gymnasium burnt down quite mysteriously. He was sixteen when he set fire to his parents' house. This was down in Rajpur, where they lived at the time. It was a lovely old mansion, so big that Alexander's parents were able to use part of it as a guest house. But the guests did not stay very long—not with Alexander around. He would introduce snakes into their rooms, or monitor lizards, or stink bombs that he made himself. The paying guests were happy to pay their bills and go elsewhere. He would even torment his little sister. One day, while she was asleep, he cut most of her hair off, leaving just shreds and patches. He was well thrashed for this by his father.

'Vengeful by nature, he waited until they had all gone out to a Sunday church service. Then he sent the cook and the gardener out on errands and set about making a pile of all the best furniture in the front room before setting it alight.

'"I am Guy Fawkes today," he declared, addressing an invisible audience. Guy Fawkes, who had once tried to burn down the English Parliament, was his history-book hero.

'The furniture made a great bonfire. It spread from the sofas and tables to the costly rugs that his mother had collected and then to the curtains, and then from room to room, upstairs and downstairs, rapidly spreading through the entire house.

'The cook returned from his errand to find his kitchen ablaze, and flames leaping from the bedroom windows. Was the Baba safe? He was a good man and feared for the safety of the errant youth. He could not believe that it was Alexander who had started it all. He dashed about, calling out to the Baba, the name by which Alexander was known to the servants. Presently Alexander emerged from a wing of the house, covered in soot.

'"House on fire," he said calmly. "Better call the fire brigade."

'But there was no fire brigade in Rajpur. And there was not much that the cook and the gardener and the helpful neighbours could do with buckets of water. When Alexander's parents and sister returned from church, they were confronted by the smoking ruin of their old home. And their pet Alsatian had disappeared in the flames.'

~

Mr Lobo poured out another glass of nimbu paani for Miss Ripley-Bean, and she in turn gave Fluff another cracker.

'So what happened to Alexander? Did they send him to a reform home?'

'Oh no, they doted on him and wouldn't accept that he was responsible for it, although in the back of their minds they must have known that he was the devil incarnate. We can never believe the worst of our own progeny, can we?'

'I wouldn't know,' said Mr Lobo, a confirmed bachelor.

'Nor would I, really,' said Miss Ripley-Bean. 'But over the years I've seen it in so many people who rush to the defence of their beloved Tom, Dev or Danny, in spite of their having committed the most heinous of crimes. So Alexander's parents covered up for their diabolic boy even though it was their own house he'd burnt down!

'Well, he couldn't go to college. He'd already been expelled from two schools. So they sent him to a Bible school in Landour, run by a couple of homely American missionaries. Poor boy, they said, he has had a bad time of it—misunderstood by his parents and teachers; we'll put him in the Lord's way and, who knows, one day he might make a good preacher! And they put him in charge of the community library.'

'That should have cured him.'

'Hardly. Books! All those books. Such a temptation to the little firebug. What could make a better fire? Books burn so well—and who needs them anyway, or so reasons Alexander, who values everything on the basis of inflammability. Some of the world's greatest libraries have been lost to fires, or so he's heard, so why not add this little one to the list? Most of them are religious books anyway, and no one bothers to read them. The ragman buys up the old ones and turns them into paper bags.

'So there is quite a conflagration, and although the students of the nearby Pinewood School turn out in force, with buckets and jerrycans of water, they can do nothing to put out the fire. And meanwhile, Alexander is sitting on the hillside singing an old sea-shanty that he'd learnt in his nursery days:

Fire in the galley, fire down below,
Fetch a bucket of water, boys,
there's fire down below.
Fire up aloft, and fire down below,
Fetch a bucket of water, boys,
there's fire down below.

'He'd also heard the good missionary lady speak of this wicked old world being consumed by "fire and brimstone", and he felt that this was a good beginning.

'Once again, no blame attached to Alexander. It was a short circuit, obviously. Or a careless smoker. And Alexander did not smoke.

'But with the library gone, some other occupation had to be found for him. And since he was the outdoor type, why not appoint him as assistant to the estate manager of Pinewood School, Mr Rajan, who was due for retirement in a few months? The missionaries were directors of the school and could easily arrange things. The estate was extensive, taking in the entire hillside and a large tract of pine forest. Mr Rajan had a hard time keeping away the villagers who would slip in at night to cut branches for firewood. He needed help.

'And Alexander turned out to be a handy helper. He kept the villagers away by strutting about with a loaded rifle, occasionally firing it at random. In the autumn, pine needles covered the ground, and by December the pine cones were falling.

'The school people used the pine cones in their fireplaces, and Alexander kept them well supplied. He had also discovered that pine cones burn beautifully. School was about to close for winter when a fire broke out in the forest. It hadn't rained for weeks, the grass had turned yellow, the pine needles dry and brittle, and Alexander had made a little bonfire of cones just for his private amusement, and he couldn't resist watching it spread.

'A boy stuck his head out of a dormitory window and exclaimed, "Look! There are flames in the forest!" And soon, everyone was running around, eager to see the forest fire and speculating on whether or not it would reach the school building.

'The village was actually more in danger than the school, for the trees were close to the fields. But a strong wind carried the flames towards the school, burning leaves and floating embers leaping from one tree to another, while the grass beneath was a carpet of fire. A flock of sheep, returning to the village, perished in the smoke and flames. Their attendants, two youngsters, were lucky to escape. The school servants and some of the bigger boys ran about with buckets of sand or water. Several pine martens and a barking deer fled the forest in panic, as did a party of flying squirrels and several large brown owls.

'Alexander was very prominent in all this activity, at times directing the firefighters and at times running about wildly and without any clear sense of purpose. Standing on a cliff edge and waving his arms to a crowd of spectators, he slipped on the pine needles and went tumbling down the steep slope into the burning undergrowth. His clothes on fire, he ran here and there screaming for help, but he was overcome by the smoke and flames and vanished from sight.

'Eventually the wind shifted and the fire burnt itself out. Mr Rajan and his helpers went in search of Alexander and found his charred body at the edge of the forest.'

'So all things wicked must come to an end,' commented Mr Lobo. 'It's all a matter of time. And time must pass . . .'

'Time has nothing else to do, except pass,' said Miss Ripley-Bean wryly. 'And as for Alexander, he was accounted a hero and, being dead, he could not change his status to that of villain. They gave him a grand funeral and a headstone with an inscription that mentioned his bravery in helping to prevent a forest fire from enveloping the school. His grave is up there in the Landour cemetery.'

Miss Ripley-Bean gave Fluff the last of the crackers and rose to go. 'Time for my afternoon nap,' she said. 'It's always nice to talk to you, Mr Lobo.'

~

That evening Mr Lobo went for a long walk, which took him to the Landour cemetery. After wandering around for some time, he found Alexander's tombstone. As he returned to the hotel, the sun fell away to the west, which now reddened to receive it. He looked very thoughtful as he tapped on Miss Ripley-Bean's front door.

He found the old lady sipping a crème de menthe. She made her own liqueur and treated herself to a couple of glasses every evening.

'Have some crème de menthe, Mr Lobo. There is nothing else, I'm afraid,' she said by way of greeting.

'No, thanks,' said Mr Lobo, who hated crème de menthe. 'I won't stay. Just wanted to tell you that I visited the Landour cemetery.'

'And did you find the grave?'

'Yes, I did. It was quite clearly inscribed. But it gave his full name. John Alexander Bean. Is that correct?'

'Yes, that was his name,' said Miss Ripley-Bean. 'He was my brother.'

STRYCHNINE *in* *the* COGNAC

Sick was she on Thursday,
Dead was she on Friday,
Glad was Tom on Saturday night
To bury his wife on Sunday

Miss Ripley-Bean was reclining in a cane chair in a corner of the Royal's beer garden, reciting old nursery rhymes to herself, when Mr Lobo, the resident pianist, walked over and placed a glass of lemon juice beside her.

'Oranges and lemons,' he said, sitting down beside her. 'Which do you prefer, Aunty May?'

'Both,' said Miss Ripley-Bean. 'Oranges for the complexion and lemons for the digestion.'

'Words of wisdom. But that nursery rhyme sounded a bit wicked. I can only remember the innocent ones like Jack and Jill.'

'Not so innocent,' said Miss Ripley-Bean. '"Jack fell down and broke his crown"—he wouldn't have survived a broken head. Maybe Jill pushed him over a cliff—and then went tumbling after!'

'Like the judge who fell into the Kempty waterfall. Was he pushed, or did he fall?'

'We shall never know. No witnesses. But here come the Roys—what a handsome couple!'

The Roys were indeed a handsome couple, as you would expect them to be. Dilip Roy was in his mid-forties, but still a name to be reckoned with in Bollywood. He was greying a little at the temples, just below the edges of his wig; but he remained lean and athletic-looking, and the meaty, romantic roles still came his way. His wife, 'Rosie' Roy, was two or three years younger than him, but inclined to plumpness. When she was in her late twenties and early thirties, she had starred in several very popular films—two of them opposite Dilip Roy, whom she had married while on location with him in Kashmir. But of late she had been having some difficulty in getting parts to her liking. She hadn't been feeling well and had taken to sleeping late in the mornings. Her doctor had suspected diabetes and had advised a complete check-up, but she kept putting off the necessary tests.

'You need a change,' Dilip Roy had said, showing his concern about her health. 'A change from Bombay. A fortnight in the hills will do wonders for you. I'll spend a few days with you too, before I start shooting in Switzerland. Where would you like to go—Simla, Mussoorie, Darjeeling, Ooty?'

'Why not Switzerland?'

Dilip Roy laughed uneasily. 'It wouldn't be much of a holiday. I'd be shooting all the time and you'd be pestered by hangers-on and loads of admirers.'

'Former admirers.'

'Well, better an old admirer than none at all. And I'm still jealous.'

They had settled on Mussoorie—partly because Dilip Roy's father was an old friend of Nandu, the owner of Royal Hotel, and partly because Rosie had spent an idyllic summer there as a girl, staying with an aunt in Barlowganj.

When the couple arrived at the hotel, the first person they encountered was Miss Ripley-Bean, watering the potted aspidistras in the porch of the Royal.

'Hello,' said Rosie, smiling curiously at Miss Ripley-Bean. 'Are you the new gardener?'

'I'm the old gardener,' said Miss Ripley-Bean. 'A resident, actually. But the gardener never waters these aspidistras—he thinks they are hardy enough to go without. But plants are like humans—they need a little attention from time to time, otherwise they die of neglect. I've seen you somewhere, haven't I?'

'Only if you go to the movies,' said Rosie. And added, 'Old movies.'

'You're Rosie Roy!' said Miss Ripley-Bean. 'I've seen you in *Cobra Lady*.'

'Wasn't it terrible?'

'It was so bad that I enjoyed every moment of it. And this must be the great Dilip Roy,' observed Miss Ripley-Bean, as the well-known actor joined them, followed by the room-boys loaded with luggage. 'The hero of *Love in Kathmandu*.'

But the hero ignored her. He continued up the steps to the lobby, followed by his wife and the room-boys. Miss Ripley-Bean returned her attention to the aspidistras.

'Friendly heroine but not so friendly hero,' she said to the nearest potted plant. The aspidistra appeared to agree.

~

The couple settled in and, over the next few days, Miss Ripley-Bean saw quite a lot of them although she took care not to intrude in any way, for it was obvious that the Roys were not looking for company.

In the evenings Dilip Roy would plant himself on a bar stool and work his way through several whiskies, occasionally answering polite questions from the bartender or a casual customer, but always rather morosely—his mind obviously elsewhere. In the background, Mr Lobo, the hotel pianist, would play popular numbers but without receiving any encouragement or applause.

Rosie did not join her husband in the bar. But occasionally a martini was served to her in her room— sometimes two martinis—it was obvious that she liked a gin and vermouth cocktail now and then. Nandu presented her with a bottle of cognac, and she kept it on her dresser, intending to open it only when her husband was in the mood to drink with her.

They went out for quiet walks together, avoiding the mall where they would be recognized by both locals and visitors. Sometimes they passed Miss Ripley-Bean, who was herself a great walker. As they were fellow residents of the Royal, they would stop to exchange comments on the weather, the view, the hotel, the town, sometimes even the country and the rest of the world. But from the quiet of the mountains, the rest of the world can seem very far away.

Rosie Roy liked the look of Miss Ripley-Bean and was always ready to stop and talk. Dilip Roy was polite but brusque. The local gossip did not interest him, and he thought Miss Ripley-Bean a rather quaint and rather foolish bit of flotsam surviving from the days of the Raj. But then (as Rosie argued) the hotel, the cottages, the winding footpaths, the hill station itself, were all survivors of the Raj, and if their old-world atmosphere did not please you, it might have been better to holiday in Goa—and soak up the Portuguese atmosphere!

India would always be haunted by its history . . .

~

One day the Roys had a violent quarrel. Miss Ripley-Bean was no eavesdropper but couldn't help overhearing every word that was spoken.

Her favourite place was a bench situated behind a tall hibiscus hedge. It looked out upon the snows, and Miss Ripley-Bean liked to spend half an hour there with a book, while Fluff, her little Tibetan terrier, investigated the hillside, looking for rat holes. You couldn't see the bench from the beer garden, and it was in the beer garden that Rosie and Dilip Roy were confronting each other.

'You're off, because of that woman in Bandra.' Rosie's voice was quite shrill. 'A week away from her and you're beginning to look like a real Majnu—all pale and melancholy!'

'Don't make up things.' Dilip Roy sounded impatient rather than melancholy. 'You know they start shooting the new film next week. And it's in Switzerland, not Bandra.'

'You're not the star. They can do without you. You're getting too fat for leading roles. And you're drinking too much.'

'I'll end up an alcoholic if I stay here much longer. The doctors advised rest for you, not for me. You've given yourself ulcers and you won't get any better if you worry over trifles.'

Here the couple were interrupted by a group of youngsters seeking autographs, and Miss Ripley-Bean took advantage of the diversion by slipping away, taking a roundabout path up to her rooms. Fluff enjoyed the extended walk.

That evening Dilip Roy opened the bottle of cognac. He was leaving the next morning, and he was in the mood to celebrate. But he was not particularly fond of cognac and did most of his celebrating with his favourite Scotch. Rosie poured herself a wine glass of cognac, then put the bottle away on the dresser in their room. There it remained all night.

~

Dilip Roy breakfasted alone in the dining room, then sent for a taxi to take him down to Dehradun. Rosie did not see him off.

'She's sleeping late,' explained Dilip Roy. 'She has a headache. Don't disturb her.'

'Enjoy yourself in Switzerland,' said Nandu, the affable proprietor.

'Look after Rosie,' said Dilip Roy. 'Let her get plenty of rest.'

And everyone did their best to make Rosie comfortable and welcome, because she was the more gracious of the two. The manager and the staff fussed over her, and Mr Lobo played her favourite tunes, especially the one she always requested.

> *Whatever will be, will be*
> *The future's not ours to see . . .*

Even Miss Ripley-Bean was drawn towards Rosie and joined her on an inspection of the garden, for they both were fond of flowers, and in late summer the grounds were awash with bright yellow marigolds, petunias, larkspur and climbing roses. They had coffee together and Rosie recalled her parents and happy childhood days spent in Mussoorie; she did not talk about her marriage.

As evening came on, Rosie would retire to her room and send for a martini; it would be followed by a second. She would have a light supper in her room—usually a chicken or mushroom soup with some toast—followed by a few sips of cognac as a nightcap, and then to bed!

This routine continued for three or four days, and the cognac bottle was still half full because Rosie preferred martinis. Dilip Roy made a couple of calls from Bombay—the crew would be off to Switzerland any day, and meanwhile they were shooting some scenes in Lonavala.

He had been away for almost a week when Rosie suddenly fell ill. At about ten o'clock, after her dinner, she rang her bell. A room-boy answered her summons, found her on her bed, still dressed, and having a fit of sorts. He ran for the manager.

The manager hurried to the room, followed by a concerned Mr Lobo. They found her still having convulsions.

'I'll go for Dr Bisht,' said Mr Lobo, and hurried from the room. Minutes later they heard the splutter of his scooter as he took the winding driveway down to the mall. Dr Bisht had a scooter too—this was the Age of the Scooter—and he arrived in time to give Rosie some basic first aid and arrange for her to be taken to the local hospital. He was cautious in his diagnosis. 'Looks like food poisoning,' he said, and then his eyes fell on the open bottle of cognac, of which about half still remained.

There was still some liquor in the glass, and he sniffed it and made a face. 'Or something else. We'd better have this bottle examined,' he said. But that would take time . . .

A call was put through to Dilip Roy's studio in Bombay, but the actor was in Switzerland now, and flights were not very frequent in those days. It would be two or three days before he could return.

Miss Ripley-Bean visited Rosie Roy every day, and so, occasionally, did Nandu and Mr Lobo. And to everyone's relief and amazement, Rosie made a good recovery.

There were crystals of strychnine at the bottom of the bottle, it was found, but they had only just begun to dissolve. Another evening's drinking, and Rosie would have reached the fatal dose lying there in wait for her. For it was obvious that someone had placed the poison in the bottle, and that someone could only have been Dilip Roy, before he had left Mussoorie. Far away at the time of his wife's expiry, he would have the perfect alibi.

Of course nothing could be proven—all was surmise and conjecture—but Rosie was certain in her own mind that her husband had intended to do away with her in absentia, so to speak, and had very nearly succeeded.

She and Miss Ripley-Bean had now become fast friends, and Rosie found herself confiding all her fears and suspicions to the older person, and turning to her for advice and guidance.

~

They sat together on the lawns of the Royal, Rosie reclining in her easy chair, Miss Ripley-Bean quite at ease on a wooden bench. From indoors came the tinkle of a piano as Mr Lobo played the 'September Song'. Miss Ripley-Bean sang the words softly, almost to herself:

> *For it's a long long, while from May to December,*
> *But the days grow short when you reach September.*

'That's a pretty song,' said Rosie. 'A little sad, though.'

'September is a sad month,' said Miss Ripley-Bean musingly. 'The end of summer. The end of all those lovely picnics. Holding hands and paddling in mountain streams. Hot sunny days. And then all that rain—weeks of endless rain and mist. September brings back the sunshine if only for a short time, and then those icy winds will start coming down from the snows.'

'How romantic!' exclaimed Rosie. 'You are lucky to have lived here most of your life. Well, perhaps I'll come and join you when I've finished with that wretched husband of mine in Bombay.'

'What do you intend to do, my dear? Put arsenic in his vodka?'

'Arsenic is too slow. But if he eats enough of those chocolate-coated hazelnuts of which he is so fond, he could well come to a sticky end!'

'What do you mean, dear?'

'This is only for your ears, Aunty May.' Rosie addressed Miss Ripley-Bean by her first name whenever she became trustful and confiding. 'I know you won't give me away— just in case something happens.'

'What could happen now?'

'Well, these last two years, I've been so miserable that I've always kept a little cyanide pill with me, just so that I can put an end to my life if it becomes too unbearable.'

'Oh dear. Do throw it away. Don't even think of doing away with yourself.'

'Well, actually, I did throw it away—got rid of it, rather. I took the pill and gave it a nice coating of chocolate and then mixed it up with all the little hazelnut chocolates in the tin that Dilip always carries around.'

'Oh, but that was wicked of you! Quite diabolical! Understandable, though, when you think of what he tried to do to you. But he could get to that chocolate pill any day—pop it in his mouth, and then . . .'

'Pop off?' said Rosie, a glint in her hazel eyes.

'But it's been some time, hasn't it? Almost three weeks since he left. Someone else might have helped himself or herself to a chocolate . . .'

Just then they saw Nandu advancing across the lawn. It wasn't his usual amble—he looked very purposeful.

'Bad news,' he said, when he reached their sunny corner. 'I've just had a call from Dilip Roy's manager. Your husband died last night, Mrs Roy. Suicide, it appears. Cyanide. He must have been feeling very guilty about what happened to you. I'm so sorry for you . . .'

~

That evening Miss Ripley-Bean dined with Rosie Roy in the old ballroom. It was the end of the season, and only a few tables were occupied. Mr Lobo was at the piano, playing nostalgic numbers.

'What will you have, Aunty May?' Rosie said. 'You're my special guest today. It's not that I want to celebrate or anything like that . . .'

'I quite understand, my dear.'

'So you must have a decent wine, instead of that dreadful crème de menthe you make in your room. Here's the wine list.'

Miss Ripley-Bean ran her eye down the wine list. She was no blackmailer, but she couldn't help feeling a little surge of power as she made her choice. And it was such a long time since she'd enjoyed a really good wine. So she went for the most expensive wine on the list, and sat back in anticipation.

THE
BLACK DOG

We usually think of black cats, black panthers and black dogs as rather ominous creatures, associated with witchcraft or hounds baying in the night or leopards leaping upon you in the dark. But Miss Ripley-Bean assured me that black dogs, even ghostly ones, were benevolent creatures who looked after lonely travellers, provided of course that the travellers were well intentioned and pure of heart.

I met Miss Ripley-Bean when I came to live in Mussoorie in the early 1970s. She had rooms in the old wing of the old Royal Hotel, above the Library Bazaar, and I was living in a small cottage near Kempty village, just above the waterfall. The village was some three or four miles from the town, and in those days there was no motorable road, just a steep footpath going up through fields and an oak forest.

I visited the Royal quite often. I liked talking to Miss Ripley-Bean, who was an upright, active, seventy-year-old, and regaled me with stories of her childhood in the west of England, and her grown-up years in Mussoorie and the Doon valley. She had a lot of folklore at her disposal, ranging from mermaids off the coast of England to tree-spirits and fairy glens in the Himalayas.

Another friend at the Royal was Mr Lobo, who played the piano every evening in the lounge or ballroom. He was always ready to oblige me by playing some nostalgic old number of my choice: 'September Song' or 'I Kiss Your Little Hand, Madame'. After a couple of whiskies at the bar, I'd head home, torch in hand, because the path to Kempty was dark and full of shadows. I was usually home by eight. A boy from the dhaba across the road would bring me something to eat—green beans from the village, cooked with potatoes, or a small fish from the little river below Kempty. The place was then still something of a wilderness, not the messy tourist destination that it has become today.

One day I was invited to a small party being given by a well-known newspaper editor who was staying at the Royal: Shashi Sinha of the *Diplomat*. He'd been publishing some of my short stories in the Sunday magazine. I knew the party would only get started around eight, so I left home later than usual, just as the sun sank behind the Chakrata range and dusk fell softly across the valley.

The walk took me through a cultivated area, then on a path through a mixed forest, and finally through the oaks and pines below the Mussoorie ridge.

From the beginning I was aware that I was being followed by a dog, a large, black creature of no particular breed. This did not bother me, as I was used to the village dogs, most of whom were rather scrawny, timid specimens. They barked a lot but kept their distance.

This dog, taller and larger than most, did not bark at all. He made hardly a sound as he padded on, occasionally looking right and left but never in my direction. And unlike most dogs, he made no effort to get to know me. I too kept my distance. I wasn't afraid of the dog, but I could tell that he was different from other dogs and I refrained from making any friendly overtures.

When I got to the hotel entrance, I was met by Miss Ripley-Bean and her little terrier, Fluff, who had been barking furiously at my approach.

'Did you have a dog with you?' she asked. 'I thought I saw a large black dog accompanying you.'

'You did,' I said looking round. 'It's gone now. One of the village dogs, probably. But it didn't bother me.'

Miss Ripley-Bean did not attend the party, which was quite a noisy affair. A lot of liquor was consumed, there was some singing and dancing, and Mr Lobo was kept busy at his piano.

'Your cheque's in the mail,' said Shashi Sinha, in connection with the most recent story I'd written for his paper.

'I'm sure it will reach eventually,' I said politely, quite accustomed to cheques being inordinately delayed and sometimes even vanishing in the mail.

It was almost eleven o'clock when I bade my host goodnight and left the party. I may have been a little unsteady on my feet, but the moon had risen over the mountains and I could see the path distinctly, even without the help of my torch.

And there was that dog again!

It loped along beside me, sometimes in front, sometimes to my left or right; never too far away, never too close. Even when I quickened my pace, I could never catch up with that elusive but ever-present dog.

It looked real enough—a tall black hound, quite at ease in the forest, familiar and yet unfamiliar, staying away from me and yet so near . . .

It took me almost an hour to get home, and the dog was with me all the way.

Finally I was there.

I opened the gate, unlocked my front door, and looked around. The black dog had gone.

And I never saw it again.

So what was so special about my experience, I wondered. A dog had followed me up to the town, and back again, and had then disappeared. True, it was a strange sort of dog, remote and uncommunicative, and I had never seen one quite like it; but it had been real enough, padding beside me in the dark forest.

And for some reason I couldn't put the black dog out of my mind.

~

Several months later, I was in the Royal bar, having a drink with a couple of new acquaintances, one of whom was the chief warden of Haridwar jail. The conversation turning to crime and criminals, the warden turned to me and said, 'You are Mr Bond, the writer, aren't you? Do you realize that you had a narrow escape from being waylaid and robbed—possibly even murdered?'

'First I've heard of it,' I said.

'Well, there are two undertrials down in Haridwar who were caught after breaking into the local bank, and they were overheard talking about a plan they had to follow and rob you while you were on your way to this very hotel, or on your return, sometime last year.'

'Really? But why?' I asked. I am hardly prosperous enough for it to be worth someone's while to rob me.

'You are so well known in the town that they must have assumed you are very prosperous,' the chief warden smiled. 'Anyway, they followed you all the way from Kempty and back again, but you had this large dog with you, and they were reluctant to take on both of you at the same time. Very wise of you to keep a dog. Is it a Labrador or one of those big Bhutia mastiffs?'

'I don't keep a dog,' I said. 'But there was one with me that night. A big, black dog. I had never seen it before, and I've never seen it since.'

Mr Lobo had been listening to our conversation. 'A guardian spirit,' he said. 'We don't always recognize them, but they are always there.'

ENVOI

THE JOY
of WATER

Each drop represents a little bit of creation—and of life itself. When the monsoon brings to northern India the first rains of summer, the parched earth opens its pores and quenches its thirst with a hiss of ecstasy. After baking in the sun for the last few months, the land looks cracked, dusty and tired. Now, almost overnight, new grass springs up, there is renewal everywhere, and the damp earth releases a fragrance sweeter than any devised by man.

Water brings joy to earth, grass, leaf-bud, blossom, insect, bird, animal and the pounding heart of man. Small children run out of their homes to romp naked in the rain. Buffaloes, which have spent the summer listlessly around lakes gone dry, now plunge into a heaven of muddy water. Soon the lakes and rivers will overflow with the monsoon's generosity.

Trekking in the Himalayan foothills, I recently walked for kilometres without encountering habitation. I was just scolding myself for not having brought along a water bottle, when I came across a patch of green on a rock face. I parted a curtain of tender maidenhair fern and discovered a tiny spring issuing from the rock—nectar for the thirsty traveller.

I stayed there for hours, watching the water descend, drop by drop, into a tiny casement in the rocks. Each drop reflected creation. That same spring, I later discovered, joined other springs to form a swift, tumbling stream, which went cascading down the hill into other streams until, in the plains, it became part of a river. And that river flowed into another mightier river that kilometres later emptied into the ocean. Be like water, taught Lao Tzu, philosopher and founder of Taoism. Soft and limpid, it finds its way through, over or under any obstacle. It does not quarrel; it simply moves on.

A small pool in the rocks outside my cottage in the Mussoorie hills, provides me endless delight. Water beetles paddle the surface, while tiny fish lurk in the shallows. Sometimes a spotted fork-tail comes to drink, hopping delicately from rock to rock. And once I saw a barking deer, head lowered at the edge of the pool. I stood very still, anxious that it should drink its fill. It did, and then, looking up, saw me and leapt across the ravine to disappear into the forest.

In summer the pool is almost dry. Even this morning, there was just enough water for the fish and tadpoles to survive. But as I write, there is a pattering on the tin roof of the cottage, and I look out to see the raindrops pitting the surface of the pool.

Tomorrow the spotted fork-tail will be back. Perhaps the barking deer will return. I open the window wide and allow the fragrance of the rain and freshened earth to waft into my room.

RAIN

After weeks of heat and dust
How welcome is the rain.
It washes the leaves,
Gives new life to grass,
Draws out the scent of the earth.
It rattles on the roof,
Gurgles along the drainpipe
Collects in a puddle in the middle of the lawn—
The birds come to bathe.
When the sun comes out
A lizard crawls up from a crack in a rock.
'Small brown lizard
Basking in the sun
You too have your life to live
Your race to run.'
At night we look through the branches
of the cherry tree.
The sky is rain-washed, star-bright.

SOUNDS
I LIKE *to*
HEAR

All night the rain has been drumming on the corrugated tin roof. There has been no storm, no thunder just the steady swish of a tropical downpour. It helps one to lie awake; at the same time, it doesn't keep one from sleeping.

It is a good sound to read by—the rain outside, the quiet within—and, although tin roofs are given to springing unaccountable leaks, there is in general a feeling of being untouched by, and yet in touch with, the rain.

Gentle rain on a tin roof is one of my favourite sounds. And early in the morning, when the rain has stopped, there are other sounds I like to hear—a crow shaking the raindrops from his feathers and cawing rather disconsolately; babblers and bulbuls bustling in and out of bushes and long grass in search of worms and insects; the sweet, ascending trill of the Himalayan whistling-thrush; dogs rushing through damp undergrowth.

A cherry tree, bowed down by the heavy rain, suddenly rights itself, flinging pellets of water in my face.

Some of the best sounds are made by water. The water of a mountain stream, always in a hurry, bubbling over rocks and chattering, 'I'm late, I'm late!' like the White Rabbit, tumbling over itself in its anxiety to reach the bottom of the hill, the sound of the sea, especially when it is far away—or when you hear it by putting a sea shell to your ear. The sound made by dry and thirsty earth, as it sucks at a sprinkling of water. Or the sound of a child drinking thirstily the water running down his chin and throat.

Water gushing out of the pans of an old well outside a village while a camel moves silently round the well. Bullock-cart wheels creaking over rough country roads. The clip-clop of a pony carriage, and the tinkle of its bell, and the singsong call of its driver . . .

Bells in the hills. A schoolbell ringing, and children's voices drifting through an open window. A temple-bell, heard faintly from across the valley. Heavy silver ankle-bells on the feet of sturdy hill women. Sheep bells heard high up on the mountainside.

Do falling petals make a sound? Just the tiniest and softest of sounds, like the drift of falling snow. Of course big flowers, like dahlias, drop their petals with a very definite flop.

These are showoffs, like the hawk-moth who comes flapping into the rooms at night instead of emulating the butterfly dipping lazily on the afternoon breeze.

~

One must return to the birds for favourite sounds, and the birds of the plains differ from the birds of the hills. On a cold winter morning in the plains of northern India, if you walk some way into the jungle you will hear the familiar call of the black partridge: *Bhagwan teri qudrat* it seems to cry, which means: 'Oh God! Great is thy might.'

The cry rises from the bushes in all directions; but an hour later not a bird is to be seen or heard and the jungle is so very still that the silence seems to shout at you.

There are sounds that come from a distance, beautiful because they are far away, voices on the wind—they 'walketh upon the wings of the wind'. The cries of fishermen out on the river. Drums beating rhythmically in a distant village. The croaking of frogs from the rainwater pond behind the house. I mean frogs at a distance. A frog croaking beneath one's window is as welcome as a motor horn.

But some people like motor horns. I know a taxi-driver who never misses an opportunity to use his horn. It was made to his own specifications, and it gives out a resonant bugle-call. He never tires of using it. Cyclists and pedestrians always scatter at his approach. Other cars veer off the road. He is proud of his horn. He loves its strident sound—which only goes to show that some men's sounds are other men's noises!

Homely sounds, though we don't often think about them, are the ones we miss most when they are gone. A kettle on the boil. A door that creaks on its hinges. Old sofa springs. Familiar voices lighting up the dark. Ducks quacking in the rain.

And so we return to the rain, with which my favourite sounds began.

I have sat out in the open at night, after a shower of rain when the whole air is murmuring and tinkling with the voices of crickets and grasshoppers and little frogs. There is one melodious sound, a sweet repeated trill, which I have never been able to trace to its source. Perhaps it is a little tree frog. Or it may be a small green cricket. I shall never know.

I am not sure that I really want to know. In an age when a scientific and rational explanation has been given for almost everything we see and touch and hear, it is good to be left with one small mystery, a mystery sweet and satisfying and entirely my own.

SOME NIGHT
THOUGHTS[*]

The mountain is my mother,
My father is the sea,
This river is the fountain
Of all that life can be.
Swift river from the mountain,
Deep river to the sea,
Take all my words and leave them
Where the trade winds set them free.
Oh, piper on the lonely hill,
Play no sad songs for me.
The day has gone, the night comes on,
Its darkness helps me see.

---

[*] Written after one of my nocturnal walks.